I0763465

FAR FOREST SCROLLS

Earth on Fire

Ocean of Blood

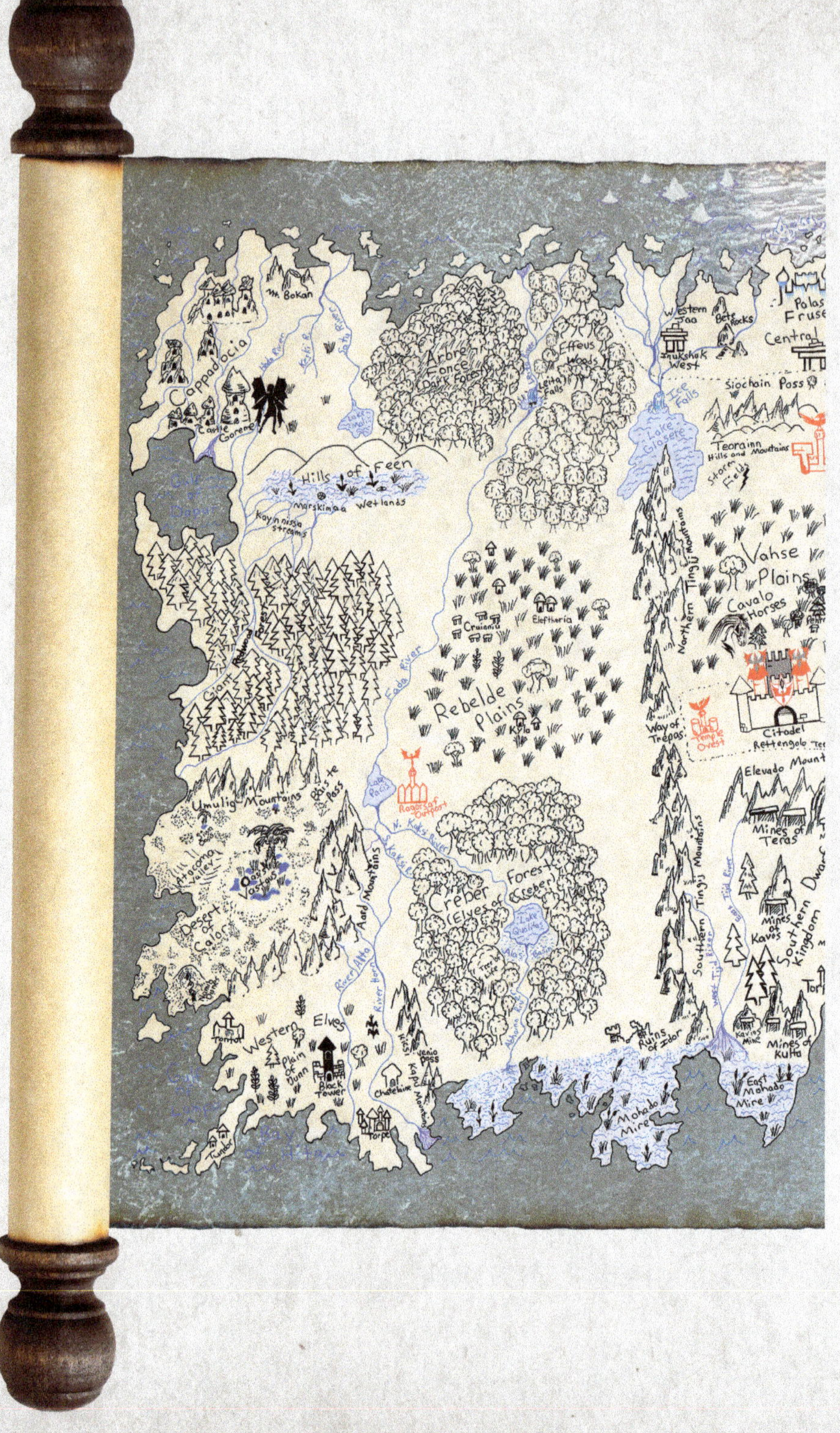

Cappadocia
Castle Gorne
M. Bokan
Arbre Foncé Dark Forest
Effeus Woods
Hills of Feen
Narskimaa Wetlands
Western Jaa
Bete Rocks
Polas
Central
Inukshak West
Siochain Pass
Ice Falls
Lake Glasere
Teorainn Hills and Mountains
Storm Fell
Northern Tinjü Mountains
Vahse Plains
Cavalo Horses
Elepheria
Fada River
Rebelde Plains
Citadel
Way of Trepas
Temple Ovest
Elevado Mount
Mines of Teras
Umulig Mountains
Aragona Valley
Desert of Calor
Aarl Mountains
Creber Forest (Elves of Creber)
Southern Tinjü Mountains
Mines of Kaves
Southern Kingdom
Mines of Kulta
Ruins of Idor
East Mohado Mire
Mohado Mire
Western Elves
Plain of Dunn
Black Tower
Torpe

Tebeotho Springs
Nord
Eastern Jaa
Inukshuk East
Jaa
Inukshuk Mitte
Koori Mountains
Northern Dwarves
Mount Honoo
Keha Haudella Volcanos
Kino Mountains
Storten Flower Fields
Anen
Temple Palvoa
N. Azul River
Haj
Ryba
Kala
Piscium
Iso
Taiheart
Glan
Piscium
Pescore
Haavi
Miksi River
Ruins of Murbh
Kippe
Pollen Lake
Toil Shaor
Cosan Bridge
River Vita
Dark Sea
Proliator Channel
Proliate Archipelago
Tallcon Temple
Kissa Tukea Mountains
Proliate Islands
Temple Dalia
Kovo Cliffs
Ager
Maatilo
Liberum
S. Azul River
Azul Delo
Oroite Mountains
Jalo Kivi
Temple Ensjel
Eluvies Delta
Cliffs of Karst
Torpen Sea
Isle of Hirmulisko
Dark Sea

The League of Truth takes the direct path through the Arbre Fonce and quickly regrets the decision—barely surviving against the arboreal Fionain. Scouting for food, Scelto and Gimelli come across a village of horrors. Will the League survive long enough to find the first set of Macht Crystals?

FAR FOREST SCROLLS

Earth on Fire
Ocean of Blood

BOOK FOUR

The external struggle is but a wisp of any war. Raging under muscle and metal, mental battles bristle, nourished by anxiously accelerated heartbeats and bated breath. On every battlefield those internal conflicts broiling beneath armor often rise above the physical, determining victory or defeat. Each warrior combats their own demons, wrestles their own special brand of fear, overcoming their dread, fighting nerves. On and off the battleground we must attempt to balance mind, body, and spirit. Despite their power, our minds, our will, are still but lowly shackled prisoners of our frangible mortal forms—fettered to gasp their emblematic last breath when the body falls.

The embryology of fate before the event is but an ethereal wish, gestating into existence only upon the conclusion. A construct about the past, fate only coagulates into physical form once the outcome has been determined. Only looking backwards from the cozy confines of the future can destiny materialize to be dispensed as an explanation—a fallacious attempt at justification—righteous rationalization for the victor and feeble crutch for the defeated.

Jumeaux fails his test, but Veneficus' disappointment ebbs after discovering Jumeaux converses with his sister and can monitor Bellae's path to the crystals. In remittance, Veneficus tutors Jumeaux on advanced magical arts.

Fear.
Ghostly.
Ephemeral.
The greater the distance from the act or exploit,
the less fear seizes us...
Until the moment arrives, and thumps into
your core.
Only with terror resonating through the body
can courage be born. Bravery, the offspring of
fear, arises from panic and stress. The musician,
athlete, and poet should be commended and
honored for their sacrifices while
striving for success.
Yet the warrior
Stands alone
Overcoming true terror:
Merging will, body, spirit, and mind to
stand and fight
Within the fiery forge of life and death: battle.
Death, a concept usually relegated to the
unconscious—
A problem for another day.
Such unawareness is a luxury upon which the
warrior cannot be afflicted.

The Knights find themselves in a fight for their lives against a vastly superior force lead by the Proliate. Will Friar's intricate battle plan overcome the massive armies descending upon them?

For more information please visit:
www.FarForestScrolls.com

Scrolls from 1,000 C.E.
discovered during an archeological dig
in the Far Forest region of England,
the soul of this ancient fantasy tale
is reborn in your mind's eye.

Author: AAAA (Alpha Four) Illustrations: AAAA and Paganus
Scroll translation to English: Radek Novotny PhD Image Restoration:Altier Restoration

*A sincere welcome back to the world
of the Far Forest Scrolls.
Return to its embrace, increasing
(we humbly hope) your Wisdom of How to Live.*

Copyright © 2021 All rights reserved, including the right of reproduction in any form, or by any mechanical or electronic means including photocopying or recording, or by any information storage or retrieval system, in whole or in part in any form, and in any case without the written permission of Far Forest Scrolls LLC. The fictional content in this work of literature extends beyond the words and illustrations to all translations, websites, origin stories, and blogs about *The Far Forest Scrolls*, dating back to 1,000 AD and the discovery of the scrolls you are about to read. This is a work of original fictional and with the exception of veritable languages-including their manipulation and conglomeration, authentic historical, nonfictional, and mythological figures-constructs-quotes-personage-etc., and satirical observations of the aforementioned and their works-used in fictional ways-is completely the innovation of the author and any similarity to actual persons, living or dead (except aforementioned), or events (except aforementioned), historical or fictional, is coincidental.

Library of Congress Control Number: 2020918811

ISBN (Hardcover, color edition) 978-1-7357528-0-8
ISBN (Paperback, black & white edition) 978-1-7357528-1-5
ISBN (e-book) 978-1-7357528-2-2

Named after the Norse god, Tyr, who volunteered to lose his hand in order to bind the savage wolf Fenrir. Teiwaz is the rune of sacrifice and courage. It represents the power of sacrifice given freely. It epitomizes the warrior spirit offered up by soldiers in a time of battle. War, with its insatiable appetite for the blood and spirit of the combatants, is always happy to oblige the leaders sending orders to march and die. It speaks perfectly to the upcoming battlefields about to be drenched in the lifeblood of its combatants. The required sacrifice will scour Verngaurd on an individual and societal level.

Reverse Teiwaz (from the underside of chest four in the Far Forest of England) speaks to the questionable causes of this war as deceit weaves its disruption through the leaders of Verngaurd.

(Aside on Norse mythology: wolf Fenrir was the third child of god Loki. The other gods, considering Fenrir dangerous, wanted to bind him. Fenrir, suspecting a trick, refused to be bound in the chain forged by the dwarves {out of the sound of a cat's footsteps, the beard of a woman, the breath of a fish, the roots of mountains, the sinews of a bear, and bird spittle}. Fenrir agreed to be bound only if a god would place their hand in his mouth. Tyr freely did so, and when the dwarf chain called Gleipnir bound the wolf, he chomped Tyr's hand off).

At the end of the day, even those of us who have never fought in a war have battle scars, visible and invisible, repressed and haunting, external and internal, public and confidential. Regrets can cling to our souls like invasive dew. A spirit dropped by adversity, if encouraged by hope and driven by resolve, can be reborn. For when we stand up after each failing, molded by the courage to endeavor again, a new version of ourselves does rise.

Table of Contents

Peractio

End of Book Three

Gathering the last of his wits, Scelto moved over to Ichor. With all his might he jumped up, and using his weight and power, thrust the sword down into Ichor's neck. With a sickening crunch and then a fleshy squish, Scelto's blade severed his spine and plunged deeply into his chest cavity. Ichor's eyes shot open in terror as blood gushed everywhere. With his neck cut apart and spine severed, he could not move, and his arms and hands went slack. Some of the countless appendages fell off Gimelli and began thrashing around violently, some whipping Scelto.

Yelling, Liha rushed towards Scelto. He quickly yanked his sword free and slashed horizontally with all his might across her neck. Her head flew up and to the side as her body continued forward for a few steps. Both disconnected pieces were pumping blood randomly about the room. Her hands grasped out desperately for Scelto and momentarily held on to his cloak before her body crumpled to the ground.

Turning back to Gimelli, Scelto's initial adrenaline rush was wearing down and the drugged incense was starting to take hold. With a massive stroke he severed Ichor's hand and wrenched the remaining tentacles off Gimelli's neck. It reminded him of pulling vines off Liberum's wall. Hundreds of wounds began to ooze blood as Ichor's hand fell lifelessly to the ground. The thin rope-like projections were still writhing angrily on the floor, fangs within his palm chomped angrily. Scelto kicked and stomped on the tentacles closest to him as they shot forward, still mindlessly rummaging for blood.

Moving quickly, Scelto sheathed his bloody sword and hoisted Gimelli onto his shoulders. He had to get out of the hut and away from the intoxicating smoke. As he left the doorway, the fresh air felt invigorating.

Just as his head began to clear, Gimelli moaned loudly, drawing the attention of one of the feasting undead. Scelto quickly ran between two huts into the forest. The heavy footsteps of the undead could be heard plodding after them. Carrying Gimelli slowed him down, and he could tell they were gaining.

"Unchain the Wasted Undead!" Ichor's mother howled. "Let them loose!" she cackled. "Let the wasted loose!" she repeated before howling into a maniacal laugh.

How in the world am I going to get out of this? Scelto wondered.

Their bloodthirsty calls began echoing around the trees as more undead joined the chorus. Their cry was cut off by a blood-curdling scream fracturing out of the village.

Ichor's mother had discovered her son's body. Her shriek was quickly followed by a series of depraved howls, as all the undead of the village were now awake and enraged.

The feeble skirmishes of book three fade—mere kindling for the larger violence erupting. Sacrifice, freely given, is the fabric of the warrior. Stepping forward unwaveringly into battle despite the rattling armor and battle cries of the army assembled to kill, that is a warrior's offering and courage melding into acceptance. Teiwaz symbolizes the warrior's consent to the brutality of war despite its propensity to choke out compassion, embroiling the world in blood and fire.

Take heed, all who would proceed.
The stripped-bare violence of war strains, breaking from its chains.
Those of flesh and sinew, with the courage to continue:
It is time to strap on your armor.

Figure 1: Carrying Gimelli is slowing Scelto, adding to his fatigue. The thought of the torture and death that awaits if caught spurs him to overcome exhaustion and keep moving.

Chapter One
Battle Begins

Scroll 1: Oh, Shii...!

Scelto struggled to keep ahead of the undead in the thick Arbre Fonce. His breathing was loud, forced, his chest heaving over burning lungs as he struggled to carry Gimelli's limp and bleeding body. Scarlet colored him from head to toe, a mix of Liha's, Ichor's, and now Gimelli's weeping blood.

"We can smell you, boy!" one of the vampire's henchmen yelled. "There's no need trying to be quiet."

Great, Scelto thought. The only conclusion rattling around his mind was the desperate need to stay ahead of them.

"What?" Gimelli groaned.

Scelto stole a quick glance at her pale face bobbing on his chest as he ran. Blood oozed from countless puncture wounds the vampire had used to drain her blood. Scelto's arms and legs howled in desperate pain, shaking from the exertion. Grunting, he willed himself to continue.

"You can't run from us forever, boy!"

They're right. I can't keep this up, and no way can I outrun them carrying Gimelli. His tired brain whirled for a solution. He remembered several large rocks they had glimpsed when heading to the village and shifted course to the left, making for the shelter the outcropping could provide.

"We're going to boil and eat you, boy!" an undead yelled.

"Get ready for pain!" another cried.

Scelto could hear their heavy footsteps, punctuated by occasional shrieks, closing in.

Surrender is not so much an option. Think what they'll do to Gimelli, his brain screamed in a vain attempt to motivate his protesting muscles.

The rocks.

Reaching the small clearing in front of three large boulders, he gently set Gimelli down, propping her up against the largest rock. He allowed his eyes to dwell on her for just a moment. The blood on her neck and upper back had turned dark, blending with the black stone. The most substantial boulder jutted out, tilting slightly forward, making it impossible for anyone to circle around and get at them from behind.

Scelto jumped back as her eyelids snapped open, revealing a terrifying pair of completely white eyes. "What the...?" He knelt down to get a closer look, but they had already closed. A small hissing sound leaked from her mouth as her body convulsed in a quick spasm. The sound, and her movement, gratefully stopped. Reaching out, he gently brushed his hand against her cheek. "Stay with me...please."

The rocks around its base, like everything else in the forest, were inky and rough. Many had jagged edges, but being oblong and thin, they were perfect aerodynamic projectiles. Tossing one in the air, he smiled. "Thanks for these, at least, you stupid petrified forest!"

Hearing the undead moving closer, he pocketed a few rocks then heaped a pile near Gimelli before sprinting to his right.

Let them come.

Crouching silently within the forest, he waited while desperately trying to slow his breathing as the pursuers crashed through the forest. Suddenly, the several undead who had been feasting around the cauldron burst through the edge of the small glade, stopping about ten feet from Gimelli, staring hungrily at her flaccid figure.

"Where's boy dinner meat?" one said, his lips curling into a menacing snarl. All bared their yellow teeth, showing the black pincer-like fangs writhing out from their gums.

"Lovely smile," Scelto whispered, heaving one of the stones over their heads. It sailed high in the air before landing on the opposite side of the forest, crashing through the trees, causing them to turn to the noise.

"Hiding won't help. We'll find and kill you!" one yelled to the empty side of the forest.

Stealthily, Scelto moved through the trees, coming out just behind them. When he was close enough, he hurtled forward, quickly cutting the head off the closest undead. Thick, dark blood spurted out in a putrid stream before degrading into a wild splay of frantic, disoriented droplets as the head fell. The next closest turned just as Scelto slammed his sword through his midface. A salvo of blood ejected around the sword, splattering upon the layers of dried blood already residing on Scelto's clothes. Bringing his right foot up, Scelto kicked the undead in his chest with all his might. The still-twitching body fell, pulsing out blood in raining arcs as the sword slurped out.

The last undead spun towards the squire, howling angrily, baring his monstrous fangs. Scelto could see the chunks of flesh still dangling between his filed teeth and the deep black circles under his vacant, hateful eyes.

As the attacker lurched forward, Scelto stepped to his right and slashed the charging undead's left arm off. Screeching savagely, he dove at Scelto with surprising speed. Scelto brought up his left knee and slammed it into the creature's face, snapping it backwards. The undead was stunned long enough for Scelto to bring his sword over in a slicing arc that removed his head. As the body hit the floor, three more undead burst into the clearing.

"Hey, nice of you to show up," Scelto said, his confidence blossoming. There was something strangely calming in the reality that there was nothing left to do but fight and win, or fight and die.

The first one into the small clearing snarled, "Wipe that smile off your face, flesh bag, the Wasted Undead have been released. Soon they shall descend upon you and unleash true horror."

"Can't wait," Scelto replied.

Confused by the squire's untroubled attitude, the three undead stared at the body parts and seeping, fetid blood from their former comrades as Scelto took a few leisurely steps towards Gimelli. Stealthily, he took hold of one of the rocks from his pocket and without warning whipped his body around, throwing it with all his might at the closest undead. It hit right between his eyes, snapping his head backwards. Using the momentum from the throw, Scelto spun forward in a three-sixty revolution, cleanly decapitating the surprised undead. He quickly retreated to stand over his friend's unconscious body.

The two remaining undead howled with unbridled fury.

"I thought you might be the type to lose your heads," Scelto said, smiling.

The two creatures growled, rage boiling over.

"We're gonna pain you, boy!"

"Wait until the hordes of Wasted Undead come," the other said.

"Yeah, so you said," Scelto replied icily.

"We should just injure this fool then make him watch us have fun with the girl before we eat him," the first snarled as they moved toward the squires.

The mention of what they would do to Gimelli lit a fire, Scelto's rage blazing through widened eyes. Scelto stabbed his sword into the ground before reaching down to pick up a handful of rocks. The undead crouched low, raising their hands at the ready. He threw one hard at the undead furthest from him and then tossed the rest in the direction of the closer one. Reflexively, the undead raised his arms to block the cascade of rocks as Scelto smoothly grabbed his sword before bounding forward to pierce his neck.

With the sword still embedded, Scelto slashed hard to his right, cleaving the undead's neck half off, his head lopping forward, blood spurting out in a surreal strobe pattern. The other had recovered from the thrown rock and charged headlong at Scelto, who skillfully slashed up then quickly back down against the advancing undead while backpedaling. Both strikes cut deeply, and it crumpled to the ground with blood spurting everywhere, splattering the ground in a torrent, some spraying the already-saturated-with-blood squire.

Gurgling, and fueled with adrenaline, the undead with his head dangling rushed forward. Scelto slashed furiously: right—left. Even with his chest and abdomen opened up, he continued moving forward. Slicing his blade horizontally with all his might, Scelto completely severed the undead's neck. With his head tumbling in a blood-sprinkling arc, the mutilated body finally fell.

A hand grabbed at his ankle. Despite his blood drenching into the earth, the one Scelto had slashed across his thorax crawled forward, his mouth open, teeth bared, two crazed black feelers hungrily thrashing at Scelto. Jumping, spinning, Scelto brought down his sword onto the back of the neck of the crawling savage. A loud *crack* was quickly followed by a shower of blood as the spinal cord shattered and both carotids exploded.

Breathing heavily, Scelto scanned the forest for others. Seeing none, he backed towards Gimelli. She suddenly seized his leg, hissing loudly—her eyes, completely covered in white sinewy strands, were wide and frenzied as her hiss turned to a deranged howl.

"Oh, shiiite!" he screamed, quickly stepping away. Thankfully, she quickly passed out again. Bending down, he tenderly moved the hair out of her eyes. "You *have* to be okay."

Suddenly, a spasm quivered through her body as a bloody froth spewed from her mouth.

Is she turning? The idea she would become an undead was more frightening than battling them. After pausing to look for other attackers, he quickly wiped down then sheathed his sword. Gently picking Gimelli up, he took off running towards the meeting place.

A distant but roaring rumble of inhuman shrieks began to echo through the trees, sending flashes of the Wasted Undead chained by madness and fettered by shackles in their own excrement blazing through Scelto's mind.

They're right. I can't fight a mob of Wasted Undead, he thought, unsure of exactly how many there were. With a fresh dose of adrenaline he willed his tired legs to move forward.

Scroll 2: Now They Shall Know

"King Abernan, you honor us, leaving your besieged Kingdom to personally lead your army," Friar said, beaming.

"My Dwarves will hold the Kingdom, especially now that we've unleashed the Saatana—payback for the Tournament loss of three of our beloved dragons. I almost pity the griffins and Magicians who try and step up. Almost," the king said as he embraced Friar warmly. "Plus, all Dwarves know how important this battle is to Verngaurd."

Friar sat astride his horse, watching the Northern Dwarves stream into the Allied camp. The red Saatana divisions, better known as dragon warriors, marched first. They drew their famous Draak swords with razor-sharp spikes up the entire length of the blade. Their equally fearsome helmets bore a pair of red dragon wings and black horns.

They were followed by the green Vioma infantry divisions carrying axes and S-curved swords. Friar knew that the Aer Ridire were patrolling the skies and setting up their own camp complete with dragons.

Even in the distant shadow of the walled Proliate fortress, Friar felt it was the enemy who should be afraid. The Northern Dwarves had arrived to join the small contingent of Knights of Liberum and a few Dwarves of the Rebelde Plains. The battle plan was materializing as Friar planned. All were being cloaked by prestidigitation. As the Dwarves continued to march into camp, he rode to check on Lovag.

"How are the siege engines coming?" Friar asked.

Lovag spun around, the strain boiling within the Knight instantly obvious. Sorea had so much to attend to west of the Tingij, she could not be in front of the whitewashed Proliate fortress. It was hard to tell who was more disappointed, Sorea for missing this phase, or Lovag for having to lead it.

"I wish Sorea was here."

"I have faith in you. The time for wishing, for better or worse, is long past," Friar answered. He spent the rest of the night moving around the camp, checking the war preparations. Even as fatigue pulled at his body, he kept moving, helping where possible.

During the uneasy time of the eve of battle, Friar returned to his tent, his outward quiet belying the agitation whisking below the surface. Warriors, faced with abrupt end to their time on earth, confront such a brusque potential shortage of time differently. Some become introspective, while a few boast, physically or verbally—a sort of piteous self-pep talk striving to mask the coagulating fear.

Friar unfurled his map. *Is this plan too complex? My Allied forces are scattered around Verngaurd like seeds in the wind.* Large forces, like his, were hidden while small contingents were made to look like massive armies to confuse the enemy. *Going against the old tenet of never dividing your forces in hostile territory? If the Proliate find us before my plan unfolds, all Allied forces will be obliterated.*

Hitting the table and maps hard, Friar stood up, fear recharging his exhaustion. *No more planning. From here on out, I react to the enemy's responses.* He ran his fingers over his chronically aching shins. The rubbing didn't help, but he continued the motion anyway.

Whose hands are these? he wondered, gazing on the withered and wilted look time compelled, wringing the youth from his hands.

Slowly, he retrieved a pair of greaves and carefully laced them over skin littered with scars and age spots. He would wear armor into battle for the first time. After covering the outward signs of his age, he smiled. With the bluster and athleticism of youth corroded by the ravages of age, his armor could cover some of his lost speed.

"All the troops transferred from the eastern front against the Dwarves are tucked into their barracks here in the Citadel," an overexcited Proliate captain declared to Lidenskap. "They were unsuccessful in engaging the Knights' army, which is still at least a couple days march away from reaching the Citadel."

"What of the Northern Dwarves and the Rebelde Plains?"

"The Dwarves are on the move but heading towards us in relatively small numbers. We are seeing activity in the Rebelde Plains, but they have not moved out in force."

"What about dragons?" Lidenskap asked.

"The good news is we believe we have greatly reduced the Vioma ranks, as the Dwarves have started bringing out Saatana dragons to defend against griffin attacks. The bad news is the kill ratio has gone from twenty griffins dead to every dragon killed to thirty-five to one."

"Those losses are unacceptable!" Lidenskap howled. "Tallcon, curse all dragons!"

"High Commander Storlax is adjusting the strategy to improve the kill ratio in our favor. He wanted me to ask if you were going to summon the other nations in our Confederacy to the Citadel before the Knights arrive."

Lidenskap, feeling betrayed, stared at the young captain. *Did Storlax send him to spy on me? Am I in charge of the Citadel or not?* There was also a pang of regret after he had somehow, and unintentionally, ended up telling Veneficus he didn't need help from the Magicians. *While it's true I don't think too highly of the Knights, I want a quick and decisive battle to end this nuisance before it turns into a prolonged civil war.*

"I will not be summoning any other Confederate nations," Lidenskap answered.

"Perhaps it would be wise," the captain said.

Lidenskap smiled smugly. "I won't be summoning them because griffin riders were sent weeks ago."

Obviously annoyed, the captain left. Lidenskap's smile quickly faded as he unfurled the map. His trap was evolving perfectly. The Knights and their paltry Allies were walking right up to the impenetrable Citadel. He would let them bang their heads against its mighty walls until the nations making up the Confederation could fall down upon their rear, cutting off their thin supply lines, and demolish them.

Say no to Tallcon? Now you shall know our wrath. We shall slaughter them all.

Scroll 3: Stand Your Ground

Before dawn, Friar reviewed his plans one last time before leaving his tent.

Figure 2: Friar's complex series of maneuvers and the decision to divide his forces potentially leaves the Allies vulnerable.

"The Proliate are falling for your deception," Ritari greeted. "While they think the main Allied forces are heading to the Citadel, and days away, we sit hidden in front of Temple Ovest."

"True, but we are putting a great strain on the Rebelde Plains Dwarves and their prestidigitation. They are conjuring a vast 'army' marching on the Citadel," Friar said, worry wearing across his face.

Ritari nodded, handing Friar the enchanted Huuto. "The troops are ready."

Taking the shell, Friar began, "It starts now. We did not ask for this war, but we are ready to fight. Overcome all fear. Transcend all doubts. To withhold your best is the same as letting life drain from your soul. With wisdom and temperance we fight with courage to defend justice. This day they may kill your body, but only you can harm your true self, your soul!

"Make no mistake, this fight is for our survival. Even though we are not in our mountains or castles, we fight for their defense. Even though our families are not here, we fight for their lives. Think of all the Proliate have taken: land, castles, Knights, dragons, Dwarves, squires. It ends here. It ends now. For the sister or brother who stands next to you, we fight. For our families and our very way of life, we fight! Hold nothing back. Unleash your soul!"

A roar of approval burst from the assembled Allies.

Friar nodded. "It begins!"

Ritari signaled the Northern Dwarves. Using their fastest Vioma Dragon, a single rider shot out of camp from Ovest to the small force outside the Citadel, followed by half a dozen slower moving transport dragons, each with a single driver and empty carrying platforms. For protection, four fully armored Vioma Dragons complete with five Aer Ridire Dwarves flew with them.

"Load the siege engines!" Friar shouted, part of his mind drifting to the feint at the Citadel that was about to be unleashed.

Lovag rode Behalen hard up and down the lines as the various machines of war being loaded groaned in feverish anticipation.

General Lidenskap ran to the walls as the alarms rang. Shaking his head in disbelief, he stared at the large force of Knights and siege engines that seemingly appeared out of nowhere. Their intelligence had estimated they wouldn't be in position to attack the Citadel for several days. *Let them try to take down these walls,* he thought.

The Vioma Dragon sent from Ovest by Friar had arrived at what looked like the entire Knight army in front of the Citadel but, in actuality, was only a small group of Knights, a few siege engines, and several Dwarves skilled in prestidigitation.

"Unleash the mechanicians!" the Aer Ridire yelled. Thousands of imaginary troops and siege engines summoned by the Dwarves seemed to begin firing. The Citadel's whitewashed walls and flags shimmered in the Mardin sun as the repelling forces of the Proliate awaited fire from what they thought were hundreds of siege engines. In reality there were only two trebuchets aligned against the mass of the Citadel. As the two projectiles bounced harmlessly against the wall, the Proliate looked around in confusion. Repeatedly, the Knights manning the trebuchets launched large boulders at the walls of the Citadel, with little effect.

"Add some heaviness to the counterweight," Bly, the sergeant in charge of the small force of Knights, yelled. "It's time for the next phase."

"Hurry it up, guys," one of the Dwarves groaned. "Prestidigitation this large is harder than it looks!"

Bly, a seventh-generation Knight, sighed. "If the Proliate figure out how few of us are here, we all die!"

"The extra weight has been added," a Knight mechanician yelled.

"Good, that should carry our gifts over the wall. Iseal, put on your wools and load the boltinns," Bly ordered. "If you were better at dice, you wouldn't have gotten the lowly job of loading the trebuchet with our gifts!"

"Who wouldn't want to pack rancid meat, excrement, and entrails?" Iseal said, tying on a linen mask before putting on a woolen vest, chaps, and gloves. He had purposefully not eaten that morning but was still wracked with dry heaves as he opened the barrels of rancid material.

"Smells like the latrine after Bly used it!" Iseal said through his mask.

"Funny. Now get loading," Bly replied dryly.

Despite the covering, Iseal felt the horrid refuse wicking its way into his skin. *I will never wash this slop off!* he thought, his head pounding at the wretched smell. The putrid meat and rotting entrails of long-dead animals were placed in the boltinn—spherical containers made of thin wood specifically designed to throw the foul and decaying matter over the enemy's walls.

"Gently. Remember, they're meant to shatter, spreading our fetid garbage gifts," Bly said.

"Ready," the queasy Iseal said after latching up the boltinn.

"No, no. We have special orders from Friar," Bly yelled. "Open them up."

Iseal opened up the boltinn, and the sergeant dumped in a bag of metal shards. "That should spice things up a bit," he said, smiling.

The first noxious loads of the boltinn smashed behind the walls of the Citadel. Screams and cries ripped through the air as shards of shrapnel and excrement sliced into soldier and civilian alike—each wound a death sentence. Septicemia and high fevers would quickly set in, signaling death was dancing close by.

"Sir, the dragon rides are ready," Iseal said, hopeful they could depart.

"We aren't done yet," Bly said. "We have more presents to deliver."

Behind the walls, Lidenskap seethed. The idea of sticking to his plan was becoming harder to swallow. "Throwing entrails and feces over the walls? Spineless."

"I'm not surprised," a lieutenant replied.

"Why are we taking so few hits with that many siege engines laid out before us? It could mean factions of our enemy are convulsing in unorganized chaos and ripe for the picking," Lidenskap said.

"The troops are assembled and await your order to attack," the lieutenant said, his words coming out quickly, spurred by excitement.

"The Knights have chosen good, high ground and are sure to have many gutless archers," Lidenskap said. *What if the other siege engines are aiming towards the gates, waiting for us to exit before hammering us?*

Another round of the rancid projectiles smashed around Lidenskap as he struggled with the decision blocking his way.

"General Lidenskap," a scout interrupted. "We have a visual on the contingent from Jaa heading for the Citadel. Your orders?"

"How many?" Lidenskap asked.

"All of them, sir."

This is my answer. Praise Tallcon! Lidenskap thought. "Quickly now, send a messenger. Tell the warriors of Jaa to attack the Knights' right side, flanking them. Assemble our troops at the gate. When the Jaa contingent is closing on the enemy's flank, we will break forth and attack from the front. We can roll up their lines and crush them all!"

"Yes, sir," the soldier said, sprinting off.

General Lidenskap impatiently paced upon the littered walls of the Citadel. Anticipating ending the Knights in one swift blow made time crawl. "Where are the rest of the civilian patrols? This rancid mess needs cleaning up!"

"More arrive each minute," the lieutenant said.

"Have you summoned Veneficus and his Magicians?"

The lieutenant hesitated. "Twice, but…no reply."

The warriors of Jaa looked like a giant white caterpillar inching along the plains towards the Citadel. Lidenskap smiled. They had sent their entire contingent of fierce women warriors. *This will be a quick victory.*

"Attack, sir?"

General Lidenskap gazed into the lieutenant's animated eyes, blazing with youthful excitement.

"Dashing in at the wrong time is sure formula for defeat. A little more patience is required. The Jaa Warriors need to cover another half mile before—"

He didn't finish, as the lieutenant tackled him to the wall-walk. A loud crack echoed in their ears as the wooden boltinn disintegrated into a shower of splintering shards. Their ears rung as the slivers jingled and tinked off of armor, their noses quickly filling with the putrid smell as refuse rained down on them.

Infuriated, Lidenskap stood up, throwing the lieutenant off his back. The startled lieutenant landed hard against the battlements. He stared up at Lidenskap, who was gazing at the warriors of Jaa, willing them to move faster.

"Lieutenant! Gut the Knights! Attack!" he screamed. "Get me a runner! Veneficus better get here right now! Their dragons will obliterate us without the Magicians and griffins to cover the air."

Iseal looked up to the quivering siege engine wearily, sighing heavily through its stroke of death. *The forces of Jaa are getting close, too close.* Sweat poured outward, weaving its way through his heavy wool coverings, intertwining with the foul fluid wicking inward, soaking his skin in rancid liquid. *Give the bloody order to retreat! Do they expect a handful of Knights and a few Dwarves skilled in prestidigitation to stand against two armies?*

"Get back to loading the boltinns!" Bly yelled. "That slop won't pack itself!"

Without speaking, Iseal pointed to the Citadel. A stream of Proliate Red Guard flowed out of the castle gates with blazing efficiency. Despite the bottleneck of the bridge and barbican, the Proliate were surging through at a full sprint thanks to their ordered, well-practiced discipline. All along the top of the gates and white towers the Red Guard could be seen raising their arms and chanting "Tallcon!"

"We have to take off now!" one of the Dwarves yelled. "Now!"

At that moment, the warriors of Jaa gave a fearsome shout—raising their menacing guanduo weapons and breaking into a sprint.

"To the dragons!" Bly yelled. "Retreat to Ovest!"

The Dwarves stopped wielding their loitsia sticks. Instantly, the facade of a massive Allied army dropped away, leaving two trebuchets, a handful of Knights, a few exhausted Rebelde Plains Dwarves, and Vioma Dragons. Confused, the women warriors of Jaa slowed. Perplexed but undeterred, the Proliate continued to fly towards their position. Recovering from their shock, the women of Jaa were quickly moving again.

"Hurry up, you fools!" one of the Aer Ridire Dwarves howled, struggling to keep his Vioma Dragon calm at the approach of two armies.

Iseal struggled to get the wet, foul wool off as the others bolted for the Vioma Dragons with open platforms. They quickly began scurrying up the wobbling rope ladders as the nimble warriors of Jaa dashed closer.

"Iseal, here now!" Bly yelled frantically. The four armored Vioma serving as escorts took off and showered the warriors of Jaa with bursts of flames as the Aer Ridire added crossbow bolts. A large dent scorched through their front lines as the lucky ones fell by bolts and the unlucky by the slow, painful sear that is dragon's breath. Other Jaa Warriors struggled to douse the flames, only stopping when the dragon naphtha ravaged the flesh of their comrades, eventually charring down to bone. Many had the burning naphtha transferred to their own bodies, beginning their own convulsions of pain.

"Bloody hell, Iseal! Move *right* now!" Bly screamed as the enemy closed in on the restless dragons, shuffling tensely.

"The rest of you, get moving," an Aer Ridire on a transport dragon yelled. "I'll stick around…at least for another minute."

"Don't wait too long. That number of Jaa Warriors will quickly flank, and overwhelm, your dragon," another replied.

The rest of the dragon riders urged their Vioma Dragons into flight. Five of the transport dragons made it into the air while the last grounded dragon snorted enviously at those soaring to safety. His nervous stomps began to shudder with increasing apprehension as his driver struggled to provide reassurance. The single rope ladder quivered nervously under the dragon's agitated movements.

"There are too many warriors to slow them all down! We need to leave!" the Aer Ridire yelled as the four covering dragons continued spewing fire.

Iseal had his gloves and chaps off but was tangled in his rancidly soaked woolen vest.

"You, run to me right now!" Bly yelled. "That's a direct order, Knight!"

Obediently Iseal began to run to the last grounded dragon as the army of Jaa closed in. With their heavier armor the Proliate were still minutes away.

"Speaking of right now, we need to take off, Bly!" the Aer Ridire driver pleaded.

"Hold."

As the word came out, Iseal tumbled, slipping on a puddle of the refuse he had helped fire at the enemy. As he skidded to a stop, he looked up, knowing his fate had been sealed.

One of the escort dragons lit up the Knights' two trebuchets, and the flames shot up behind Iseal, instantly turning him into a struggling silhouette. Bly stepped off the dragon platform onto the ladder just as the first guanduo sliced into Iseal's leg.

Iseal screamed as the Aer Ridire driver jerked the reins up and the dragon frantically exploded into the air. Bly managed to strap in at the last second, watching in horror as the warriors of Jaa engulfed Iseal in a sea of vengeful blades. Long after his body was a lifeless pile of severed flesh floating in a lake of blood, the strikes continued to pierce and shred. Somberly, the dragons flew towards the real camp of the Knights and Dwarves, outside Temple Ovest.

"What devilry is this?" Princess Hamaza shouted.

"What did you expect from a bunch of criminal traitors? They sold out to the Dark Warriors to save their own skin. We should not be surprised they are resorting to deception," Lidenskap said as the two met in his office after the battle.

"I lost over fifty warriors and they but *one*!" the princess howled. "My warriors still burn with unquenchable naphtha even as they enter their graves. Every fiber of my being, and that of my country, demands revenge! That a handful of Knights and a few dragons could play such a trick in front of the home of the Magicians is absurd, if not a signal of your own corruption!"

Lidenskap refused to blame Veneficus, even though he had summoned him repeatedly. "I take responsibility and assure you we want vengeance as well. They have fouled our sacred city and spilled your hallowed blood. Our scouts are scouring the countryside looking for—"

He was cut short by a knock. Without waiting to be told to enter, the door burst open.

"Storlax!" Lidenskap blurted, fearing repercussions of his failure. Then he noted the scorched appearance of the High Commander. "What…?"

"You first," Storlax retorted.

Lidenskap related the Knights' duplicity.

"Tired of hearing these ridiculous stories from scouts about the Knights and Dwarves appearing and disappearing, I rode out to see for myself. We found and killed a few Northern Dwarves and handful of Dwarves from the Rebelde Plains using the false black magic. After listening to your tale, I can see deception *is* their plan," said Storlax.

"We were just about to rout them when a blasted Vioma Dragon dropped out of the skies. We were trounced, and I barely escaped with my life on a griffin. Our experiences are a wake-up call. In all ground battles we need to have air support to deal with dragons, or we burn. I—"

The High Commander was cut off by a frantic knock on the door.

"Come!" Lidenskap yelled.

A disheveled-looking scout stumbled in. "Sir…and High Commander," he said, giving the Proliate salute. "I have urgent news. There's a *massive* army attacking Temple Ovest."

"Another trick…perhaps?" Lidenskap wondered, looking questioningly at Storlax. "What say you?"

"I don't believe so, sir. The walls are taking a tremendous beating from a huge array of siege engines, and I personally saw the size of their army. I barely made it through, and only after my squad took massive losses."

"It looks like we know where you get your revenge, princess," Lidenskap said.

Scroll 4: West, Meet East

Time, and the distance he covered, seemed to grind forward while his breath and heart rate soared. *Keep moving,* Scelto repeated. His lungs' complaints reshaped from a burn to stinging fire as his throbbing muscles, not to be outdone, closed in on exhaustion. Scelto slowed as Gimelli abruptly groaned. Tenderly laying her down, he cradled her head.

Gimelli's eyes frenziedly opened wide, a white film covering them. The coating quickly disappeared, and her face softened. "What… where?" she mumbled, her yellow eyes looking hollow and vacant within her pale face. "Why do I feel so weak?"

"It's a long story."

"I love you, Scelto," she said, her eyes brightening briefly.

A storm of emotions surged through his body and mind, tumbling and climbing until rolling out of his mouth as an inept, "Hey."

Her eyelids fluttered as a white web rose to obscure her eyes before she passed out.

"Is all you can think of? Seriously, you're a moron," Scelto huffed to himself as unwelcome flashbacks of soiling himself with Princess Hamaza flashed in his mind. "Undead I can handle. Girls, not so much."

Just before he was about to pick her up, he froze. Closing his eyes, he cocked his head sideways, straining to listen. A series of demented howls scorched the air, quickly followed by a loud rustling sound as hundreds of the Wasted Undead crashed through the forest not far behind them.

"I'm going to eat you slowly while you're still alive!" Ichor's mother howled. "So you killed a few undead. Can you beat an army of Wasted Undead?"

A furious, inhuman series of growls and shrieks stung the air. After taking a deep breath, he opened his eyes, picked Gimelli up, adjusted her weight, then took off running. *No. No, I can't beat an army of those things.*

"I smell your blood and sweat!" one of them yelled.

Keep breathing, Scelto told himself, his chest heaving under the strain. Just like when in their gruesome village, his heart thumped in his chest. Despite his best efforts, he could feel his heart racing faster as his breath became labored.

"No cooking this one, boys!" Ichor's mother screeched. "We eat him alive!"

"First, we devour the girl!" an undead bawled. Ichor's mother howled with laughter, apparently thinking that was both a funny and great idea.

"I really hate these things," Scelto huffed.

Gimelli's body spasmed, throwing off his stride. He lurched to his left—luckily, a black oak tree was near. Tucking Gimelli in to protect her, his shoulder rammed into the hard bark. He shifted her over, using the tree to leverage her weight while taking several deep breaths.

A deep cackle from somewhere behind woke him up to the reality he had no time to rest if he wished to survive. Letting out his own primordial scream, he started off again.

"Good! Use your energy screaming. We're gaining!"

Without looking back, he called on all his strength to push his body forward. Despite the effort, his pace rapidly started to slow. His mind raced for solutions. If he stood to fight, he would quickly be overwhelmed. There was nowhere to hide Gimelli. With the monstrous black fangs sticking out of their gums he thought it likely they could smell him.

Eventually, exhaustion's momentum grew, teaming up with gravity to weigh down, then slow, his increasingly wobbly legs until he was no longer able to run. Soon even walking made every muscle shake under the strain, burning in protest. His right knee buckled briefly, and his body lurched to the right. He was barely able to compensate and keep upright.

Abruptly, someone grabbed his shoulder, Scelto spun around so quickly he nearly dropped Gimelli, struggling to make sense of what he was seeing. Finally, he recognized Arend. Scelto smiled broadly. With the last of his strength he shifted Gimelli over his head, thrusting her towards the Eaglian before promptly collapsing, his muscles aching, screaming as his breath rattled.

"Kainen!" Arend yelled, cradling Gimelli.

"Hey…" Kainen paused, taken aback by the sight of Gimelli looking pallid to the point of death, and Scelto, his muscles quivering in exhaustion, his entire body splattered with blood. "What the actual…?"

"No time," Scelto huffed. "Arend needs to fly Bellae and Gimelli to safety, we are about to have a shit-ton of undead on us."

"Gimelli!" Bellae cried out, dropping to her knees and sobbing at the sight of her sister. Her eyes scoured over the seemingly endless puncture wounds, some still oozing, others coagulated black, as Crann came over, tenderly rubbing his nose against Bellae's back.

"Wait," Kainen said. "Did you say un…dead?" *I knew the rumors about this forest were true,* he thought, more than a little angry with Sankari for forcing them into this heinous forest.

"Undead is what the vampire guy called them, but they're partially alive."

"Just rest a minute and then…" Kainen was interrupted by a series of savage cries.

"Do you want the girls to end up chained in a pool of their own shit?" Scelto asked.

"Wait, why is that even an option?" Lontas asked, helping Scelto take a drink.

"Listen, we need to move *right* now," Scelto gasped after taking several large gulps, the cool liquid feeling amazing worming through his parched throat. "Vampires and undead—partial-dead, zombies, freaks, whatever you want to call them—are coming, and they are pissed. I may have killed their leader…and like a half a dozen or so."

Sankari huffed, "He's cray-cray-craaaazyyy."

Thunderous crashing sounds echoed along with inhuman howls. They could now hear a large group rumbling through the forest directly for them.

"Maybe we should listen to Scelto," Lontas said.

"If we stay and fight, we all die," Scelto added.

"What about going north? South? Try and get away," Lontas asserted.

"I'm pretty sure they can smell us and won't stop until they kill me and Gimelli," Scelto said, slowly rising.

"Let's go towards the Fionain," Kainen suggested. "Listen, listen!" he said over their protests. "They obviously hate…whatever those things are. The Fionain freaked out over those weird wooden masks hung up as a warning. The creatures Scelto ran into must have put them up as an impromptu border. If we lead them close enough to the Fionain, maybe those things will stop, just like the tree creatures did."

"What are we supposed to do then?" Sankari asked, fluttering hotly. "What if the Fionain show up and attack? We'll be stuck between two groups trying to kill us."

"We'll sort that out later," Kainen answered, glaring angrily at the Fairy, but equally upset at himself for not trusting his gut to avoid this forest. "When I look around, the only semi-safe direction is east."

"I trust his Elf eyes," Arend said, nodding.

"Didn't help us with the Fionain!" Sankari huffed.

"Actually, I did see them, just too late…"

"Enough!" Scelto yelled. "All I know is that we can't stay here. No way am I ending up in one of those feces huts."

"What's with you and the—"

"They're close. Move right now," Arend interrupted Kainen, adjusting Gimelli and heading back to the east.

The others followed, Lontas helping Scelto, Sankari fluttering in the rear, keeping watch. As they popped between the pervasive forest shadow and scarce bursts of light, it seemed as if they, and time, were drudging forward.

"Pick it up, guys!" Sankari warned as the Wasted Undeads' wailing howls grew closer. "Who's that screaming lady?" she asked of the cackling voice.

"The mother of the head-guy, vampire thing. She's a little upset."

"You think?" Sankari hissed. "The mission was to find food, not make us someone else's."

"We were so hungry, and their food smelled delicious...until we found out it was people being cooked in green slop."

Lontas dry-heaved, his face shuddering in revulsion while they continued to move as fast as possible away from the wretched swarm pursuing them.

"Guys, I don't know if we can—" Kainen was cut off as they all came to an abrupt halt.

The grating screech of the Fionain directly in front of them crashed against the furious wailing of the undead closing in behind. Bellae stepped forward, her normally melodic talking-to-animals voice transforming to a guttural grating sound.

After listening to them for several moments, she pivoted to the others. "They hate the 'dead' who inhabit the west woods and say it's time to reclaim their forest."

"That's good," Lontas replied as Bellae swiveled to listen again.

She suddenly nodded vigorously. "We agree."

"What did we consent to?" Kainen asked.

"If we fight those they call the dead, and then leave their forest immediately, they will help us defeat them and not kill us. After seeing us battle two of their kind so fiercely, they decided to head west to help us rid the forest of the dead."

The Fionains' jarring words were mostly unrecognizable to everyone but Bellae. However, several creaked coherently, "Revenge" and "our forest."

Sagely laying Gimelli down behind them, the others drew their weapons and turned to face the coming horde. The Fionain stomped forward, making space for the League in their swarming line.

"I'm glad they're fighting with us," Lontas said, staring up into the vacant black holes that served as eyes of the one closest to them. The Fionain opened its mouth, and hundreds of filamentous cirri shot forward in tune with a rolling screech that sent a shiver of fear through the young squire.

"Kill!" the creature moaned, using his vine-like arm to point towards the approaching undead.

"Yep, got it," Lontas replied, holding his sword a little tighter.

Looking back at Gimelli, still passed out behind them, Scelto let loose his own rumbling growl. Shaking out his muscles, he took a deep breath, trying to suppress the horrific visions from the village. Sensing Lontas' gaze, Scelto's head whirled, wide-eyed, towards his fellow squire and whispered, "Kill them all."

Lontas swallowed hard, nodding as Scelto's mind drifted to the black fangs, roasting humans, chains of the feces-filled hovel, and Liha attacking despite her wounds. "Brain shots or take off their heads. Cutting open or cutting off anything else is useless," he warned.

The racket from the legion of undead crashing through the forest grew, and they could now see flashes of them hurtling through the frames of branches, needles, and leaves. Abruptly, the forest around them exploded with activity as dozens of undead burst through the undergrowth to stand across from them—stunned to see Fionain.

Ichor's mother emerged, pushing through the agitated rows of the soulless. The front lines of undead were still in relatively good shape, the stragglers bringing up the rear, the wasted ones, were littered with lacerations, deep sores, and oozing wounds, brushed with a greenish hue. The smell of death and excrement wafted through the forest as the hundreds of Wasted Undead joined the others.

"They literally smell like rotting flesh and shit," Sankari retched.

"I warned you about the dung huts," Scelto said.

"Be gone, Fionain!" Zlota shouted. "You're in *our* side of the forest, and we will have that food." A heinous smile ripped across her face, revealing pointed teeth and wriggling black fangs as she pointed to the League.

Suddenly, one of the Fionain lurched forward, lifting Bellae up with the many tentacles of its arms. Before Scelto and Kainen could come to her defense, the Fionain gently set her down in front of them before speaking in his scraping language.

Bellae nodded, then translated, "They're going to kill all of you, Zlota, all your sick underlings, and reclaim their forest. The peace accord is broken."

Ichor's mother laughed. "Your harpy friends killed my boy. I will not rest until you are all dead. We shall rip the flesh from your bones with our teeth. Your death shall be slow and painful. If I have to kill all the Fionain to do it, so be it—more room for us."

Bellae smiled. *I've heard those ultimatums plenty of times from the Nishi.* "What an original threat."

Zlota spoke in her own halting language, shouting orders. After finishing, a greasy smile spread across her face. "We shall drink the blood of those brats and bathe in the sap of you overgrown shrubs!"

The Wasted Undead moved forward, through the rows of healthier ones, howling and screaming. Some scurried on all fours, others lurched in jerking spasms, a few limped, but all had green eyes radiating hatred from within faces of sallow complexion. Massive sores littered their entire bodies while erosions circled their legs and arms where shackles had chained them in their huts of horror. As the wasted neared the Fionain, the healthier undead moved backwards before heading to their right, towards the left flank of the Fionain.

Kainen let loose a barrage of arrows. Two were direct headshots, instantly dropping the targets. As Scelto predicted, body shots did nothing to slow them down. As Kainen continued to fire and kill, the Fionain shuddered with pleasure as each undead target fell.

Despite his weakness, Scelto was the first to step forward as the undead rushed towards them, his sword impaling through an attacker's eye socket. Scelto's thrust combined with the undead's momentum pushed the blade through the skull until it hit the sword's cross guard. Blood gushed out, rushing onto the countless sores on the undead's disfigured face. Some lesions percolated with active infection. A few were so deep you could see through sinewy windows into his festering mouth.

Before he could withdraw his sword, Scelto roared as one of the Wasted Undead running on all fours latched onto his leg. In a panic he ripped his sword violently upwards. The decomposing neck muscles snapped, and Scelto found himself with a detached head impaled on his sword, receiving another blood bath as spurts of gore shot out of the headless neck while the twitching corpse dropped. He stepped back as the one on all fours continued to lunge forward, violently clawing at Scelto. The undead's left eyelid had decayed, resulting in a wide-eyed look—giving his already maddening expression a beefy, psychotic appearance.

The undead thrust himself upwards. Now clutching Scelto's shirt, he shrieked a deranged cackle. His decayed mouth flung ajar, his filed teeth set to bite when Scelto began beating him with the head still affixed to his sword. Repeatedly, the blows rained down. Loud cracks filled the air as both skulls began to fracture. Finally, the undead fell to the ground. Scelto pointed his sword down and speared through the attacker's skull…repeatedly.

"Think he's dead there," Sankari said, fluttering anxiously. She moved to flitter around the head of an attacking undead, distracting him long enough to give Lontas time to react.

Lontas whipped his sword around, its blade chopping into the neck. It was enough of a blow to drop the undead assailant but not sufficient to completely decapitate him. Bellae moved forward with her small sword. Twisting with all her might she hacked at the tissue still clutching the head to the body.

The nearly headless attacker was still alive and with one hand grabbed Bellae's cloak, while the other landed several blows to her face. Grym and Borb angrily skittered across her arms and began chewing on the undead's eyes while scratching into his ragged and swampish skin. The two mice chewed mercilessly into his eyeballs, occasionally shaking their heads side to side in order to rip out larger sections as ocular fluid and blood flooded their fur. Their claws continued to dig and shred the scabrous skin of his face.

Blinded and enraged, his blows became much less effective. He let go of her arm to swat at the mice. With the distraction, Bellae managed to finish the decapitation, and his body descended into inactivity.

Grym began spitting out the repugnant flesh. "*This guy tasted dead and seriously needs a bath.*"

"For once I agree with Grym," Borb said. *"Now we seriously need a wash. Dead-guy eye goo is, as you might expect, disgusting."*

"Thanks for the assist, guys," Bellae said, holding the sore and reddening spot on her face.

Crann used his whip-like tail to upend an undead coming for Bellae. Spinning around, he began mercilessly stomping on its head until it was crunched into flattened gore, and all movement stopped.

"Thanks," Bellae said, gently patting the horse's neck.

"Move back, Scelto!" Kainen shouted, warning of an undead vaulting towards him.

As Scelto withdrew, Kainen slammed a side kick into the attacker's face before performing a three-sixty spin, his kama weapon cutting into the undead's heart. As the zombie fell, Kainen rained down blows, the sharp beak from Creber easily obliterating the zombie's neck, relieving it of the responsibility to hold the head in place.

The Fionain closest to the League threw down one of the undead, then rammed one of his spider-like legs through its skull. Another simultaneously shot his arm tendrils through the eye sockets, up the nose, and into the mouth of an undead before whirling and rotating the filamentous fingers until the zombie's brain liquefied and his body went flaccid.

To the left of the League sudden screeching howls of agony from the Fionain were followed by a cackling laugh from Zlota. Dozens of the sturdier undead had moved around to their left flank and were overwhelming the arboreal creatures. Using sheer numbers to overcome individual Fionain, they were rolling up the line.

Some of the undead threw clay pots, which shattered on impact, releasing noxious gas, which slowed the Fionain, as it had Gimelli. The arboreal creatures hit by the toxic vapor went flaccid, their viney arms falling slack at their sides. Although most had not brought weapons, a few undead had axes and quickly moved forward with blurring speed to rain down vicious blows. In reality they were not moving faster, but the dazing gas altered the victims' perceptions.

Sap exploded out as they mercilessly chopped and slashed at the Fionains' faces. After their trunk bodies hit the ground, the undead continued hacking until their tree-faces splintered. As other Fionain moved in to assist, they too were greeted with the smoke-filled grenades.

Even without the gas several of the tree creatures had fallen and were being gouged and torn apart by the crazed undead. Numerous zombies were teaming up, pulling, ripping, and detaching limbs and branches. Brutal screeching howls of pain and heinous shrieks oozed out of the maimed and dying Fionain.

Scelto made a move in that direction to help but was restrained by the tendrils of a Fionain. He soon discovered why as loud cracking sounds exploded all around the forest. Hundreds of new Fionain descended from all sides. They rolled onto the undead like a wave, many using the masks that had served as a restrictive barrier to bludgeon the overwhelmed zombies.

The last of their gas-filled containers were thrown, but other Fionain emerging from the forest simply moved past their stunned comrades. Using their innumerable tentacle arms, they quickly took possession of all axes. One undead was held up by his arms while an axe bisected his head. Harsh howls of revenge bellowed out of the arboreal creatures.

Four Fionain grabbed the cursing and thrashing Zlota. Their writhing tentacles became taut, lashed onto each of her extremities, and began viciously pulling. Their arachnid roots serving as legs surged backwards, wrenching her body taut. Her scream joined the dying shrieks of the other undead. With a ripping slurp they dismembered her, throwing her appendages and letting her body fall. Wriggling on the ground, she continued to scream as blood streamed out from where limbs were absent.

"My other sons shall rise and seek revenge! We shall repopulate the forest, and the world, with undead!" Zlota screamed, her eyes flashing pure hatred as her lips snarled. A heinous laugh echoed from her as she glared at the four Fionain standing over her.

After listening to her for a moment, they took turns stomping on her until only a beefy bloodbath remained. As the last of the undead were crushed, a resonant silence echoed off the gore-soaked forest floor, taking the place of the now-silenced screams and howls still chiming in their ears. The Fionain looked around fiercely, gazing for any more of the undead. Satisfied none remained, they joined their tendrils together. Lifting their heads back, they let out a piercing howl. The grating noise sounded like a thousand trees scraping and grinding off each other.

Arend hustled over to Gimelli, quickly lifting her up. "Let's get out of here."

The others nodded and began heading west.

Several tendrils whipped out, wrapping around Bellae's neck, lashing her backwards. As the howling stopped, a Fionain that had not been fighting hobbled forward from the forest shadows. His movements were slow, disjointed, painful. Several of his arm tendrils were immobilized, dangling flaccidly. Two of his leg roots were disabled, dragging tediously behind.

Bellae was forcibly twirled around to face him as Lontas restrained Scelto. "Let's see what happens. They let us go once. There's no reason to think they won't keep their word."

"I don't see malice around them," Kainen added.

"But they have Bellae," Scelto seethed despite his exhaustion.

"I know, but look around," Lontas replied, nodding to the hundreds of Fionain closing in around them, many moist with blood and fleshy splatters from the undead still coloring their bark. "We're in no position to fight them."

Standing excessively close to Bellae, the ancient Fionain used some of his working tendrils to hold up her chin, turning her head side to side. Gently he rubbed the redness around her eye, which was quickly swelling. In a gravelly, scratching voice he spoke to her for a long time.

Eventually, Bellae nodded, hugged him, then slowly moved to the others. "Time to go."

The League headed west through the forest.

"The elder Fionain recognized Gimelli's wounds and gave me a suggestion," Bellae said.

"Right now, let's get some distance between us and them," Kainen said. "We'll get the details later."

"Let's give the dead village Scelto and Gimelli blundered into a wide berth," Sankari said, fluttering pridefully, as if their stumbling into the village was worse than her insistence they enter the forest in the first place.

"Definitely. That lady who had her arms and legs amputated screamed there were more who could rebuild," Lontas added.

"Exactly. Those vampire creatures, like Ichor, didn't fight," Scelto said.

"What the?" Arend howled as Gimelli shrieked, her eyes exploding to reveal haunting white fibers. After her body spasmed several times, her eyes closed and her screaming stopped.

"Yeah, her eyes look like that now." Scelto sighed.

"Are all those spots bite marks?" Sankari asked.

"Yes," Scelto said, explaining the barbed tendrils of Ichor that leached from his fanged hands.

"I thought vampires bit people with their teeth," Lontas said.

"No. His teeth were blindingly bright white because he eats through the tendrils and fangs within his hands," Scelto said.

"Does this mean she's going to turn into one of…whatever they were?" Sankari asked.

"Absolutely not!" Scelto steamed.

"We should stop and rest," Lontas said.

"We're too close to that village of the damned," Kainen said. "We keep going."

After several hours of travel, Scelto paused before taking several deep breaths, his face shuddering in discomfort. Letting out a gasp, his body collapsed to the ground, his hands clasping his hamstrings as they seized in painful cramps.

"We have to rest," Kainen said. "We should be far enough from that village."

"Agreed," Arend replied. "It's time to take care of Gimelli."

"We should keep going. Scelto can suck it up," Sankari said.

"We rest!" Kainen said, his anger with Sankari boiling over.

"Gimelli's running a fever," Arend informed, gently setting her down.

"Is that good?" Lontas asked.

"No clue. What *would* have been good was to avoid this horror show of a forest," Kainen seethed, still glaring at Sankari. "What do we need, Bellae?"

"The elder Fionain said we need arnebia plants," she said, wiping the sweat from Gimelli's forehead before starting on the monumental task of cleaning her wounds.

Kainen nodded to Arend. "Arnebia, that's a good thought."

As those two and Sankari headed out to look for medicines, Lontas and Bellae huddled near the now-moaning Gimelli. Scelto fell asleep, and Crann stood guard.

"She looks super pale," Lontas said.

Bellae nodded, tears welling in her eyes. "I don't think I could handle it if she dies."

Not knowing what to say, Lontas gently rubbed his friend's back. After several moments, he spoke, "What are the Fionain?"

Bellae looked up. "A long time ago, they were more animal than tree. At first, I thought they were humanoid, but they are kind of a mix, which is why I could talk to them. They adapted to draw nutrients from trees, never taking enough to kill them. They—"

"A symbiotic relationship!" Lontas interrupted excitedly. "You know, a lot of people mistakenly think *both* need to benefit from a symbiotic connection. Not true. It's simply a close relationship between two different beings or species where at least one gains an advantage. It could be protection, food, anything really. The other in the dyad could have a negative—parasitic, positive—mutualistic, or neutral—a commensalism outcome in the relationship. Some examples of each kind of symbiotic relationship include..."

Lontas stopped at the sight of tears and disinterest radiating from Bellae's eyes, one swollen and turning black from being hit. He murmured, "Oh, sorry."

"Many generations ago, the Fionain apparently began spending more and more time attached to trees, and now they spend most of their lives with just one."

"Did that old Fionain tell you that?"

"Yes. He also mentioned his ancestors referred to a group of human friends who could talk to them. He says they are the ones who taught them some words of the common tongue. Because of their connection to each other, they have kind of a collective knowledge. So what one knows, they all know once they connect."

"So they were friends with the Ainmhi Caint?"

"Apparently. He remembered them as kind. I was a big reason they didn't kill us. He actually thanked us for helping them rid the world of what he called 'spirit assassins.' It was his life's goal to reclaim the entire forest for the Fionain before he died."

When Scelto came to, Gimelli was lying next to him. She was sleeping, and her skin was heavily bandaged, each injury oozing an orangish-yellow hue underneath.

"We used the arnebia plant," Kainen said, holding up bunches of small yellow flowers, each with five petals, giving them a star-like appearance. Every stalk had hundreds of small tendril-like leaves that gave Scelto a chill, reminding him of the vampire's whip-like appendages.

"Arend flew to get them. Luckily, there are few griffins and no Watchers this far west. Obviously, the stories are true and the Fionain elder knew about these ancient plants as a cure. It seems vampires don't like arnebia, so they must have had the undead pull it from the forest."

"I think we caught the change in time," Arend added.

"You *think*?" Scelto said, sitting up quickly. "Does that mean you believe there's a chance she *might* turn?" He moved protectively closer to Gimelli, staring at her anemic face, longing to see her famous smile. "Are the bandages orange because the plant's mixing with her blood?"

"No," Arend answered. "We mixed in sap from the dragon trees of the Marskimaa Wetlands."

Scelto looked up in surprise. "You flew all the way there?"

"Yes. Our warriors regularly go and cut open the bark to collect the healing red-orange sap."

Scelto nodded. "I'm eternally grateful, my friend."

Gimelli's eyes suddenly burst open, the sinewy white film stretching across them, giving her a tortured appearance. Her mouth extended into a blood-curdling scream.

"It's okay," someone was saying, but Gimelli saw only darkness. *What's happening?* she wondered, desperately wanting to ask why she couldn't talk or see. *I feel like I'm stuck in a giant well of mud.*

"That's it. Calm down, calm down," Kainen said as Lontas wiped the sweat from her brow.

"She's burning up," Lontas said. "Her fever's higher."

Their voices barely registered with Gimelli as Ichor's eyes materialized out of the darkness encasing her mind. Slowly, the drugged incense of the hut materialized. She could hear his mother's cackles. Soon his face took shape, his mouth contorting into a devious smile before opening insanely wide. A hand whipped out of his mouth. Initially, a closed fist, it snapped open to reveal several sets of fangs and tentacles shooting out by the thousands. The black barbs began attaching to eat into her face. She began shrieking louder while hitting, striking out. Thinking she was fighting Ichor, she was actually pummeling the League trying to restrain her.

"She's going to hurt herself or someone else!" Sankari hissed. She was about to suggest dispatching Gimelli to protect the rest of the League when Scelto shot her a blistering look and she thought better of it.

Eventually, Gimelli's eyes closed and she passed out.

"We need to take turns watching her," Kainen announced.

"I'm first," Scelto said protectively.

"That last shriek woke me up," Bellae said, moving next to Scelto. "Thanks for taking first watch. How's it going?"

"Intermittently, she screams and spasms. She lashed out at me several times," Scelto replied, worry etched across his forehead as he nervously rubbed his face. "Her eyes…"

"Still white?" Bellae asked.

He nodded. "She cannot turn, Bellae. She can't."

"I know," Bellae said, moving to embrace Scelto, letting her cloak brush away his tears.

Gimelli's hand clutched the back of Bellae's leg as she let out a vicious bellow. Bellae moved to the other side as Scelto leaned over her, whispering calming words. Gimelli's body began thrashing violently, her teeth bared, biting aimlessly as her eyes splintered open, revealing a pulpy white stare hauntingly gazing out in blind rage. Scelto moved to hold her down as her feverish body convulsed combatively. Her temperature soared as sweat erupted prodigiously while her vacant, ivory eyes flashed frenzied rage.

"Again, again, again?" Sankari whined. "She's like a cracked bard who keeps singing the same line of a song."

"Nice," Kainen said, glaring at the Fairy as Lontas moved to assist.

"Her fever's really up," Arend added, joining them.

"Switch!" Scelto called out after trying to hold the pale, but surprisingly strong, Gimelli for half an hour.

Arend stepped forward and took his place. Scelto moved back, shaking out his tired muscles. He could feel the weight of Kainen's stare. Angrily, he snapped his head towards the Elf, "She *will* be fine!"

"She's absolutely not, by any sane definition, 'fine,'" Sankari hissed. "We don't know what's going to happen, but we should prepare ourselves..."

"She...will...be...fine!" Scelto seethed deliberately.

"I-I know, but you...we, we all need to prepare ourselves for the worst-case scenario," Kainen said gently.

Scelto shook his head, not allowing his mind to settle on the possibility she could turn.

"I think her fever's breaking," Lontas said after another half hour of fitful thrashing. "Finally, she's settling into real sleep."

"For her to recover we have to let her rest, so you might as well get some sleep," Sankari said, fluttering anxiously around Scelto's head. There was a streak of annoyance in her voice, but it was tempered with an unexpected amount of compassion. "I'm not sleeping anymore tonight, so I can help Bellae with the next watch."

As if on cue, Scelto felt a wave of fatigue. As Bellae anxiously watched, he curled up next to Gimelli, quickly fading into sleep.

"How in the world did they get away from those undead?" Kainen wondered.

"Lots and lots of blood. I found six decapitated bodies in a blood-stained clearing with a large rock formation. Looks like the Proliate gave him a really nice weapon during his time with them," Arend said, nodding to Scelto's sword that Lontas began sharpening.

"It's good quality," Lontas replied. "I wonder if there are any more of those undead creatures, and how many vampire things?"

"That's why we avoided the village. After what that lady screamed, I bet there are more."

"Are we safe here?" Bellae questioned, nervously petting Grym and Borb.

"Two of us should keep watch through the night, and we won't risk a fire," Arend said. "Come what may, we move out tomorrow, so you'd better get some rest."

Bellae nodded, but the idea of falling asleep seemed ridiculous. Tenderly, she touched the swollen, throbbing skin around her eye. *Stupid undead.* Besides being worried about her sister every time she closed her eyes, she kept seeing the dead bodies of the zombies. She wasn't sure what they were, and her imagination whipped fear into a frenzy.

Scroll 5: Proud Papa

"This one?" Jumeaux asked.

Irvikuva, the golden gargoyle, crossed his arms. "Yeah. Again, yeah," the living statue said as one of the sealed doors opened. "No one will accuse you of being a scholar."

"This is a cool room," Jumeaux said, entering one of the side chambers off Veneficus' office.

"Actually, you aberration, this room is the exact same temperature as it was in the other chamber. Genius here thinks the temperature changed. This room is not 'cool,' you fool! Amazing that some people think this new generation is lazy, dull-witted, and talentless. You really buck the trend there with your astounding intellect," a Valo stated, rolling his eyes.

"It's my special training center," Veneficus said, ignoring the floating light. "The walls are coated in mindre crystal dust designed to absorb spells."

"That's cool…er, awesome," Jumeaux said glancing at the floating orb as the light rolled its eyes. "I wondered why the walls sparkled." There were all manner of wooden contraptions, from hoops, to people, and monsters, around the room. Several stones ranging in size from small to enormous rose up as well.

Several Valo in the room carried on mumbling insults to Jumeaux as Veneficus continued, "I wouldn't want you blowing up my office or killing yourself."

"Oh, I don't know, boss. I, personally, would love to see this guy blow himself up!" a Valo said, chuckling.

"Are you getting enough to eat? How's the food?" Veneficus asked.

"Yes, and great, thanks. So much better than Liberum."

"Classes going well? Keeping up?"

"Yes."

"What an elegant response, youngling. 'Yes.' How profound," a Valo asserted. "You really paint the picture of how classes are going with your delicate yet thorough descriptions. I feel like I'm living through the experience with you. In fact—"

"Excellent," Veneficus said, interrupting the Valo. "I knew you could handle starting out as an Apprentice."

Jumeaux beamed at the compliment.

"Alright, let's get to it," Veneficus said, handing Jumeaux a crosier.

"Oh, master, I could have done that for you!" a Valo stated, his expression suddenly turning to one of mock surprise. "Oh, that's right! With no arms, I guess I can't. Thanks again for that mildly irritating, and never inconvenient, oversight."

"Let's start with moving things around," Veneficus said.

"I think you have the ex agito hic spell down, Jumeaux," Veneficus said after hours of moving increasingly heavy objects.

After starting with small boxes, by the end, Jumeaux was moving the largest boulder in the room. The former squire wiped the sweat from his forehead, taking several deep breaths.

"You know, big master guy, I think he should work on that spell a little more. I most definitely see room for improvement," a Valo said, looking at Jumeaux with mock concern.

"That's a lot harder than it looks, especially with the heavier boulders," Jumeaux huffed.

"The greater weight requires extra concentration and effort. However, the more you practice, the easier it will become," Veneficus said. "You're learning the first lesson of Magic, stay hungry. You must—"

"You know, I could go for something to eat," a Valo interrupted. "Oh wait, once again, thanks to your incredible kindness, I have no stomach or digestive system. That's fine. You two go ahead and eat if you're hungry. We'll just float around aimlessly."

"I could teach him the ekrixi spell and have him obliterate you into nothingness. Would you like that, my floating menace?" Veneficus asked.

Seeing the rage in his eyes, the Valo floated back silently but continued miming insults.

"Magic and life are successful when desire to achieve your goal encounters concentration. It all starts with having an objective. Once you commit to achieving it, you must ravenously attack it while maintaining clear focus. As your studies progress, you will start to see connections. Desire and focus are strength. Persistence is power. A hunger, a focus, and never giving up, this is the recipe for triumph." Veneficus smiled, placing his hand on Jumeaux's shoulder. "Enough for today. Are Kaveri and Chy treating you well?"

"They've helped me a ton."

"Excellent. You come to me if you have any problems."

"Becoming a Magician and studying with you has been spectacular. It's my dream to become a Master Magician."

"Dreams, which can seem so hardy, even sturdy, within the fortified confines of our skull, acutely become fragile and vulnerable when exposed to the outside world. Each time we fight to achieve a dream, we uncover part of our heart. It takes courage to reveal a dream and diligent fortitude to achieve it. We will try to contact Bellae again soon, and you will continue your studies."

Jumeaux nodded, trying to digest the words. Before he could turn to leave, Veneficus spoke again.

"Remember, don't tell anyone, especially your friends, about this extra training," Veneficus stated.

"I feel guilty about that."

"Do not ever confuse being selfish with looking out for self."

Smiling, Jumeaux nodded before exiting through the door, which magically sealed behind him.

"He's making excellent progress. The Ainmhi Caint blood flowing within will make him an excellent Magician," Veneficus said. When the Valo did not make a snide comment, he pivoted towards them with raised eyebrows.

"Oh, did you want one of us to say something?" a Valo said. "Sorry, I get a headache after pretending to care for so long."

"I told you to let me know if my facial expression gave the impression I cared. I never want to portray the wrong appearance," another Valo added. "Plus, sometimes silence is the only way I can stay out of trouble. Remaining quiet is better than spreading a thick load of bull excrement."

"Although," a third Valo said, "you know our motto: 'Silence is for people too dim to discharge a thriving dose of sarcasm!'"

"You should stop persecuting him and help out that boy," Veneficus said.

"Oh, sure, I would love to help him *out,* but he already *left*!"

"You really don't like him?" Veneficus asked.

"Let's just say if gangly and awkward looks made money, he'd be super-duper rich," one replied.

"In my opinion he looks best when I close my eyes," another said to laughter.

"Enough," Veneficus ordered. "Jumeaux's parasitic self-victimization made it hard for him to feel attached to his sisters, although, now that he is gaining confidence, his fragmented sense of family seems to be healing. He's starting to come into his own, realizing that maturing is a long and arduous path."

"Aww, and people say you don't care," a Valo said while sneering.

"You sound like a proud papa!" Another Valo laughed, his face quickly turning serious as Veneficus' eyes blazed with anger. "I meant that as a complement! Congratulations...er, Dad!"

Scroll 6: Unleash

Lovag rode Behalen to Friar. Even with the sweat pouring off of him he wore a thin smile. The attack had been going well, extremely well. The siege engines had been pounding the walls of Fortress Ovest for hours.

"The group attacking the Citadel has returned," Friar informed. "Since the Veli and their Knights arrived earlier today, we are finally at full strength."

"Any casualties at the Citadel?"

"Unfortunately, one," Friar said somberly.

"No sign of movement from Temple Ovest, as of yet."

"The Proliate forces at the Citadel were eventually drawn out by the decoys, but you never know what's going to set these Red Guard off."

"Friar, I'm seeing more troops patrolling the curtain walls and request permission to unleash the rakknivs," Lovag asked.

Smiling, Friar nodded. "I think Finn would be proud to have you unleash his invention. Plus, it may be what we need to draw them out."

"I'll give the order."

"Wait, I'll join you. I want to see this."

Riding to the siege engines, they passed the Dwarves of the Plains feverishly working their loitsia sticks.

"What are rakkniv?" a Dwarf taking a break asked.

"They consist of two extra-large ballistae whose behemoth bolts are connected by razor-sharp wire. Both bolts within the rakkniv are fired at the exact same time with a single trigger mechanism," Friar said.

"As the bolts fly through the air, the razor wire stretches between them, cutting the enemy in two," Lovag added.

"You Knights have waaay too much time on your hands," the exhausted Dwarf huffed.

What the walls of Temple Ovest lacked in style they made up for in thickness. It had two massive flanking towers that soared sixty feet. A tall circular tower with a red phoenix, representing Tallcon, was visible in the distance beyond the massive gate.

"We have been pounding the areas around the gate. It's relatively weak there, at least compared to their colossal walls. If we can't entice them out, we can pound that area into falling, but it could take weeks," Lovag stated.

"We don't have that kind of time, but they don't know that. Keep these siege engines running twenty-four seven!" Friar stated with an edge of excitement.

Friar, Lovag, and some Knights from Liberum were in the center, running the siege engines. A ditch ten feet deep sat in front of them, followed by an earthen rampart complete with wooden spikes. Using night and prestidigitation as cover, they had built the defenses without detection. The Northern Dwarf infantry was stationed behind the siege engines while the Vioma Dragons and their Aer Ridire were hidden up in the Tingij Mountains. The Veli, with the Knights from their castles, were in charge of the eastern flank, protecting it from attack by reinforcements from the Citadel. The intimidating walls of the Way of Trepas rose up on their left.

"Unleash," Lovag said in a quiet but menacing voice. The sharp, tangy snap of the ballistas firing contrasted the slow, aching groan of the trebuchets.

The pairs of bolts fired from the ballistas surged forward, aimed just above the crenelated curtain wall of Ovest—the razor-sharp metal wire in between imperceptible. The right missile of one pair sank into one of the merlons at the top of the battlements while the left swung around, and the razor wire took out several of the defending Proliate. One was decapitated while two others were sliced in half as the wire whipped around and behind the wall. The other razor wire bolts from the rakkniv had similar results.

"Keep the rakkniv unpredictable. Target various parts of the wall, then give it a break before coming back to them," Friar instructed, leaving to find Ritari.

"What are you thinking?" Friar asked upon finding his captain.

"Your plan had better work."

Friar shrugged. "If it doesn't, we won't be around to worry about it."

"Is that supposed to be humor?" Ritari asked with a dash of a smile.

"During battle, it qualifies. Either way, get ready—the night is just about to heat up."

Just then, streaking flames and shrill screams bit through the air as hundreds of Knights unleashed a barrage of fiery, whistling arrows. Behind the pointed tip of each arrow was a rounded section with holes. As the arrows flew, air rushed through the holes, making a high-pitched screeching sound. To make it more terrifying they were presoaked in naphtha and lit on fire. Friar couldn't help smiling at the musical symphony of terror and destruction. The harmonious sounds of devastation were occasionally highlighted by the screams of those on the receiving end.

"Beautiful music tonight," Friar stated, wearing a smile of satisfaction rivaling that of any successful composer.

"It's quite the sight," Ritari said, following the arc of the flaming arrows. "We have reports that the Proliate in the Citadel have taken the bait and are mobilizing with other members of the Confederacy to move against us here at Ovest."

"Excellent. Things are going nicely."

"Why don't you lie down and get some rest?"

"Not a chance. I've never felt more alive," Friar beamed. "The wind has picked up and is blowing into the Temple. Let's unleash the kites."

"At night? In the dark?"

"Why not?" Friar replied. "Make it happen. With the light from the arrows and moons, the images should be fairly unnerving to the Proliate."

After an hour, the melodic barrage abruptly stopped.

Friar smiled, the resonant silence signaling the giant kites were ready. The Knight Kiteer teams had silently moved around the earthen fortifications. The most difficult part was getting the massive kites and their loads off the ground, which was achieved using a modified ballista.

The kites were forged in the shapes of dragons and phoenixes and controlled with two strings. One thick cord flew the kite, the second went to a ring mechanism that, when pulled, would release a payload on the enemy.

"What are we delivering to our Proliate friends tonight?" Friar questioned as Ritari returned from overseeing the kite's deployment.

"Ah, you know, standard welcome baskets: caltrops, excrement, pig heads, and animal entrails—all of which has been marinated to perfection in spoiled food."

"I'm sure the Proliate will enjoy."

"One of the Kiteers asked me what they should do if the wind suddenly changed and the payloads dropped outside the walls."

"What did you say?" Friar asked.

"I told him not to eat any of it."

Friar burst out laughing louder than he had in ages. It echoed around his troops and up to the Proliate on the wall, the cheerful cackle striking more fear than any battle cry. After a few moments, the adapted ballistas fired, sending the kites and their payloads into the air. Their extra-long tails flapped in the wind, helping with stability given the extra weight. Once caught by a current, it took four soldiers to control one kite. The wind stayed favorable, blowing them over the fortress walls. Terrified, the Proliate raised torches, trying to figure out what the strange shapes were.

"Restart the naphtha arrows!" Friar yelled.

The flickering light from the flaming arrows and the Proliate torches gave haunting, strobe-like glances of dragons and phoenixes as the kites fluttered over the walls.

"Ritari! The Proliate are sending reserve troops to the walls, trying to figure out the kites. Run to Lovag! Order him to fire the rakkniv after we release the payloads and reel in the kites! Hurry, now!" Friar yelled.

After dropping their foul payloads, the Knights attached the ropes to a winch, slowly pulling the kites to the ground to be reloaded. The Proliate cries of fury and queasiness were still ringing out as the razor-sharp wires of the rakkniv ripped into the unfortunate Proliate on the walls. The ballista-razor wire combination was wrenching, slicing, and throwing them off the ramparts, leading to fresh screams. The barrage started again as Lovag ran up to Friar.

"Friar, your suggestions *are* adding terror but are killing *us*. None of my men have taken a break, much less slept. We all want victory but…"

"All right, son. Get the Knights some rest," Friar said reluctantly, his voice dripping with disappointment. Despite his soulful knowledge of the horrors of war, he had to admit, there was pleasure in his plan coming together.

"There you are!" Lovag shouted.

Feeling as if he had never slept, Friar's eyes snapped open, his body slouched between two creaking trebuchets. Rolling over to stand, his bones cracked and muscles ached.

"Sorry to wake you, but we have some action. We've been looking for you."

"I'm ready to go," Friar said, despite feeling exhausted, old, and stiff.

Lovag smiled but could see the age in his leader and was pessimistic about the ravages the coming war would unleash. Handing Friar a water skin, Lovag pointed to Ritari, who was gliding towards them.

"Don't scare us like that," Ritari said sincerely.

"I didn't plan on sleeping…it just happened," Friar said, shrugging.

"Our Eaglian friend Aquila has informed one of the Elf runners that the Proliate army from the Citadel *and* the warriors of Jaa will be upon us from the east very soon," Ritari said.

"How did they get here so fast?" Friar answered his own question. "Magic. Any movement from within Ovest?" Friar questioned as he stiffly walked with his captain.

"No, I imagine they'll wait for their reserves before attacking."

"We have to encourage them to come out before they arrive," Friar stated.

"Lovag, spare some of your onagers to the Veli on our flank. They will be the ones to take the first hits when they attack," Friar ordered. As Lovag left, Friar walked up to King Abernan. "Looks like we're going to see action soon."

Abernan nodded excitedly and warmly clasped Friar's arm. "We fight with you. To the end. Whatever happens, to the end."

"Thank you," Friar said, smiling at the intimidating Dwarves.

Scroll 7: Come Out, Come Out

"That's a lot of reinforcements," Ritari mumbled later that day. Friar and the others watched the seemingly endless line of Proliate and Jaa reinforcements march into Temple Ovest. Suddenly, the warriors of Jaa stopped. Those closest to the Knights performed a series of backflips towards them, landing on their knees and thrusting their guanduos menacingly at the Knights while yelling, "Death to you all!"

"I don't think they like us anymore," Ritari said.

"It's hard to see former Allies lined up against you based on lies and deceit," Friar said.

The warriors of Jaa reformed and marched into the Temple but continued gesturing rudely. The Proliate marched in their typical silent, efficient way.

"General Lidenskap is there," Friar said.

"Looks like they aren't going to attack," Ritari stated.

"Either they want to regroup inside Ovest, or they are waiting for even more reinforcements," Friar replied.

The rest of the day went without more excitement as the Knights bombarded the Temple walls near the gates without any Proliate response.

"There's some visible cracking along the gates and corners of the towers, but the blasted rounded towers deflect the force of projectiles," Lovag said.

"Friar!" an urgent yell rang out. Ritari had already been on his way to give his leader some bad news when the messenger sprinted in front.

"What is it, son?" Friar asked. Breathless, the messenger handed Friar a note. The color drained from Friar's face, and his knees trembled. Seeing Ritari approaching, he added, "We've got serious trouble. The army of Ager and the Southern Dwarves are nearly upon us. How did they sneak up on us? Aquila and the Eaglians should have seen them approaching."

"The Eaglians are busy preparing for their upcoming role. Unfortunately, that's not the half of it. We knew the Proliate sent a sizable force out for training exercises in Western Jaa. What we didn't know is that they were given marching orders to move south *before* our attack," the messenger said.

"When?" Friar asked.

"They've been marching for days."

"How did they know to move south before we attacked?" Ritari wondered.

"It's likely they were to be at the Citadel before our fake forces arrived. Either way, they are moving south, along the *western* edge of the Tingij Mountains!"

"They could then strike at our left flank after crossing through the Way of Trepas!" Friar stated.

"That will ruin your plan!" Ritari said.

"Ruin it? That will get us all killed. If they come through Trepas, our escape will be cut off, and we'll be surrounded and crushed in a pincer movement by the armies of Ager and the Southern Dwarves," Friar replied, pacing nervously.

"What are your orders?" Ritari asked, grateful he was not Friar.

"Tell Aquila I need details on the size of the Proliate army coming down from Jaa and accurate information on when they will reach Trepas. We have no choice—we move now!" Friar yelled. "Bring me Pumilus."

"Don't you think it's odd we haven't seen Watchers or Dark Warriors?" Ritari asked.

"No, actually," Friar responded. "I think they've withdrawn, happy to let us kill each other before swooping in to mop us up. The Vioma Dragon scouts have told us they are no longer casting their nets around the mountains."

As Pumilus walked up to Friar, his eyelids fluttered with exhaustion. Gone was the edgy temperament that usually served as an abrasive decoration on his ill-tempered personality.

"We have an emergency," Friar said. The Dwarf just shook his head and let his tired eyes close fully.

"Pumilus, unless you want your rest to come through death, I need you, and I need you now," Friar declared.

Pumilus raised his eyes and nodded.

After they had a chance to talk, Friar stood next to Ritari as they waited for Pumilus and his prestidigitation Dwarves to start. It was only a few minutes, but it seemed like an eternity.

"Should we have Aquila risk direct landings for messages in order to get rid of the delay using the Elf runners?" Ritari questioned.

"Oh, no! Eaglian involvement *must* stay a surprise. Remember your shock at seeing one. Imagine the enemies' fright at a thousand swarming the skies. We will have to go on our wits from here on out."

Ritari was happy to see the mischievous gleam back in Friar's eyes.

"Finally, Pumilus is ready. He looks thinner than usual, and his sparse red beard looks even rattier than normal," Friar said as Ritari nodded.

Suddenly, a large object appeared just to the side of the siege engines. It was covered in a flowing black drape.

The enchanted huuto made Friar's words bellow out. "Behold a stolen sanctus kivi!"

At that Pumilus banged his loitsia sticks, and the fictitious black drape he had created fluttered away, revealing a massive, glowing orange stone.

"We will defile your sacred rock unless you immediately come out from behind your cowardly walls and fight!" Friar continued.

"I saw the sacred stone during the ceremony at the Citadel, and this is an excellent recreation," Friar said to just Ritari. "The Proliate believe the divine volcanic rocks are residue from Tallcon's rebirth."

With no response, Friar nodded to the Dwarves in charge of the prestidigitation. They conjured imaginary Knights defiling the rock. All sorts of nasty substances, including animal blood and waste, were splattered on their holy rock. Several fictitious Knights were also pounding at the rock with war hammers and axes. After twenty minutes without a response, a Knight runner approached at a dead sprint.

"They're coming," he said breathlessly. After a few slow deep breaths he continued, "The army of Piscium is here, and Ager is not far behind!"

"We need to get the Proliate out of that bloody Temple now!" Ritari yelled.

"Friar, I have an idea," Lovag said. "Have Pumilus use the prestidigitation to imitate someone from Piscium being tortured."

"No!" Friar yelled. "That will feed into the lies about us and play right into the Dark Warriors' hands!"

"I also hate the idea, but we don't have a choice. If we're going to follow your plan, especially the phase with the Eaglians, the Proliate *have* to come out of Ovest. Defiling the sanctus kivi was a great idea, but it didn't work. You said we should take advantage of their piety, so..." Ritari added, letting his voice slowly recede.

"If I were them, I'd sit in that Fortress until the Proliate troops coming from Jaa made their way south, moved through the Way of Trepas, and fell upon our left flank," Lovag said. "With Piscium and Ager on our right flank, they have us in a death pincer," Lovag uttered. "I say we fake the torture or retreat."

"If we retreat without drawing them out of Ovest, all the planning, all the surprises we spent years preparing, will go to waste," Friar announced. "However, if we go through with this, there's no turning back. All of the lies told about us torturing and destroying villages will be confirmed in their minds. The point of this war was to force them *back* into an alliance, not destroy any hope of a relationship with the Proliate and all the countries of their Confederacy."

"Was there really any chance of an alliance with the Proliate after all the lies? After these battles dripping with deception and death?" Ritari asked.

"Then why are we here?" Friar thundered.

"When there are no choices left, you fight."

Friar nodded. "I guess deep down, even when I was planning this battle, I knew I was deluding myself all along that peace and unity would ever be an option."

"I can't tell you what to do, but those are the two choices," Ritari stated.

"When you're fighting the wrong war, there can be no victory, no matter the outcome." Friar paused, letting his chin fall heavily on his chest. His brain felt hazy, his mind spinning over anemic knees. Feeling completely off balance, it seemed he was having an out-of-body experience yet, perhaps for the first time, truly seeing the predicament he was in.

Have I led my Knights to their doom? Scanning the faces of those staring expectantly, Friar's breath quickened. His heart bounded as panic showered its pollution across his brain. Everything seemed wrong as his mind played out the coming battle complete with brutal combat and cruel traps. *There are no answers to impossible questions.*

Ritari steadied him.

Although destiny is a myth, sometimes you find yourself with your back against the wall and no choice but to fight. "After all our preparations, there's no way we're walking away. If the stories about the power of the diezmar siege engines are correct, our walls won't hold out. We came here to provoke Lidenskap's self-righteousness until he's ruled by anger. Fake the torture," Friar said with more conviction than he felt.

Pumilus and the others began the difficult prestidigitation. Soon large wooden stakes were conjured, complete with images of Piscinians with various illusory wounds tied to them. Cries of outrage could be heard from behind the walls of the Temple complex.

"Now you will see a truth of war manifested. There can be infinite power in restraint and unadulterated weakness and defeat in attacking," Friar said. "We shall see which path the Proliate choose."

Ritari nodded as Ovest exploded with activity. "Since they swore to protect all those in their Confederacy, the Proliate should have no choice but to advance and rescue the victims being fabricated by the Dwarves."

"Their unwavering conviction is easily sculpted, manipulated," Friar murmured as a loud gong rang from the Temple.

With impressive precision the Red Guard infantry were lined up just inside the gates of Ovest. General Lidenskap strode in front, his eyes wide with rage.

"Each and every one of you, as well as your weapons and pieces of armor, were forged from the sacred fire given by Tallcon. We, the chosen, were spewed forth from the rocky volcanoes making up our home. We are born of righteousness and cannot be intimidated!

"All of us marching into battle have cause to give thanks. No matter our fate, we are victorious. The luckiest amongst us are blessed to die in sacrificial service of Tallcon. Those who live have the honor to carry on his fight another day. So together, in complete faith, let us march against those who defile our land, our friends, and our god. To victory!"

The Proliate roared back their support in voice and rattle of spears against shields. The gates opened, and they flooded out, forming lines to the east to avoid the earthen wall and trench in front of the Temple. Their lines slanted towards the southeast to match the Knights led by the two Veli. The various Red Guard regiments took up the middle and right flank.

"Piscinians," Ritari seethed.

The Piscinian warriors gyrated forward, forming the left flank of the Proliate line. The warriors of Jaa followed the Proliate out of Ovest, taking up a position in reserve.

Directly opposite the Confederate troops were the two Veli from Taiheart and Toil Shaor. Veli Falciss took up position on the right, and Veli Pingius took up the left. Behind the earthen works were the siege engines, and behind them were the Northern Dwarves. A cavalry made up of a combined force of Knights from all three castles had been off to the west, but Friar ordered them back as the situation began taking shape.

"Should we move the Northern Dwarves?" Ritari questioned.

Before Friar could answer, the massive battle horns, the same ones used to pass messages deep in the mines of the Southern Dwarves, blasted into the awkward pre-battle silence. Any remaining birds flew far from the field of battle as their arrival blared across the field.

"Blasted magic, speeding their arrival!" Friar howled.

Directly east, across from the Veli, a long line of Southern Dwarves appeared in their pretentiously gaudy armor. They aligned in six regiments representing the major mines of the Southern Dwarf Kingdom.

"The Veli are going to get flanked and enveloped!" Friar screamed. "Pull them back to re-form here with the Dwarves!"

Immediately, the communication flags and drums of the Knights went to work. However, fierce and cavernous drums of Ager overwhelmed the Knights' message. To the south of the Southern Dwarves the hulking infantry of Ager appeared.

"You've got to be kidding!" Pumilus bellowed, his voice burdened with exhaustion.

Figure 3: Battle of Ovest Battle Key

Figure 4: Battle of Temple Ovest Icon I: The Knights and Northern Dwarves stand against the armies of five nations.

TABLE ONE Battle of Ovest

Allies		Confederacy	
Knights of Liberum:	2,000	**Proliate Red Guard:**	20,000
Knight Cavalry:	1,500	**Piscinians:**	
(lightly armored from all three castles)		**Retiarian Division:**	3,500
Knights of **Taiheart:**	7,500	**Suoli Division:**	3,500
(led by Veli Falciss)		**Warriors of Jaa:**	5,000
Knights of **Toil Shaor:**	5,000	**Southern Dwarves:**	10,000
(led by Veli Pingius)		**Ager:**	8,000
Northern Dwarves:		**Auxiliary Cavalry:**	2,000
Vioma Division: (Green)	7,500	(Heavily armored-inside Temple Ovest)	
Saatana Division: (Red)	5,000		
Rebelde Plains Dwarves: (skilled in prestidigitation)	250		
Total	**28,750**		**52,000**

"Fire onagers!" Friar yelled. "Lovag, get any siege engine that can turn trained on their lines. If they can't turn, keep pounding the Temple!"

"If the Veli don't fall back, they're going to be slaughtered!" Ritari yelled.

"Resend the bloody order to fall back!" Friar shouted.

The onagers Lovag had moved to support the Veli creaked into ferocious action. Their throwing arms slammed into the wooden cross beams propelling large rock projectiles towards the Confederate lines. The large boulders exploded into the Piscinian and Southern Dwarf lines. One rock slammed into an unsuspecting Southern Dwarf's head, thrashing his neck backwards with such force the spine cracked and the muscles tore. His gooey, unrecognizable face hung down by the thinnest of strands of skin down past his shoulder blades, what was left of his eyes staring lifelessly backwards, before his entire body crumpled.

"Abernan, get your Northern Dwarves formed up perpendicular to the end siege engines. As the Veli retreat, they can re-form to the right of your lines. The siege engines and earthen works should protect our flank to the north. Ritari, move the cavalry on the far-right flank!" Friar shouted.

While Ritari informed the signalers, Abernan immediately took off to organize his fierce Northern Dwarves. The meager force of Knights and Northern Dwarves were hopelessly outnumbered against the armies of Ager, Piscium, Jaa, the Proliate Islands, and the Southern Dwarves.

"I need Iontaofa!" Friar yelled. The fastest runner in all of Liberum glided his thin athletic frame to Friar.

"He learned to run before walking and never saw reason to try the latter," Friar said to Ritari before whispering to Iontaofa. "It's time. Alert Aquila and the Eaglians."

Iontaofa smiled and nodded before sprinting off, his feet seeming to barely touch the ground. On his back he carried the tightly rolled signaling flags they needed.

"Hurry!" Friar yelled, but Iontaofa was already far away.

Another messenger arrived. "Veli Falciss is refusing to retreat!"

"Repositioning, *not* retreating," Friar said, pivoting to see Veli Falciss of Castle Taiheart thinning his lines to match the massive army spread out before him. His men moved efficiently and unquestioningly.

Veli Pingius of Castle Toil Shaor, however, was quickly retreating with his forces towards the Northern Dwarf lines—his sizeable body fighting gravity and lack of conditioning as sweat poured off. Friar felt a tinge of embarrassment at the panic in the undisciplined movements.

"You taunt us to come out and then run like cowards!" Lidenskap yelled.

"Send the order to retreat *again*!" Friar shouted. "We must choose our ground wisely."

From across the battlefield Falciss glared back at Friar, blatantly ignoring the signals.

"Runner, now!" Friar shouted. When one sprinted up, he continued, "Tell Falciss I can't help his Knights without endangering my own troops. He is to retreat right…bloody…now!"

Time oozed forward as the two armies closed in on each other.

Sweating profusely, the runner bolted back to Friar. "His reply is, 'I shall never retreat in front of these lowlife red birds!'" Friar seethed, but the runner continued, "'Standing alone I keep alive the Knights' fighting spirit.'"

"We need to help Falciss right now!" Ritari cried longingly.

"He needed to follow orders. His arrogance is going to cost his Knights their lives. If we send troops to his position? Lambs to slaughter. The ground down there is horrible, and the numbers are ridiculous in our enemies' favor. We would be quickly enveloped and destroyed."

"We can't lose one third of our Knight force!" Ritari cried out.

"At this point, we're trying to *only* lose one third. Horrible ground, massively outnumbered, and positioned to be enveloped…they are beaten before it begins," Friar said.

"We must help!"

Friar sighed. "That's your warrior's heart speaking, not your captain's brain. Brave is what is forced upon us when there are no other choices, or when we must stand against evil. Stupidity is choosing to throw yourself, and your troops, into the jaws of defeat under the falsity of valor and frailty of bravado disguised as courage. Falciss will find what he has so longed for—a heroic death, created in his tangled web of a self-fulfilling prophecy."

Ritari looked down, his eyes a mix of rage and aggravation.

"I know what you're thinking, but there's no honor in suicide, and that's exactly what an attack would be. Only a fool throws good troops after bad into a doomed plan. If we attack now, the enemy will kill us all and spit on our graves. Falciss' obstinance, however misguided, is giving us time to form up proper battle lines. Now get over there and organize the mess that is Pingius' troops!"

Ritari left, understanding Friar's reasoning but loath to accept the consequences.

The Confederate troops consisting of the Proliate, Piscinians, and warriors of Jaa were lined up slanting towards the southeast. The armies of the Southern Dwarves and Ager lined up straight south. Veli Falciss spread out his Knights in a thin line across from the Proliate, Piscinians, and Southern Dwarves.

Figure 5: Battle of Temple Ovest Icon II: Veli Falciss disregards several desperate orders to retreat, instead throwing himself, and his Knights, into the jaws of impossible odds.

The Confederate armies paused, confused by the thin line of Knights in front of them.

"Are the Knights really going to sacrifice an entire castle to be butchered?" Emperor Fanga of Piscium wondered aloud.

"Hold the onagers!" Lovag yelled across the battlefield. "We'll risk hitting our Knights. If we aren't going to help, what do we do now?" Lovag asked Friar.

"We watch them die," Friar said, sadness at the reality coiling with anger at Falciss for disobeying orders. "I swear I can see a giant smile on his face even from this distance. Warriors enraptured with a 'glorious' death in battle often find it."

Falciss raised his sword and let out a loud yell. The Proliate Red Guard formed a shield wall anticipating his charge. Falciss turned towards his Knights. "From the time of your birth there was nothing for you to do but die. Now do it with glory. We shall flame out like shooting stars, streaking across the sky until there is nothing left for us to give. To victory! To death!"

"To death!" his Knights shouted.

He led his Knights from the front in a desperate charge. Instead of heading straight ahead, towards the Proliate, they swung to their right and made for the gap between the Piscinians and Southern Dwarves. The Knights crashed into the enemy lines. The Confederate soldiers were caught off guard, surprised to find themselves taking the brunt of the assault.

The Knights initially made headway, hacking through the startled lines. However, they were quickly enveloped as the Piscinians and Southern Dwarves closed in around the vastly outnumbered Knights. The well-organized Falciss had his disciplined troops form up in a square despite the chaos.

General Falciss moved to the center of his encircled Knights. "Do you think you are the only ones who are crazy?" he yelled to those surrounding them.

His troops screamed as one, "Death!"

"Do you think you are the only ones who are fanatical?" Falciss wailed.

"To die!" his Knights shouted back.

The armies of Jaa and Ager misinterpreted Veli Falciss' motives and moved to block any possible escape route for the Knights. He was not trying to break through the lines to escape, but, at least in his mind, sacrificing himself and his Knights to save the Knights' honor while giving the rest of the army time to reform.

Once Falciss and his Knights were surrounded, Lidenskap saw the Northern Dwarves across the field. With a satisfied smile he yelled for the Proliate to advance. Before joining them, he signaled the tower guards. Like one giant shield, the Proliate infantry moved—swinging clear of the Piscinians battling Veli Falciss and his hard-fighting Knights. The Knights who had been manning the siege engines moved to form up lines to avoid having the Proliate move through and around the trebuchets, potentially rolling up the Northern Dwarves' flank. Even after the creaking and groaning complaints of the trebuchets fell silent, the sound still replayed in the ears of the Knights who had been manning their unceasing assault.

When the Proliate were just over a hundred yards from the Knights and Northern Dwarves, their red shield wall suddenly stopped before parting to reveal a hard-charging cavalry leaving the gates of the Temple.

"Heavy cavalry!" Ritari yelled.

Friar called out several commands. As his orders were being carried out, he reveled, "A novice using cavalry, Lidenskap made a crucial error revealing his plan so early! He should have waited to have the infantry part so we didn't have so much warning."

The Knights' lightly armed cavalry was out, heading towards the gap in the Proliate line that had occurred when they separated. Secondly, the Knights quickly passed forward their enormous rectangular stoova shields designed to hold up to a heavy cavalry charge.

The shield's lower edge had four spikes facing straight down, giving it the appearance of "fangs." Two conical spikes in the middle and two larger spikes with barbs on the outside were all driven into the ground. Halfway up the shield two bracing poles angled backwards and were also pounded into the ground.

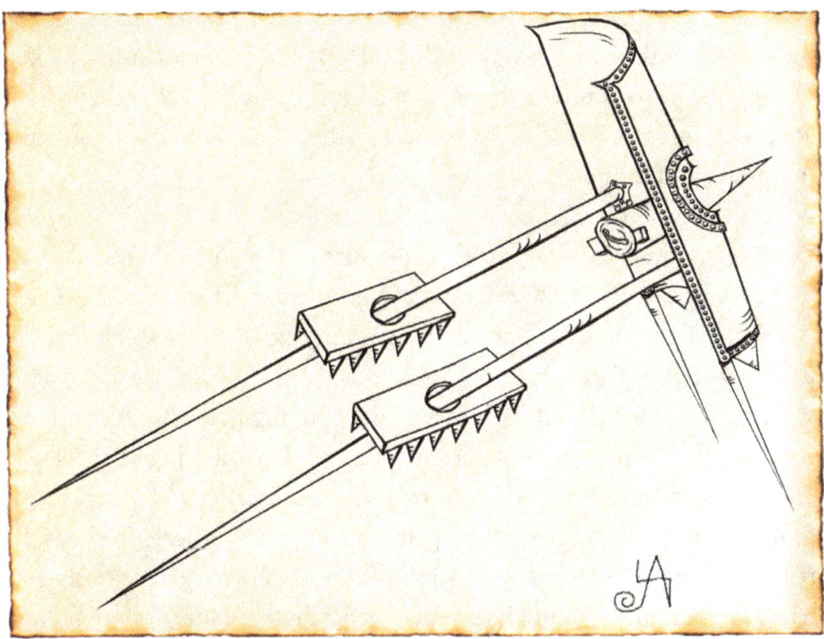

Figure 6: Although unwieldy and time consuming to place, the stoova shields provide a fearsome wall of steel against a heavy cavalry charge. What appears to be a small central prong transforms into a three-foot-long spike when pushed forward and locked into place.

All Proliate heavy cavalry finally exited the temple, forming up in two lines before toiling towards the Knights.

"We need more time to set up the stoova shields," Friar cried.

He and Ritari ran to the front line to assist the squires and Knights pounding in the spikes, anchoring both the front of the shield and bracing it from behind. The center fallaciously appeared to have a small, pointed, brass boss.

"Remember your training on the stoova!" Ritari called out from the front line. "Do NOT push the central spike forward until I give the order. Doing it too soon will alert the enemy and potentially give them time to divert their attack."

"Just before the charging cavalry hits our shields, slam the large cone-shaped spike forward," Friar added.

"Do not forget to lock it in place by twisting. You don't want it flying back and knocking you out," Ritari stated. "Remember to quickly insert your arms through the double argive grip of the shield and put your weight into it. With no time to stop, their horses will impale themselves on a three-foot spike."

As the much lighter cavalry of the Knights closed in on the gap of Proliate infantry, they began riding in a circle. They fired their composite bows repeatedly at the infantry around the gap. This served to block the Proliate cavalry's view of the installation of the stoova shields while thinning the Proliate ranks.

As the Proliate cavalry burst into the opening made by their infantry lines, the composite bows began firing at them, aiming at the sides and backs of the horses where they had no armor. Arrow after arrow found its mark, instantly creating havoc for the inexperienced cavalry's discipline. The horses were strong but too new to be true destriers. Many horses bucked and kicked into the Proliate infantry. Some bolted back towards the Temple.

"Falciss and his Knights are putting up a monster fight," Friar commented to Lovag after the stoova shields were secured. "They're keeping their square and giving us the precious gift of time."

"It's not worth losing an entire castle of Knights," Lovag replied.

"There's a hefty price for lusty hubris," Friar said, looking toward the Tingij Mountains for their relief. The timing had to be perfect. Lingering in the back of his mind were the nagging doubts about the force of Proliate moving down the western side of the Tingij. If they arrived through the Way of Trepas before them—the entire plan would crumble and every Allied soldier east of the Way of Trepas would be slaughtered.

"We may not need Sorea's stoova shields if our arrows keep landing," Lovag commented.

Friar shook his head. "Enough cavalry will make it through. They always do."

"Friar, as Captain I am again formally requesting permission to relieve Veli Falciss!"

"Sacrificing good troops to failure is like adding naphtha to a fire you want to put out—it makes the situation worse."

General Falciss began shouting passionately from inside his Knights' squared-up formation.

"We trade our lives for…" Falciss started.

"…everlasting honor!" his Knights finished.

Ritari huffed away in frustration as the number of Knights from Taiheart surrounding Veli Falciss continued to shrink. A wave of Proliate infantry moved forward and, using their infamous merja spears, forced the Knights' light cavalry to abandon their wheeling maneuver that had allowed almost constant fire on the approaching heavy cavalry.

Friar signaled his cavalry to feign retreat. A large cheer rose up from the Proliate, believing they had forced them back. Once the arrows stopped, Lidenskap berated the heavy cavalry. The only thing he hated more than cavalry was archers, viewing both as spineless.

The Proliate cavalry began moving east, as if they would circumvent the stoova shields. Friar quickly signaled for the light cavalry to move back and fire, forcing the Proliate cavalry towards the waiting stoova shields. Once the herded Proliate cavalry was funneled towards the waiting Knights, the archers shifted their fire to the rear of the heavy cavalry, compelling those in back to push forward. Once the Knights' cavalry saw the Proliate in a full charge towards the fortified shields, they retreated once again.

Out of nowhere, Ritari was among the front-line Knights, encouraging and reassuring those in front bracing the massive, anchored shields. The Proliate heavy cavalry shook the ground, their massive hooves roaring forward as they thundered towards the Knights.

"You will fight like Knights!" Ritari yelled as they braced for impact.

"Knights!" they replied back.

"We *will HOLD!*" Ritari called out.

"Hold!" the Knights howled.

"Steady your hearts!" Ritari shouted.

"Steady!" the Knights roared as the stoova shields rattled at the behest of the reverberation of the cavalry.

Figure 7: Battle of Temple Ovest Icon III: Unfamiliar with cavalry, General Lidenskap shows his intention too early—allowing the Knights to set their stoova shields. Veli Falciss and his Knights fight in forlorn desperation.

"Advance spikes!" Ritari bellowed.

"Advance!"

"Lock spikes!" Ritari ordered.

"Lock!" the Knights hollered in reply.

Each front-line Knight pushed the three-foot spike in the center of their shield forward, twisting to lock it behind a metal ridge. The cavalry was too heavy and traveling too fast to stop. The first line of horses slammed into the spiked shields. Whinnies of fear and pain stung the air as the violent crashing of metal, wood, and flesh rang across the battlefield. Most of the shields held, but some shattered, sending splintered shards of metal and wood slashing through Knights' flesh. Others had the metal ridge holding the cylindrical spike break, the force of the horse sending the metal whipping back, obliterating the Knights' forearms and smashing their ribs. They crumpled to the ground, in a blur of pain, gasping for air, lungs filling with blood.

The spikes of the shields that did hold easily penetrated the peytral armor protecting the horses' chests. Many of the heavily armored riders were tossed from their saddles, some thrown over the massive shields. Once down, their heavy armor prevented them from easily rising, and the Knights made quick work of them. Those with swords probed the Proliate armor for weaknesses, while those with maces and war hammers did not bother, denting the downed riders' helmets repeatedly until blood pooled beneath and their spastic movements stopped.

As line after line of the cavalry piled into one another, the force transferred into the groaning shields. Friar moved next to his signalers. His first order was to have the light cavalry move forward. They did, firing into the rear of the heavy cavalry, forcing them to scrunch ahead into the claustrophobically tight mass of armor, horses, and men. This effectively negated their maneuverability and momentum. The second order was an infantry flanking maneuver. The Knights to the rear of the stoova shields swung around the western edge of the shields to attack the cavalry's right flank.

Using halberds, the Knight infantry pulled off the Proliate riders. Once dismounted, they were easy fodder for war hammers and maces. A few loud snaps rang out as sections of the stoova shields began to fragment and sliver behind the enormous pressure pushing forward.

"Knights, fall back!" Friar yelled. "Mechanicians ready!"

With a tumultuous crack, the shields began to shatter and fracture as the Knights manning the shields and directly behind quickly moved back and to the sides.

"Wait until your fellow Knights are clear!" Friar ordered.

The Proliate cavalry closest to the shields were thrown forward and hurled off their horses. As the shields continued to completely break apart, many of the riders were trampled as the horses stomped over them. Several Knights did not move fast enough and were crushed.

"Fire!" Friar screamed.

The Knight mechanicians from the west opened up fire with ballista and onagers. The large bolts and stones crushed and fractured anything they hit. One particularly fast Proliate horse made it close to one of the ballistas just as it fired.

The massive bolt demolished the horse's armor and sent it slamming into the horse's chest. Its legs and head continued moving forward, wrapping around the bolt before its lifeless body crumpled to the ground in a heap of blood. The Knight cavalry concentrated their fire on those horses breaking through the ranks. One of the ballista shots slammed into a Proliate rider just as he was thrown forward off his dying horse. The huge bolt impaled him sideways, pinning him to a passing horse, killing both. Shot after shot from the Knight mechanicians crashed into the panicking Proliate cavalry. Soon, most were dead or dying.

"Hold, my excellent mechanicians! Knights, finish this!"

Chaos ensued with an overall rout of the cavalry as Veli Pingius and his Knights moved forward to help clean up any survivors. The Knights mopping up the field walked among the injured littering the ground, drawn to the howls of agony and groans of pain. Inverse gardening, they plucked the life from the dying enemy as mace blows dented armor and skulls while war hammers pulverized flesh with little regard for metal or bone.

Friar Pallium turned to see the blue flag of the Knights under Veli Falciss wavering. The large white dove of peace flying over two crossed swords and a single castle tower fluttered briefly before it was violently ripped down. Suddenly, Falciss emerged above the fray, violently swinging his sword, sending the front line of attackers rippling backwards. One of the Southern Dwarves picked up the Knights' banner, brandishing it scornfully.

Falciss leapt up with his sword held high, his raging wide-eyed stare glaring with resolve to take as many of the enemy with him as possible yet tempered with a practical conviction that he would soon be swaddled within death's embrace. His helmet off, blood and dents obscured his once pristine armor. With a primal scream he drove his sword into the Dwarf holding the Knights' banner. It pierced just above the chest plate and quickly plunged into the chest cavity, exploding the heart. Falciss grabbed the banner.

Figure 8: Falciss Falls. Despite his valor and determination, the wide-eyed Falciss dooms himself, and his Knights, to die.

A spear lanced into the side of the Veli's head, shaving off his left ear and shearing his scalp to the bone. An amalgamated scream of pain and rage bellowed from Falciss as he used the flagpole like a lance and shoved it through the face of the attacker. Before he could withdraw his makeshift weapon, a mace blow shattered his jaw, showering his already bloody and soiled chest plate with bone, fragmented teeth, and a deluge of blood. Swords and axes hacked into the Veli from all sides as he fell.

Shouts of joy and loud cheers erupted from the Piscinians and Southern Dwarves as those closest to Veli Falciss continued to rain down gratuitous blows on his long-dead body. A Southern Dwarf greedily held up the severed head of the former leader of Castle Taiheart, prompting more cheers.

"One entire castle contingent destroyed!" Lidenskap yelled heartily.

Across the field Lovag murmured, "Did we just lose *all* the Knights from Taiheart?"

Friar nodded numbly.

A fresh round of cheers from the Piscinians and Southern Dwarves made Friar realize they were now free to turn and attack his Knights and Allies.

"Fall back and reform lines!" Friar yelled. "Square up perpendicular to the siege engines and ramparts! Knights from Liberum, to the left flank! I want the Northern Dwarves to hold our center! Veli Pingius, you and your Knights to the right flank! We may need to thin out our ranks to match our enemies' lines!"

Pingius waddled nervously amongst his soldiers, his hands fumbling anxiously as he directed them to spread out, his usual mirthful expression masked in rigid fear.

Our traps! Friar suddenly remembered.

"Pingius! Do *not* move any further south!" Friar yelled.

"I thought you said to spread our lines?"

"I have a few tricks to the south reserved for the Proliate and their Confederacy. You will have our cavalry just behind you, but do *not* move further south!"

Forming up in lines directly across from them were the fresh Proliate and Ager troops. Behind them were the Southern Dwarves, Jaa, and Piscinians who had finished mopping up every Knight under Veli Falciss.

General Lidenskap suddenly stopped. "What are they doing?"

"It appears they're falling back to reorganize," a lieutenant stated.

"They've lost over a third of their Knights, and I don't see any Elves of Creber or warriors from the Rebelde Plains. They should be afraid!" Lidenskap offered. "We need to stop them from retreating so when our forces from the north come through the Way of Trepas, we will have them in a pincer and kill all the traitors!"

The two armies stood facing each other, anticipation shivering through the very air. It was tempered by fear sweating up and acting like an unreachable itch under hot armor. For just a moment, an eerie silence settled on the battlefield. Even the flags representing each country seemed to open and close like quiet butterfly wings, giving brief glimpses of their emblems.

TABLE TWO Battle of Ovest

Dead *Reduced number*

Allies		Confederacy	
Knights of Liberum:	*1,850*	**Proliate Red Guard:**	*19,735*
Knight Cavalry:	*1,350*	**Piscinians:**	
(lightly armored from all three castles)		**Retiarian Division:**	*3,200*
~~**Knights of Taiheart**~~**:**	~~7,500~~	**Suoli Division:**	*3,150*
(led by Veli Falciss)		**Warriors of Jaa:**	*4,300*
Knights of Toil Shaor:	5,000	**Southern Dwarves:**	*8,700*
(led by Veli Pingius)		**Ager:**	8,000
Northern Dwarves:		~~**Auxiliary Cavalry**~~**:**	~~2,000~~
Vioma Division: (Green)	7,500	(Heavily armored)	
Saatana Division: (Red)	5,000		
Rebelde Plains Dwarves:	250		
(skilled in prestidigitation)			
Total:	**20,950 (7,800 casualties)**		**47,350 (4,650 casualties)**

"We can wipe out the Knights and most of their Allies in one day!" the lieutenant said, his voice full of excitement.

"Praise Tallcon!" Lidenskap stated just as the Knights and Northern Dwarves began to rapidly retreat.

"Should we order the attack?" the lieutenant asked longingly.

"Not yet, son," Lidenskap answered. "We'll chase them down once they move past their siege engines—their left flank won't be protected. Then our superior numbers can sweep around both of ends with plenty of time before they get to the Way of Trepas."

"They do have cavalry in reserve, while ours was destroyed."

"Even more of a reason for us to spread out our lines once we get away from their siege engines and have some breathing space," Lidenskap pronounced. "Have the warriors of Jaa, the Southern Dwarves, and Piscinians take up our left flank. We don't want their cavalry trying to move around us."

Before the Knights made it past the siege engines, they began to contract their lines. "Move north," Friar extolled frantically, removing small markers delineating his traps as he went. Few knew his reasoning. The Knights under Veli Pingius of Toil Shaor and the Vioma Northern Dwarves moved backwards to take a reserve position.

"Why are they making it easier for us to surround them?" Lidenskap asked.

"Maybe they're getting ready to make a move through the Way of Trepas?"

"Seems early," Lidenskap replied. "They're still quite a ways from its entrance."

Once they passed the siege engines, the Knights continued to retreat while deepening their ranks. The Confederacy, on the other hand, was spreading out from right to left: Proliate, Ager, Jaa, Southern Dwarves, and Piscinians. Their huge force outnumbered the Allies more than two to one. Even with their cavalry intact, the Allies were in serious jeopardy of being outflanked.

"The fools continue to bunch their lines. They must assume we're content to let them escape," the lieutenant repeated. "If we let them get to the other side of the Tingij Mountains, they'll be able to spread out and, if our forces from the north are delayed, they could bottleneck us at the opening of the pass and negate our superior numbers."

Lidenskap paused. *Do they know about our troops from the north? Where are the dragons? Where is Veneficus and his griffins?* Lingering doubts rattled in his mind, raising an internal alarm. He shook the uncertainty away, yelling, "Sound the attack! Charge!"

Once the order went through, the Piscinians let out a howl of rage, spurred by their taste of Knight blood when killing Veli Falciss and his Knights. They charged forward recklessly.

"Stay together!" Lidenskap yelled. "A hole in our front lines will split our forces! Signal the order for Jaa and the Southern Dwarves to move forward. Keep the line unbroken!"

"The Southern Dwarves and warriors of Jaa can't keep up. The line's breaking!" the lieutenant yelled as the heavily armored Southern Dwarves struggled to keep up with the passionate Piscinians.

"Send another order for the Piscinians to slow their advance! Those delinquent neophytes could ruin everything. We can't afford a breakdown in discipline when we're this close to victory."

Despite the lieutenant's frantic signals, their line was becoming more unbalanced with their left flank swinging forward, away from the Proliate troops, who were advancing with shields locked in an orderly march.

"Sir, it appears the Piscinians are about to outflank them. Should we order a faster charge?"

"We'll lose our shield wall and we know the Knights and Northern Dwarves have plenty of bolts and arrows. Plus, the Knight cavalry is just sitting there," Lidenskap said. "In the future there will be a Proliate commander with each Confederate army to control those hot heads. The impetuous Piscinians are the worst of the lot and are going to get us killed by exposing our lines."

Before the words slipped away from his lips, a loud creaking sound was followed by an immense crack as the ground crumbled under the feet of the front line Piscinians and Southern Dwarves. Screams of terror and agony filled the air.

"What's happening?" King Abernan demanded.

"My Knights, under prestidigitation, dug a large trench and then constructed flimsy wooden and rope supports before replacing the soil and grass on top. As the Piscinians and Southern Dwarves marched forward, their weight became too much, and it snapped," Friar said as momentum pushed several more rows of shrieking infantry into the pit.

"How deep is it? They scream horrifically!" Abernan said.

"It's not the depth," Friar answered.

Figure 9: Battle of Temple Ovest Icon IV: Friar's elaborate plan is coming to actualization, resulting in an abundance of pain and death.

"There are punji sticks in the pit," Friar said, his ears assaulted by more intense screams of pain erupting as the soldiers fell onto the sharpened stakes.

"You're dedicated to victory, I'll give you that," Abernan said.

Friar shook his head. "Whatever the reasons for us ending up here today, we still have to fight and win."

"Of course—" Abernan started, interrupted by Friar's yell.

"Cavalry, forward, and fire!" *No choice but to fight and win. Regret will have to wait.*

Arrows from the Knight cavalry began to pour into the Piscinians and Southern Dwarves.

"Vioma warriors! Move forward and loose your crossbows!" Abernan commanded.

The green-clad Dwarf warriors quickly moved ahead, sending bolts gushing into the Proliate lines. The front row would kneel and fire before shuffling to the rear to reload as another line of warriors moved up to fire. They continually repeated this rotation of death.

"Remind me never to get on your bad side, Friar," King Abernan said, cringing at the howls of pain and stench of death.

Chaos erupted up and down the Confederate lines, except for the well-disciplined Proliate.

"The Proliate are something," Abernan commented to Friar. "They have amazing restraint. I don't think they ever break ranks."

Friar couldn't help smiling. "Oh, there's a way to break their discipline. There's a key to turn everyone's heart from calm to rage, from control to fear. Some take more planning, but I shall make their strength a fatal weakness."

King Abernan turned to him questioningly.

"Our goal is to unnerve, transforming the backbone of their toughness into frailty. I shall unfocus their minds, deform their spirituality, and command victory," Friar remarked ominously.

Across the battlefield the Proliate lieutenant turned to Lidenskap. "What do we do?"

"Obviously, they narrowed their lines to avoid their iniquitous pit. Once again, they prove they have no honor."

"Praise Tallcon!" one of the Proliate soldiers yelled—his words followed by howls of unadulterated joy as the Proliate turned their eyes towards the skies.

"Tallcon! Tallcon!"

Floating high in the sky behind the Knights, there appeared a gigantic flaming sword. Several Proliate dropped their shields and weapons in disbelief. The sword was so vast it was the size of a large temple. Orange-red flames bristled and flared off as it slowly moved through the blue sky, closer to where the enemies were facing off.

Scroll 8: Tallcon has Come!

“The sword of Tallcon, straight out of the Sanctus Kirja Flamma. The fire of retribution shall be laid down upon you!” Lidenskap yelled, his voice trembling as pride and exhilaration wove together into a knot of self-vindication.

“These dealers in deception will get what they deserve! Chapter twenty-one, Rune fourteen,” Lidenskap quoted from memory. “He shall divide His infinite body and send down from the sky a terrible fire of retribution, a blazing sword, against your enemies. Behind the sword shall emerge innumerable images of the one true Tallcon, and your enemy will burn!”

Across the battlefield Friar smirked, reciting the same passage underlined in the book, given to him by Veneficus, that Bellae had read so long ago in his office.

“Word of Tallcon, speak to these non-believers in the language they understand, death!” the lieutenant howled.

Friar signaled the stunned Knights and Northern Dwarves to restart their retreat while the cavalry formed a thin line in front to help mask their withdrawal. The devout cries of the Proliate scattered, mingling with the sickening howls of pain from those dying in the punji pits. The uninjured warriors desperately tried to help their fallen comrades get out without falling in themselves. It was a bloody, painful mess as they tried to hoist out the impaled. Many of the injured had their armor skewered onto the impaling sticks, making it difficult to lift them out. The pit quickly became slippery with splinters, blood, screams, and death.

Suddenly, explosions of fire and lightning ripped the sky around the flaming sword soaring overhead as storm clouds rippled out, scampering across, spreading a curtain of darkness. Angry-looking flares arched towards the raging clouds as the sword tilted downwards, directly towards the Knight cavalry, causing the horses to neigh loudly in protest.

The sword suddenly fractured into hundreds of glowing sparks bathed in fire. As the flames died down, the outlines of hundreds of flaming phoenix shapes crisped into view.

Overcome with emotion, Lidenskap whispered, "It's happening! 'Behind the sword shall emerge innumerable images of the one true Tallcon.'"

Shouts of joy exploded from the Proliate lines as they gazed upon the intimidating scene. Hundreds of fiery phoenix-shaped figures flew through the sky, inching ever closer to the battle lines. As they flew nearer, they began to change color, from red to orange to yellow and finally white with a soft flame surrounding them. The flying phoenixes passed over the Knight cavalry, continuing towards the Proliate lines.

"It's magnificent!" Lidenskap murmured. "Tallcon has come!"

The hundreds of white phoenixes stopped and hovered. Outlined vividly against the stormy sky they seemed to glisten. The awe-inspiring sight sent tingling sensations through the spines of combatants on both sides of the battle. Some Proliate dropped to their knees in prostration as others stared in wonderment. Almost all of them had thrown down or lowered their shields. Many chanted songs of worship. A unique atmosphere undulated across the battlefield: extreme excitement balanced by calm reverence. The glinting phoenixes gently floating through the sky gave a dreamlike feel to the whole scene.

Without warning the sky was fractured with piercing shrieks that skewered the air from high above the phoenixes as the storm clouds began to break up. Abruptly, the flames surrounding the white phoenixes were quenched as the prestidigitation stopped, and rapidly the shapes flipped over. Strapped to the back of the hundreds of metal phoenixes were the Northern Dwarf Vasama warriors, each one wielding several loaded crossbows.

Friar couldn't help smiling as he continued to retreat, the dark clouds disappearing to reveal blue skies.

"What just happened?" King Abernan gasped.

"Those are the metal kauhistaa gliders I developed. They are carried by Eaglians via a series of ropes. One set of cables supports the weight of the glider and Northern Dwarf during the flight while another set of ropes are used to flip it over!"

"When you asked for my Special Forces, I had no idea this is what you had in store for them."

Friar smiled. "Your Dwarf warriors were initially lying on the side facing up, carrying three loaded crossbows, while the Rebelde Plains Dwarves used prestidigitation to concoct the sword breaking into flaming phoenixes—that's right out of their holy book. The goal was to catch the Proliate in stunned, pious bewilderment by deception. They had been so sure Tallcon came to kill us 'deceivers' that they are unable to comprehend what's happening." *They can't help but believe.*

The side of the gliders now facing down was blue, blending in with the azure sky, further adding to the confusion of the Proliate. With a sharp war cry the Dwarves let loose bolts of terror on the stunned Proliate. The projectiles rained down, slamming into the dazed warriors before they could recoup their wits. Their lines had fallen into righteous disorder when the flaming sword had appeared. Many had their helmets off and shields down, making easy targets.

With gravity aiding the powerful weapons, the bolts easily pierced through any armor they happened to meet. The Proliate fell by the hundreds. Those who did not die instantly had the metal of their armor peeled into and around the wounds—adding to the pain.

Friar gave an order. Taking advantage of the Proliate looking towards the sky, the cavalry galloped forward, swiftly firing several volleys into the dumbfounded Proliate before sprinting back towards Friar and the retreating infantry, which had long ago picked up their pace.

The Vasama Dwarves strapped into the gliders reloaded their crossbows, which were connected to the phoenixes, and repeatedly fired death volleys. The normally rigid discipline of the Proliate wavered under the shock of the duplicity. The other commanders of the Confederacy were still trying to heave and tear their soldiers from the punji pit. Without knowing the extent of the pit and its direction, they were not anxious about rushing after the Knights. Abruptly, dozens of new Eaglians dropped out of the sky, their fearsome appearance adding to the mayhem.

"What in Tallcon's name are they?" a lieutenant howled.

Lidenskap shook his head, still having trouble coming to grips with what happened.

"Eaglians!" King Tarha of Ager yelled.

"I thought they were a myth," Lidenskap whispered.

"Wake up, Lidenskap, and get your men organized!" Tarha screamed.

Pairs of the newly arrived Eaglians carried large barrels. They began dumping a sticky, black liquid on the border between the Proliate troops and those of Ager, making a thick stripe of the viscous fluid. A single Eaglian swooped down from the opposite direction and dropped a torch, lighting the liquid concoction that included dragon naphtha. A huge surge of heat and flame burst forth and quickly traveled down the line of the dark liquid, completely separating the Proliate from the armies of the other countries.

The Eaglians flew off with the Vasama warriors riding the kauhistaa gliders just as fresh screams joined the fray from those unfortunate enough to be anywhere near the naphtha. Men were struggling to get their burning armor and clothes off as they were slowly cooked alive. Those caught directly in the fire had their screams quickly melt to gurgling sobs. Thick black smoke, followed by the sick smell of burning flesh, exploded. As the warriors of Ager tried to move away from the fire, they pushed into other Confederate warriors, unleashing a chain reaction in which scores were pushed into the lethal punji pits. Fights broke out along the lines separating the countries—struggles to get away from the pit on one side and fire on the other.

The Vasama Dwarves flying on gliders returned, but this time from the back. The gliders had been flipped again, and the now unstrapped Dwarves were air surfing on top. The Eaglians carrying them let go of the gliders directly behind the Proliate line. The metal gliders smashed into the backs of the Proliate soldiers, causing a horrific boom followed by a series of nauseating *cracks* as their bodies snapped under the force of the gliders. Most of the rear lines of the Proliate were knocked over, and those that weren't had the surfing Dwarves jumping on them, quickly hacking at the Proliate with two curved, medium-length swords. The Proliate turned to meet them, struggling to form lines in the pandemonium. The disarray was too great for the Proliate to form their shield wall, and the skill of the Vasama Dwarves rapidly began to cut a wedge of death through the Red Guard.

"They have turned our reverent dream into a nightmare, one from which we cannot wake," Lidenskap whispered to King Tarha. The two stared helplessly through the wall of fire at the massacre of the Proliate warriors. Before the naphtha was lit, several warriors from Ager had pulled the dazed General to the Ager side. The young lieutenants left to lead the Red Guard were inexperienced and overwhelmed.

"Turn and form up in your lines!" a Proliate lieutenant finally yelled, flames and death surrounding them. As those at the front of the lines were cut down, the discipline and training of the Proliate kicked in and many remaining Proliate formed up into tight enough lines to create a shield wall.

"For Tallcon!" the lieutenant yelled as they surged forward, slamming into the advancing Vasama Dwarves. Slowly, the lightly armed and colossally outnumbered Dwarves were pushed back.

Just as the Proliate were getting the upper hand, hundreds of startling squawks filled the air as the Eaglians who had been carrying the kauhistaa gliders descended with a vengeance upon what was now the rear of the Proliate lines.

This unanticipated attack flustered the struggling Proliate, especially when their remaining lieutenants were quickly reduced to shreds by the powerful talons of the Eaglians. Parts of them went flying in different directions as the Eaglians tore them into shredded bits. The Eaglians began to claw and rip their way through the back of the Proliate lines. The shield wall quickly disintegrated, and the Eaglians and Northern Dwarves soon met in the middle of the blood-drenched battlefield. Once every Proliate north of the fire had been killed, the Eaglians swooped around and picked up the Dwarves, flying off towards the Tingij Mountains.

As the Eaglians were leaving the carnage, the retreating infantry of the Knights and Northern Dwarves reached the Way of Trepas.

"A little warning about your traps would have been nice!" King Abernan said. "When those gliders flipped over, I almost shite my saddle!"

"Surprise was crucial," Friar replied. "If our plans leaked, we would have lost the shock. Deep, pious betrayal, after stirring up devout feelings, created the magnitude of trauma needed."

"Plus Eaglians? After all this time?"

"They're intimidating, no doubt," Friar answered.

A wave of excitement ran through the Allies. The complete devastation of the Proliate Divisions emboldened their spirits, tempered only by the sacrifice of the Knights under Falciss.

While the Eaglians carrying the Dwarf Special Forces crested the peaks of the Tingij Mountains, the stunned troops of the Confederacy were still struggling with fire and punji pits. After the Proliate, the Piscinians had taken the second worst beating, sustaining fierce casualties from the punji pits and the arrows from the Knights. The armies of Jaa and the Southern Dwarves were not much better off. Ager's army was in the best shape, having taken only mild losses.

"You!" Lidenskap thundered. "Get to the Temple and have them send an urgent message to Veneficus. Tell him to fill the skies with his blasted Magicians and griffins!"

TABLE THREE Battle of Ovest

Dead *Reduced number*

Allies		Confederacy	
Knights of Liberum:	*1,850*	**Proliate Red Guard:**	*1,150*
Knight Cavalry: (lightly armored from all three castles)	*1,350*	**Piscinians:**	
		Retiarian Division:	*875*
~~**Knights of Taiheart:**~~ (led by Veli Falciss)	~~7,500~~	**Suoli Division:**	*2,000*
		Warriors of Jaa:	*3,500*
Knights of Toil Shaor: (led by Veli Pingius)	5,000	**Southern Dwarves:**	*5,000*
		Ager:	*7,500*
Northern Dwarves:		~~**Auxiliary Cavalry:**~~ (Heavily armored)	~~2,000~~
Vioma Division: (Green)	7,500		
Saatana Division: (Red)	5,000		
Rebelde Plains Dwarves: (skilled in prestidigitation)	250		
Total:	**20,950 (7,800 casualties)**		**20,025 (31,975 casualties)**

There were fifty casualties for the Northern Dwarves Special Forces (Vasama Division) and five Eaglians killed {7,855 total casualties}.

Scroll 9: Death Sickness

"Come on, Kari. Eat something," Arend encouraged.

Shaking her head, Sankari's wings drooped in despondency.

"Hey, Gimelli's eating!" Bellae announced. "Take the ropes off her legs."

"She needs to be bound to protect us, and we don't want her running off. Besides, look at her eyes," Kainen said.

Bellae walked around the slightly damp ground inside the Dark Forest. "Still white," she said, tears forming at the corners of her own eyes. Everyone but Sankari watched Gimelli eat in an unconscious stupor. Her innumerable wounds were covered with arnebia and dragon sap, but her yellow eyes and smile were missing. Her muscles seemed to be moving in automated fashion as Lontas put pieces of peccary into her hand.

Finally, Sankari fluttered over, her eyes puffy from fitful crying. "We, Fairies, were aware of this illness, but we didn't know it was from creatures in the Dark Forest. I genuinely didn't know they existed. We thought those with this illness were poisoned or possessed. There was an unwritten rule to never cross the Satu River, but most thought it was nonsense. In Cappadocia we call this the death sickness. I'm sorry Gimelli isn't getting better."

Everyone froze from a mixture of surprise at her emotional apology and hesitation to respond that it was "okay" in deference to Bellae when it seemed Gimelli might not recover. Lontas looked to Bellae, hoping she would answer, but only awkward silence roared in his ears.

"Thank you, Sankari," Bellae finally said. "I know you wouldn't lead us to this on purpose."

Sankari was cut off before she could reply as Gimelli spoke, "Bellae."

Even though her eyes had the white film over them, she stared towards her sister.

"I'm here," Bellae said, kneeling. "You're going to be okay. I want to—uhhg."

Bellae's words turned to a gasping gurgle as Gimelli began choking her. Her breathing turned to short, ragged gasps as Gimelli's hands tightened around her throat. Bellae's head exploded in pain, still sore from the beating she took from the undead.

Scelto quickly removed her hands, but Gimelli began scratching and clawing at Bellae and him, violently drawing blood. Lontas pulled Bellae away as Arend moved in to help. Eventually, the two managed to tie her hands behind her back.

A sickening gurgle erupted from Gimelli's throat as she lunged at them, teeth bared. Kainen moved in, tying cloth around her chomping mouth as Gimelli unleashed a loathsome, muffled scream. After several minutes, she stopped fighting, drifting into restless sleep.

"Kari, have any infected Fairies ever recovered?" Kainen asked.

The Fairy looked uncomfortable. "No…but," Sankari cried as Bellae began to sob, "we never tried arnebia or dragon sap."

Kainen looked at Arend, who vigorously shook his head. The Elf mouthed, "We might have to."

"What?" Scelto seethed. "Might have to do what?"

"All I'm saying is we need to be realistic. If she gets worse, we have no choice but to deal with it."

"By 'deal with it' do you mean kill her? Because you'll have to finish off me first," Scelto raged.

Kainen sighed. "Our mission comes first, over any of us. If it were me, I would want to be killed if I turned into one of those monsters."

"Well, it's not you, and you don't get to touch her."

The young Elf put his hands on his head, sighing. The whole trip had not followed the script written in his imagination. *My father trained me to take control. I rarely have it. I should have respect, but don't.* He was beginning to question the whole idea of a youthful, small group that the League elders had espoused given Bellae's age. They had almost died multiple times and didn't even know their first quest. *My dad, or Aquila, Arend's dad, should be here.*

"It's going to be okay. You are doing good," Arend encouraged, reading the doubt on his friend's face.

Kainen fought back tears. The pockmarks on his face from fighting the Fionain were starting to heal but still painful. "After all the training, all the sacrifices, to have it…this quest…I don't know, turn out so badly, this early?"

"It's because of our training we will succeed."

"Do you ever wonder if we should have had an army of Eaglians and Elves instead of us?" Kainen asked.

"No!" Arend answered emphatically. "*If* such a group made it through the enemy-filled skies, it would not have survived the Dark Forest. If they saw an army of Elves or Eaglians, or both, the Fionain would have seen them as a threat and instantly killed them."

Kainen's head remained tethered by doubt.

"Do you remember when strange things started happening around Verngaurd, including Nishi? Our fathers sat us down and told us the timetable for the plan had to be moved up a decade because Na Cearcaill was here. There wasn't time to let her, or us, grow older. They asked if we were ready, and we both answered a resounding yes. I left to watch over Bellae while you continued training."

"I remember."

"Good. Keep in mind our size was chosen on purpose. We are lethal enough when we need to be but can slip by undetected and are not seen as a threat to large armies. The elders knew what they were doing. We're young, mobile, and going to triumph. Sacrifice for success."

"Love you, crazy bird," Kainen said, unable to stop a few tears from leaking.

"Don't make this weird, Elf." Arend laughed.

Scroll 10: Blodskogur

The entire garrison of the Ragorsaf outpost had been ordered to move out and meet up with the Proliate troops coming down from Jaa in the north. Together they would march through the Way of Trepas and attack the Knights from the flank or rear as the Proliate and their Confederate allies assailed them from the front and side.

"The Red Guard coming from the north had been stationed on the upper frontier of Jaa," Velox, Scelto's former mentor, stated as they continued their forced march.

"I cannot believe the Knights think they can take the Citadel," Fenik said. "With the Piscinians, Jaainians, Agerians, and Southern Dwarves coming from the East, we will absolutely crush them all."

The griffin and Magician who had given them their orders did not know the attack on the Citadel was a diversion, nor had they been updated of the massive defeat at Ovest.

"They will get what's coming soon enough," Velox said confidently. However, he silently prayed to Tallcon that Scelto, the squire he had grown to admire at Ragorsaf, was not amongst them.

Even the disciplined and well-trained Proliate garrison was feeling the effects of the blistering pace. They had been traveling nonstop save for prayer breaks. Despite the cooler weather, all of them were drenched with sweat and covered in dust and grime as they traveled between two enemy territories.

"Luckily, no sightings of the ragtag warriors of the Rebelde Plains to the north or the Elves of Creber from the south," Gozador said.

"I would love to face the shambles that is the army of the Rebelde Plains," Velox replied. "The Elves, however, are brutal." Velox had been trying to forgive Gozador, still blaming him for driving Scelto away during the late-night clarification process.

"We should be coming up on the Blodskogur Woods," Gozador said.

"Time to read from the raamattu!" Fenik bellowed before Velox could answer. The Proliate garrison came to a grateful stop, anxious not just for the spiritual restoration it would bestow but the needed physical break. The Proliate formed an oval with the large Proliate champion, Fenik, in the center. They had a few soldiers on watch in every direction and scouts ahead and behind. Just as Fenik cleared his throat to start reading, large arrows began raining down. The Proliate watch had been the first to fall, the sizable arrows piercing their throats and denying them a chance to call out. Wave after wave of arrows rolled down on the Proliate from the southwest, wreaking havoc as many had taken off their helmets for prayer.

"Shield wall!" Fenik yelled as they scrambled to escape the torrent of arrows.

"How'd they get past our scouts, and where did they come from?" Temere, the Proliate who had helped Scelto with the diezmar, questioned.

"We may have outrun our scouts to the south," Fenik answered as they efficiently formed a shield wall.

"There's one of the forward scouts," someone yelled over the clink of arrows on armor and shield. Standing on a small hill to the east was one of the Proliate forward scouts. His winged helmet was bobbing with urgency as he motioned for them to come.

Velox stared at Fenik, wordlessly asking if they should move towards the scout.

"I don't see much choice," Fenik answered. "If we stay here, we'll be pulverized."

"Cowardly arrows!" Gozador screamed. "You have no honor!"

They moved as one towards the ridge, fighting to keep their shield wall. Their training and discipline kicked in to keep the arrows out. Dozens of Proliate lay dead or dying from the initial arrow barrage. The scout's gesticulations for them to hurry became more exaggerated as they inched closer to the hill. Suddenly, the scout disappeared behind the slope.

"The regiments coming from the north must be in trouble!" Velox said.

"Do you think the scouts can see them?" Fenik questioned. "Aren't we too far away?"

"Not sure. Let's step it up anyway," Velox replied.

"Agreed." Fenik yelled, "Stay together but double time it to that hill."

Once on top of the hill, the arrows thankfully stopped, but there was no one there. "Where's that bloody scout?" Velox asked.

"Not sure. Let's square up until we find out what's going on," Fenik ordered.

"Should we go back and get our supply train?" Velox questioned.

"After we figure out what's happening."

"There. In the trees…I saw, I think, our scout," Temere stated.

"Are you sure?" Fenik questioned.

"No."

"That's Blodskogur Woods," Gozador said.

"It'll provide cover from the archers," Fenik stated.

"Is it safe?" Velox questioned.

"Should be. It's not part of Creber."

The garrison moved towards the large grove of trees. As they moved closer, arrows from the tops of the trees began to pour down on the Proliate. Because they were in a square, the arrows targeted the backs of the Proliate facing away from the forest. Within minutes, the entire far wall of Proliate was killed. The remainder formed up a shield wall facing the forest just as the hill behind them filled with hundreds of Elven archers letting loose arrows into the back of the shield wall, quickly decimating the rear lines.

"Run for the forest!" Velox yelled.

The Proliate garrison sprinted towards the thicket, still under fire from above and behind. As they made it to the forest, they saw the trail of dead stretched back to the hilltop. Some were still writhing in pain while others gurgled out blood, fighting for absconded air.

"Stay together!" Fenik ordered the remaining three thousand troops—down from five thousand.

"What now?" Velox whispered.

"Keep your eyes open. Look to the tops of the trees for archers," Fenik ordered. Turning to Velox, he whispered, "I think we should move through the grove and see where we're at on the other side. Perhaps our scout did the same?"

The Proliate moved through the thick woods. Their labored breathing, along with the crunch of sticks and leaves below their feet, broke the silence. Their clumsy merja spears were constantly getting caught on branches in the dense woods.

"Oafish Proliate are noisier than a thousand siege engines!" a heavy voice called out.

"Who said that?" Velox questioned.

The Proliate strained their senses, searching for the source of the speech. Darkness, tree trunks, and golden, fluttering fall leaves silently greeted them. Slowly, they began to move again, quickly becoming disoriented in the thick trees.

"What's that noise?" Fenik asked.

"Sounds like scratching."

Several trees and larger branches began nodding, bending, and straightening as the gratingly abrasive scratching sound continued.

"Someone's rubbing tree bark. I think—" a Proliate soldier was abruptly cut off. He fell flaccidly to the ground. As his body crumpled to the earth, several other loud thumps followed as a handful of other Proliate hit the ground with crashing thuds.

"Talk to me! What's happening?" Velox shouted.

No one answered.

"What's happening?" he screamed.

"I saw a wooden staff come out of nowhere and hit them," a soldier answered.

"They're not dead!"

"He's right," Velox said gratefully. "They're only knocked out. Pick them up, and let's keep moving."

"That noise is back," Fenik whispered.

"Stop that bloody scratching!" Velox bellowed, panic blending with the darkness and confusion they bathed within. As he spoke, the scraping sound intensified, quickly followed by the bending of branches and smaller trees, loud cracks as wooden staffs met Proliate helmets, and finally, thumps as bodies hit the dirt.

"Same as before—they aren't killing, just knocking them out!"

"Get them up and move!" Velox yelled.

This cycle repeated until all of the Proliate were either carrying or being carried.

"We're no longer a viable fighting force. We have to get out of here, now!" Velox seethed, supporting two injured Proliate.

"We aren't getting out of here," Fenik said darkly.

"The trees are alive!" Temere yelled. Suddenly, the Elves of Creber, who had been hiding amongst the trees, opened their eyes and stepped in front of the Proliate. They calmly removed their kama weapons. Several Proliate on the edges had the bird-beak weapons rip into their necks, blood spurting everywhere.

Screams of panic burst through the Proliate like a shock wave as they realized the trap they were in. With their bodies already shaking with exhaustion and alarm, the Proliate set down their injured brothers, took out their swords, and hacked wildly at anything and everything around them. They watched in horror as Elves appeared and disappeared at will, sometimes scampering up the trees, sometimes seeming to magically emerge from the bark itself, striking quickly before retreating. The clumsy swords and spears of the Proliate were constantly hitting branches or vines in the thick forest.

After a few hours, the few hundred Proliate that were left put their backs together in a crude circle of desperate exhaustion. Dying soldiers clawed to get in the fraudulent safety of the middle of the circle but were ignored. Some began to sob, any veneer of pride or invincibility long evaporated. As the wounded scratched and swatted at their legs, the abrasive scuffing of Elfin skin against bark surrounded them.

"Finish this!" Velox yelled.

Abruptly the chafing sound of scratching stopped, plunging the forest into a deafening silence. Those Proliate able to stand froze, staring into the darkness of the forest, scanning and searching for any sign of movement from the Elves in the unnatural silence.

After hours of listening to the cutting sounds of the Elves moving amongst the forest, the corpulent quiet seemed as terrifying as the previous racket. The Proliate frantically tried to quiet their rapid breathing, straining their ears for any sign of the Elves. Many were bruised and cut, and all splattered with the blood of their dead and dying comrades. A burning rage simmered within, but with no outlet it simply churned their stomachs, brewing into dense anxiety.

"What can we do?" Velox asked.

"The forest is their world, not ours. We die," Fenik answered.

The helplessness they swam in soaked into them so thoroughly, their spirits wrinkled in frustration and their battered morale evaporated. With eerie silence ringing in their ears, they startled when someone shouted, "Our scout!"

Slowly, the gleaming red armor of a Proliate scout moved through the thick underbrush. There was something odd about his movements—awkward, unnatural.

"Hi, it's me! Your friendly scout here to rescue you," a strange voice called out.

"What the…" Fenik mumbled.

About ten feet from the last of the battered Proliate, the scout began to dance bizarrely, like that of a puppet—movements irregular and jerky. Suddenly, he stopped, and a sickening chorus of laughter echoed through the forest from all sides. The body of the scout slumped to the floor to reveal several Elves of Creber who had been supporting his dead body like a marionette.

Throwing their arms up into a self-congratulatory "V," they shouted, "Ta-da! It was us all along, silly Proliate!" Shrill cackling rang through the forest, vibrating from everywhere and nowhere. A chill ran through the spines of the meager remaining Proliate.

"Oh, crap," Gozador mumbled.

Suddenly, the darkness around the bleeding warriors scattered, replaced with the stern faces of the Elves of Creber who had been mercilessly torturing them. Their features seemingly materialized out of thin air to surround the Proliate.

One Elf stepped forward. The Proliate in front of him held out his sword, but it shook with fear and exhaustion. The Elf stared at the Proliate for a while before speaking.

"You threaten our forest. You endanger our families. You make up lies accusing us of betraying Verngaurd! You condemn us as traitors who side with the bloody Dark Warriors. Did you think such blasphemy would go unanswered? There is a sharp price for such indiscretions."

The Elf paused and paced back and forth several times before stopping to examine the two closest trees. "Your pride, your pompous over-confidence...they will be your undoing. Amongst the trees, that is our world. The forest is *our* home! It's time to finish your welcome."

Suddenly, the abrasive scratching sound shocked the air above the Proliate once again as the Elves' rough hands and feet scampered down the bark. The scant light piercing the forest canopy was completely blacked out as the sky exploded with Elves.

They gracefully bobbed down just long enough to strike a blow before shooting back up. Hundreds of them alternated moving up and down to completely disorient the Proliate. Howls of pain and fear rung out, only to be methodically silenced by the Elves.

As the Proliate slashed and thrust their weapons blindly skyward, the ring of Elves on the ground tightened the noose, hacking their way forward. It was only a matter of moments before the blood-curdling screams gave way to gore-soaked silence. The Elves of Creber were covered in the splattered blood and fleshy debris of their enemy.

Only one Proliate remained alive. Fenik stood, a shaky red figure, exhaustion, pain, and injuries yoking his normally formidable body. His feet drenched in the bloody lake of dead friends, he stared at the thousands of Elves surrounding him on all sides and above. His helmet gone, he briefly glanced at his lifelong friend, Velox, grimacing at his dead companion's wide-eyed stare of pain. Gozador had his face smashed in, almost unrecognizable.

Fenik's chest plate was riddled with dents and fissures. Looking down again, to see what happened to his shield, he stole a glance at his left arm, quickly learning why it would not move as it dangled lower than normal. His left vambrace was gone, his mutilated lower arm barely dangling by a few strained tendons as blood gushed out of the hacked remains. With a resigned attitude and realistic awareness of his impending death, his weary eyelids fluttered back up to the Elves. A shredded arm was of little consequence.

Soon, it would all be over.

Tallcon, I shall see you quickly, he thought wearily.

Kempe strode up to him, and the two warriors stared at each other. Kempe could see by Fenik's pale complexion that he had lost an enormous amount of blood.

"We just wanted to live in peace within our forest," the large muscular Elf said. "But you had to accuse me of killing children? Accuse all Elves of dishonor? Your arrogance shall be your undoing."

Wishing it to be over, Fenik used his right arm to slash with his sword. The strike had none of its usual speed or power. Kempe easily slashed it away with his kama before driving his weapon's sharp beak right into the mid-face of the giant warrior. There was a sickening crunch, a spray of blood, and a heavy thud as the last of the Proliate of Ragorsaf fell into the basin of blood and lifeless bodies on the forest floor.

"I see no evidence of Tallcon here!" an Elf said in a forbidding tone. He emerged from the background and pulled back his hood. It was Ailante. His green eyes stood out even in the darkness of the forest, their grey streaks shining with determination.

"Tallcon must not like forests," Kempe said to laughter.

"They should rename this Blood Forest," the first Elf said, stomping in the bloodied ground.

"Friar's right—pride blinds them. To march straight into our trap is testimony to this fact. This bodes well for today's battle. Now, to the rest of Friar's plan," Kempe encouraged.

Scroll II: Protracted

"I can't wait to get out of this forest!" Scelto seethed.

"We're seriously moving soooo slow. This trip through the forest was supposed to be the 'fast' way," Sankari lamented.

Kainen held his tongue but mentally berated her for convincing them to take the forest. Her surprisingly authentic statements of regret had shriveled long ago.

"We're losing daylight. Plus, there'll be plenty of food on the Cappadocia Plains. Three rivers, a lake, plenty of game, and wild berries," Sankari tempted.

Arend was going to say something, but Gimelli's screaming interrupted. Scelto quickly wiped away some frothy spittle foaming out of her mouth once she quieted.

"She's alerting anyone and everyone to our position." Kainen sighed. "We still don't know if those vampire things are coming after us." He paused, looking up to the dark canopy above. "This forest is so thick there are few windows for light. It's not just the bark that's black, but a general absence of light."

Arend motioned for Kainen, and the two walked a short distance away.

"What are we doing about Gimelli?"

Kainen looked away, as if the answer might be somewhere in the forest. "Absolutely no idea. Losing her sister is going to seriously put Bellae off balance, and then there's Scelto…"

"Welcome to the gray that is life and leadership. Answers do not come easy, and there is rarely a clear path."

"Is that supposed to be helpful?" Kainen complained.

Arend chuckled and shrugged his shoulders. "The truth doesn't have to be."

"I'm totally fine! Untie me!" Gimelli pleaded, her voice cracking from her previous shrieking. "It's hard to walk tied up."

The League had made ploddingly slow progress due to Gimelli alternating states of vegetative sleep and raging attacks.

Sankari had lost her cursory patience and misplaced her ephemeral humility. "Gimelli's definitely turning into one of things and needs to die."

"Sankari!" Arend berated. "Patience and rest are what she needs. Plus, she's herself much more now—her eyes are even normal."

The Fairy huffed. "We should have ended it back when you attacked Bellae."

"I would never attack her!" Gimelli rustled, stumbling on a rock.

Arend held the rope leading her bound hands. "You seem to be getting better, but you still have times where your eyes glaze white and you become infuriated."

"It's great to see your…yellow eyes again," Scelto said, evading the insertion of "beautiful," wavering under embarrassment.

"Your color looks better. You've been eating a ton, and peccary are high in vital fluids to replace what that vampire guy sucked out of you," Lontas added.

"I'm starting to see Ichor's face less during my blackout times. I'm truly sleeping now, and only partly in a weird trance state," Gimelli said, shuddering. "Those half-conscious times feel more claustrophobic than being tied up."

"You still screamed most of last night," Kainen said skeptically.

"But her wounds are looking better. The arnebia and dragon sap have really been helping," Lontas added. "Thanks, Arend."

"Speaking of food, night's about to fall, and I'm hungry," Sankari voiced.

"Why do we say night falls?" Lontas wondered. "It's the suns that 'fall' as they rotate out of our vision while darkness hungrily fills the void. It is interesting to think of the suns and the evidence showing that we are actually spinning and traveling around them. I remember…"

Lontas trailed off as Sankari fluttered close, her face red and peccary sword drawn. "Do not test me! I will cut you! I'm seriously not in the mood for another science lesson."

Scroll 12: Cracked

Friar paced nervously outside the western entrance to the Way of Trepas. Through the dark and misty gorge the path took on a ghostly, undulating appearance as if it were a vision in a dream, threatening the Knights with revenge.

"It's okay. We're ready," Sorea reassured with a smile.

"I need them to come through before their northern reinforcements arrive," he said anxiously. "Plus, we've had no sightings of the Western Elves."

Even being back with the full force of his Knights of Liberum was not easing his pain at the loss of Veli Falciss and his entire castle of well-trained Knights. Shaking his head, he brought his mind to the present. *Focus.* "How's Gleoi Dea?"

"Feeling guilty for being here helping me and not with the Knights from her castle when they died," Sorea answered. "That said, she'll fight well when battle comes."

"I have every faith in her," Friar stated as Ritari strode up.

"Large numbers of reserve Proliate infantry from the Citadel are on their way. I don't think they can get here in time to impact this battle. However, the blasted Magicians and their griffins will be arriving on the other end of the Way of Trepas shortly."

"We must make sure the Eaglians stay away from the griffins at all costs! They are more evenly matched than they will admit, and we can't have them getting distracted from their future assignments. Let the Vioma Dragons and their Aer Ridire take care of griffins," Friar said.

"I'll personally talk with Abhac," Ritari answered.

"What news of the Proliate coming from the north?"

"Depending on how fast they march, they may get here before the troops on the other side of the pass come through. It could be trouble if we are engaged with them when Lidenskap decides to march through."

"Can we divert the Plains troops up north to harass them?"

"No. Their forces are already in camp," Ritari answered. "Plus, I'm not sure they're the best choice to face four seasoned regiments of Proliate. I don't doubt their courage, but their training and discipline are different matters."

"The Elves better make it. We need them after they deal with Ragorsaf," Friar stated. "Let's head to the war council."

Standing next to several massive siege engines, the various leaders of the Alliance awaited Friar's arrival.

A loud squawk from Eaglian General Orel broke the tense silence. His neck swiveled around beneath the uncomfortable gaze of the others, still in shock at the sight of Eaglians. After centuries hiding, their emergence was a thunderous surprise. He spread out his wings, revealing his desire to get back in the air.

"Congratulations to General Orel, his Eaglians, and the Vasama Dwarves on their wonderful victory at the Battle of Ovest. Their skill is stunning and potent," Friar said as he arrived. He forced a smile, trying to remain calm in the face of the apprehensive looks of the other leaders.

The rulers from the Rebelde Plains stood nervously next to Friar. The Elf Kelig anxiously thumbed his bow as the human, Teyol, fretfully rubbed his stubbly chin. The Dwarf Vakava's eyes darted furtively.

King Abernan of the Northern Dwarves growled, "We're hungry for battle! We want some payback for all the attacks they've dished out to us."

"We shall all have our fill of battle," Friar said ominously. "We stick to the plan, while being flexible."

"Where are the Elves?" King Abernan demanded. "Or is it just Knights and my Dwarves who spill their blood today?"

"They'll be here. Remember, everyone has different assignments."

"After this battle, what will we have gained?" Teyol of the Rebelde Plains asked. "What are we supposed to do?"

"We fight until they all die!" Abernan growled angrily.

"Please. That's vague and insulting, even for the King of Dwarves," Kelig stated.

"We have enough enemies to fight. We don't need to start on each other," Friar admonished as King Abernan snarled angrily. "It's a valid question, but our priority is to survive today. Once this is over, we'll reexamine our situation. We could negotiate…"

"Negotiate?" King Abernan yelled. "They just wiped out Veli Falciss, and they are constantly pummeling my home, and you want to discuss terms?"

"Verngaurd still has to deal with the Dark Warriors," Friar said as a din of separate conversations erupted around him. "Enough!" Friar yelled. "We didn't ask for this. They declared war *on us* based on false information! Today we focus on killing as many of them as we can while losing as few of our troops as possible. After the battle, we regroup. We have Eaglians and dragons to rule the skies. We must keep this advantage. Air superiority is key to our communication and strategy. Let's review the battle plan and seize victory."

"We need to get the Confederate force into the Way of Trepas before we unleash our plan. What news?" Friar asked, addressing Ritari and Eaglian Orel.

"The griffins are closing quickly," the Eaglian said. "The Proliate regiments that had been stationed in Jaa have stopped, for some unknown reason, north of here. Maybe they are waiting for the Proliate from Ragorsaf. If so, they'll be waiting a *very* long time!"

"You have news of the Elves?"

"My scouts state the Proliate regiment from Ragorsaf fell into the Blodskogur Woods trap. They were decimated with *zero* casualties from the Elves!"

"Wonderful!" Friar said. "Fighting Elves in a forest? Suicide."

"Ragorsaf is in ashes. The Elves sent a small force to burn it," Orel finished.

"If the Proliate from the north have stopped, we still may have time to send a carrot into the Way of Trepas to lure the main Confederate troops to come through," Friar stated.

"Who did you have in mind?" Ritari questioned.

"Me," Friar answered, quickly holding up his hand to silence any protests from his captain.

On the other side of the Way of Trepas, the Confederate rulers were meeting. In his flowing yellow cape, Emperor Fanga of Piscium paced back and forth, using his large scepter as a hammer, as if punishing the ground beneath him. King Tarha of Ager stood in his simple leather clothes and cape. His enormous girth rested on his large, gold scepter. Campesino was next to his king.

The massive man of Ager had his armored pole flail out, absently swinging it around—impatient to head through the Way of Trepas to harvest revenge on the Knights and Dwarves. Princess Hamaza stood with quiet elegance while whispering to several of her trusted advisors. In their ornate armor, the representatives for the Southern Dwarves, Dverg and Dvergur, stood in quiet but heated discussion. The rulers of the four countries had been discussing strategy when General Lidenskap rashly took off to scout the Way of Trepas.

"Lidenskap is acting cracked," Dverg said. "After the deception with Tallcon, and loss of his soldiers, we should just leave."

"None have lost more than Lidenskap and his Proliate," King Tarha of Ager said.

"Do you really think there are Proliate regiments coming down from Jaa and the west? Even if there are, Friar surely knows," Emperor Fanga said.

"The Proliate were doing military exercises with our forces to the north," Princess Hamaza stated. "However, I highly doubt Friar is unaware of their movements. He has obviously been planning this for an extremely long time."

"If we move through the Way of Trepas, do you think we could catch Friar and the Knights in a pincer trap with our troops and then the Proliate marching from the north and west?" Tarha wondered.

"Even with the griffins and Magicians finally deciding to show up, this smells of another Friar setup," Dvergur huffed. "We should leave!"

"Agreed," the others said, nodding.

"Just in case, I sent a couple Piscinian squads to check out Trepas. I don't trust Lidenskap or—" Emperor Fanga of Piscium started, interrupted by Lidenskap running towards them, eyes wide with elation.

"There's nothing there! Prepare your troops and follow me!" he screamed, with the last part morphing into an animal-like cry. After several large strides back towards the gorge, he turned to see them standing firm, staring in contempt.

"What's wrong with you? I just returned from going up and down the blasted gorge. Look at the carnage behind you! We avenge this treachery!"

"Everyone wants revenge," Princess Hamaza said. "However, we can't afford to walk into another trap."

"I already told you there's *nothing* there."

"Friar has been ten steps ahead all day," the princess replied. "There's no reason to think otherwise now. We should regroup, not rashly rush in."

"Agreed. Just because you don't see anything doesn't mean it's not there," King Tarha of Ager said, pointing to the punji pits. "We learned that painful lesson today."

Without a word, Lidenskap marched up to the king. Even though Lidenskap was a good-sized man, the massive King from Ager dwarfed him. Unexpectedly, Lidenskap backed away, cheering zealously. Pointing upwards, he said, "Here they come."

The others turned to see the sky filled with a lone white figure and thousands of brown streaks. In a few moments, the white Pegasus touched down with such grace and beauty as to take your breath away, quickly followed by legions of griffins screeching and squawking.

"Good job, Runor," Veneficus told the large white stallion with two powerful wings.

"We surveyed the skies," Veneficus started, forcefully cutting off Lidenskap. "There are no Vioma Dragons or Eaglians. Our griffins will allow quick communication. I have already sent a platoon of griffins and riders to the Proliate regiments on the other side of the Tingij to alert them of our presence.

"I'm sorry to see the carnage behind us. However, we can still win the day. There have been sightings of large forces of Dark Warriors to the far east, so we can't afford a drawn-out battle."

Turning to the rulers of the Confederate nations he stated, "For your safety, I insist you ride next to me on a griffin. At least until we get your troops through the Way of Trepas." His voice thundered with such conviction the rulers could only look helplessly at each other. Many had experienced his power when he slammed them to the floor and allowed them to lie in suffocating agony.

Even the fiery spirit of Princess Hamaza was quiet as Lidenskap said, "Now, here's our strategy."

Scroll 13: I Hate Vegetables

"You okay, Friar?" Lovag asked Friar outside the Way of Trepas.

"It feels as if we are drowning in a sea of lies, the tentacles of deception pulling us down into a nightmare. The more we gasp, the more watery deceit we swallow."

Lovag nodded.

Friar forced his face to soften, easing the worry adhered to it. "Battle has the unique power to rip death from its dubious, foggy, often ignored position hidden obscurely in the future and bring our demise bitterly into focus, a razor's edge away." Friar paused, looking at the Knights and their allies. "War brings together a million discrete stories hidden within each individual combatant. We all carry victories, defeats, goals won, dreams lost. Each of us bears tales of parents, family, friends, enemies, being bullied, bullying ourselves. All those narratives broiling, simmering, coalescing under our individual armor entwines with those standing next to, and across from, us. Those innumerable accounts braid together for one moment in time. An unbelievably complex set of backstories coalesce to create one storyline, one outcome. Victory or defeat, life or death."

Lovag sighed. "That's pretty deep. I thought I was the studious one."

Friar continued, "Once the entropy of war is tipped forward, it is impossible to control the devastation. Think how many stories are about to come to an end on both sides."

Before Lovag could speak, Luchar came rushing up. "Let's go kill them all!"

Lovag began laughing. "Friar and I were just talking about something fairly profound."

"This is *not* library hour. No time for profundity, time to pound!"

Lovag laughed. "I didn't know you knew 'profundity.'"

"Looks like we're ready," Friar announced. "Let's go."

Friar, Luchar, Lovag, and the Ulven squad led by Varg, representing the Knights, were joined by a platoon of ten Vioma Northern Dwarves. The group cautiously made their way into the claustrophobically high walls of the gorge.

"Friar, you know I hate vegetables," Luchar growled after they had been walking for some time.

"What?" Lovag asked, chuckling at the odd statement.

"We're being used as human carrots," Luchar said without cracking a smile.

"Who knew you were so funny?" Lovag replied.

"Tighten up," Friar said, his eyes darting unceasingly. "We're about three-fourths of the way through the Way of Trepas."

"We should hold," Varg said. "I feel someone watching us."

A pang of regret rocked Friar. He couldn't help looking for Finn, missing his special vision, which could sometimes warn of danger.

"I should have brought Gleoi Dea," Friar whispered.

"I can feel them," Luchar said in an ominous tone. The weight of the hidden eyes suddenly feeling overwhelming, he unconsciously bounced side to side, his axe twirling as his eyes swiveled.

"Watch your head today, buddy," Lovag said, jokingly tapping his friend's helmet. "I don't want to have to pry another of these off."

Luchar ignored the comment, suddenly looking above the soaring canyon walls. Something was streaking across the opening. "Are they Eaglians or griffins?"

Before Friar could answer, inhuman screams echoed off the canyon walls—coming from everywhere and nowhere.

"Circle!" Friar called—but too late.

Light blue and yellow streaks of the Piscinians were streaming out of hidden crevices from behind. With their large fin-like crests and manicas (shoulder and arm guards) the Retiarians crashed down on them from the left. Their deadly anclas weapons were out. The very sight of the curved trident and bladed weapon could not help but produce fear. The Suoli washed on them from the right with their shields and iaculum, or disemboweling spears, out.

The Dwarves and their crossbows did not turn quickly enough. The Dwarf furthest back was just rotating when the curved end of an anclas slammed into his face and chest. His green helmet split from the ferocity of the attack. As the Piscinian warrior repeatedly slashed with his weapon, ripping flesh and armor completely off, the Dwarf slumped into a bloody heap, his tissue stripped to the bone.

The right side was also suffering the ambush. The longer reach of the iaculum spear made that side of the Dwarf line fall almost instantly. The backwards-facing barbs of the iaculum lived true to their name, and the entire canyon floor was quickly crowded with blood and freed intestine.

"Fall back!" Friar yelled. The Knights and four surviving Vioma

Dwarves quickly formed a defensive line a few yards back. "Fire at the Retiarians with no shields!"

The four surviving Dwarves unloaded their bolts with three direct hits and one that bounced off a manica and back into the gorge. They then went behind the Knights to reload their crossbows. The small band of Allies saw they were facing about thirty vengeful Piscinian warriors. Seeing Friar's strategy to target the shieldless Retiarians, the Piscinians alternated them with the shield-carrying Suoli fighters as they formed up in three lines.

The Knights lined up with the five Ulven squad members led by Varg on their right and Friar, Luchar, and Lovag on the left. The four Dwarves would step up when they reloaded.

"Revenge-revenge..." the Piscinians chanted as they moved forward. The melodic tone and resulting echo off the canyon walls combined to make it disorienting and terrifying.

"Fire on their left flank," Friar whispered to Lovag and the Dwarves. He stole a quick glance behind. They were caught between the Piscinians on one side and a large Confederate army beyond the gorge. Lovag was letting his arrows fly every few seconds, his fire making the lines bunch to their right. With only four crossbows and taking twenty seconds to reload and fire, it was taking too long to have the impact he wanted.

Scroll 14: You Don't See That Everyday

Bellae couldn't help smiling at the sight of Lontas sleeping soundly when all she could manage were stumbling fits of restless dozing. A few weeks ago, he would have been terrified to walk, much less sleep, in the Dark Forest's clutches. The blue dragon Stralande's words echoed in her head as the first whispers of morning peeked through the dark branches of the forest, transfiguring complete darkness into dirty gray.

Kainen had been rustling around for some time, and Bellae could tell they would move out soon. As a cruel joke, her eyelids started feeling heavy just as Borb and Grym started squeaking for breakfast. She might have been able to ignore them but for Crann's nuzzling.

All eyes turned to Gimelli. When she began to stir, Scelto was over her in a flash. Her eyes fluttered open as she began licking her lips.

"Hey!" he said.

Gimelli smiled weakly before mumbling something. Her eyes were their normal yellow. "I kept dreaming I couldn't see—at least not anything real. Ichor attacking me and his awful, incense-loving mother kept replaying in my head."

"We're just glad to see and talk to you," Kainen said. "Let me look at these wounds." He carefully applied more of the mixture of salve from the arnebia plant's yellow flowers and the orange-red sap, or blood, of the dragon tree over the seemingly endless puncture wounds.

"They look way better. Does it sting when I apply this?"

"Not now. At first it burned like crazy," Gimelli commented in a hoarse voice, still strained from screaming.

"That's good," Kainen added. "It likely means the poison from the bites is gone.

"Can we risk a fire?" Scelto asked as Arend prepared a large hare he had killed.

"No choice," Kainen answered. "Gimelli must keep eating meat to replenish the lost blood. Thank goodness you ate, even if reflexively."

"I regret to tell you," Arend stated, "this catch is just for Gimelli."

Gimelli surprised everyone, including herself, devouring the entire hare with blistering speed. After swallowing the last bite, she burped. "Sorry," she mumbled before instantly falling asleep.

"Let her nap while we get ready," Kainen stated.

The cold morning had given way to a comfortable day, and the League had not stopped. Everyone was relieved to finally be out of the forest. After days of fitful walking, Gimelli was finally getting some color back, thanks to Arend's hunting. The Satu River was just ahead, and even Sankari was in good spirits.

"I'm so itchy," Scelto said.

"You'll feel better after washing up," Kainen advised. "Dried blood and mud are not good when left on your skin. As an Elf I feel weird saying this, but I'm grateful to be out of that forest and have a chance to clean up."

"How about today?" Gimelli asked, nodding to the ropes binding her.

"She didn't scream at all last night, and her eyes have been normal for a while," Scelto added.

"Okay," Kainen said as Arend nodded, "untie her."

They sought different areas of the crystal clear Satu River to clean up. There were a few scattered trees but mostly wild prairie grass around them. The distant outline of Mount Boken was visible to the northwest.

"That was so refreshing," Bellae said, glad to have the grime washed away.

"We have two more chances," Sankari said. "Plenty of bath time, and plenty of fish!"

"It's just a little bit farther," Sankari said the next day, her voice rising with enthusiasm. She had been perpetually talking, her excited chatter increasing exponentially with each step closer to home.

"Cappadocia is *the* wonder of the world. The area used to be full of volcanoes, in a time too long ago to imagine. That's where our homes, the Fairy Chimneys, came from. We Fairies mostly stay up in the middle and upper sections where everything's brown.

"The real action is below, around the Sprite Streams. They run in between our rock spire homes. It's so beautiful. You really can't imagine how ravishing it looks, even if you've been to the Storten Flower Fields. Now you won't be able to see the Rite of Desumo since that happens in the spring..."

"What's that again?" Lontas asked with a huge smile. Bellae squeezed his hand and flashed a razor-sharp look of disgust.

"What are thinking? You *want* to hear about this again?" she whispered.

Lontas patted her hand. "What? It's interesting," he claimed while suppressing a laugh. "Actually, it's just really nice to see Sankari truly happy. I guess she was homesick."

"I'm most happy to go over it again!" Sankari announced, her wings fluttering incredibly fast. She darted back and forth between the members of the League as she chattered, making sure they were paying close attention.

"So, as I said, Sprites live along the colorful rivers and streams that weave their way through our Fairy Chimneys. The Sprites live in the larger mushrooms that grow along the banks of the stream. Oh, they are just indescribably gorgeous—bursting with color and surrounded by flowers and vines.

"The Rite of Desumo happens in the spring when spriggans are born. They are funny little creatures that can fly and swim with equal skill. Spriggans are born with completely clear skin—you can actually see their blood vessels, organs…everything. The newborn spriggans meet with three-year-old Sprites—who have to pick a spriggan to be their kindred spirit for the rest of their lives. After the choice is made, the spriggan takes on the color of the Sprite that chose them, and they will be together as friends until death. The spriggans can only communicate with their Sprite. If the matched Sprite dies, the spriggan passes away quickly from the loss of their one confidant."

The skies were clear of griffins and Watchers, so Arend circled above, elated to fly freely. Gimelli was riding Crann, Sankari fluttered, and all the others—Bellae, Kainen, Lontas, and Scelto—walked. Later that day, well after crossing the Hada River, they came to a steep hill.

"We're here!" Sankari shouted, pirouetting in the air euphorically.

After walking up the knoll, they found themselves staring into a valley. The dale's incline was broad but gentle as it slopped down and back up again. On the other side of the valley, they started to see the famed

Fairy Chimneys hiding behind the second hill. Conical dark brown to black rooftops of stone sat on the cylindrical light brown homes.

"We carve our homes right into the Fairy Chimney rocks!" Sankari stated with more than a little pride. "Come, let's go! Oh, I forgot to tell you, Crann can't come. Larger animals aren't allowed in Cappadocia. He could kill someone or destroy the Sprites' homes."

Bellae nodded and informed Crann.

"See you soon," Bellae said, squeezing his neck. *"Love you, Crann. I wish Finn could see this."*

"Love you too, and I miss him as well," Crann said.

Bellae choked back tears over Finn and the emotions of the quest that had been thrust upon her.

"We'll get through this," Crann added, seeing the depth of her sadness.

"Take one step," Bellae said. *"Just one step at a time. That's what Stralande told me,"* she added, noticing his confusion.

"Let's go before Sankari explodes," Kainen said with a small chuckle.

"Do you guys want to come or stay with Crann?" Bellae asked the mice.

"We'll take our chances with the Sprites and Fairies," Grym stated. *"Better prospects for food,"* he added quickly.

The League of Truth, minus Crann, made their way up the steep and slippery rock face. The craggy surface was hard, but there was a dry, almost spongy softness to it that made you think it might not be too bad to carve into. Reaching the top of the hill, it became apparent that part of the defensive spiked top was missing, enough to let them squeeze through.

"No sentries? No guards?" Kainen asked.

Sankari shrugged. "Few come this far north."

Upon cresting the top, their breath dropped away. The brown Fairy Chimneys stretched out far into the distance like castle spires. They came in an astonishing array of shapes. Instead of streets, the Fairy Chimneys had magnificent streams weaving their way between them. Each stream was accessorized on both sides with ridiculous colors that wavered as if alive. The dazzling hues took the form of flowers and something else—alive and extremely active.

Figure 10: The League of Truth arrives at the fabled Cappadocia: land of Sprites and Fairies. The impressive, but relatively monochromatic, brown towers of the Fairies stand in stark contrast to the flowing streams of color that harbor Sprites and spriggans.

What looked like large butterflies and small birds were careening around with abundant energy. The streams were awash in reflected color from the magnificent hues lining their banks and zooming overhead.

"You don't see that every day," Scelto murmured, amazed by the beauty and wonder of Cappadocia.

"Now you understand! Once seen, this place never leaves you," Sankari said, quickly performing aerial summersaults before fluttering down the hill to the closest stream. Suddenly, the color collecting around the stream swarmed up like a flock towards the fairy.

"Bellae, what's this?" Lontas questioned, pointing to what looked like a wisp of white cotton floating near his face. "I thought it was tree pollen except it's hovering." He reached out his hand, but Bellae quickly grabbed it.

"Hello!" Bellae tried, instantly sensing it was alive.

"Where'd Sankari go?" Kainen interrupted, overwhelmed at the sight of Cappadocia.

Looking down, the League saw only a swarm of color swirling frenetically.

Seeing their hesitation, Sankari zoomed back up. The haze of color followed her a short distance before dropping back towards the stream in a cloud of iridescence. "Come on!" she coaxed, waving her hand energetically, an enormous smile cutting across her normally critical face. "Oh, that's a cotton bird. They're nice but rather dull."

Lontas and Bellae looked at each other, knowing it was one of the coolest things they had seen. Its large, soft-looking white threads protruded all around, and two small black eyes in the front sat over four small legs. Instead of wings, the wisps of cotton-like strips vibrated and contracted to keep it afloat. As it flew away, they were magnetically pulled towards the burst of color around the stream by Sankari's sheer will.

"The smell's intense. It's like you're tasting a bouquet of beautiful flowers," Bellae said as an elegant medley of aromas thrust into their nostrils.

"Oh wow!" Gimelli said, feeling a tinge of lightheadedness as a blistering array of colors engulfed their eyes in flashing waves. Soon they were completely surrounded by vivid shades pouncing around in feverish swirls.

"It's breezy," Bellae laughed as the gusts of thousands of fluttering wings vibrated all around them. "It tickles when their wings sweep against you!"

"Enough. Enough!" a rough voice bellowed some distance away, the source of the vocalization blocked by the rainbow of commotion. However, the words held power as the barrage of colors immediately began to blur, scrambling this way and that before fading.

Relieved at the breathing space, the League began to take stock of their surroundings. The stream flowing confidently in front of them glowed a radiant bluish green—coated in a viscous color palate of pollen. On either side of the stream sprouted innumerable flowers of every shape, height, and color. Rows of magnificent, but comparatively drab, Fairy Chimneys rose up in the distance. The colorful figures previously besieging them once again moved in mass to hover closer. Wingless creatures were riding odd animals with furiously beating wings and long snouts.

"Those are Sprites riding their spriggan," Sankari informed.

The Sprites were about six inches tall, and no two held the same color. Some were solid while others were streaked or splattered by a tremendous number of tints. Their whole bodies gave off a sparkling appearance. Their elongated faces were almost insect like. Despite this, they wore cheerful, mischievous smiles. Two antennae sprouted next to flattened ear structures on their foreheads. Several sharp fangs spilled out over their lower lips.

Sankari pointed. "They use their antennae to greet one another and their spriggans."

"Are they drinking the water?" Bellae asked.

"Yes, a tube-like proboscis feasts on the water, which is ripe with nutrition from the constant supply of thick pollen from the surrounding plants—see the steady flow falling to the stream?"

The League gazed at the perpetual snowfall of pollen fluttering and flitting downward. Once mooring upon the stream, colors coalesced into a flowing, but constantly morphing, rainbow.

"They also eat small fish and insects," Sankari added as the polychromatic throng of hovering creatures occasionally bumped the flowers, cajoling an extra cascade of brightly colored pollen to escape.

"Like I said, each Sprite rides a spriggan of matching color," Sankari said, fluttering feverishly while pointing out examples.

The spriggan had long snouts and tongues, useful for getting at nectar. A small pair of wings protruded from their heads and two large sets from their sides. Spikes crowned the tops of their heads and ran down most of their backs save one section where their Sprite sits. The most distinctive feature of the spriggan was the fact they had no arms or legs.

"See their long, spiked tails? They use them hold onto vines or plants either above or below the water," Sankari informed.

Figure 11: Companions for life, spriggan take on the color scheme of their counterpart Spriggan.

"Oh!" Bellae howled when, as if on cue, a spriggan dove into the river.

"They are at home on either side of the border: under or over the stream, as their wings are functional in and out of the water," Sankari informed. "They're excellent swimmers, and the smaller wings on their heads are useful for maneuvering."

Trumpets blared, startling the League. Their mesmerized stares broke loose from the enchanting Sprites and spriggan to see a group of Fairies approaching.

"It's King Kuningas, the one who told everyone to leave you alone," Sankari said. "We Fairies were here first. The Knights transported the Sprites and spriggan here when the Proliate tried to wipe them out from the flower fields."

The squires nodded, remembering the story from when they visited the Storten Flower Fields so long ago. The king, relaxing on a large litter, contrasted sharply with the four Fairies struggling to carry him while flying. The open sedan chair had ornately carved wood and was escorted by twelve Fairies blowing trumpets circling the perimeter. Eventually, they landed and, at a mere eighteen inches, short even by Fairy standards, the king stood up, his girth more than compensating for his lack of height. His stretched golden-brown garment sweat from the pressure of his jostling belly. The typical bland brown wings fluttered above his intense face.

"Welcome, honored guests!" he bellowed, his voice resonating below his large and meaty nose. Hanging lazily from the middle of his face it lingered, seemingly waiting for someone to prop it up. "We're honored to have the great and mighty League of Truth join us in Cappadocia. Our tradition is to welcome you with a feast. Come, it's time celebrate!"

Scelto smiled at the idea that the League was great and mighty. *I guess we are compared to six-inch Sprites and two-foot-tall Fairies.*

The League walked through Cappadocia as if in a dream. The colors of the streams and Sprites balanced the relatively unadorned Fairies and their unique tan rock spires.

"Ow!" Bellae cried, doubling over, holding her stomach.

"What is it?" Lontas asked.

Bellae didn't answer, too busy scanning for the source of pain she felt. She searched the bursts of color crowding and zig-zagging, but she couldn't localize the injured creature. She began walking away from the others, who continued following King Kuningas and his entourage.

"Bellae!" Lontas pleaded. "We need to follow him. All this is for you."

She stopped, hurt radiating from her eyes. *All for me?* She did not know everything, but she understood enough to realize this was no holiday. *No one would choose what lies ahead*, she thought. The sting of what Stralande told her in confidence bit into her anger, emboldening it. A sharp pang of pain brought her back to the suffering animal.

The king can wait. Turning, she walked into the shadowy base of a Fairy Chimney. Her eyes adjusted, the darkness giving way to amazing details previously obscured by shade. There were countless brawny mushroom homes hugging the base of the Fairy Chimneys. Sprouting at odd angles, some appeared frozen in the middle of a raucous dance. Each enormous mushroom was surrounded by a series of vines crawling up the sides of their houses and onto the rock they backed up to. Delicate bursts of color flowered their way up each vine. Moving closer, she saw smaller rows of crop mushrooms growing out from a terraced section above each house. Some were fat and juicy, while others were tall and thin. A few had wet-looking patterns zig-zagging over their tops.

Shuffling forward, she began to make out carved doors in each of the large mushrooms. Occasionally, a Sprite would poke its head out and stare wide-eyed at her for a second before quickly retreating to the presumed safety of their mushroom homes.

"Those are TaiMadarch mushroom houses," Sankari said, fluttering over. "They are tough, like trees, and the Sprites carve them out to make their homes. It takes over a hundred years for them to grow that tall. Anyway, we can look at them later."

Bellae ignored Sankari. Something was moving in the flower-lined vines. It took her a moment to realize it was spriggans hanging upside down. Closing her eyes, she focused on the feeling of pain, blocking out Sankari's continued protests. Opening her eyes, she moved to the source and knelt. A red spriggan with yellow splotches was swaying on a vine with its wings tucked back and both eyes closed.

Nausea, pain, frustration, fear, loneliness—Bellae could feel each and every emotion as they gashed into her.

"Are you okay?"

The spriggan's eyes shot open in horror, having never communicated with anyone but its matched Sprite.

A small hand vibrated on Bellae's shoulder. "This spriggan's Sprite was killed several days ago, and it has not eaten since," a Fairy stated sadly, nodding at Sankari.

"Will you come and eat with me?" Bellae pleaded.

The spriggan's long tongue flicked in and out, slowly dragging along its dry and gaunt skin. It was well past the point of hunger—that sensation disappeared long ago as its stomach shriveled under neglect. Its wings began to sputter—buzzing briefly as its tail let go of the vine. Its undernourished body quivered briefly before plummeting towards the ground. Bellae let out a scream while desperately reaching forward to catch it.

"Thanks," the spriggan buzzed before dying in her hands.

Closing her eyes, Bellae began to sob softly. Overwhelming emotions squeezed her mind: hunger, fatigue, pressure, grief, expectations, death. She closed her eyes. Lontas knelt down, supporting her as she leaned into him. The tears came, harder, faster.

"I'm already tired, Lontas," she said. "We haven't even really started, and I'm exhausted. Fatigue sidled behind her sobs, and she drifted off to sleep, still gently cradling the spriggan.

A loud clanging noise woke Bellae. She sat up, disoriented, head spinning. Looking up, the ceiling was only a few inches above her.

Gimelli quickly slid over on all fours to give her a hug. "You're in a Fairy's house right next to King Kuningas' royal hall." The room was sculpted out of stone with intricately carved wooden furniture, miniaturized for Fairies.

"Scelto carried you here," Gimelli said, pointing to the low ceiling. "He left with more than a few bumps to his head!"

"Oh no," Bellae said.

"You missed the party, and the king was sad but understood how tired you were," Gimelli said as a loud sound rang out. "That gong means King Kuningas has left the banquet. The nice Fairy who lives here said you could lie down in the lower level of their house. Lontas and I took turns watching you."

"Thanks," Bellae said, her stomach gurgling.

"I understand that sound. Let's head to the royal hall and get you some food."

The two sisters hunched their way out of the quaintly decorated front room of the Fairy's house. Carefully avoiding the TaiMadarch houses, Sprites, and spriggan, they headed into the banquet hall.

"Sorry I missed everything," Bellae said, licking her dry lips. She reached out to steady herself against her sister. "I'm feeling a little lightheaded."

"It's okay. Let's just rest here," Gimelli said. The two sat against the corner wall, leaning heavily against one another. The great hall was empty save for Fairies cleaning up the enormous mess and sticky residue of what had obviously been quite a feast.

Suddenly, Gimelli began mumbling, an agitated look sprouting across her face.

"Jumeaux...telepathically?" Bellae mouthed.

"Yes, he keeps bugging me. He always wants to know what we are doing and where we are. At Liberum he could care less about us. He claims he's an 'influential' Magician and has learned to appreciate us," Gimelli scoffed, but instantly blushed. "Sorry, he's still our brother." Pausing, she stared at Bellae, concern etched on her face. "He relentlessly wants to know about you." Gimelli bit her lower lip, desperately wanting to believe Jumeaux cared for them but unable to deny the feeling he had ulterior motives.

"Did you tell him where we are?"

"Didn't have to. He sees us now, using magic, when we talk telepathically," Gimelli said.

"Can't change it, I guess. How are you feeling? Your color's better, and the wounds look a ton better."

"I feel healthier, and while you slept, a Fairy healer checked me. She said I'm cured," Gimelli answered, flashing her celebrated smile. "Look—no white eyes, and no black fang thingies! I'm more worried about you. I feel terrible I choked you."

"That wasn't really you."

"Thanks for that. I also feel bad about eating so much food through the forest. You have to be starving."

"Not really. I guess I'm just tired…and nervous," Bellae said.

"I know. Me too. What exactly we are supposed to do? How do we get to the crystals?"

Bellae nodded, tears bristling in the corners of her eyes.

"Sorry, I didn't mean to make things worse."

"You didn't," Bellae reassured, laying her head on Gimelli's shoulder. Gazing around the king's hall, she could see it was carved into the same tan stone that made up most of Cappadocia. The most impressive feature was its size, especially considering the diminutive Fairies and Sprites. A series of ornamental arches and columns, all carved from solid rock, bounced around the large room.

"What did I miss?" Bellae asked.

"Lots and lots of mushrooms, tasty, sweet water, and did I mention mushrooms? No sign of Patuljak," Gimelli said before getting up to fetch a pitcher and cup, offering Bellae water.

"Oh, my!" Bellae gasped. "This is amazing."

"I know! It's honeyed from all the nectar. It's like a banquet itself. Apparently, there are underground volcanic springs so flowers bloom year round."

Gimelli paused, staring at her sister. *We're supposed to save the world? We barely made it here.* "I'm nervous about meeting the Grand Master Elf, Patuljak, and this quest," she said out loud. "However, we'll do it together."

"Just…no more trying to make 'friends' with vampires and zombies!" Bellae said.

Gimelli laughed. "I promise. Did I mention there were a lot of mushrooms?" Gimelli said, reaching up for a platter on a nearby table. "Those brown ones with the white powdery mold are cogumelos. It sounds disgusting, but it's not bad. The tan ones with the milky, jagged streaks are faixa-cogumelo. You dip crisp bread into the milky part and eat it." Gimelli made a disgusted face and began laughing again.

"I don't remember the names of the others. Actually, the one with the slimy stripes is pretty good. There's also peccary meat and some weird-looking fruits and vegetables. I'll find some."

Bellae nodded, drinking more of the wonderful water.

"Sorry to interrupt here!" Grym squeaked, raising his paws to his mouth outside her pocket. *"You picked the absolute perfect, really ideal time to nap—while everyone else feasted! Now I'm so weak, I can barely move…food!"* Grym said, feigning dizziness.

Bellae chuckled, grabbing a mushroom and crisp bread. Setting it down, her mice ravenously ate. Finding a cup that still had some of the stream water in it, she helped them drink. After gorging themselves, the two crawled contentedly back into her pocket.

"I'm so glad you're here," Bellae said, snuggling in next to her sister, who had returned with another salver of food.

"Peccary and fruit as promised," Gimelli said.

"May I sit with you?" a new voice pierced their serenity.

Scroll 15: An Answers Reward

Standing over the sisters was an elderly Elf. His rough skin drooped, sagging beneath the burden of age, especially around his eyes—giving him a tired expression. Despite his years, there was an unmistakable twinkle of vitality in his deep brown eyes. With a loud grunt, he sat down on the floor next to them. Even while seated, the hunch in his spine was apparent. His knobby legs stretched out before them, but they could tell he had been tall and strong in his youth.

He flashed a warm smile, and Gimelli saw something familiar in his face. "I'm Patuljak, and glad to see you again."

Bellae jumped up with surprise. "The Grand Master Elf?"

He smiled, adjusting his simple white cloak. "The title's nothing, especially these days. Please, sit. I walked with you long ago, when Bellae was just a baby, to deliver you to Liberum," the Elf said, looking down despairingly. "My son, Kempe, was with me. I know you met him again. My grandson, Kainen, has been traveling with you. I hope he isn't giving you too much grief."

"I remember you," Gimelli said before reassuring him how great the two Elves were.

Bellae felt a bit disappointed, expecting to meet the Grand Master Elf in an ornate hall full of warriors and great pageantry. This Elf, these circumstances, seemed anticlimactic. *That's vain,* she thought, blushing. Patuljak smiled brightly as if he could read her mind.

"I'm supposed to say hello from Stralande. He said you were friends," Bellae said.

A despondent, almost pained look spread across his creased face. "I was sorry to hear he died. I'm pleased he saw you before he did. These are dangerous times, and much depends on you." As he spoke, his eyes bore deeply into Bellae. They moved side to side as if judging every square inch of her.

Bellae couldn't help focusing on the haunting secrets Stralande whispered. *Someday I'll tell someone what he said…but not today.*

"I was in the town of Torpe, meeting with Western Elves, when the first attempt on my life occurred. After that, everything spiraled out of control. Piscium, Ager, Jaa, and the Rebelde Plains were temporary stops before travelling here. An evil has gripped Verngaurd, and I fear my presence is putting the Fairies and Sprites in danger." The Elf looked around the great hall as if reminiscing.

"As you know, Magician's mindre crystals ultimately depend on Macht Crystals—the true source of magic in the world. If the lesser mindre crystals lose contact with the Macht for too long, they lose all power. Your ancestors, the Ainmhi Caint, made the supreme sacrifice to steal and hide these Macht Crystals to avoid a great evil, the cycle of destruction—Na Cearcaill. They were relentlessly hunted. As their numbers dwindled, they enlisted others who could not speak with animals to help keep the secret of the crystals safe. Hence, the League of Truth was born.

"When no pure-blood Ainmhi Caint remained, your direct forebearers, distant relatives of the animal talkers, were hidden in the Giant Redwoods for safety. There we waited for the gift of the Ainmhi Caint to reemerge. The Eaglians agreed to withdraw from Verngaurd, pretending to turn into isolationists, in order to protect and nurture the heirs of the Ainmhi Caint, for only an animal talker can complete the prophecy and discover the Macht Crystals."

"How did I get the ability? Why not Gimelli or Jumeaux?" Bellae asked.

An intensely tortured look flashed across his face, only to be quickly replaced by a forced smile. "Some are born to be tall, others to run fast, another to jump high. We all inherit different gifts, and sometimes talents coalesce into something special."

"Thank you for the background," Gimelli commented. "Our time with Stralande was much more abbreviated than we expected. To be honest, we came away with more questions than answers. A big one is why the Ainmhi Caint stole the crystals from Veneficus in the first place? Isn't he on our side?"

Patuljak sighed, as if it was a question he had hoped to avoid. "The Ainmhi Caint somehow discovered a great evil was about to descend upon the world, causing global destruction. The cycle, it alarmingly turns out, has repeated a large number of times, Na Cearcaill. Those ancient writings are long gone, but I have heard they spoke of the slaughter and extermination of almost the entire world. This 'evil force' could only carry out their plan if they could acquire the Macht Crystals. Therefore, they stole and hid them."

"Couldn't Veneficus have stopped the 'evil' if they had left the crystals with him?" Bellae asked, remembering his awesome power.

"Apparently not. Or at least the Ainmhi Caint were convinced he couldn't," Patuljak replied. "Remember, this all took place eons and eons ago."

"The evil you speak of, the White Wizard?" Gimelli questioned.

Patuljak rubbed his forehead as if he was wiping away the early appearance of sweat. "He's undoubtedly part of the evil. However, it's much more complicated. Many of the writings with those details were lost generations ago. More will be revealed to you as the journey progresses. I'm but a lowly servant of the League of Truth."

"I don't understand!" Bellae exclaimed, becoming irritated by the mystery surrounding their quest. "Is he or isn't he the evil you speak of?"

Patuljak laughed. "You'll need that spunk, believe me. But you have to understand, I simply don't know. There will be clues along the path you are about to embark upon." He smiled apologetically. "The Ainmhi Caint left much out and divided our responsibilities, purposefully keeping us, and our knowledge, segregated. The overall picture was known only to them and will become clear only once you complete the task."

Bellae rolled her eyes. "You know...this whole Chosen One, secrecy thing is getting annoying. We need to find Macht Crystals to defeat some sort of evil you can't even tell us about? Something 'wicked' is going to destroy the world? I still don't understand Na Cearcaill thingy."

Patuljak's smile disappeared. "I'm afraid, my dear, annoyance will be the least of the trials you are about to face. Your ancestors purposefully kept this knowledge secret to protect us for as long as possible. Anyone knowing the ultimate truth is long since dust in their grave.

"Na Cearcaill means 'never-ending cycle.' A pattern of destruction that occurred on such a monumental time scale that an average being could not possibly notice these repeated devastations as a pattern. Somehow, the Ainmhi Caint discovered this cycle and made it their life's mission to end it, to free Verngaurd from its evil grasp."

Gimelli squeezed her sister tight. "From the beginning of this... whatever it is, every step leads to more questions than answers."

Patuljak laughed. "Welcome to life. Welcome to the reality of every scholar, scientist, and seeker of knowledge. Every cave we illuminate reveals ten more offshoot chambers to explore. Each bit of knowledge we garner reveals dozens of questions we hadn't even thought of. That is the glorious, and frustrating, thing about scholarship—there is no end point. There is always more to know." He paused, looking down for several moments before looking up. "That is the underappreciated audacity of the scholar. We march forward into the dark caverns of ignorance, desperately searching for the ultimate answers, knowing we will never live to see the end.

"Perhaps, the intellectual and warrior have more in common than either wishes to admit. The warrior heads to battle, facing darkness and death, while the scholar, already swimming in the murkiness, and seeing the reality of death, fights for answers. Maybe if we could see more of ourselves in each other, we wouldn't need to kill each other so often in war.

"Growing older has its own cycle. Find an answer and have ten more problems tied to your consciousness. You have to trust your predecessors. Have faith that they knew more than I. The emergence of the Chosen One signals a return of hope, optimism that the evil cycle, Na Cearcaill, can finally end. Know that innumerable ancestors died setting up this elaborate prophecy just for this moment. You must find a way to finish the job and end the threat once and for all."

Bellae paused, remembering Stralande's secret words. Perhaps she knew more than even the Grand Master Elf. *That's discouraging,* she thought, looking into his kind eyes.

"I just *LOVE* it when you guys put that much pressure on my little sister. It's sooo reasonable, so compassionate," Gimelli said, clenching her jaw.

"Pressure is an interesting concept," Patuljak mused. "If a house falls on you, that is external pressure. Anxiety, however, is an internal construct of our creation, and one, fortunately, we control."

Gimelli tilted her head. "Fancy words, but it's still more than she should have to bear."

"That I agree with. Words are easy, while activating them within your mind is a different matter. Still, choosing to see, and attack, the hardships in front of you, freeing yourself from excuses and justifications, is true strength. I know it will be hard, but your success will depend on you, not fate or circumstance."

"What exactly is 'success'?" Bellae asked. "What happens when we find these Macht Crystals?"

Patuljak paused, his eyes locked on Bellae's with such ferocity she had to blink and turn away. *Does he expect me to know what to do with them?*

Finally, after an uncomfortable silence, he spoke. "That knowledge is revealed *only* when all Macht Crystals have been gathered."

"How about a hint? Do we give them to Veneficus to fight the White Wizard? Do we 'use' them? Is that even possible?" Gimelli questioned.

"Sure," Patuljak answered with infuriating, and ambiguous, simplicity.

"What does that even mean?" Gimelli questioned, irritation leaking from her words.

"It means you need to survive and solve the riddles to find all five quests, for five separate pairs of Macht Crystals," the Elf answered.

"Wait, what?" Gimelli roared. "Five separate quests?"

Patuljak nodded.

Bellae fought tears. *Five quests? Not one?*

Gimelli rubbed her eyes, suddenly feeling dizzy.

Bellae remembered some of what Stralande had said to her. *"You will not want to see or learn most of what is coming. Some of it will be downright painful, mentally, and physically. It does no good to try and gloss over the truth. It will, sooner or later, always break through."*

"Pressure and stress can be excitement and enthusiasm," Bellae said out loud.

"What?" Gimelli asked.

"That's one of the things Stralande wrote to me in the note before we left. He also told me, 'Move forward with your family and friends, taking one step at a time for them. Let the outcome work itself out.'"

Patuljak nodded as if he was impressed and proud of her. "He clearly gave you better advice than I."

"She's supposed to magically know what to do with the *five* sets of Crystals when we're done?" Gimelli inquired.

"I'm sure you're sick of hearing this, but with each step you learn more. Listen to Stralande, have faith, keep moving forward. Here." Reaching into his knapsack, he carefully removed a leather pouch. Tenderly, he pulled out a scroll and handed it to her. Standing to leave, he said, "Good luck with your first mission scroll."

"Wait!" Bellae cried out. "Aren't you going to help?"

He smiled. "I'll be back to check on you, but this is your burden."

"That's incredibly unfair," Gimelli stated, anger rising in her voice.

"Perhaps, but my job is to give you that. Your role is to solve it."

"Speaking of such things," Gimelli said. "You know we almost died, like several times, just getting here?" She whooshed her hair over, showing her neck before rolling up her sleeves to reveal the healing wounds from the vampire. She had several flashbacks to Ichor and the thousands of little barbs shooting out on tendrils to suck her blood. Shuddering, she continued, "Shouldn't we have an army? Or at least more help."

Patuljak nodded, seemingly genuinely concerned. "I...have often wondered that myself. However, the architects of this prophecy, your ancestors, have passed down the proclamation that a small group not only has the best chance to triumph but the *only* chance for victory."

He moved to leave before stopping. *Only the young would keep going with this quest, moving forward despite the absurd odds, and not become discouraged.* Partially looking back, he added, "That is where the faith part comes in. Remember, I send with you my grandson. I can tell you I wish for, with all my heart, your triumph and safe return."

The further away he walked, the more despondent the two sisters felt, despite his enigmatic message. They both realized cryptic was the currency of this quest. Bellae looked up to see Kainen, Arend, Lontas, and Scelto walking in. They were staring at the girls with a protective glare she recognized so often in Finn's face. Lontas, his pants suspended high above his ankles, looked like he had grown another inch in size and a mile in maturity since they had left. She wondered what would happen if Lontas ran into the bullies that used to torment him back to

Liberum. She battled tears knocking to come out. *I know I will never see Liberum again.*

The invisible target of self-doubt that all who are bullied carry, that trawled his expressions into caution, and yanked his movements into nervous twitches were gone. His growing coordination teamed up with his cultivating self-assurance to form proof that invisible forces can affect your physical being.

Bellae inspected the scroll. *This is it? So much fuss over a rolled up, blah-looking, yellow sheet of paper.* She gently touched the curved lines and felt its brittleness crackling under her fingers. The girls cautiously unrolled the scroll, bits of its edges flaking off.

"Ah-ahh! Careful!" Gimelli said as pieces fragmented off.

Scroll 16: Have Fun...

Once the flaking ancient scroll had crunched into an unrolled position, Gimelli read:

"Cleared the dragon's test.
Now you are ready for your quest.
Carefully follow each clue.
Courage and persistence will see you through.

Let there be no doubt,
Nothing shall be freely given out.
Each step will be a fight,
Bringing secrets to light.

Five sets of Power Crystals to seek.
Succeed, and the strong shall fear the weak.

Recover them and deny Evil.
Undo millennia of savage crimes and upheaval.

First, crystals of **Sight**.
Sometimes you need more than light.
Seek the crystals of **Perception**.
Beware it's joined opposite, **Deception**.

Go where there is no time for seasons in the land.
Half each day ruled cool—half it's banned.
Within the ocean of brown,
Sits a gem fit for any crown.
Beware apparitions or in the dry drown.

After wading into this desolate sea,
Few areas of life can be.
Find the area that is lower down.
Follow birds, and it can be found—the rock crown.

Go between the sprigs,
Of dates, olives, apricot, and figs.
There, discover a mystery you must solve,
Before the door will revolve.

Once you enter and stand,
Try and hold it in your hand.
Open your fingers, and there it's not.
Squeeze it tight, and you lose a lot."

The girls groaned in exasperated unison.

"Can't they just tell us where to go?" Bellae questioned.

"I guess not," Gimelli replied, feeling tired and desperately wanting to lie down. The run-in with Ichor and the undead had taken more out of her than she wanted to admit. Instinctively, she rubbed her neck, still struggling with feeling lightheaded and sluggish. Although the small puncture wounds were healing externally, internally, she felt a chill at the dark memories of the slimy tentacles and their piercing needles.

"Not good?" Lontas asked tentatively.

Without thinking about it, Bellae stood up quickly and gave Lontas a warm hug.

"Need help then?"

Bellae nodded emphatically. Kainen, Arend, Scelto, and Lontas all joined the two sisters around the ancient scroll and read it themselves.

"Clear as mire sludge," Kainen said.

"Why does it always have to be a rhyme?" Bellae wondered.

"It's easier to remember that way," Patuljak stated calmly, his sudden appearance startling them.

"Grandpelf!" Kainen said, spryly jumping up to give his grandfather a long hug. "I was so sad you weren't at the feast."

"Every second I get to see you is a blessing, dear child," Patuljak said, then, as if it was a ritual required of all elderly relatives, he held his grandson at arm's length and studied him. He nodded proudly before embracing him again.

When they finished, the aged Elf looked to Gimelli. "I thought about what you said, and I wanted to give you something. Before I do that, let me answer about the rhyming. There's only one copy of each scroll, and only one person at any time that knows what it says. We have to memorize it in case we need to destroy and rewrite the scroll."

"I couldn't memorize that," Bellae stated, staring at the long-dusty scroll.

Patuljak laughed before settling into a reflective smile. "It took me a while, but as with anything, if you put your mind to it and practice long enough, there's nothing you can't do. Plus, like all the guardians of the scrolls, I just had to memorize this one. I know it forwards and backwards.

"Want to hear it backwards?" he asked. Without waiting for an answer, he began, "Lot a lose you, and tight it squeeze. Not it's there, and fingers your open. Hand your in it hold and try, stand and enter you once. Revolve will door the before, solve must you mystery—"

"Grandpelf, really?" Kainen interrupted, embarrassment infusing amusement.

"That's nice, sir, but I'm not sure it adds much," Arend stated directly.

Patuljak laughed, nodding his head in agreement. "The one keeper or guardian-one scroll rule has been the norm for thousands of years. I have no idea what any of the other scrolls will say as you journey to find all five sets of Macht Crystals."

"You can't tell us what's coming?" Bellae clarified.

A look of sadness flashed across his face, quickly replaced, with exertion, with one of optimism. "Unfortunately, you're on your own, but I have every faith in you."

"It's good your ancestors are dead, girls, or I might kill them myself," Scelto scoffed.

"You mean, you don't know if the other scrolls even still exist?" Lontas asked incredulously, the reality of the keepers or guardians only knowing their part finally sinking in. "If one of them didn't pass on their knowledge, our quest comes to a crashing halt." He quickly glanced at Bellae. There was a steely look in her eyes articulating determination. No storm was going to shake her resolve, no matter what Patuljak answered. He sighed. *I'm with you, my friend, all the way.*

"That's correct," the Elf stated. "In the beginning, when these rules were forged, the Ainmhi Caint were being relentlessly hunted. Once they were wiped out, things slowed down. It has only been in recent generations that those of us in the League of Truth have been pursued again."

"We have to take one quest at a time and not worry about what comes after. The prophecy was quite specific about protecting these clues," Kainen stated.

"Can you tell us anything about this riddle?" Gimelli asked. "You know it so well."

Patuljak looked concerned. "Unfortunately, I'm forbidden from offering verbal assistance. The Chosen One, and her companions, must figure it out. I know it seems unfair, but there's a reason. You have a long road full of many trials ahead. You must overcome them on your own. Trust *no one* but those walking this path with you."

"Hello, hello!" the booming voice of King Kuningas rang out as he was carried on his litter. On either side of him Fairies carried various platters and bowls of food.

"Hello—" Patuljak began, only to have Kuningas interject hungrily.

"That scroll's the reason it was so important for us to protect our Grand Elf brother. We Fairies and Sprites were happy to do so…" His voice trailed off as he took an obscenely large ladle of mushroom pudding.

A female Fairy quickly fluttered over to wipe a dribbling splash from his chin.

"How long will this quest take?" Bellae asked.

"No one knows. You have to discover the rest," Patuljak replied.

"Do we know who specifically wrote this prophecy anyway?" Gimelli pressed.

Nodding approvingly, Kuningas paused as a Fairy again approached to wipe away drizzle. "Good question, but to be honest, we just don't know. Most believe it was the last Ainmhi Caint together with the earliest members of the League of Truth."

Patuljak added, "Keep in mind these prophecies go back to the earliest recorded history of our turn on this world. Countless generations have been born and died since this was handed to us. The leaders of Elves, Eaglians, Fairies, and dragons have protected the prophecy through innumerable generations after the last of the pure Ainmhi Caint died."

"Well, I hope you enjoyed the feast, my friends. I must be off for official duties…" Kuningas said as his eyes cravingly massaged the various foods around him.

"Official duties," Patuljak said once the king was out of sight while quickly shoveling imaginary food into his mouth. The squires suppressed a laugh.

"What will you do now?" Bellae asked Patuljak.

He sighed deeply. As the breath escaped from his lips, you could almost see the burden of carrying the scroll wafting away. "I'm relieved to have done my part. I will still try to reconcile the differences between the Elven countries. Those with whom we have the most in common are often the ones it is easiest to find fault. It is mentally simpler to see our own imperfections in those who share them. When we find shortcomings in others, it is often our subconscious throwing us a warning, one that we all too often ignore. Would you mind if I sit in as you try to figure out the location?"

"Of course not," Gimelli said, smiling. *None of this prophecy is his fault.* Any anger she felt towards him vanished. It was hard to imagine some mysterious evil and almost impossible to fathom Na Cearcaill.

Squeezing her sister tight, Gimelli whispered, "Let's take the next step, and all yet to come…together." Smiles were shared as the League turned to the scroll. Everyone silently reread the contents.

"Look here, 'desolate sea,' and then, 'drown.' It must mean we need to find a lake, or something," Scelto stated.

"I don't think so," Kainen said. Scelto shot him a defensive glance. "Look, it talks about being 'desolate of life' and mentions '*dry* drown'. Lakes are obviously not dry, and they are teeming with life."

"Kainen's correct. It says 'ocean of brown.' That doesn't sound like water," Arend stated.

"Maybe a dried-up lake?" Lontas remarked.

"That's a good thought. If the water dried up, 'ocean of brown' could be mud," Gimelli said.

"Exactly!" Lontas replied excitedly. "And you could 'drown' in the mud. You could get stuck and sink." He paused and frowned. "Wait a second. If it's so 'desolate,' why does it talk about birds and trees?" Momentarily baffled, the League paused to review the scroll.

"Wait, wait," Kainen said. "Think about the trees mentioned, 'dates, olives, apricot, and figs.' They all thrive in areas that are hot and dry."

"I see where you're going," Lontas announced eagerly, grabbing Bellae's arm to steady himself. "A desert!"

"Exactly. A desert is a desolate 'sea' of sand that's tannish brown. Some creatures survive there, including birds," Kainen stated.

"Look," Gimelli said, pointing to a section. "It talks about trying to hold 'it' and you can't if your hand is open or if you squeeze it. That has to be sand."

"Yes," Scelto agreed. "Sand would slip through your fingers if you opened them or closed them in a fist."

"Also, the desert doesn't have a change of seasons, and it's hot in the day but gets cold at night," Bellae added, pointing to a section and reading, "…there is no time for seasons in the land. Half of each day ruled cool—half it's banned."

"There's only one desert in Verngaurd, Calor," Arend stated.

"That was quick!" Patuljak exclaimed. "You're a sharp group. I expect you will have no trouble figuring out the details of where you are going within the desert."

The Elf suddenly looked down briefly before continuing. "Although I couldn't tell you where, I have been there and would like to give you something I made." Patuljak went back and grabbed a large brown sack off a table. Returning, he pulled out a beautiful shield, handing it to Kainen.

"It may come in handy in the desert," he said, winking at his grandson.

"I can remember seeing you work on this for…a long time," Kainen said. It was highly polished, like a mirror on the inner, concave side. Even in the soft light of the hall it reflected vivid shafts of brightness, which danced into their eyes and across the ceiling.

"That's totally impractical as a shield," Sankari said. "It would blind the bearer and all standing behind!"

"Sankari!" Arend said as the Fairy shrugged her shoulders.

"You will probably want to carry it in the bag," Patuljak stated, waving his hands to block the reflected light. He motioned to Bellae. "Come with me for a moment, please."

Bellae obliged.

"I have something to whisper to you alone," he said.

Bellae sighed. *Here we go again.* "You know Stralande already told me lots of secrets."

"Did he?"

"Yes, and they were mostly painful. He told me a prophecy is nothing but a wish, a hope for the future, and that the Chosen One thing is for *others* to believe in me. I'm just a girl who happened to be born with the gift of the Ainmhi Caint. My ancestors wanted to make sure only an animal talker solved the riddles. There's nothing 'Chosen' about me—just blind luck. Sometimes I wish it wasn't me."

"But, why *not* you? It's easy to be a reductionist, but that path quickly leads to depression. Why me for this? Why am I even here? What does it all mean? Trimming life down with questions that, for the most part, can't be answered reduces existence to something that owes us answers and promises of hope, of prosperity. Life only offers a solitary *opportunity*, a chance to succeed, or not, but never promises anything except a hard-stop end. Also, don't so easily underestimate the power of hope and belief.

"Even if you don't agree, the mere prospect of using your gift to save untold lives and end Na Cearcaill is amazing. Before you can see that life itself, as well as this opportunity, is a gift, you have to start with acceptance. Accept you cannot control the situation, but you can determine your response. Don't be an observer of life. Be a participant. Take responsibility for the problems in the world. Try to fix them. See life's challenges as opportunities to be tackled with gratitude."

"It doesn't feel like a 'choice.' Pretend to be some 'Chosen' and follow a quest to save everyone, *or* let them all die," Bellae sneered.

"Oh, but it *is* a choice, one of many you will have to make, and there will be innumerable opportunities to stop and take the easy way out," Patuljak said. "You'd be surprised how many in your situation would come up with excuses and not even attempt this quest. Fear and anxiety are powerful deterrents while pain and sorrow can seize good intentions and freeze our hearts."

Bellae shivered in dread, longingly looking towards the exit. *Run!* her mind screamed in fight-or-flight overload. Standing before this immense task, her choice seemed clear—battle for months, maybe years, in an extreme quest, or spring out in an instant.

Bellae looked back to Patuljak. "How would I live with letting Na Cearcaill kill so many? Running away might give temporary relief, but ultimately, it would haunt me for the rest of my life. When I ask about Na Cearcaill, I get told, 'You have to figure it out,'" Bellae said, trying to mimic Stralande's voice. "Or, 'The answers will be revealed as you move forward on the quest,'" she uttered in the Elf's voice. "It gets super old."

Patuljak chuckled. "I know it's frustrating, but realize how ancient Na Cearcaill is, and how countless generations have fought to end it.

Even if you stopped searching for the crystals and spent the rest of your life studying all the texts and rumors about this cycle, you would only get through a fraction of the narrative.

"Your ancestors, the Ainmhi Caint, failed to stop the cycle and suffered greatly for the attempt. We planned to let you get older before beginning, but time did not allow this. The White Wizard and Veneficus have been increasingly desperate to find the crystals, sending increasing numbers of minions to find you."

Patuljak paused, seemingly lost in thought. "I had a dream last night that you failed and never made it here."

Bellae tilted her head, eyes widening. "Thaaanks?"

"You made it, obviously. In plenty of dreams you succeed. Dreams are an invitation given at night, but to be fulfilled into true substance, must be conjured through hard work in the waking hours. I know this seems overwhelming, but the true danger is in being ordinary. That is the great lie within the whisper of fear and murmur of anxiety—the greatest deceivers in the world. Fear never tells you the repercussions of *not* acting, not moving towards your dream. Dread and anxiety are begging you to be satisfied with the common, the safe, the known. I sincerely wish I was young enough to go with you, but I am grateful my grandson gets to travel with you."

"Stralande said something similar," Bellae said.

"From the precipice of old age, the wonderment of a true adventure shines perfectly clear." The Grand Master Elf looked down. "Unfortunately, there will be more surprises ahead, each carrying their own brand of pain."

"Not really heartening. I still want to know more."

"Unfortunately, especially when great distances and many have touched it, no matter the original truth, there will inevitably be lies folded within its core. Perhaps the greatest dangers are half-truths and lies of omission."

Bellae raised her eyebrows in displeasure.

Patuljak laughed. "Simplified, I don't know. However..."

"Let me guess, this prophecy is really old so you can't know everything?" Bellae said, her expression softening.

Patuljak nodded before leaning in. "There's a price for everything. A life of adventure demands we give up security and normalcy. A life filled with the ordinary provides stability, but it lacks thrilling exploits. Both will dispense their own forms of regret, manifesting as the shapes of the choices we made and the phantom notions of the ones we didn't. The blade is always sharper in the other armory, as they say. Don't let regret leech joy from your chosen journey."

Bellae scrunched her nose, feeling overwhelmed and sick of philosophical lectures.

Patuljak laughed. "I can see I'm not the first to try and offer wisdom, but remember, many of us have waited our whole lives to meet you. Can you blame us for sermonizing?

"Even though you did not choose this path, it is still an adventure, and for some reason, it is in our nature to think, 'If only we had taken the other road, things would be better.' Each track has its own problems we simply can't see, unless we walk it."

Stepping back, Patuljak smiled. "This part's just for you.

If hope is to breathe a chance.
Ever onward advance.
If you fail,
We continue beneath the evil veil.
The cycle of death, Na Cearcaill, will repeat,
Until the One ends in defeat.
Be careful of untrue friend and perilous stranger,
You will never be far from danger."

Bellae's breathing quickened. Her heart rate bustled forward as the room started to spin. Smiling, Patuljak gently steadied her by the shoulders.

"What if I fail?" Bellae huffed.

Complete with crackling joints, Patuljak bent down to make eye contact. "In life, and on this quest, do not lose sight of the importance of the journey itself. Concentrate on your heart and dedicated effort. Those are the things you can control. Isn't your best all that you, and the world, can ask?"

Bellae chuckled. "Now you really sound like Stralande and Friar."

"Ah, how flattering! Shall we?" Patuljak said, turning to rejoin the others, Bellae trailing behind. They were met with expectant stares and strained silence, the others unsure of what was to come. Finally, Patuljak said, "Hey, at least I stopped reciting it backwards." Everyone laughed as some tension floated away.

"Thanks, Grandpelf," Kainen stated, holding up the bag with the shield before embracing Patuljak.

"I'm proud of you, and confident you'll figure out when to use it," Patuljak stated, smiling tenderly to camouflage the depth of his concern at the dangers the youth would soon face.

Shaking the forearm of each and every one of them, he stated, "Well, I'm off. For the first time in many years I'll sleep well, confident in your ability. You are the League of Truth, and don't forget it. May the spirits of the forest and good luck ride with you."

"Thank you," Bellae stated. She threw her hands around the Elf, squeezing him tightly. Smiling, he turned and left, hoping he had spun around fast enough to hide his tears.

"Have fun in the desert," he stated with a parting wave. Nearing the door, he stopped and turned. "Remember, your perception does not change the reality."

As he exited through the doors, a crafty grin stared out from his face.

Chapter Two

From Bad to Repugnant

Scroll 1: Kill the Boy

Jumeaux slipped into the training chamber off Veneficus' office. As he moved through, the wall behind him magically re-formed.

"Welcome," Veneficus said.

"Oh boy, are we glad to see you!" a Valo said sarcastically, floating over the former squire. "Hey kid, do you know what the best thing is about obtuse students coming in here?"

Jumeaux shook his head.

"When they leave!" the Valo said, laughing.

"Yeah, our alone time isn't to recharge—it's for your safety!" another added.

"You are the human equivalent of a pain in my butt…if I had one," a third admonished.

Veneficus, ignoring the Valo, stared at the young Apprentice. Jumeaux tried to maintain eye contact but had to look away under the intense gaze.

"Are you enjoying your time here?" Veneficus asked.

"Of course. This place is amazing," Jumeaux replied, suddenly becoming animated. "I love this practical training. But…sometimes the studying we do doesn't seem relevant."

Veneficus chuckled. "If becoming a Magician was easy, almost everyone would sign up. Those classes, and the required untold hours of study, are barriers placed in front of you to confirm your commitment to the craft. All the classes and years of training do as much to weed out who *shouldn't* be here as to confirm who should."

"I get it," Jumeaux said.

"How are things going with your sisters?"

Jumeaux wobbled his head. "I think good. They seem suspicious, but we're getting along better."

"Excellent. Although hate can be a powerful emotion, it tends to flame out, leaving us exhausted and hollow. Try to move past any pain they caused you, build a bridge of trust." Veneficus examined Jumeaux intently, feeling as if he could see the boy's wounds slowly congealing together in healing. "Our souls are like gardens. If you water and fertilize hatred and anger, weeds will soon choke out compassion and reason. However, cultivating caring and concern will allow us to harvest happiness."

Veneficus paused as Jumeaux processed his words and the Valo mockingly rolled their eyes. Eventually, Veneficus looked up. "Na Cearcaill is coming. I would like you to join me in surviving it."

"You can do that?"

"Did you just ask *the* Supremiest Grandiest Masteriest Magicianiest person in the world if he could do that?" a Valo asked incredulously.

"Of course he can!" another answered. "He has many times before."

"True," Veneficus answered. "If we collect the Macht Crystals, I'll have the power to persevere through the cleansing cycle of Na Cearcaill."

"Oh, yeah, totally a cleansing cycle!" a Valo said mockingly. "It certainly is a disinfecting personal hygiene cycle if your idea of 'cleansing' involves bathing in blood and fire!"

"I agree, my distinguished, light-giving brother!" another added. "It is so utterly *not* evil. Who would consider that genocidal bloodbath of a horror show as a negative?"

Veneficus calmly looked at the Valo. "Men create their own evil every time they awaken. On a small scale they partake in a million wicked acts every day in the form of lies, cheating, swindling, laziness, debauchery, and rage. Every so often they create major depravities such as slavery, large-scale war, genocide, and the like. The destruction of Na Cearcaill pales in comparison to the evil of men who often attribute, and explain away, their actions based on some higher power or justified cause."

"Okay, boss, I get it. It's not the *most* evil thing in the world. Therefore, it must be okay?" a Valo said sarcastically. "What are hundreds of thousands of dead and dying?"

Before Veneficus could exact revenge, Jumeaux spoke, "I get what you are saying about different evils in the world, and it would be nice to outlive Na Cearcaill."

"Was it a tough choice, kid?" a Valo chided while hovering close. "Is it hard for your underfed, miniature brain to figure out the options?"

"Let's see, tough decision: be protected by magic and live, or die like a dog in the 'cleansing' cycle?" another Valo said contemptuously. "Imagine, if you will, I have arms and I am moving them up and down like a scale. I can see how those two alternatives, which are so close in weight, would be incredibly tough to choose between."

"Dumbeaux, are you imagining his arms moving?" the first Valo asked.

"Enough," Veneficus said, stepping in. "Jumeaux will soon be an immensely powerful Magician. You floating irritations may want to be careful. I'm proud of you, Jumeaux."

"Thanks Daa…"

"Wait, wait, wait! Did you almost call him dad?" a Valo howled as all the floating lights burst out laughing.

"What did I say last time about being a proud papa? Hmmm? Told you!"

Veneficus gave them a death stare, and they slowly bobbed away. *Part of me wants to become attached to someone again. I have blocked people from getting close for so long—could I let me guard down again?* The idea was so tantalizing, Veneficus' insides seemed to smile. *A magical gargoyle statue and floating menaces passing themselves off as lights only go so far fulfilling the role of companions.* Just as the notion began to gain traction, a flashback of the bitter betrayal at the hands of the Ainmhi Caint came flooding in. *He's a descendent of those duplicitous rats. No, keep your distance.*

"The problem we all have with death is the totality of what it targets," Veneficus said. "It's like the ruthless, unstoppable villain in a fairy tale: uncompromising, unforgiving, unwilling to bargain or barter. Death is full-stop nothingness—all plans, all loves, the whole narrative of our lives are demanded by dying."

Veneficus paused, a pained look digging its way across his face. "I find that unacceptable. I hope you will join me in escaping the wrath of Na Cearcaill."

"Oh, but bright eyes there is still thinking about it. Aren't you, genius?" a Valo said angrily.

"The big storm of Na Cearcaill is coming!" another Valo chided. "Good riddance!"

Veneficus looked at the floating light for a minute. "Vicious storms have a way of finding weakness, don't they? Trees without strong roots will be torn from the very ground."

"Yeah, rip out the weak trees, you cycle of destruction!" a Valo cheered.

"Yet!" Veneficus said, his voice rising with excitement. "The opposite is also true. In weeding out the weak, a storm finds strength. Those still standing are worthy. In the storm of Na Cearcaill, Jumeaux, we can be the strong who continue."

Jumeaux nodded.

"Oh wow, wow, wow. What a profound response there, kid," a Valo sneered. "You're really a true erudite of unsurpassed intelligence!"

"No more talk of Na Cearcaill or storms. Let's get to work," Veneficus said. "Most Magicians master thirty to fifty percent of known spells. You will bridle all of magic."

He went over to several wooden figures. After chanting for several minutes, five of them animated into real-looking humans. Veneficus whispered something, and instantly, they glared angrily at Jumeaux.

"Prepare yourself. There are five. Might I suggest fire orbs—conveniently packaged to deliver quintuple bursts?"

A Valo hovered next to the increasingly nervous Jumeaux. "I could ask you to give me a piece of your mind to understand what you are thinking, but I would hate to take the last piece."

The Valo floated away from Jumeaux, joining the others next to the high ceiling. "No offense, kid, but we have a rule: don't die this early in the morning."

The five animated humans grabbed weapons before spreading out across the large room.

"Kill boy!" one yelled before breaking into a sprint.

"Now would be the ideal time to react," a Valo chided from high above.

"Eldur hnottur!" Jumeaux yelled. Nothing.

"They're getting closer, genius!" another Valo added.

Jumeaux took a deep breath and concentrated, repeating the enchantment. This time a fireball exploded from his crosier, sidling him backwards in recoil.

As the first attacker exploded, his form reverted back to shattered wood that splayed backwards in blackened splinters, a few still ablaze. The second orb discharged before Jumeaux had a chance to aim, shooting through the debris of the first assailant. Veneficus quickly put up a shield spell, and the orb bounced away to be absorbed by the magically coated walls.

Jumeaux was ready for the next, disintegrating the closest attacker. The third and fourth combatants also fell—leaving one, charging hard.

"The kid's gonna die!" a Valo yelled gleefully as Jumeaux began to back step.

Using his crosier, Jumeaux blocked a sword thrust, spun around, and slammed the staff down on the attacker's head. Suddenly, ice exploded out of Veneficus' crosier, and the figure froze, anger still etched across his face.

A loud crash startled Jumeaux as Veneficus used a dropped sword to smash the frozen assailant. Ice splayed outward as the animated figure morphed into frosted, splintered wood.

"The timing of fire orbs can be inconsistent and tricky," Veneficus said. "You did good improvising, but you need to protect your crosier. Use magic *or* a weapon, not your crosier *as* a weapon. Let's go over the lightning spell. It's devastating."

"Not as devastating as his face!" a Valo chuckled. Seeing Veneficus' withering gaze, the light added, "I mean, you beat that fire ball spell like a Saatana Dragon does a griffin!"

Veneficus' clenched jaw and throbbing neck veins made the Valo back up. "Well, I mean, I must be mistaken—the griffins are doing great against the dragons, just really, really great."

Veneficus' face softened. "You are correct—we have been losing griffins at an alarming rate, but we have already groomed their replacements."

Scroll 2: A Way Out?

Of the eight Knights, five were the Ulven squad along with Luchar, Lovag, and Friar. They, and four remaining Northern Dwarves, were making a dent in the thirty Piscinians arrayed before them in the cavernous Way of Trepas. Even though the shield-carrying Suoli had moved to protect the shieldless Retiarians, Lovag and the Dwarves were doing damage.

Concentrating their fire on the Piscinians' left flank caused their lines to rotate as the forces approached. The Piscinians bunched to their right, away from arrows and bolts. The Knights mirrored their movements, and the two lines were in danger of turning in a half circle when the Piscinian commander screamed, "Charge!" Lovag slung his bow and drew his scimitar.

"Vioma, to our left flank!" Friar ordered. The four Dwarves moved left, taking their large shields off their backs and pulling out axes.

With a scream of, "Revenge!" the Piscinians rushed forward.

A burst of speed by the Piscinians brought the two lines crashing together. Two of the four Dwarves and one Knight were too slow reacting—the fearsome iaculum spears plunging into them. An Ulven squad Knight was pierced in the abdomen. As the spear retracted, it hooked rings of intestine, flinging blood and bowel out and up. The Dwarves were hit with glancing blows on the arms and shoulders.

Luchar was rampaging, swinging his large axe wildly. He slammed it into the shoulder of one enemy, sending his now-limp body plunging to the ground. Removing his heavily embedded axe, Luchar used a quick upstroke and swipe to the side to decapitate another—adding to the splattered blood varnishing his armor.

"Maintain a disciplined line!" Friar yelled. However, the disorganized Piscinians started fragmenting into two groups with the Knights driving into the center like a spear tip. With their smaller numbers they could be surrounded and cut down.

"Fall back!" a Piscinian yelled.

To Friar's delight, they made no move to envelope them but regrouped. "Reform our line. Luchar, that means you!" Friar's outraged words echoed off the gorge walls.

Seething with fury, Luchar reluctantly moved back.

"We must keep them in front of us, Luchar," Friar said quietly.

Two of the Ulven squad and one Dwarf were dead, leaving nine Allies. The Piscinians were down to fifteen.

"We're going to kill you all!" the Piscinian commander yelled. "Stay together and...*gurgle*."

In mid-speech one of Lovag's arrows seared into the commander's throat.

"Charge!" Friar yelled, taking advantage of the confusion within the Piscinian lines. While the Piscinians watched their superior struggle for air, two more of Lovag's arrows found targets. The Piscinian leader's body thrashed in the dirt as he arched back—his hands frantically grasping at his bleeding throat, desperately trying to hold in the soft hissing and gurgling escaping his gashed neck.

"Ceannaire! My friend!" a Piscinian screamed, kneeling next to his waning leader. Removing his helmet, he sobbed, "Ever since—"

His words were cut off as Luchar's axe bisected his head. As blood spewed out from the cleaved brain in massive arcs, the Piscinian's body hung for a moment, giving Luchar time to swipe his axe horizontally, beheading the already cleaved cranium.

"No weeping, babbling, or poignant speeches during battle!" Luchar wailed, adding a brutal whack to the Piscinian's dead body.

The remaining Knights and Dwarves surged against the leaderless Piscinians. Shrill shrieks suddenly pierced the air. The canyon walls magnified the terrifying sounds. Both sides looked up to the ribbon of sky above as waves of Eaglians slammed into squadrons of griffins. The shrieks were soon joined by blood, feathers, and falling bodies as a brutal aerial battle raged. The Piscinians tensed in horror as griffin after griffin smashed into the ground around them.

A few Eaglians abruptly dove towards the bottom of the ravine. Aquila and two of his trusted warriors sped towards the Allies. The three let out fierce squawks, plunging fear into the remaining Piscinians.

"What do we do?" a Piscinian yelled in terror.

Luchar jumped at the opportunity. Screaming, he rushed headlong into the muddled enemy—using his axe to crash down an iaculum spear before slamming the end of his weapon into the helmet of the Piscinian. The metal dented, compressing into his battered face. Lovag and the Dwarves moved up with their arrow and bolts. After a quick glance at each other, the Piscinians quickly threw down their weapons in surrender.

"You don't get off so easy," Luchar yelled, swinging his axe in a crisscross pattern, hacking and slicing into the nearest Piscinians. Lovag and Friar dove in to restrain him. Only when Varg joined did they manage to pull him away from the cowering Piscinians.

"We accept your surrender," Friar said, wiping blood from his lip, courtesy of Luchar's elbow.

The Eaglians landed with a series of loud shrieks, startling the Piscinians into grabbing their weapons. Four of them instantly fell from arrow and bolt.

Luchar turned, his chest heaving. The adrenaline rush coursing through his brain slowly faded, and the frenzied light of battle in his eyes flamed out. The group stood silently listening to the gurgles of the dying Piscinians.

"They were surrendering, Luchar. You're evil!" Lovag yelled.

"While actions can be good or evil, very few people are truly just evil or good," Friar said breathlessly as the last Piscinian fell. Grabbing Luchar's helmet, Friar put his face against the blood-splattered metal. "Never forget who we are and what we stand for! Remember our code contains temperance, self-restraint, for a reason."

"Friar!" Aquila yelled, exposed flesh outside his chest plate streaked with bloody lacerations, alternating shallow-deep-shallow, compliments of griffin talons. After a last glare at Luchar, Friar moved to the Eaglians, tensing at the alarm in their keen eyes.

"The Magicians used prodisiosis volo to get here quickly and bring griffins in numbers we did not think possible," Aquila said. His wings fluttered nervously in the deeply claustrophobic gorge.

"Where are the Vioma?" Friar asked.

"Exactly!" Aquila said irately. His eyebrows raised and his lower lip curled back, revealing the full power of his yellow-orange beak. "Besides the griffins, they brought reinforcements from the Citadel."

"How many?"

"Four regiments of Red Guard and two Silver Ultor with their freakish spraks."

"If we can crush this force…" Varg let his words trail off, superstitiously not wanting to jinx their victory.

"Friar!" Aquila yelled as a large force of Proliate Red Guard rushed towards them from the eastern opening of the Way of Trepas.

"Rubbish," Lovag said, quietly readying his bow.

"Yes!" Luchar roared, excitement flooding back.

"We succeeded in drawing them into the pass—time to leave," Friar called.

"We can fly some of you out," Aquila offered.

"No thanks, my friend," Friar answered. "We'll stick together. You attend to your Eaglians and watch yourself. I'll get the Vioma Dragons going."

Aquila gave a quick nod, and the Eaglians rose into the air as the Knights began to sprint towards the western end of the pass.

"We're not going to make it," Varg said practically.

"We don't have a choice," Friar said, huffing. In addition to his age, he was not used to wearing armor.

"Can—" Luchar started.

"No! We *can't* fight here," Friar hissed. "Stick to the plan. Sorea is waiting at the other end."

As they ran, the ravine path seemed to elongate. Luchar's huffs let Friar know he wanted to stop and fight.

"There's Sorea!" Lovag called as they finally neared the western end.

"Whoa!" Varg yelled as three griffins suddenly dropped down between them and Sorea. Their tousled manes bristled as they flashed their fearsome beaks and pawed the ground with their front talons. To add to the Knights' panic, a chilling scream went up from the Proliate closing in behind. A griffin charged. Lovag quickly put an arrow through its right eye. Luchar bolted forward, planting his axe through its skull for good measure. The griffin's head split, splaying out blood and brain on either side of the menacing blade.

"I'd say that was excessive," Lovag commented.

"I'd say 'shrewd caution,'" Luchar growled, struggling to release his axe.

Sorea could be heard yelling, but none could make out what she was saying. The two remaining griffins let out a wrathful screech, half flying, half running towards Luchar. Fluttering low, their legs occasionally pushed off the ground. Releasing his axe from the dead griffin, Luchar charged forward, wide-eyed. The largest one was only a few feet away when it suddenly reared up, its eyes shooting open in a mix of terror and pain before they closed. Its body flopped lifelessly to the ground—several bolts and arrows sticking from its neck. Feeling despondently cheated out of killing the griffin, Luchar was caught off guard by the second one bounding over the body of its fallen companion. Springing off the lifeless body, it slammed into Luchar. Its front talons clenched Luchar's shoulders, and with a powerful beat of its wings the two back lion paws flipped forward, slamming into Luchar's helmet. A high-pitched *tink* was quickly followed by a sickly crunch as Luchar's head shot rearward. His body followed, flipping over into a series of backward summersaults. Varg and another Knight toppled to the ground as his body crashed into them.

The griffin moved with lightning speed, bounding straight for the unconscious Luchar. Screeching, its talons dug between his chest plate. Rushing forward, Friar's sword sliced through the back of the griffin's neck just as blood began leaching out from Luchar's armor. Friar hacked viciously as arrows and bolts flooded in. With a mighty blow Friar released the griffin's head. Its headless body flopped around, spraying blood all around the canyon. The Proliate let out another fierce cry—the closeness startling them.

"We can't make it if we carry Luchar," Varg declared.

"Let's try," Lovag said, pulling Luchar up. Varg joined him, and they began moving towards Sorea. Looking puny, framed by the towering Way of Trepas, she frantically waved them forward.

Struggling to carry Luchar, the Knights could now hear the harsh breathing of the Proliate in addition to the marching thud of their boots and rattling armor.

"We won't make it," Friar said. "Varg and Lovag, carry Luchar to safety. The rest of us will turn and fight."

Just as Friar stopped speaking, Sorea's voice came booming towards them. "Drop now!" she yelled in a panic. "Now! Now!" she kept screaming.

"Hit the dirt!" Friar bellowed as the tired group dove. "Keep your head down if you want to retain it. Get ready to move on *my* command in between."

"In between wha…?" a Dwarf started, just as the air above them filled with flashing projectiles whizzing overhead.

"Sorea fired a rakkniv. Those were two large bolts and connected razor hurtling above," Friar said.

"Oh! In between that," the startled Dwarf said. "Good idea."

"Run!" Friar yelled. Behind them they could hear the giant bolts from the ballistas ripping into the shields and bodies of the Proliate. Those unfortunate souls were instantly whipped backwards, wrapping the razor-sharp wire into the Proliate in the middle. Several were caught between their breastplates and helmets and instantly decapitated. Blood spurted in spasms with each witless heartbeat. A few growls of anger went up from the Proliate but otherwise they continued in their usual stoic professionalism.

"Down!" Friar yelled again.

Stealing a glance up, they could see a massive machine behind Sorea that had been previously hidden by prestidigitation. Spread out across the opening of the gorge was a wooden structure, ten feet high, named the sidus heulwch, or sun star. Multiple A-frame supports braced a large wheel holding beams running the length of the triangle construction covered with rows of crossbows.

A single string instantly released hundreds of crossbows on one side of the weapon. The Allies on the ground could hear, and feel, the bolts rushing overhead. This was quickly followed by a series of thuds and high-pitched clings as they pierced into shield, armor, and flesh. These sounds were instantly followed by sharp exhalations and dry thuds as those hit cringed in pain, some falling to the ground.

"Double time!" a Proliate yelled.

"Stay down but get ready to run!" Friar bellowed.

The group cringed at the sound of the Proliate closing in quickly as they lay prostrate on the ground. Sorea turned the large crank on the sidus heulwch, rotating the circle of wood and bringing new, loaded crossbows into view.

"We need to move!" a Dwarf said, panicking. As he started to stand, Friar pushed forward, grabbing, but missing, his arm. Friar fell heavily to the ground as the Dwarf ran towards the opening of the ravine. The sidus heulwch fired, sending flocks of bolts down the ravine. Six bolts tore into his chest, flipping him backwards. The Allies on the ground

Figure 12: Sorea's sidus heulwch, or sun star, is said to unleash as many bolts as a sun does rays at a single time. After a quick crank, it is ready to fire two more times.

pushed their faces into the dirt, hearing the same whir, shrill exhalations, and thuds as the Proliate line was once again smacked by the volley of bolts.

The cycle repeated a third time before Friar yelled, "Now!"The Allies quickly stood running towards Sorea. Lovag and Varg were struggling with the now-waking Luchar.

"Hurry!" Friar chided. As they ran, a team of horses pulled the sidus heulwch away—Sorea riding on the end. She gave a tense smile before giving a signal only Friar understood.

"Curve sharply left as we exit the pass," he said, breathing heavily.

"Their fiendish contraption is gone! Break formation and kill them!" the Proliate commander yelled.

The Proliate dropped their shield wall, moving as fast as their armor would allow. A line of Knight archers moved into the pass and began firing over the heads of their friends—each volley achieving good hits. However, because the Proliate were now close on the heels of the Allies, they were unable to shoot those closest in pursuit.

"Keep going," Friar encouraged as Varg struggled to keep Luchar up and moving.

"AHHHHHHHH!" One of the Dwarves screamed in pain, speared from behind by one of the Proliate merja.

"Die, cowards!" a Proliate yelled.

Turning to help his comrade, the second Dwarf quickly fell as the Proliate overwhelmed him with blows of retribution.

"Hard left!" Friar yelled as they finally reached the end of the gorge.

"I'm fine!" Luchar howled. "Let's turn and fight."

"Not here, not now," Friar advised.

"Follow me! Step *only* where I do!" Sorea yelled fearfully.

The remaining Knights turned left and moved single file behind Sorea as she carefully chose their path.

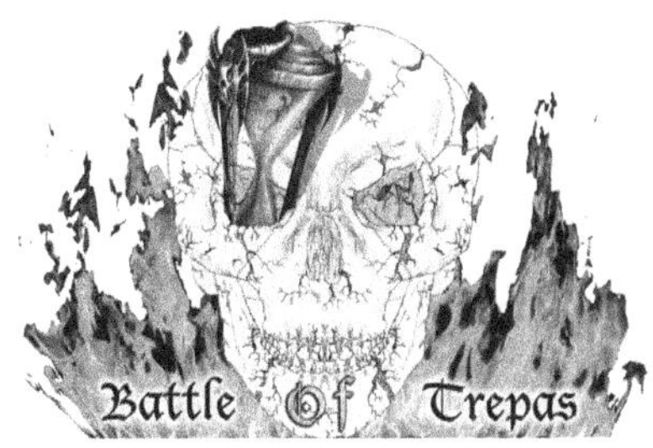

Scroll 3: Overcast, with a Chance of War Birds

Entering the sunlight with their polished armor, the Proliate slowed.

"Move aside!" the commander yelled, pushing forward.

As he left the darkness of the pass, he turned to see what looked like the entire Allied army arrayed before him. He fruitlessly searched the north and west for the Proliate reserves. His Proliate comrades stretched back, eventually swallowed by the darkness of the giant gorge. A chill ran down his spine. *Lambs to the slaughter. There's no way we can get our troops through in time.*

The Knight cavalry was directly in front of them. The Allied infantry was stretched out south of their cavalry in a perpendicular line to the Tingij Mountains. In order they stood: the army of the Rebelde Plains, the Knights of Liberum, the Knights of Toil Shaor led by Veli Pingius, and finally, the Vioma and Saatana Divisions of the Northern Dwarves.

The first Proliate regiments were the precious few Red Guard who had suffered the many trials of the Battle of Ovest. The reinforcing regiments from the Citadel were right behind, filling the entire Way of Trepas. Ager was next, followed by the reluctant and tattered remains of the Piscinians, the Warriors of Jaa, and the Southern Dwarves. The Proliate Ultor or silver divisions brought up the rear with their dreaded spraks.

TABLE FOUR Battle of Trepas

Expected (not at battle yet*)

Allies		**Confederacy**	
Knights of Liberum:	7,500	**Proliate Red Guard**	
Knight Cavalry:	3,500	(a corp + survivors):	31,150
(lightly armored from all three castles)		**Proliate Silver**	
Rebelde Plains:	7,500	(Ultor-with spraks):	10,000
Eaglians:	1,500	**Piscinians:**	
Knights of Toil Shaor:	5,000	**Retiarian** Division:	*875*
(led by Veli Pingius)		**Suoli** Division:	*2,000*
Northern Dwarves:		**Warriors of Jaa:**	*3,500*
Vioma Division: (Green)	10,000	**Southern Dwarves:**	*5,000*
		Ager:	*7,500*
Saatana Division: (Red)	5,000	***Proliate Red Guard-** coming from the north:	12,000
Vasama Division: (Blue)	2,000	**Magicians:**	1,500
		Griffins:	5,000
Rebelde Plains Dwarves: (skilled in prestidigitation)	400		
Vioma Dragons + Aer Ridire	650		
Total:	**43,050**		**78,525**

The Proliate commander frantically, but unsuccessfully, searched for General Lidenskap. Before he could make a decision, Sorea walked towards them, her right hand twirling a thick rope in an easy, unhurried manner.

"What's happening?" the Proliate commander asked, the strangeness rendering the rest speechless.

Sorea stopped twenty yards from them. Cocking her head to the side in a questioning way, she held up the rope and smiled. Fierceness suddenly jumped onto her face as she quickly sprinted away, pulling the rope as she ran. Once the slack was gone, she slung the rope over her shoulder, leaning forward under the strain. In confused silence the Proliate watched the rope straighten from her shoulder to about ten feet in front of them, where it dove underground.

"What's this treachery?" a Proliate asked, walking towards the rope, intent on cutting it. When he was five feet away, a loud creaking noise came from below the earth in front of them.

BOOM! An intense noise from underground was quickly followed by a loud snap as a huge section of earth instantly rose up before traveling in an arc, crashing down upon the commander and the first twenty Proliate.

"That thing snaps to attention like Veli Pingius on fresh pastry," King Abernan of the Northern Dwarves said with a chuckle. Everyone around the king laughed while across the battlefield the Proliate were awash in rage.

"That contraption is the reka sla," Lovag informed. "It's a modified torsion-based catapult lowered in the ground that slams a rectangular platform down on the enemy rather than throwing a projectile. The end of the catapult has a rectangular piece of metal reinforced with wood and studded with spikes."

"I'm glad you Knights are on our side," Abernan said, his eyes widening.

"It kills small numbers but breeds fear," Lovag added.

Fifty Proliate began struggling to get the rectangle off their mangled comrades. The tension was so tight it barely budged. Many slipped and fell in the copious pools of blood and innards, which had once been their comrades, squishing out. However, more and more Proliate came until it began to move upwards. Once it was five feet off the ground, a large snapping sound streaked across the battlefield as the lever arm shattered, sending countless small pieces soaring everywhere.

"What exactly were they expecting to find under there?" Abernan questioned of the congealed Proliate coalescing in a lumpy swirl of unrecognizable blood and body parts.

The Proliate troops stuck in the claustrophobic gorge pushed forward, trying to get out of the stifling pass just as Friar ordered the Knight archers and cavalry to advance. Some used long bows, others composite. Knight archers furthest from the Proliate used massive, twelve-foot-long toten bows capable of shooting a thousand yards. The toten archers lay on their backs, their outstretched feet secured in wooden holders on the shaft of the massive bows. Assistants helped the shooters load the massive arrows as they strained to row the string backwards before launching the massive projectiles.

As the Knight infantry unleashed a merciless hail of arrows, the cavalry moved forward to wheel and fire. The combining shower stormed the gorge with seemingly endless projectiles. Dead Proliate and mounds of arrows piled up around the entrance. General Lidenskap finally appeared twenty yards from the opening. "Move forward! To victory and revenge!"

"Sir, we have reports of massive numbers of arrows and enormous dead," a young sergeant informed.

"Then form a *shield wall* as you near the exit!" he blared. "Do I have to remind you to breathe as well?"

Slowly, the Proliate formed a shield wall and climbed over the dead to get out of the gorge. The number dying from Knight arrows slowed to a trickle.

"Form lines in front of the dead and remove them," Lidenskap ordered. Slowly the dead and dying Proliate were tossed to the north, clearing the opening.

Having regrouped after briefly skirmishing the Eaglians, the griffins stormed back in mass. Five thousand griffins formed up into five separate Air Wings stacked vertically. Twenty-five squadrons of forty griffins each flew in smaller V-shaped formations within each of the Air Wings.

"Maneuver around to attack the rear of the Knights' line!" a Magician in charge of the air attack yelled. "Keep in your levels!" she added. "Maintain a hundred feet above and below each Air Wing."

"The bloody Vioma Dragons and Aer Ridire are supposed to rule the skies," Friar lamented on the ground.

"No sign of dragons. What are your orders, General Orel?" Aquila asked high up in the mountains.

"No choice—attack!" the general commanded. "We have to get above them. If they pin us between the mountains, with their numbers, we all die."

The air on the south side of the mountain erupted with powerful wing beats as fifteen hundred perched Eaglians shot into the skies, screeching, "Yee-weeent-weeent-weeent-yee-weeeent!" Some wore silver chest plates, courtesy of the Northern Dwarves.

"Release!" Orel ordered. The air between the two giant war birds filled with conical black throwing darts. Screeches of pain erupted. The power of the Eaglians' throws, multiplied by the speed of the griffins flying towards them, propelled the darts deep into the griffins' bodies, and they began to fall in droves—their dead bodies dropping on the advancing Proliate, creating chaos in the gorge below.

"Draw swords!" Orel screamed as the distance between the two groups closed.

The brisk grinding of metal as the Eaglians unsheathed their swords mixed with their fierce screeches. The Eaglians advantage of weapons initially overcame being outnumbered nearly five to one. However, the griffins were moving so fast, the Eaglians did not have time to get above them, only reaching the third level of the five-tier griffin formation. As the two forces met, the Eaglians were instantly engulfed, their swords and talons slashing and ripping into the griffins. In the initial clash, a fresh round of lifeless griffins plummeted to the ground.

As the aerial battle continued, the multi-leveled formation of the griffins proved its worth. They swooped down from above and up from below, while those on the flanks enveloped the Eaglians, wrapping around to attack from the rear. The griffins assaulted the Eaglians with their razor-sharp beaks and dagger-like talons of their front legs.

"Form sphere!" Orel yelled while slashing at the seemingly endless supply of griffins. As soon as one fell, several appeared to take its place.

"Where are the blasted dragons?" Friar challenged King Abernan, his voice rattling with anger and panic.

"They should be here!" Abernan bellowed, furiously scanning the skies as the Eaglians disappeared, swallowed by the cloud-like swarm of griffins. Eaglians weighing, on average, 250 pounds, and griffins, weighing between 300 to 500 pounds, were falling like rain, pummeling and crushing the Proliate below. The confusion allowed the Knight archers to increase their kill rate.

"Oh, no," Friar whispered. Up above the gorge, streaks of destructive light and orbs of fire began shooting across the sky. Magicians riding griffins were feeling comfortable enough about the aerial battle to join the fight. "Abernan, I don't care how you do it, *get* the bloody Vioma up there before the Eaglians are massacred!"

He nodded, and several Vioma infantry immediately fired two large ballistas into the air. Tied between the massive bolts was a banner with a green dragon. Time dribbled forward as the Eaglians fought for their lives, their bubble sanctuary ever shrinking.

"Again!" Abernan yelled.

As the second banner fell, enormous green streaks could be seen flying across the tops of the Tingij Mountains. A loud cheer went out from the entire Allied army.

"Watch out for the Eaglians!" Friar yelled, knowing they couldn't possibly hear him.

Within seconds the speeding Vioma Dragons hit the cloud of griffins. Instantly, fire thundered into the surprised griffins just as the bolts from the Aer Ridire's crossbows spread through the sky. A fresh downpour of griffins, many charred, plunged downward. As they fell, the naphtha oil secreted by the dragons began splattering the Proliate soldiers stuck in the gorge. Those on fire frantically began the difficult task of taking off their burning armor, made more difficult in the packed gorge. The smell of burning flesh, smoke, and roasting armor made the already claustrophobic atmosphere even more agonizing. Those in the middle of the pass shoved forward, pushing more and more Proliate into the fresh deluge of arrows from the Knights' infantry and cavalry.

Above, the Magicians retreated as the dragons began to dominate the skies. Occasionally, a few aerial combatants separated from the main battle, giving those on the ground a clear view of the life-and-death struggle. A large Vioma Dragon had been isolated from the main force with a dozen griffins buzzing in pursuit. Three latched onto the wooden structure holding the Dwarves and were ripping and clawing savagely. Other griffins joined in from the other side, and all the Dwarves were quickly killed.

With no orders coming from the Aer Ridire, the Vioma Dragon began to spin in circles to dislodge the griffins. While the rest moved in and out to bite and claw at the dragon, five griffins continued to yank on the wooden structure on its back. Several of the already dead Dwarves plummeted to the ground as the structure was ripped to the side. This threw off the dragon's balance and dug into its left wing.

Howling in pain, the dragon let out a massive flame, incinerating two of the clinging griffins. The circling pattern became erratic, degenerating into wild, squiggling ovals. A giant puff of smoke wafted out of its mouth, signaling it was out of fire. With a series of high-pitched screeches all the griffins converged, digging and biting into the dragon. Their front talons ripped and dislodged heavy green scales before sinking their massive beaks into the exposed flesh.

The dragon's wings were shredded so badly they floundered, sending the dragon into a death spiral. Faster and faster it spun. The entire way down the griffins were intent on doing as much vengeful damage as possible. Just before it crashed into the earth, the remaining griffins burst off, shooting into the air to rejoin the battle. The bloodied body of the dragon unleashed a massive splatter of blood and flesh.

"Signal the Eaglians, AGAIN, to retreat! We cannot afford to lose them!" Friar screamed, even though the Knight signalers were continually relaying the message.

"They're leaving!" a Knight announced as the Eaglians began exiting the melee, heading back to the top of the Tingij Mountains.

The dragons conjured a wall of fire to cover the withdrawing Eaglians. With their formation broken, the griffins quickly found themselves overwhelmed by the enraged dragons. Squawks of pain filled the air as the griffins bathed within the dragon inferno. Soon, their numbers drastically reduced, they fell into chaotic retreat.

With the griffins put to flight, the Vioma Dragons began patrolling the skies in large arcing circles, occasionally spurting fire as a warning.

"What now, sir?" one of the lieutenants asked of General Lidenskap.

"The griffins and Magicians were supposed to provide aerial coverage and negate the Knights' archers. We have to get our troops out of this death trap. If we engage their armies in close quarters, the arrows will stop."

Scroll 4: Leaves for Leaving

Far away to the northwest, the League was getting ready to depart for the desert. About thirty Fairies and dozens of Sprites came to see them off. Standing just outside the border of Cappadocia, Bellae nestled up to Crann while Grym and Borb played with the Fairy children.

"These kids are attacking me!" Grym complained. *"This isn't playing—it's assault!"*

Bellae giggled, ignoring his protests, as she could feel how much fun he was having.

Lontas stared at Bellae, a worried edge behind his eyes. With each step down the path of the prophecy, she seemed to be descending deeper into herself. Lontas ducked as Sankari flew by, fluttering off to give hugs and kisses to the family and friends who had come to see her off.

"Hello, hello!" a now-familiar voice boomed lustfully—bellowing well before it would be prudent. King Kuningas continued towards them, a large goblet sloshing around as the sedan chair he was riding in jostled. "Well, Patuljak's already off, so I guess it's your turn."

"We can't have you leaving empty handed now, can we? Well, I guess we could, but that'd be rude," the king said, laughing earnestly. The members of the League exchanged quick glances, unsure of what to make of this loud king.

"Anyway, we have some things you'll find useful," Kuningas said. Clapping his hands, a dozen Fairies flew forward with various baskets and skins. "I know you filled your water skins, but trust me, you'll need more, many more. So here you go." The king paused, staring and leaning forward.

Sankari whispered something to Arend, and he said, "Thank you."

"Ah, it's nothing," the king said, cheerfully sitting back, obviously having paused for credit. Bowing to the king, Scelto took the skins and began to load them on Crann.

"Take a drink of water. What do they call you? Scrip-oh or something?" Kuningas said.

"Scelto, sire. My name's Scelto."

"Ah, sure. Just drink up, my thirsty boy."

Scelto, who was not actually thirsty, glanced at Sankari, who nodded furiously.

Apparently, I have no choice. After taking a drink, he could see Sankari fiercely mouthing, "Thank you." The second thing was harder to pick up on. He thought it was, "wonderful."

Taking the hint, he said, "Thank you so much. It's wonderful." His tone was monotonous, but the king howled joyfully.

He clapped his hands again. This time, Scelto tried to act like he was busy as a fresh set of Fairies flew forward with more gifts.

"Let someone else finish that, Skip-toe," the king said in a boisterous tone.

Scelto paused, unsure if he should tell the king he had gotten his name wrong *again*. He had no time to think as a fresh round of bags were thrust into his face.

"These are our world-famous mushrooms. Just so you know, I went ahead and had them wrapped in molted Fairy wings from my own personal stock. That keeps them moist and fresh, which will be handy for you. Why don't you taste one of them? You seemed to enjoy the water so much. Taste the freshness."

Annoyed, Scelto carefully unwrapped a mushroom. Out of the corner of his eye he could see Gimelli and Kainen snickering. *Glad you're having fun.* "Delicious! Thank you, sire." Scelto said, initially intending to be sarcastic, but it was actually very good.

King Kuningas ate up the praise, clapping his hands as the process repeated itself. Each time something new was brought forward, Scelto's name would be butchered while he was forced to try whatever they were getting before heaping compliments back upon the king.

"And now, the final gift!" Kuningas said.

Two Fairies came forward, each holding a bag. Scelto reluctantly took it.

"Oh, Scrip-oh, those will be a treat on your journey!" Kuningas winked.

Grudgingly, Scelto opened the bag, peering inside. It was full of yellowish-green leaves. With his over-filled stomach protesting in violent gurgles, he slowly picked one out and took a large bite. He couldn't help grimacing as he began to chew the bitter and tough leaf.

"Oh, man. That's horrible!" Scelto cried.

"What do you think you're doing, Skip-lo?" the king asked.

Thinking he had offended, Scelto quickly apologized. "I'm sorry your highness. I'm just not used to the taste. I appreciate your generosity."

"Of course you do, boy. But the truth is, those leaves are for the *other* end! You use them for wiping your arse, not for eating," the king said, laughing wildly as the Fairies joined in.

Turning red, Scelto spit out the leaf. Wiping his mouth on his sleeve, he turned to see Gimelli coming over.

"Who would have known?" Taking the bags of leaves, she packed them on Crann, trying, but failing, to hide her snickering.

"Someone get this starving boy something more to eat. He's so hungry he's gobbling down the shite-wiping leaves! We can't have you leaving the bounty of Cappadocia on an empty stomach, can we, Skip-no!"

Motioning for Scelto to lean forward, the king whispered, "The leaves were my idea. When I was young, I went to the desert on an 'adventure.' What a bloody mistake that was. When I left my butt was so sore…ouch! Let me tell you, sand is more than a little rough on the old backside. Really, the desert is just the worst place in all of Verngaurd." Seeing the look of horror on Scelto's face, he quickly added, "I'm sure it will be fine for you though."

Motioning for the straining Fairies carrying him in his sedan chair to move out, he yelled, "Goodbye and good luck!"

"Thank you, great king," Sankari said as a chorus of less distinguishable, "Thanks," emerged from the League.

Gimelli put her hand on Scelto's shoulder. With a serious look in her eye, she held his gaze. Scelto blushed under the scrutiny.

"I have something to ask you," she said.

"Okay."

"Can I call you Skip-toe?" she asked, bursting out in laughter. "Please?"

"Very funny."

"I kind of like 'Snow-ho the Leaf Eater' myself," Kainen added, doubling over in laughter.

"Scelto will do," Lontas said forcefully. Walking up to Scelto, he winked. "I know all about unwelcome nicknames," he whispered. "Thanks for all the times you helped me."

Scelto smiled at Lontas and nodded his head, but there was a tinge of something deeper. Was it jealousy? Here Lontas was, self-assured in a role reversal, standing up for him. With a handful of Fairies still trying to force feed the bloated Scelto, the League set out for the desert.

"Seriously, I'm going to need those leaves sooner than later if you keep this up!" Scelto protested as the others laughed. *I definitely don't want a repeat of the torahammas milk trots!*"

With Verngaurd in the midst of all-out war, the true hunt for the Macht Crystals had finally begun.

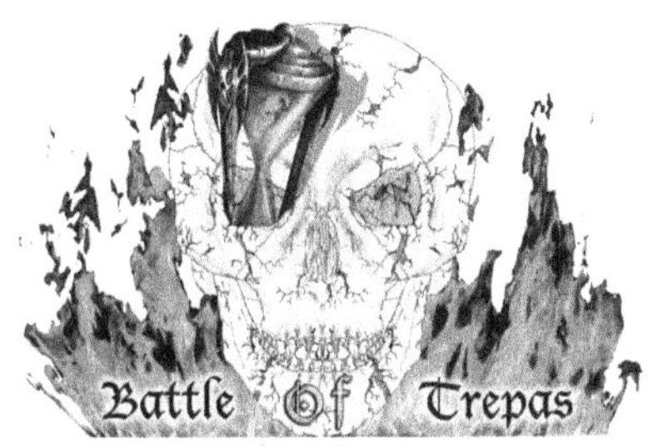

Scroll 5: A New Battle Order

"Maintain shield wall and advance," Lidenskap yelled, sacrificing speed for security. "We need to crush those archers and allow room for our troops. Lieutenant, stay with the front lines. I'll direct those coming through the pass."

"If we advance now," the lieutenant whispered, "our troops could be outflanked or overrun with their cavalry. Shouldn't—"

"You have your orders," Lidenskap interrupted. "Our brothers from the north and Ragorsaf from the west should be here any moment."

The arrows continued to rain down on the shield wall of the Proliate as they slowly advanced towards the Knights. The speed of Proliate coming through the pass greatly increased now that the skies had stopped raining giant, often flaming, birds of war.

The advancing Proliate heard a *click*. Within seconds, three more reka sla strikers were activated by trigger plates. Their powerful platforms, laden with spikes, bit deeply into the front lines of the Proliate, mercilessly shattering armor and bone, instantly reducing them to flaccid, perforated, formless vessels. A relatively small number of Proliate were killed, but it created a chink in their shield wall, setting up those behind to archers' fire.

"Re-form and advance!" Lidenskap ordered.

The Proliate struggled forward, around platforms oozing gelatinous rivers streaked with blood, and the exposed pits, which had held the reka sla. After taking heavy losses from Knight archers, the Proliate reformed a shield wall. The discipline of the Proliate took over, and they were now rushing out of the Way of Trepas as the warriors from Ager finally entered the pass.

Figure 13: Battle of Trepas Battle Key

Figure 14: Battle of Trepas ICON I. Thirsty for revenge, the Confederate army storms through the Way of Trepas to find the Allies have plenty of surprises waiting.

"Once we get closer, I want a full assault on the Northern Dwarves. The Knights will have to stop their arrows once we move close enough. Reinforcements arriving through the gorge will head out to protect our right flank as we advance," Lidenskap said.

"But our flank will be vulnerable..." a lieutenant stopped under the rage-fueled eyes of Lidenskap.

"Many have to die today, a price welcomely paid for revenge!" Once most of the well-trained Proliate streamed out of the pass Lidenskap yelled, "Charge!"

Breaking their tight shield wall, the Proliate took off towards the Northern Dwarves. The prestidigitation that had been hiding one Knight was released. Suddenly, between them and the Dwarf army stood a solitary female, head down, obviously unconcerned with the approaching horde of enemies.

"You attack our honor. You unjustly accuse of us of evil," Sorea yelled, knowing few Proliate could hear. The horrors of the punji pits and flames punctured into her ears, tore at her heart, and weighed on her mind. Doubt leached through her body as other traps sat impassive and emotionless, patiently waiting to unleash savagery. *It's one thing to stand in front of an army, but this...?*

The sheer brutality of the traps fought with her justifications. *I'm a warrior, and the Knights did not start this fight.* The immense indifference of the traps and weapons stood in stark contrast to the ponderous, restless anxiety coursing through the soldiers rustling in their armor—the warrior's canvas for blood and gore. Only time would tell what combination of theirs, and the enemy's, war would paint.

"Get back, you crazy Knight!" Abernan yelled from the Dwarf line, still unaware of all Friars' plans.

The army thundered closer. Sorea held...until she could no longer. Grabbing a solitary rope lying comfortably on the grass below her feet, she suddenly sprinted towards the Dwarf line. The single cord branched out to dozens of connected ropes in a pyramid shape. A massive groan rumbled underground.

Despite their trepidation the Proliate continued advancing. The rope bit deeply into Sorea's shoulder, her steps slowing under the burdensome resistance. Two Dwarf warriors broke ranks, running to her aid. The Proliate let out a well-timed yell, startling the pair sprinting forward. The Knight was leaning so far forward her body was horizontal over the ground as her steps slowed under the weight.

"Pull!" she wheezed as the Dwarves arrived. They added enough strength to jerk the rope forward. A loud *snap* was followed by a massive six-foot wall of spikes shooting up in a ninety-degree angle. Because Sorea had struggled, slowing the springing of the trap, some in the front row of Proliate were flung fifteen feet up in the air, while others flipped forward, over the torsion driven wall.

"That's pretty handy," one of the Dwarves said.

"Wait for it," Sorea cautioned. As her words ended, another *crack* pierced the air. On the other side of the wall the coiled power of the trap was unleashed, releasing a second, facing wall. As the opposing wall snapped into place, it crushed any Proliate unlucky enough to be in between the barriers, while others fell into the open pit housing the torsion machines. The force of the advancing army had pushed many Proliate forward, squishing them into the trap. The mass of humanity within was quickly transformed into proteinaceous goo punctuated by shards of armor.

Several of the Proliate who made it past the barricade were quickly brought down by bolts, courtesy of the Dwarves.

"Well done, Knight!" King Abernan congratulated.

"Thank you," Sorea said. "We set up the extended facing walls under a series of tightly coiled torsion machines, then covered them with earth."

"It will slow them down, but they will soon be upon us," a Dwarf said.

Sorea shook her head. "That is but part of the trap."

Friar frantically signaled the Eaglians, who began streaking from the top of the Tingij Mountains. The Eaglians descended, carrying large buckets in their talons. The battered griffins were held on their perches by the bellowing roars of the shielding dragons. Once nearing the ground, the Eaglians dumped the thick sticky naphtha behind the Proliate lines advancing on the Northern Dwarves.

"I can't get over the sight of those Eaglians," Abernan said, chuckling.

"They're impressive," Sorea agreed.

The Knight cavalry let loose a series of flaming, whistling arrows. Their high-pitched whine sounded like an evil laugh as they flew through the sky, flame immediately erupting behind the majority of the Proliate through the Way of Trepas—trapping them between a wall of flame and six-foot torsion walls. The Knights of Liberum infantry and cavalry moved north to continue firing on those Proliate still streaming out of the gorge, while the Knights of Toil Shaor, led by Veli Pingius, and a regiment of the Northern Dwarves Vioma moved around the wall to attack the trapped Proliate's flank.

As the Knights and Northern Dwarves rounded the torsion wall trap, the Red Guard turned on them like the cornered beasts they were. To soften up their lines the Dwarves poured bolts from their crossbows while a mix of arrows and bolts rained in from the Knights.

"Should the Knights of Liberum and the cavalry move that far north?" Abernan questioned.

Sorea shook her head. "I assume Friar has his reasons."

"Revenge for their deception!" a Proliate screamed as the trapped Proliate charged from their peninsula of death, surrounded by flames, a mountain, and a wall.

A deafening impact of shield and armor concussed around the battlefield as the two forces collided. The stout Dwarves held up well, even managing to push the Proliate back a short distance. Veli Pingius' troops were thrust in reverse almost instantly.

"Ritari! Take a battalion to help Pingius," Friar yelled frantically after looking back.

A thousand Knights from Liberum quickly followed Ritari to where Pingius' troops were faltering. Initially, there had been about ten thousand Proliate troops in the trap. Around a thousand had died or been disabled by the wall and flames. The chaos amongst the Knights of Toil Shaor allowed Ritari's troops to move forward. As he neared the fighting frontline, he readied his fierce tarvella panther spear.

Suddenly, two Knights were killed in front of him, his eyes instantly looking upon three heavy merja, the giant spears of the Proliate. Ritari quickly swept his spear down, then circled up and around to clear the three spears before slamming the sword-like tip of his weapon into the throat of one Red Guard. He dodged a spear thrust while withdrawing his own. Flipping the bottom of his spear forward, he jammed the heavily weighted bottom of it into the helmet of a Proliate, smashing the two wing-like projections before crushing the mid-face. Ritari saw his eyes squint in pain before the center of his face cavitated backwards.

The third Red Guard crashed the weighted tip of his own spear towards Ritari. The Knight captain slammed his shield into the incoming spear and up before twirling his own blade forward. Quickly slashing right and left, he opened up both femoral arteries, dropping the Proliate to his knees. Ritari slammed a sidekick into the warrior's face before slicing the blade of his spear through the ocularium of the helmet, carving through the eyes and the top of the nose, a shower of blood birthing through the opening.

Pain instantly seared up Ritari's arm, his spear falling after a Proliate shield slammed into his hand. He quickly spun his shield around to block a spear thrust from the new enemy. His hand felt too battered for his broad sword, so he settled for his short one. As it was unsheathed, his right arm was hit again by the weighted end of the spear, and his sword dropped.

The thunderous shouts, cries, and screams of battle became louder, yet the newly Knighted Tempaus of the Tilkeri squad became less aware of them as he focused on Ritari and the Proliate warrior over him. The Proliate's eyes were ablaze, accentuated by the red wings of his helmet flaring out around them.

Clutching his sword with two hands, the attacking Proliate raised it over his left shoulder.

An opening, Tempaus thought, gazing at the gap between the top of the Proliate's chest protector and the armor encircling his arm. He saw the warrior's muscles flexing forward as Ritari frantically reached for his sword.

With a loud grunt Tempaus thrust his sword into the unprotected axilla just before the space vanished. He felt the recoil as the sword sliced brutally into the man's shoulder—squishing as it severed flesh before jarring into the top of his pauldron, the armor protecting his shoulder.

With surprising violence, a massive spray of blood blasted back in a shower splattering over his face and chest. The Proliate's arm immediately slumped, rendered futile as the blade shattered the head of the humerus. Knight Saccade rammed his spear into the neck of Proliate to allow his friend Tempaus to remove his sword. Blood spurted in startled arcs from the Proliate's neck like travelers jumping off a cliff.

"Nice timing," Ritari said, still weary of the freshly appointed Knights, and former bullies, of Liberum.

"Operation Thunder Strike! Watch the skies for dragon's breath!" Knight Varg yelled.

"Let us through!" several hundred Knights of Liberum yelled. Ritari moved back to join them, helping them push their way to the front of Pingius' troops. Each one held two large, twelve-foot spears. Nearing the front Ritari gave the order to have the Knights briskly retreat ten feet before handing out the spears.

"Eaglians!" Ritari shouted as they once again dove into battle carrying buckets—this time aiming the naphtha directly at the Proliate. A few screamed, some prayed, and others fought like men possessed. Only a handful of burning arrows were needed, as the naphtha-fueled flames exploded. Fire manifested itself into a living being, consuming with greed and heedless brutality, swirling incarnate.

"Keep them pinned. If the burning soldiers touch you, you die," Varg yelled. He and the other Knights with long spears formed a line between the flames to the north and wall to the south, fending off the burning Proliate from escaping. Several Red Guard threw themselves at the wall of spears in a fit of agony.

"Hold firm!" Varg shouted. "No retreat, no mercy!"

The Proliate attacked with even more ferocity, many demented with pain. The space was so enclosed the flames quickly leapt to others as they jostled to fight and escape. Screams mixed with percolating gurgles of those near death. Some Knights began to vomit, overwhelmed at the appalling smell of burning flesh clogging the air.

Eventually the flames won, and the screaming stopped to reveal a horrific scene. Those unlucky enough to have a sliver of life left could only bubble out weak groans of scorched misery. Veiled in smoke, a heap of charred humanity laid crackling on the ground.

Friar winced at the dejected faces of the Liberum Knights returning to him in the north from the grisly event. S*uch a scene cannot help but scald the soul,* Friar thought, before yelling, "Griffins!"

About ten griffin squadrons, four hundred in total, came hurtling towards the rear of the Knights' cavalry and infantry.

"They must have circumvented the dragons," Ritari said, sprinting to rejoin Friar.

"Agreed," Friar said. "Unfortunately, some have magician riders. Our Knights and cavalry are caught between griffins to the west and the Proliate streaming out of the gorge to the east. I fear I led us to far away from our lines."

"Archers to my left, fire on the griffins. Those to the right, shoot at the Proliate," Ritari commanded.

"Slow, controlled retreat back towards our lines," Friar yelled.

The Knights fired while beginning a steady withdrawal towards the rest of the Allies. All the riderless griffins rose into the air to leave those with Magician riders a clear shot at the Knights. Fire orbs and beams rocked into the front lines of the Knights, obliterating large chunks of flesh. Smoke began to rise from char-blackened flesh and scorched ground.

Cries of "Revenge!" echoed from the Magicians.

"Shield cover for archers. Cavalry, wheel and fire to make a moving target!" Friar yelled, alarmed at the number of Knights dying.

High up on the Tingij Mountains, Veneficus sat restlessly on Runor. The beautiful Pegasus stomped, shaking its head nervously—the screams and clamor of battle far below tormenting his hypersensitive hearing.

"Let us down to our troops, now!" Emperor Fanga of Piscium demanded.

"The battlefield's not secure. Now, go back with the others," Veneficus said ominously.

Scratching his greying head, Veneficus hesitated, the burden of the unknown weighing heavily on him. After making sure no one was watching, he reached into a secret compartment of his robe, carefully removing a small, brightly glowing vial. He struggled to block the sparkling light with his hands while uncorking it. Taking a deep breath, he took a large swig. His body shuddered with an odd mixture of intense burning pain coursing through his bowels and pleasure zipping through his veins as the potent power shuddered through his body.

"Ad sistendam tempus," he whispered.

As soon as the last syllable left his lips, all pleasure instantly evaporated as his body shook in severe agony. His bones rattled and muscles ached around the fiery storm surging through his blood vessels. The magic he ingested exploded through him, into his crosier and out his crystal. Movement all around ratcheted down, clunking slower until everyone and everything but himself froze. A throbbing hiss of tortuous discomfort oozed from lungs under constricting anguish. Stopping time is a task so onerous that, before it became illegal, it took twenty Master Magicians, but Veneficus could achieve it—with help from his secret formula.

His ribs felt like they were cracking under the pressure. His true form shuddered in violent blurs as his body vibrated in sheer agony. Knowing he only had seconds, he used the last of his strength to whisper, "Salainen viesti naytaa." A small orb of bluish light emerged from his crosier and hovered before him. Gently grasping it, he whispered a message. After finishing, he spoke the guiding spell, "Ex agito hic-Friar Pallium." The blue orb traveled away with lightning quickness.

Veneficus sucked in air as the spell released its vice-like clamp on his body and time surged forward. He quickly felt his face, *I'm back,* before checking to see if anyone had noticed his actions. Convinced they had not, he smiled, wiping the profuse sweat sidling down his forehead. *The future of Verngaurd depends on the Knights surviving this,* he thought, as if trying to justify his actions.

Friar was frantically overseeing their slow retreat towards the relative safety of the Allied lines. The griffins and Magicians were slowly decimating his troops separated from Veli Pingius and the Dwarves to the south.

Friar was desperately signaling to the dragons circling above for assistance, but the dragons were embroiled in another fierce aerial battle with the resurgent griffins. Veneficus' blue orb abruptly arrived, and Friar cautiously reached towards it. Unexpectedly, a small translucent image of Veneficus appeared. Only Friar could hear its message, "Quickly withdraw your forces south. The Proliate from the north are coming with several severe surprises. I'm convinced your survival is crucial for Verngaurd's future."

As quickly as it came, the orb disappeared. Friar cautiously waved his hand where the translucent image had been but felt nothing. *I have to trust my old friend.* Turning to the signalers, he ordered a full retreat to the south where they could join the other Allies.

"All right, Knights, this is what we trained for!" Friar encouraged, willing them to move faster yet maintain some order.

A few moments after their accelerated retreat, twelve thousand Proliate from the north sped to where they had just exited, spurred on by the prodigiosis volo enchantment. The Proliate moved with lightning precision and perfect timing, courtesy of their ceaseless drilling. As one they shouted, "Honor! Revenge!"

Friar slowed to study them. They were aligned in a twelve-deep phalanx, not the normal Proliate formation, and instead of their standard merja spears they carried longer, eighteen-foot-long sarissa spears.

"Friar, the griffins are retreating!" a Knight yelled.

Watching the war birds fly higher, suddenly, a pained look spread across Friar's face. "The only reason they would retreat is—" his voice was cut off by a volley of arrows blasting towards them.

On either side of the Proliate lines stood a patchwork of bowmen from countries throughout the Confederacy, including Jaa, Piscium, and Ager. As the arrows pierced into the retreating Knights, loud cheers rose up from the Proliate. Lidenskap smiled. "No Proliate shall bear the shame of firing an arrow, but we can still combat their treachery. Signal our brothers from the north to advance. I'll lead the rest behind them and flank the Allies on their left."

TABLE FIVE Battle of Trepas

~~Dead/destroyed~~ *Reduced number*

Allies		Confederacy	
Knights of Liberum:	*6,250*	**Proliate Red Guard** (a corp + survivors):	*17,450*
Knight Cavalry: (lightly armored from all three castles)	*2,250*	**Proliate Silver** (**Ultor**-with spraks):	10,000
Rebelde Plains:	7,500		
Eaglians:	*1,250*	**Piscinians:**	
Knights of **Toil Shaor:** (led by Veli Pingius)	5,000	**Retiarian Division:**	*875*
		Suoli Division:	*2,000*
Northern Dwarves:		**Warriors of Jaa:**	*3,500*
Vioma Division: (Green)	*9,500*	**Southern Dwarves:**	*5,000*
		Ager:	*7,500*
Saatana Division: (Red)	5,000	**Proliate Red Guard-from the north:**	12,000
Vasama Division: (Blue)	2,000	**Magicians:**	*1,400*
		Griffins:	*2,150*
Rebelde Plains Dwarves: (skilled in prestidigitation)	400	**Auxiliary archers:**	2,000
Vioma Dragons + Aer Ridire	600		
Total:	**39,750 (3,300 dead)**		**(14,650 dead) 63,875**

The Magicians and griffins reappeared, attacking the retreating Knights to bunch them up—creating better kill percentages for their archers in their carefully coordinated assaults.

"They're killing us: griffins—Magicians set upon us, then briefly withdraw to allow volleys of arrows before repeating the cycle!" Friar yelled. "Pick up the pace!"

"Easier said than done with the riderless griffins diving down in V-shaped squadrons, terrorizing our back," Ritari said, still shaking out his bruised hand. "All squires to the middle! We're losing too many!"

Several Knights were ripped off the ground. A group of griffins began tossing them around—each hurl resulting in large chunks of armor and flesh detaching. With arrows streaming and Magicians and griffins shredding from above, the Knights were being decimated.

"Signalers, tell the Eaglians to loose the caltrops and have the other Allied infantry form up, but hold positions. Sorea still has some tricks to unleash," Friar ordered.

Scroll 6: Aerial Battle and Fire

"Finally, the Knights taste their own blasphemy!" Lidenskap howled as the griffins and Confederate Archers took turns dealing death. "Move behind the troops from the north," Lidenskap ordered, heading out with fifteen thousand Proliate from the Citadel. "We'll sweep around, out-flanking the Allied troops who are taking heavy losses from arrow and griffins. Any moment our troops from Ragorsaf should arrive from the west and the Western Elves from the south. Complete and total victory shall be ours."

High above the Way of Trepas the Eaglians rained down thousands of caltrops, four iron spikes sticking out from a central orb, on the enemy. The tetrahedron shape assured that one spike always pointed up to pierce foot or hoof. Normally laid down before enemy troops arrive, the cramped confines of the gorge made them beneficial to the Allies.

"Sir," a magician on a battered griffin said. The normally majestic mane and lion body were littered with gashes and throwing darts.

"Speak!" Veneficus bellowed.

"While the griffins and Magicians helping with the land battle are enjoying great success, those of us trying to keep the Vioma Dragons distracted are suffering extreme losses. Of the four Air Wings starting the battle, less than half have survived. Of those still alive, over half are severely wounded. We have to abandon the attack!"

Veneficus sighed. The griffins had put up a valiant fight, but were no match for Vioma Dragons, who were in the midst of cleaning up the last few aerial griffins.

General Orel and Aquila finished dumping the last of the caltrops into the pass when an injured Vioma Dragon broke from the main battle area and zoomed past them, six griffins in hot pursuit. An exhausted, tattered-looking Magician rode the last one with several singed areas on his robes. He glanced apprehensively at the barely glowing crystal on his crosier.

"Permission to attack?" Aquila asked, feeling the magnetic pull of animosity towards the griffins.

General Orel hesitated. They had strict orders not to engage the griffins again. He peered over the edge of the Tingij Mountains. What to a human's eye would be a blur, to the Eaglian was crystal clear. He could see the Knights of Liberum taking a pounding from the other griffins, Magicians, and archers.

"We could free up the dragons to clean up the griffins down there while we wait for our next mission," Aquila pleaded.

The two Eaglians looked to see the Magician and his griffin pulling up to perch on a protected outcropping. The other five remained in hot pursuit of the dragon.

"They're setting a trap. They'll drive the dragon back to the Magician," Aquila said as the dragon began to falter. Blackened blast sites from fire orbs and deep searing lacerations from fire beams were strewn up and down its length. The left wing was charred in several places, green fluid showering out. Three of the four Dwarves on the singed wooden carriage were flopping lifelessly, beating the timber like a drum thanks to their restraints.

"Only the pilot's alive, but his leg's badly burned. We can save that dragon and Dwarf," Aquila reiterated. Two of the five griffins on the dragon's tail had zoomed forward and to its left, doing their best to turn the beast around to where the Magician and his griffin lay in wait. The Magician fidgeted with his crosier, anxiously yearning for his prey to be driven back.

As Orel's mouth began to move, Aquila was already taking flight.

"Make it quick," Orel added.

Aquila did a circle to get his timing right before zooming towards the outcropping. He tucked his wings to decrease noise. As the dragon approached, he was a few yards from the Magician.

"Eldur hnottur!" the Magician yelled. Just as his waning crystal flashed, Aquila was on them. With lightning quickness his talons dug into the neck of the startled griffin. Quickly making a wringing motion, he was able to use his sharp talons to sever major arteries. Spurting blood exploded onto the black rock. For good measure he twisted the griffin's neck hard enough to snap the cervical spine. While his legs were busy with the griffin, he used his arms to grab the crosier. With a rapid thrust of his wings his body lurched forward, slamming the Magician against the rock he had been hiding behind. As the first fireball shot into the sky, a loud thud echoed out as the Magician's head crashed into the boulder—his caved-in skull leaving a path of brain and blood dripping down the rock as his body collapsed at gravity's requirement.

Aquila quickly aimed the crosier at the griffins herding the dragon towards his position. The second fireball slammed into a surprised griffin in front. Aquila felt himself thrust backwards from recoil as the orb crashed into the griffin's head, exploding the front half of its body and rendering it a blackened mess. The third orb slammed into the back of the beheaded griffin—its tail and thousands of small pieces fleecily floated below.

Aquila aimed the fourth orb into the side of a second griffin. Fire and pain racked its shattered body, which burst into two halves, held together by thin sinewy bands. Its fragmented corpse spiraled towards the ground. *Three griffins left.*

The other griffins saw the carnage but not the source. Flying up and around the dragon to see the cause, they instantly locked onto the Eaglian. Their eyes resonated with hatred. As the dragon zoomed by Aquila, the three griffins spread themselves out before charging the lone Eaglian.

Aquila raised the crosier towards the one in the center. As the last magical orb was about to leave, he switched aim to the griffin on the right. The griffin in the center shot higher to avoid the projectile while the surprised griffin on the right could only and raise its head backwards before the orb shattered into its neck. In a flesh-splattering, bone-shattering explosion, the charred nubbin where its proud head had been fell to the ground.

The two remaining griffins swooped down on Aquila. He brandished the crosier, swinging it at the griffins as they zoomed forward. The wood of the crosier splintered as it slammed into the one coming right towards him. That griffin was thrown into a violent spin, flying erratically up and over Aquila's head. The griffin on his left slammed into Aquila's chest plate with its lion paws. As its body arched back, its front talons sliced downwards and into Aquila's shoulder. Blood and sparks flew as the claws dug into flesh before grating against his chest plate.

Aquila let out a shriek of pain while the griffin, which had just injured him, flared out its menacing beak and slashed wildly with its talons. Drawing his sword, Aquila let out a battle roar, slashing the griffin across the chest. The griffin retreated to perch just out of sword length while screeching. Aquila sensed, more than saw, the griffin he had hit with the crosier charging at his back. Aquila reached fruitlessly for one of his throwing darts. *None left!*

The griffin continued hurtling towards his back. Given the griffin's velocity and his injured shoulder, Aquila was going to have to risk turning away from the perched griffin in front, exposing his back, to gain enough power for a sword thrust. Just as he began to turn, a green streak bolted into the zooming griffin. Aquila's keen eyes picked out the massive jaws and razor-sharp teeth of the dragon crunching into the griffin. He could hear the lone dragon-riding Dwarf yelling violent commands of revenge.

With the griffin's mangled body still in his jaws, the dragon placed his left claw down on a large boulder. Using it as a fulcrum, he spun his massive weight around in a sharp turn, which catapulted him directly into the perching griffin. Pinning it down with its immense weight, the dragon took his time, taunting the screeching griffin by putting his menacing head just out of range of its beak. He let the blood surging out of the dead griffin in his jaws pour agonizingly over the restrained griffin. Finally, he threw the dead carcass away and bared his razor-sharp teeth while loosing a roar. After a moment's pause, its jaws sliced through the griffin's neck. Indifferently, it flicked the still-convulsing body over the edge of the cliff.

"Thanks," Aquila muttered to the surviving Dwarf.

"I appreciate you taking out the Magician. Griffins alone, not too bad except in extreme numbers. However, the Magicians are ripping us up," the Dwarf said, gently patting his injured dragon.

"You should get out of this fight," Aquila advised.

"My job is to manage a fire-breathing dragon. How high do you think personal safety is on my priority list?" the Dwarf asked with a laugh. "Plus," he turned serious, "as long as the Knights fight below, we will *never* quit." With that he screamed, "Hyokkays! Hyokkays!" and steered his dragon to rejoin the aerial battle.

"Form lines!" Friar yelled below. "Cavalry, spread to our left. Move quickly, or we will be outflanked." He let his gaze head off to the west. *Please come!* he thought, wishing for the Elves of Creber.

"The Confederate arrows have stopped. That can only mean imminent frontal assault," Ritari said.

Looking somberly, Friar saw all the dead Knights and squires from the combined efforts of arrows and near-constant assaults from griffins and Magicians. "Squires, to the rear. Knights, tighten your ranks and hold! The Proliate are advancing under the prodigiosis volo enchantment."

The Knights had just formed lines when the Proliate and their massive sarissa spears slammed into them. The front lines of the Knights folded in a bloody heap. They had no defense against the ferocious weight of twelve rows of sarissa spears bearing down on them with magical speed. The spears were too numerous to be batted away and too long to allow the Knights to strike back.

"Cavalry, move around to flank them!" Friar ordered in desperation. Unless they could break up the massive spear phalanx from the side or rear, they had no chance. The move was risky with Lidenskap leading a large force of Red Guard behind the troops with sarissa spears—they could surround his cavalry. He had to risk it. If nothing changed, they would all die.

As the cavalry charged to the west and north, they were met by dive-bombing griffins and Magicians. Fire orbs and beams sliced into them just as the arrows resumed, this time focusing on the cavalry.

Lidenskap smirked. "Finally, things are going our way. Kill them all!"

"Ragorsaf is here!" his lieutenant yelled.

"Tallcon! Tallcon!" the Red Guard shouted.

Moving at lightning speed, but with less cohesion than usual, the regiment from Ragorsaf came into full view. Lining up, they looked uncharacteristically disorderly.

Friar smiled.

Lidenskap frowned.

Before the Proliate knew what was happening, the white wood bows of the Elves of Creber were drawn and firing at blistering speed. The first row of the Elven army had dawned Proliate armor from the dead Ragorsaf troops. The arrows rained into the griffins and Magicians. Using this distraction, the Knight cavalry retreated back to the infantry line and once together they began a speedy withdrawal. With the Magician's attention diverted to the incoming arrows, the Proliate could not match the speed of the Knights and keep their tight phalanx together with their long spears.

When the Knights were closer to the other Allies, Friar ordered them to turn and form up lines. The archers of the Knights joined the Elves of Creber, and the combined effort quickly forced the surviving griffins to retreat towards the top of the mountains only to find the Vioma Dragons had decimated their comrades and were now only too happy to tear into them.

The archers of the Allies turned on the archers of the Proliate army. Equipped with inferior bows and armor, they made easy targets for the better equipped Knights and Elves.

"Orders?" a lieutenant asked General Lidenskap.

"Regroup to the north. We need to get more of our troops through the pass before we advance," he said, his mind still lingering on Ragorsaf. He knew they would never give up their armor while alive. *That regiment was the best in the Proliate army.* Still, there was hope in the Western Elves coming up from the south, and the new sarissa spears had proven powerful.

With lightning efficiency the Proliate retreated around fifty yards before forming a shield wall to wait for their brothers. The warriors of Ager had already started to form their own lines, their guttural growls indicating an eagerness to fight.

"Hold here. Squires, make sure our troops get water," Friar instructed.

"Ready?" he asked after making his way to Sorea.

"Itching to release and make them all decease…ed," she replied. "Sorry, I was trying to think of a witty rhyme."

"How about, 'ready to get started to make them departed.'"

"Not bad."

"Just get going."

She laughed before gently grabbing his arm. "How are the troops holding up? It looked rough out there."

"We took heavy losses, but we are still fit to cause some trouble. If you can knock out those regiments with the sarissa spears before we have to meet up again, we would certainly appreciate it."

"Pumilus, stop prestidigitation," Sorea yelled. "Okay, Knights, time to stupefy!"

As the Rebelde Plains Dwarves stopped their prestidigitation, the previously hidden siege engines of the Knights were revealed.

"Start with plain boulders—fire at will," Sorea yelled to her team leaders. The engines creaked and moaned before hurling their projectiles.

General Lidenskap sighed in frustration. "Friar has obviously been planning this battle for years, leading us around by the nose." *Should I signal the attack to get inside of the trebuchets? Or are there more traps? Should I retreat? Veneficus, where are you?*

"Sir!" his lieutenant yelled while nervously tracking the incoming boulders. "Ager is through the pass and lined up behind us. The battered Piscinians are coming through. If we stay here we..."

BOOOOM! BOOOOM! BOOOOM!

Several thunderous crashes came raining down, shaking ground and soul alike. Some of the Proliate were demolished in the initial crash. Others were splattered out in a human shock wave as the force of the projectile concussed outward. The efficient Knight operators were already getting ready to fire again as the dust and blood settled.

His ears still ringing from the blast, the lieutenant continued. "Sir, the griffins have been killed or retreated. If we stay here, we are going to be obliterated."

Lidenskap hesitated. Friar had managed to twist his thoughts up so tightly they no longer flowed. "What do you think?"

The lieutenant faltered, stunned the normally overconfident general was floundering. "I think...if we're going to attack, it has to be now." The idea of recommending what he thought best, retreat, was not an option when speaking to the general.

The word "attack" struck a chord robust enough to stamp down the doubt rummaging in Lidenskap's heart. "Get the Piscinians out of the pass and lined up!" he yelled ferociously. As he finished, a fresh round of projectiles pounded down on the Proliate.

"Yes!" Sorea yelled. "Fire the rakkniv!" she cried.

Just as two ballista bolts with razor wire between began to fire, several of the rearguard came flying up, short of breath.

"When you're ready." Friar forced himself to remain calm despite the urgency pulsing in his heart.

"The Western Elf army is coming up from the south. They probably came through the Venio pass and skirted the bottom of the Forest of Creber."

Ritari, King Abernan, and Ailante, head Archerian of the Elves of Creber, came rushing up, and Friar informed them of the news.

Ailante hissed his disdain at the rival faction of Elves.

"How many?" Friar questioned the rearguard.

"Over ten thousand armed with halberds and long bows," the Knight answered.

"How long do we have?"

"An hour, maybe less. They're moving fast."

Friar scowled. *Battle plans quickly crumble once forces clash.* He turned away from them and closed his eyes, mentally scrolling through the forces under his command and those arrayed against him.

TABLE SIX Battle of Trepas

~~Dead/destroyed~~ *Reduced number*

Allies		**Confederacy**	
Knights of Liberum:	*5,000*	**Proliate Red Guard**	
Knight Cavalry:	*2,000*	(a corp + survivors):	*16,050*
(lightly armored from all three castles)		**Proliate Silver**	
Rebelde Plains:	7,500	(**Ultor**-with spraks):	10,000
Eaglians:	*1,300*	**Piscinians:**	
Knights of **Toil Shaor:**	5,000	**Retiarian Division:**	*875*
(led by Veli Pingius)		**Suoli Division:**	*2,000*
Northern Dwarves:		**Warriors of Jaa:**	*3,500*
Vioma Division: (Green)	*9,500*	**Southern Dwarves:**	*5,000*
		Ager:	*7,500*
Saatana Division: (Red)	5,000	**Proliate Red Guard-from the north:**	*10,000*
Vasama Division: (Blue)	2,000	**Magicians:**	*1,400*
		Griffins:	*700*
Rebelde Plains Dwarves:	400	**Western Elves-from south:**	12,500
(skilled in prestidigitation)		Auxiliary archers:	*1,200*
Elves of Creber	7,000		
Vioma Dragons + Aer Ridire	*550*		
Total:	**45,250 (7,800 dead)**		**(20,300 dead) 70,725**

"Which armies are through the pass?" Friar questioned.

"The Red Guard, Ager, and Piscinians. The warriors of Jaa are streaming out. The entire army of the Southern Dwarves is in the pass," Ritari answered.

"Signal the Eaglians to release the trap!" King Abernan cried out. "We can rid ourselves of the traitorous Southern Dwarves."

Ignoring his outburst for the moment, Friar continued. "So the Silver or Ultor Divisions of the Proliate are not even in the pass yet?"

"That's correct," Ritari said.

"Our goal, if you remember, was put a hurt on the Proliate while drawing the other countries of Verngaurd back to our side," Friar reminded them.

"I don't think waiting for the Ultor to enter the pass is realistic," Ailante said calmly.

Friar put his hands to his head. "If we let them all get through the pass, we are facing about seventy thousand. If we kill all the Southern Dwarves and cut off the Ultor Divisions, we would only be facing around fifty-five thousand."

"Considering we only have about forty thousand *and* are in a pincer, that's not comforting," King Abernan boomed. "Release the Eaglians! We can't afford to wait."

"I agree. The Ultor will escape unscathed, but it is more important that we can fight on two fronts and survive," Ritari said.

Ailante nodded.

"The Proliate and Ager are advancing!" Sorea yelled.

"Signal the Eaglians," Friar said.

"Permission to use the squires to help take on those new sarissa spears of the Proliate?" Sorea asked. "I've got some ideas on how to trip them up."

Friar nodded. "Any help would be appreciated."

Scroll 7: Sigh. Pulled Aside...Again

"When's Arend coming back?" Gimelli wondered, standing next to the towering Giant Redwoods piercing majestically into the blue sky. Not to be outdone, the soaring Umulig Mountains stuck out their chests and lifted their heads high to maximize their rocky height advantage over the massive trees.

"Arend'll be here. Don't worry," Kainen reassured the restless League.

Lontas wandered back. "I went through the Báis te Pass. You can start to feel, and even smell, the heat. The ground quickly changes from larger rocks, to smaller stones, to sand. Then, as far as you can see, it's literally just sand. Nothing but lots and lots of sand."

"How do you smell heat, dork?" Sankari seethed. "Also, you who are supposedly smart, you do know sand is part of the definition with the whole desert thing?"

Ignoring her, Lontas continued, "The Aard Mountains are super high, even taller than the Umulig range."

"I'm not excited about the desert heat," Bellae said.

"What *is* exciting to think about is how the Aard Mountains take all the rain. The Desert of Calor is actually created by their rain shadow. Think about this while we're in the arid desert—just on the other side of the Aard is a huge river system and then the lush Creber Forest."

"Take a look at the map with me, Lontas," Kainen said, unfurling an intricately comprehensive guide to the Desert of Calor.

"I've never seen such a detailed map of the desert."

"It's a secret League map from when they surveyed it using kameli eons ago," Kainen said. "So, my plan is to head west using the Darb al-Mahashas route along the spine of the Umulig Mountains to the Santarieh Oasis."

Lontas looked at him funny. "Isn't that the Siwa Oasis?"

"That's its common name."

"Well then, why not just call it Siwa in the first place?" Sankari huffed, becoming increasingly grumpy the further they moved away from Cappadocia.

"Santarieh is the map name, but I'll call it Siwa from now on," Kainen said calmly, avoiding a fight with the Fairy. "We'll pass al-Qrah Oasis, but Arend and I went there for training, and it was desolate and tiny."

"Why not head directly for Oasis Vastaus? That's by far the biggest and most likely," Sankari said, her wings fluttering wildly in irked annoyance.

Kainen blushed with anger after their near-death misadventure in the Dark Forest. "Three words for you Sankari: Fionain-Wasted-Undead."

Sankari rolled her eyes. "Like I could know those stories were real."

"That's the point. We almost died before our quest even started. If we can avoid the ferratus lanx, I will," Kainen said.

"They can live anywhere in the desert," Lontas said. "However, you're correct. They are highly concentrated around the largest oasis given that the animals of the desert, their food, flock there for water."

"What in the world is a ferratus whatever?" Gimelli asked.

Before Lontas could go into a scholarly description, Kainen interjected, "Nasty, fierce creatures that digest you on the tops of their heads while you're still alive."

Gimelli shuddered, visions of Ichor's undulating, spiked tendrils siphoning her blood pirouetted across her mind. "Yeah, lets avoid them."

Kainen nodded appreciatively.

A loud screech alerted them Eaglians were coming. Arend landed first, gently setting down an elderly man with a walking stick. Another Eaglian, the first female they had seen, alighted with a human woman. Six other Eaglians touched down away from them with swords drawn.

"I'm Ekara," the female Eaglian said. She wore a cropped cloth top but carried a sword and looked every bit as fierce as the males. "This is Kara-Rehe. She knew your mother and is one of the descendants of the Ainmhi Caint who still live within our forest."

As Kara-Rehe grasped forearms with the League, they noted a well-healed but large linear burn on her hand. They did not realize it at the time, but it was the same burn Jumeaux suffered in the Citadel.

"I knew your mothers. They—" she said.

A piercing squawk from one of the immense male Eaglians startled them all. He fluttered closer. "She means she knew *your mother*, Gimelli and Bellae."

Kara-Rehe nodded. "Of course. She was a dear friend and valued member of the Maketa." Seeing the children's questioning expressions, she continued. "Maketa means the lost. It's what we call ourselves. I thought you, Gimelli, might remember, but I guess you were young when you left."

The elderly man tottered forward with Arend's assistance. "It's correct that we Maketa are the distant descendants of Ainmhi Caint." He stopped as a faraway look flashed across his face, as if he was reliving a painful memory. "Our ancestors thought they could change the world for the better, naively flying too close to the powerful suns that rule Na Cearcaill and were burned in genocidal hatred. A steep price for fighting for what's right.

"Since the elaborate prophecy depended on the magic of an Ainmhi Caint, the world was left with a serious conundrum when the purebloods were terminated. Therefore, even those with a small dash of Ainmhi Caint blood were squirreled away in the Giant Redwoods forming our lost community." He paused, sighing loudly. "A refuge and a prison."

The massive Eaglian who had startled them moved forward. "To avoid scrutiny, and the potential that the Maketa would be discovered, all Eaglians had to isolate within our own forest. Withdrawing from the world was also a sacrifice for us. We too became captives in our home, sworn to protect the Ainmhi Caint descendants."

"True enough, KovaKotka," the elderly man said before shuffling to Bellae. "I am Cariad Anifail, elder of the Maketa. When your mother began showing amazing signs, and magical powers, we knew the full power of the Ainmhi Caint had reemerged in you."

His hand shakily journeyed towards Bellae's face, gently grazing her healing black eye. "Within you are the voices of tens of thousands of the Ainmhi Caint who came before and sacrificed their lives for what is right."

Bellae sighed under the enormous pressure heaped upon her at seemingly every turn.

"It was actually lucky timing," Ekara, the Eaglian, stated. "We were starting to see the vile Nishi and demonic Watchers encroach upon our forest in search of Patuljak and you, Chosen One. We talked of moving the Maketa, maybe to Cappadocia."

The elder Cariad Anifail laughed. "I think we might have stood out a bit! But your gifts arrival came in the nick of time. There's so much I want to say—I should have made notes. Perhaps the greatest strength is striving to accomplish what no thinks you can. Courage is standing before the wave of the impossible, diving in, and swimming as hard as you can for as long as you can. There's no bravery in an action you know will succeed. Don't focus on the burden, but the blood of your ancestors that flows through, manifesting as your gifts."

"You sound like Stralande," Bellae said. Seeing Cariad Anifail's confusion, she added, "The blue dragon that confirmed me for the prophecy."

"Ah, I see. We don't get out much, actually at all…ever. Sounds like a wise dragon. You can speak with animals, you can touch Macht Crystals, you have friends who love you, you are on a great adventure—not bad. May I speak to you alone?"

When they moved off, Bellae spoke, "No offense, and it's truly great meeting you, but I'm tired of being pulled aside. It almost always means bad news or extra pressure."

Cariad Anifail laughed. "I understand, but I, like those who pulled you aside in the past, only want to support and encourage you. This is a hefty burden to be placed upon your youthful shoulders."

"I know, but even though we're just starting, it seems like so much has happened. I'm already different and have so many regrets. I hate that Finn died, sorry so many Dwarves, dragons, and Eaglians have died just to get me here. I loathe that we got caught up fighting in the Dark Forest that almost cost Gimelli her life," Bellae said.

Cariad Anifail nodded. "Regrets can be a starting point for growth. Growth means we gain a new and broader perspective. A great man once said the most courageous and heroic die but once, but the weak die many deaths before their final one. What do you think?"

Bellae twisted sideways, thinking for a moment before shrugging her shoulders.

"I believe," he continued, "he couldn't be more wrong. In our lives we all go through innumerable small-scale deaths. Passing from infants to toddlers and teenagers to adults, parts of us die, yet rising out of the cocoon is a new version of ourselves. With each major failure, much more so than any success, part of us is destroyed, but budding from each defeat is the opportunity to regenerate and renew our mind, body, and spirit. Each time you suffer or lose, you change—growing, maturing. Failure can induce more growth than triumph. As you embark on your journey, you will fall, many times. Get up, grow, keep going."

KovaKotka began moving closer—piercing yellow eyes boring into Bellae while his wings snapped impatiently.

"What can you tell me about my parents?" Bellae asked, afraid the Eaglian would not want her to know.

Cariad Anifail's head shot towards KovaKotka, a medley of sadness and anxiety rising behind his eyes.

The fearsome Eaglian, as if sensing Bellae's question, inched nearer. "It's time for the League to start their journey."

"But I want to know—"

Bellae was cut off by Cariad Anifail, who hugged her as tightly as his aged arms would allow. "For now, let that burden go. In the end, you will know the truth. Patience can be a challenging master. Waiting for an important answer takes a lot of effort and determination."

Kara-Rehe gave Gimelli a deep hug. "Good luck. It's so good to see you. By the way, where's your twin?"

Gimelli looked down while Kara-Rehe embraced Bellae. "Jumeaux got separated."

"We are with you. We believe in you," Kara-Rehe said.

The League watched as the Eaglians flew up above the Giant Redwood forest with the two Ainmhi Caint descendants.

"I wish you could see our homes," Arend said. "Not that I ever spent much time there."

Kainen spoke to Arend in Elfish, and the two embraced. When they separated, the young Elf said in the common tongue, "We *are* the League. Sacrifice for success."

"Sacrifice for success," Arend repeated.

"Alright, let's go get our first set of crystals."

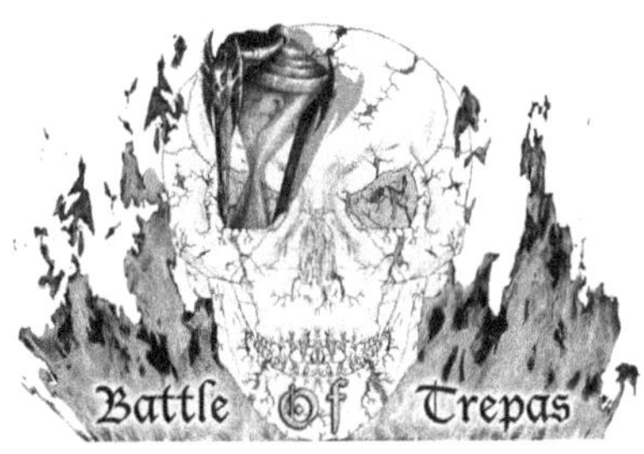

Scroll 8: What Now?

"Friar's signal," an Eaglian informed.

"Let's fly!" Orel said.

As the Eaglians moved into position, the last of the griffins and Magicians retreated from the field. Cheers from the Northern Dwarves joined the roars of the Vioma Dragons.

Moving quickly, half of the Eaglians began cutting thick nets holding boulders at the top of the gorge. The other half took off bearing nets heavily weighted with rocks.

"Release!" Orel yelled. As the last syllable echoed off the canyon walls, the final strands of net were cut. The Eaglians circling above released—the air filling with roaring sounds as thousands of boulders and rocks crashed down the sides of the gorge.

"What now?" Lidenskap yelled.

His advancing army slowed as everyone turned to watch the massive rockslide enlarge into an avalanche. Inside the Way of Trepas, chaos erupted. Screams and howls choked the gorge already clogged with panic and claustrophobic fear. The Southern Dwarves, caught in the middle of the canyon, began frantically pushing both those in front and behind.

To the west, the nimble warriors of Jaa sprinted out of the pass. The determined Ultor Division initially refused to yield, assuming the Dwarves were deserting. As the rumble grew louder, they realized what was happening and allowed them to pass. But gravity and time toiled against them. A deafening crash pierced the air as plumes of billowing smoke and debris exploded out of the gorge. Those closest to the opening were thrown forward by the impact of the blast and quickly engulfed in the billowing cloud of dust.

After the initial explosion, the fine particles from the rockslide clung in the air as if too stunned by their abrupt journey to fall further. The grey powder from the avalanche coated the Warriors of Jaa and Ager. Even the soldiers unscathed by the blast were moving their jaws to get the ringing and pounding out of their ears while coughing within the dust cloud. An uneasy silence crept over the battlefield, broken only by hacking coughs.

Lidenskap broke into the hush with a loud, painful cry of anguish. "Get back into lines, NOW!" He grabbed a steed and began riding up and down the Confederacy lines, willing the troops to prepare to attack the deceivers.

"Sorea, get those siege engines humming and then find me," Friar shouted with excitement. "King Abernan, Ritari, and Ailante, prepare your troops for battle."

"What of the Western Elves?" Abernan challenged.

"I have an idea," Friar said.

"Outstanding job! Boulders crushing the rock-mining Southern Dwarves! Joyously ironic!" Abernan boomed as Eaglian General Orel flew down.

"You're just in time. How are the skies?" Friar asked.

"We own them," Orel answered sternly.

"Excellent," Friar said. "The pass?"

"Completely blocked. Most Southern Dwarves were killed, and the Silver Proliate cannot get through."

Friar nodded. "I need Sarskil and the Special Forces Dwarves for a plan."

Time oozed impatiently forward as the two sides arranged themselves for battle. The only sound was the creaking groans of the Knight siege engines. The boulders leaving their slings screamed with high-pitched whines as they sliced through the air, their crash landings causing panic in all but the Red Guard.

"I cannot believe you kept us hostage up on the mountain while our troops were dying!" Hamaza cried out.

"It was for your protection," Veneficus replied. "Now that the skies are ruled by dragons and Eaglians, it's safer down here."

"We need to move forward and get under the range of their siege engines!" Princess Hamaza yelled. "Our troops are getting slaughtered!"

"We should withdraw!" the hulking King Tarha of Ager bellowed. "We've gone from a two to one advantage to a fairly even battle."

"The king makes a point," Veneficus added. "Perhaps it's best to retreat and fight another day—one in which Friar Pallium has not made such elaborate preparations."

Lidenskap scowled as if the Magician had just advised he stab himself.

"I change my recommendation. We should retreat to fight a different day," Hamaza said.

"Proliate don't retreat," Lidenskap seethed. "The enemy will soon bleed under our rage. They are the ones who should be afraid!"

At that moment, another round of projectiles, these with long metal spikes, rained down on the Confederate lines. They were quickly followed by the rakkniv—the many strands of razor wire brutally devastating.

"We attack!" Lidenskap howled. "Move forward, under the range of their siege engines."

"I guess the war council is over," Veneficus said cynically.

Princess Hamaza looked pleadingly at the Magician.

"You'd better advance," Veneficus replied.

"You'll let us march off to death?"

"All of you die eventually, princess. The real question is, will you follow the orders of your elected commander?"

Without another word, she moved to be with her troops. The Confederacy was arrayed in a V-formation. The Proliate took the right wing and center positions while the left wing consisted of: Ager, Jaa, the Piscinian remnants, and several hundred Southern Dwarves who had managed to push their way out of the gorge. The tattered remains of the griffins and Magicians were in reserve. The unscathed Western Elves were marching up from the south.

The Allies were arrayed left to right as follows: the Knight cavalry, Elves of Creber, Knight Infantry, Rebelde Plains, Northern Dwarves: Vioma then Saatana. They had the siege engines behind them. Sorea and a few hundred Knights of Liberum were joined by the elite Vasama Division of the Northern Dwarves and heading south to prepare for the Western Elves.

TABLE SEVEN Battle of Trepas

~~Dead/destroyed~~ *Reduced number* *Out of the Battle

Allies		Confederacy	
Knights of Liberum:	*5,000*	**Proliate Red Guard** (a corp + survivors):	*15,750*
Knight Cavalry: (lightly armored from all three castles)	*2,000*	*Proliate Silver (other side of the pass):	*10,000
Rebelde Plains:	7,500	**Piscinians:**	
Eaglians:	*1,300*	**Retiarian Division:**	*805*
Knights of Toil Shaor: (led by Veli Pingius)	5,000	**Suoli Division:**	*1,750*
Northern Dwarves:		**Warriors of Jaa:**	*3,000*
Vioma Division: (Green)	*9,500*	**Southern Dwarves:**	*500*
Saatana Division: (Red)	5,000	**Ager:**	*7,000*
Vasama Division: (Blue)	2,000	**Proliate Red Guard-from the north:**	*10,000*
Rebelde Plains Dwarves: (skilled in prestidigitation)	400	**Magicians:**	*1,400*
Elves of Creber	7,000	**Griffins:**	*300*
Vioma Dragons with Aer Ridire	500	**Western Elves-coming from south:**	12,500
		Auxiliary archers:	*1,100*
Total:	**45,200 (7,850 dead)**		**(36,920 dead) 54,105**

Figure 15: Battle of Trepas ICON II. Battle lines are drawn. The Proliate have placed their phalanx wall of sarissa spears at the tip of their V-formation.

The shadows of the two facing armies began to stretch sideways as the afternoon suns yielded to evening. To many on both sides the goodwill at the Tournament of the Flags felt like several lifetimes ago. A gust of wind snapped each country's flag into angry flutters, protesting the reminiscence and reminding them that now it was time to fight and die.

Lidenskap yelled, "Revenge! Attack!"

As they advanced, the projectiles from Knight siege engines continued hurtling into Confederate lines—the Proliate taking the greatest pounding. Those not crushed or thrown backwards by the blast moved stoically around their fallen comrades.

The Allied cavalry instantly took off to the northwest. The Elves of Creber and Knight archers continued unleashing arrows. The less accomplished auxiliary archers of the Confederates, marching behind the northern Proliate and their massive sarissa spears, were too far away to return fire. The flanking movement of the Knights' cavalry forced the Red Guard regiment to the far west to stretch, preventing getting encircled.

"Send any griffins and your lazy Magicians that are still alive!" Lidenskap yelled.

Veneficus snarled back at the insolence, temporarily thinking about blasting the general. Out of the corner of his eye he caught sight of Princess Hamaza raising her eyebrows, questioning how he liked the taste of what they had been dealing with. With a curt wave of his hand he sent the remaining griffins and Magicians towards the Knight cavalry.

"Fire at the griffins before they get entangled with the Knights!" Ailante shouted. "Once they're too close to the cavalry, our arrows will be at risk of hitting Knights."

"Cease fire. Prepare!" Lovag ordered. The Knights working the siege engines immediately began dumping a sticky liquid all over the machines.

The Proliate archers finally had the enemy in range, and their arrows were now falling on the soldiers of the Rebelde Plains—obviously targeting their softer armor and discipline. The triumvirate rulers, Teyol-human, Kelig-Elf, and Vakava-Dwarf began encouraging their troops.

"With their V-shaped formation, tipped by the long sarissa spears, they are obviously trying to split us," Ritari said.

"Agreed," Friar said. "Luckily, their right flank is being stretched. They are struggling to match our cavalry streaking around the end of their line. If they are pushed too far out, it could weaken the Confederate line and the entire side could fold."

As the archers exchanged arrows, the griffins and magicians rushed towards the Knights' cavalry to drive them back south and prevent the outflanking. As they neared, the Magicians unleashed fire orbs and beams of scorching light. The riderless griffins streaked down to fight in close quarters.

The decimated griffins had adjusted their strategy. The first few members of a flight group feigned attack before pulling up. The distracted Knights would then have griffins from a different direction slam into them, dragging them into the sky to be tossed and killed. To keep the cavalry off guard the griffins constantly changed how many diversionary flyovers they performed before attacking, and soon the cavalry was in full retreat.

"The cavalry is getting routed!" Ritari cried out.

Friar smiled. "Not for much longer."

Suddenly, loud cheers rose up from the Allies. Outlined by the setting suns, the Eaglians and dragons made a majestic and frightening display, bolting towards the griffins.

"Attacking from the direction of the suns allowed them to get right on top of the griffins before they realized the danger," Friar said.

Fueled by their natural hatred for the griffins and irritability at the constant skirmishing, the Eaglians and dragons struck with lustful ferocity. Bloodcurdling shrieks and high-pitched squawks blistered the air as the griffins began to fall precipitously.

Several of the Magicians had loosed fire orb spells only to be quickly overrun by the dragons. Many griffins attempted retreating, but the Eaglians swarmed them. With no chance to withdraw, the griffins and Magicians were quickly obliterated.

"Charge!" Friar yelled. The Elves and Knights managed to fire one more volley of arrows at the Proliate with the sarissa spears as the Confederates began attacking as well.

As the two lines hurtled towards each other, the Vioma Dwarves fired their crossbow bolts at the Proliate centerline. The armies were only a few yards apart when many on both sides let out fierce war cries. Time grew heavy as they neared. The light from the fading suns outlined their weapons' razor-sharp edges. The warriors' mouths seemed to move in slow motion as they screamed in adrenaline-filled anticipation.

Everything exploded in frantic chaos as the two lines collided with fatal violence. Once again, the longer sarissa spears at the tip of the Confederate "V" proved their worth. With twelve layers of long spears coming at them, there was little the Rebelde Plains and Knights of Toil Shaor could do, and the center of the Allied line instantly buckled.

Because the middle of their line was being pushed backwards, the edges of the Knight lines on either side were forced to backpedal to avoid having their army cut in two. Friar exhaled sharply before yelling orders to his signalers.

Sorea raced forward with hundreds of squires of Liberum.

"You're supposed to be in the south!" Friar yelled.

"They're finishing preparations. I have my cunning tricks to employ," Sorea said, winking. She then screamed, "Let us pass!" They pushed through the Knights of Toil Shaor. "Crouch and fire!" she yelled to the squires once close to the front lines.

Teams of two squires launched modified bolas weapons at the feet of the sarissa-spear-wielding Proliate. Pairs of weighted and spiked balls were connected with rope. Normally a throwing weapon, Sorea had modified pairs of crossbows to fire them, and they flew under the spears. The bolases wrapped around the legs of the Proliate tripping them.

"Steady, squires!" Sorea encouraged. "Create chinks in their spear wall!"

At the same time, Sorea directed second-line Knights to throw twenty-pound weights separated by chain over the tops of the advancing spears. The weighted chains collapsed the tightly packed spears, allowing arrows and bolts to penetrate the openings. Several Knights used the downed spears as walkways, diving into the Proliate lines for revenge.

With the griffins gone, the Knights' cavalry began circling back towards the rear of the Confederate lines. However, Friar signaled them to stop and come back to the rear of Allied line. They had some room to back up, but they were being pushed dangerously close to the siege engines.

Figure 16: Battle of Trepas ICON III. The massive sarissa spears of the Proliate are decimating the Allied Center line.

"Hold!" Ritari encouraged as the Confederate line continued pushing the Allies back. Veli Pingius was shouting orders with such fierceness even his own Knights of Toil Shaor were surprised and stiffened their resistance.

"The Plains are going to fold!" Ritari yelled.

"Although the warriors of the Rebelde Plains are individually tough, they aren't used to fighting in disciplined ranks. Facing the brutal sarissa spears is too much," Friar said.

Ritari began making his way towards them, but Friar stopped him. "I'll see to them. You take care of that," he said, pointing to a tall Proliate warrior punching a giant hole into the Knights of Liberum's front line. He wore the traditional flat-winged helmet of the Proliate with red dyed horsehair running in an arc down its center. His colossal arms were straining with each thrust of his spear.

Mester! Ritari said to himself. Silently, he moved forward, pushing his way through the Knights to take on the Proliate champion.

Friar waded into the folding lines of the Rebelde Plains just in time to see their ruling triumvirate retreat. "Hold your lines!" he yelled. "You *must* hold until the Knight cavalry arrives!"

The triumvirate didn't even look up but continued retiring. Friar rushed into the Rebelde Plains troops. "Fight! Help is coming."

Mester had impaled a Knight who happened to be a Dwarf. Seeing Ritari, he lifted the Dwarf's writhing body up. Smiling, he let the skewered body sink deeper onto his spear. With contemptible scorn, but undeniable strength, Mester flung the dying Dwarf off his spear. The crumpled and bleeding body slammed to the ground as spectators formed around the two legendary fighters.

"You're not at the Tournament—no protection enchantment to hide behind," Mester said ominously.

Ritari silently circled, his shield held on his left shoulder for some protection while allowing two hands. Mester's shield was on his back, also allowing both hands for his spear. The two felt each other out with increasingly violent spear thrusts. Each blow of metal on metal forcefully reverberated down their arms. Ritari jabbed a half dozen times at Mester's lower legs to get him concentrating low. Seeing his chance,

Ritari abruptly lunged his spear for Mester's head. Mester responded by swinging his spear up until it made contact with Ritari's, at which point he used his brutal strength to guide the panther spear up and around in an arc, pinning it on the ground. Driving his elbow down, Mester broke the panther spear.

Ritari, howling in anger, countered by drawing his sword and slashing down on Mester's arm, causing him to drop his own spear. Mester drew his sword while flinging his shield over from his back.

"Tallcon!" Mester yelled, flexing his enormous arms, branded with images of Tallcon. Mester began a punishing barrage of attacks, each violent strike designed to wear Ritari down. Ritari was countering but working hard wielding his larger sword with a sore hand.

Ritari backpedaled as Mester's blows gained force. Ritari managed a quick smile as Mester became impatient, drawing back for a massive overhead blow. Ritari used his sword to deflect the blow to the side while throwing his weight behind his shield, slamming it into Mester's arms. He howled in pain as Ritari immediately arced his sword over and onto Mester's hand, forcing him to drop his sword.

Ritari capitalized on the moment, slashing with his sword back and forth across the Proliate. Mester was able to deflect some blows with his vambraces and shield, but others were landing. Lacerations gifting blood began appearing over Mester's uncovered upper arms. He had to fight harder and harder to hold his arms up, much less block the barrage of blows. Ritari faked a head shot before spinning, striking Mester on his right thigh. The blow sliced through the muscles and notched into his femur. The stroke dropped Mester to his knees. The area around quickly filled with blood from the gaping wound.

Ritari brought his sword up and to his own right before slashing down and across Mester's left shoulder, but Mester was able to swing his shield to the front, raising it to block. Ritari began a brutal burst of strikes. Mester struggled to rise but ended up stumbling. Ritari sidestepped him and swung with all his might with his sword. He brought it arcing down, his sword cleaving just under the massive Proliate's helmet, decapitating him. The hulking body slammed forward, crashing in a heap. The only signs of movement came from volcanic eruptions of blood spurting from his neck and leaking down from his isolated head.

An incredulous gasp from the Proliate, and cheers from the Knights, plaited before the Proliate immediately closed in and the two lines re-embroiled in battle. Several Knights grabbed Ritari, moving him towards the rear, as Luchar surged forward.

"What are you doing?" Ritari questioned as Luchar handed him a replacement spear.

"I'll anchor our line. Friar needs you!" Luchar said. "The center and right sides of our line are folding."

While Ritari had been fighting Mester, the Knight cavalry had managed to ride through the siege engines and reinforce the warriors of the Rebelde Plains. However, as the horses moved forward, the intimidated Rebelde Plains warriors thought the cavalry was replacing, rather than reinforcing. Taking it as permission to retreat, the leaderless Rebelde Plains warriors sprinted through the siege engines to escape the ferocious sarissa spears. Once the cavalry came near the wall of spears, the spooked horses refused to advance. Those with bows fired upon the line, with marginal success.

As Ritari rounded the failing center of the Knights' line, he ran into Friar, who was covered in sweat and blood.

"I hope that isn't yours," Ritari commented.

"Most isn't," Friar replied. "The Elves of Creber are holding well, as are the Saatana Dwarves. The Rebelde Plains have all but retreated, and the Vioma Dwarves are not matching up well against the massive men of Ager."

"Are the siege engines washed?" Ritari asked.

"Yes," Friar answered as the Rebelde Plains troops rushed past in full retreat. The center and near right side of the Allied line was being violently tossed backwards.

"If you don't make the call now, we'll be cut in two," Ritari shouted.

Friar nodded, signaling full retreat.

Pandemonium erupted, prompting Ritari to comment, "There's no such thing as a well-ordered retreat."

"There are, however, degrees of disarray," Friar replied, directing the troops as best he could.

The Saatana Dwarves, Elves of Creber and the Knights retained decent cohesion as they fought in retreat. Every single remaining warrior from the Rebelde Plains bolted in an outright sprint, many dropping weapons and shields to speed their withdrawal. The front line of the Elves of Creber glided gracefully backwards in brilliant fashion. The Elves in the rear of the lines had nocked their arrows and stood at the ready. As those who had been towards the front of the lines passed them, they fired.

"Displace!" Ailante shouted as the process repeated. The stream of arrows forced the Proliate to maintain a shield wall. Taking off in full pursuit would leave themselves vulnerable to the lethal skill of Elven archers. The Knights from Liberum and Toil Shaor used a similar technique, although it was less pressing for the Knights under Veli Pingius, as the sarissa spear wall did not allow speed.

The Knights' cavalry had the advantage of their steeds but had to avoid the retreating Rebelde Plains troops. The Vioma Dwarves were taking a beating at the hands of the massive warriors from Ager. The Saatana Dwarves were having an easier time with the exhausted warriors of Jaa, Piscium, and the straggler remains of the Southern Dwarves.

Friar enlisted the support of the squires, and they took up position with arrows soaked in naphtha about a hundred yards behind the siege engines. To allow the retreating troops pass, they stood in single-file rows, eight deep. Every north-south oriented row had one squire with a torch to light the arrows.

"Once our troops pass, form a straight line east to west. Wait to fire until the Confederates move through the siege engines. After firing, retreat behind our lines," Friar commanded.

Many of the fleeing Rebelde Plains troops encouraged the squires to retreat.

"No squire will run!" Friar yelled. "If another coward from the Plains tells them to do so, I will personally cut off your head and stomp your yellow belly."

To the south, the two thousand Vasama Special Forces Dwarves were waiting with Sorea, who had rejoined them, and several hundred

Knights for the Western Elves. Just as some of the retreating Rebelde Plains warriors made it to them, a Dwarf scout returned.

"The Western Elves are just over that ridge!" he panted.

Sorea turned to one of the Knights. "Find Friar and inform him the Elves of the West have arrived."

"Form up lines and fight with us!" Sarskil, the Northern Dwarf, yelled to the retreating army. He had helped the League of Truth enter the Dragon Council and was in charge of the Vasama detail. These Dwarves had their tightly braided hair wrapped with scales of blue Kirvella dragons. Despite the pleas, none of the retreating Rebelde Plains troops stopped.

"Teyol, Kelig!" Sarskil shouted. "As rulers of your country, come to your senses—stand and fight. You are running right into the Western Elves."

Without answering, they sprinted past, many discarding their shoddy armor for swiftness.

"We've got this!" Sorea encouraged the Knights awaiting the Western Elves.

The highly trained Vasama Dwarves needed no motivation, stoically awaiting the enemy. The screams and commotion behind them meant things had not been going well for the Allies—there would be no reinforcements to fight the Western Elves. The last warrior of the Rebelde Plains passed over the ridge, and the Allies' southern rearguard stood in silent anticipation. Wailing breached the quietude. Some were pleading cries to be spared—others, whimpers of pain.

"Ready the horses!" Sorea called. "Knights, to your places. Sarskil, have your Dwarves raise their mantlets and prepare weapons."

While the Knights moved into position to the far right of the field, the Dwarves pulled up their mantlets—wooden defensive positions serving as portable fortifications. Like stoova shields, these mantlets had large spikes at the bottom to hold them in the ground and two slanted legs to avoid tipping over. There was an open slit in the middle to allow crossbow fire. Their work took a somber tone as they listened to the death wails and vain pleas from the Rebelde Plains warriors being massacred over the hill.

"Sorea, shouldn't we help?" a Knight asked.

Sorea glared angrily. "The deserters? No, we have to hold this line. If not, the Western Elves will storm the rear of the Allies and *all* our friends die."

For several more painful moments, they listened as their former Allies were slaughtered.

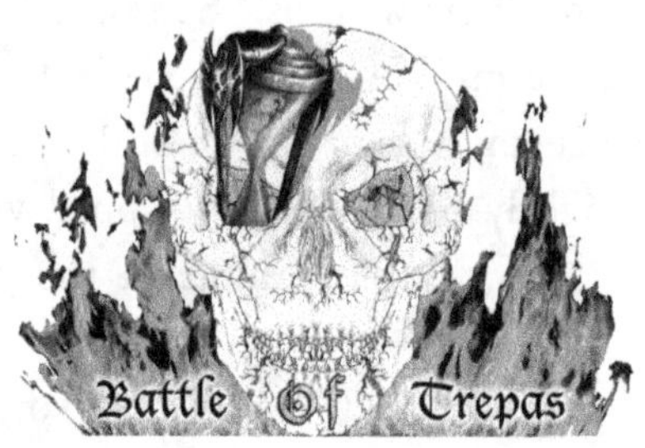

Scroll 9: The End of the Beginning

Back at the main battle, the retreat had been most costly to the Vioma Dwarves. They would have been routed save for the fact Veneficus called a halt.

"What are you thinking? We have them on the run, and the Western Elves are nearing the rear of their lines!" Lidenskap thundered.

"Have you learned nothing today?" Veneficus asked. "Who knows what surprises await? My Magicians and griffins were massacred. You'll have no air support for the rest of the battle."

"That will be a big change," Piscinian Emperor Fanga declared sarcastically.

Veneficus glared but continued, "It's only a matter of time before the Eaglians and dragons reappear, and Friar has been ten steps ahead all day. We should retreat."

"I wanted to retreat earlier," Princess Hamaza said. "However, we have them on the run, and a numerical advantage. They went through the siege engines, so I doubt there's a trap. With the Western Elves coming from the south, we can finish this. If we wipe out the Knights, the rest will come to our side. Then, the Proliate can rout the Dark Warriors like they did before."

Lidenskap nodded approvingly.

"To victory!" King Tarha shouted.

"My troops lie shredded. I'm leaving," Veneficus said, running to Runor. After galloping a short distance, the magnificent Pegasus bounded into the air.

"Archers, fire!" Lidenskap howled, his eyes awash in rage and hunger for revenge. "The rest, rush through the siege engines and reform lines. I don't trust going around the sides."

The auxiliary archers fired while the Confederates moved towards the siege engines. Friar had redeployed his troops to get better match-ups. He now had the Vioma Dwarves on the far-left flank. They were followed by the tough Saatana division and Knights to absorb the sarissa spears of the Proliate. The Elves of Creber would match up against the monstrous warriors of Ager and Piscinian remnants. He had placed his cavalry on the far-right flank in hopes they could overwhelm the fragile Southern Dwarves and Piscinians, rolling up the entire edge of the Confederate line.

TABLE EIGHT Battle of Trepas

~~Dead/destroyed~~ *Reduced number* ***Out of the Battle***

Allies		**Confederacy**	
Knights of Liberum:	*4,150*	**Proliate Red Guard**	
Knight Cavalry:	*1,050*	(a corp + survivors):	*13,450*
(lightly armored from all three castles)		***Proliate Silver**	
~~**Rebelde Plains:**~~	~~0~~	**(other side of the pass):**	***10,000**
Eaglians:	*1,100*	**Piscinians:**	
Knights of Toil Shaor:	*3,750*	**Retiarian Division:**	*650*
(led by Veli Pingius)		**Suoli Division:**	*1,350*
Northern Dwarves:		**Warriors of Jaa:**	*2,350*
Vioma Division:	*5,000*	**Southern Dwarves:**	*200*
(Green)		**Ager:**	*6,500*
Saatana Division:	*4,500*	**Proliate Red Guard-from**	
(Red)		**the north:**	*7,500*
Vasama Division:	2,000	~~**Magicians:**~~	~~0~~
(Blue)		~~**Griffins:**~~	~~0~~
Rebelde Plains Dwarves:	400	**Western Elves-from south:**	12,500
(skilled in prestidigitation)		**Auxiliary archers:**	*900*
Elves of Creber	*6,500*		
Vioma Dragons with Aer Ridire	*500*		
Total:	**28,950 (24,100 dead)**		**(45,625 dead) 45,400**

Figure 17: Battle of Trepas ICON IV: Friar realigns his forces after the complete collapse of the Rebelde Plains contingent. A large group of squires are left vulnerable to Confederate Archers.

Arrows from the auxiliary troops of the Proliate rained down on the squires. With no armor, a fifth were instantly killed and many more injured. Thinking quickly, the Elves of Creber stepped forward to return fire—their powerful arrows quickly overwhelming those of the Proliate.

"We can't match their archers," King Tarha of Ager said.

"I concur," Lidenskap said before yelling, "Double time through the siege engines! Kill them all!"

With loud battle cries the Confederate army quickened their pace through the siege engines while the tattered remnants of the auxiliary archers withdrew.

"Courage!" Friar yelled to the shaken and injured squires. He winked at a few of the squires holding the torches. "Squires of Liberum, you will stand and fight!" Several stood despite having arrows in their legs.

The Confederate army began emerging through the siege engines.

"Light the arrows?" a young squire questioned. His eyes darted back and forth between the equally terrifying army in front and his dead and dying friends all around.

"Hold," Friar commanded as healers and other squires moved forward to help pull back the wounded.

Ritari appeared on Musta-Yo. "Stand firm. We're asking you to be Knights before your time. Hold your position and remember your training!"

Friar smiled. Like all great leaders, Ritari demanded respect while radiating calming competence. Once half the Confederate army was through, Friar yelled, "Light arrows and fire!"

At first, the sight of the squires loading arrows was unimpressive. However, once the flaming arrows found their mark—siege engines presoaked in naphtha—the horror started. The wooden machines exploded into flames. The Confederate soldiers unfortunate enough to be moving through them were engulfed in a flash of fire as it roared and quickly spread.

"Get behind our lines," Friar instructed. Visions of the advancing Western Elves gleamed, and he wondered if that would be safe. Nodding to the other leaders, he ordered, "Fire!"

The Elves of Creber unleashed their arrows, and the Vioma Dwarves their bolts. Those Confederates who had already passed through the siege engines had been in tight ranks with shields interlocking. However, as their burning comrades stumbled forward, their lines broke and the scene turned into pandemonium, made worse by the shower of projectiles ripping into them.

"Kill the burning soldiers!" Lidenskap ordered as the flaming stumbled forward. The unscathed soldiers glared at him. "We need to put them out of their misery!" he bellowed defensively. "Naphtha can't be extinguished."

Just then, a massive soldier of Ager, engulfed in flames, ran blindly towards the Proliate. He flopped onto several warriors who instantly had the greasy naphtha splatter on them. "Ease their suffering and save ourselves for Tallcon!" Using their spears, the Proliate began killing anyone burning who came towards them.

Those Confederate soldiers who had not yet started through the siege engines were ordered around the edges to avoid the flames. With the screams of their fellow soldiers to spur them on, they ran as fast as possible towards the end of the siege engines. As they rounded the corner, a volley of arrows and bolts welcomed them. The heart-wrenching screams of those burning alive mixed with the cries of those falling under the barrage of arrows, creating a surreal nightmare.

"Sacrilege!" Lidenskap yelled, his face contorting in outrage. He pointed his blood-red sword towards the Knights and their Allies. "You have no honor!" Taking off his helmet, he looked to the sky as if literally expecting immediate retribution.

A mocking chuckle ran through the ranks of the Knights.

"Steady, Knights," Friar instructed as Lidenskap's eyes widened further.

"Who knew someone's eyes could get that big?" one of the Knights mused.

Despite himself, Friar chuckled, trying to disguise it by rubbing his mouth as another laugh ran through the ranks of the Knights.

"Tallcon serves us the honor of recapturing his glory on earth," Lidenskap said. "Reform our lines. Victory for Tallcon!"

Friar smiled. *Yes, throw your troops into defeat.*

"Tallcon!" the Proliate shouted, moving efficiently. The other Confederate armies moved with less cohesion and determination after enduring the myriad of blistering shocks.

Lidenskap once again turned towards the Knights. "You will dieeeee!"

"Thanks for the update. I thought we were immortal," a Knight yelled to a fresh round of laughter.

Ritari had dismounted, leaving his horse with squires. "Their rage is good for our plan." Friar nodded but kept his gaze on the enemy.

The Western Elves will be coming any minute, and then we shall rescue victory! Lidenskap thought.

The Confederate troops had been significantly thinned by fire and arrow.

"If Sorea and the Vasama can hold off the Western Elves, we're now evenly matched." Friar commented.

"More importantly, we control the air," Ritari added.

"Yes, we have the air," Friar echoed.

The Confederate armies formed ranks and interlocked shields against the Allied arrows. Suddenly, something caught the attention of Ritari. A hulking figure, even amongst the large troops of Ager, was wildly swinging his pole flail and calling out to Ritari.

"Campesino," Ritari hissed.

"I believe, my captain," Friar said, "you're being challenged."

"First Mester and now mountain-boy?" Ritari replied.

"Better you than me," Friar said with a laugh.

"Let me kill him!" Luchar howled.

"I got this," Ritari said, running to be opposite the enormous figure.

Just then, Lidenskap yelled, "Charge!"

The wind changed, and the warriors on both sides had their nostrils fill with the sickly smell of charred flesh. The Elves of Creber fired one last volley before drawing weapons—many choosing the longer reach of their five-foot wooden staffs. The Knights' cavalry rode ahead, smashing into the remaining Southern Dwarves and Piscinians. Attacking the outer edge, the cavalry forced the Confederate flank to turn left. As the two infantries exploded together, the Elves of Creber almost instantly overwhelmed the reeling Southern Dwarves and Piscinians, and the whole left flank of the Confederates was in danger of folding.

The opposite was true at the other end. Lidenskap and his Red Guard were fighting ferociously, fueled by hatred and lust for bloody revenge. The Vioma Dwarves were having trouble withstanding their charge, slowly being pushed back. The fiercest fighting was in the center where the Saatana Division of the Northern Dwarves and the Knights of Liberum were holding their own against the immense sarissa spears utilizing Sorea's new strategies.

To the right of center a space for Ritari and Campesino was carved out—this time from necessity. Campesino was flinging his spiked pole flail so wildly several of his own men were knocked senseless. Ritari maintained distance, circling with his new spear.

Even the deepest injection of energy from rage transmutes to fatigue, Ritari thought, biding his time. Seeing an opening, Ritari managed to hook and flip the chain of Campesino's weapon around the end of his spear before tugging. Campesino instinctively pulled. Feeling Campesino heave, Ritari instantly sprinted towards him. With Ritari's resistance removed and his own momentum tugging rearward, Campesino stumbled backwards into the sea of onlookers. Ritari kept pushing with his spear until Campesino lost grip of his pole flail. Seizing the opportunity, Ritari jerked his spear backwards before quickly flinging it straight towards Campesino. The large man moved sideways but the spear tip gashed his side. Campesino howled in pain while reaching for his sword.

Ritari's momentum propelled him forward, his chest smashing onto Campesino's arm just as he was drawing his sword. The strength of the warrior from Ager was obvious as he lifted the Knight up, flipping him over his head. Ritari dropped his spear while hurtling over the giant man. Ritari landed hard on his head before flopping on his stomach, flinging off his helmet and gasping for air. He drew his sword just in time to deflect a vicious downward blow from Campesino.

Ritari struggled to cope with a barrage of blows—each one sending pain up his arm. A vicious strike disarmed the still-downed Knight. In desperation Ritari kicked at Campesino's knee. It buckled, and Campesino paused long enough for Ritari to draw his dagger before surging, forward slicing his left calcaneal tendon.

His calf muscles now detached from his heel, Campesino howled in pain, hopping on his one functioning leg while blood surged from the other. Ritari scampered forward, trying to sever the tendon on the other leg, when Campesino brought his massive elbow down on Ritari's back, knocking the air from his lungs as he plummeted to the earth with a *thud.*

Campesino flopped down, quickly placing the stunned Knight in a brutal chokehold. Ritari quickly gave up pulling on the massive, unmovable arm squeezing his neck. "It's good night for you, princess," Campesino whispered. "Don't worry. I'll fill you with pain before killing you."

Lights began to flicker in Ritari's eyes and with failing strength he plunged his dagger deeply into Campesino's arm. The big man howled and released Ritari. The Knight rolled away, sputtering for air.

Campesino pulled the dagger out and tossed it at Ritari, knowing he would have trouble standing on one leg. The Knight calmly caught it and, still struggling for air, lunged at the downed warrior.

Campesino's hulking arms flailed wildly as Ritari repeatedly skewered them until they went limp. Ritari sat on his abdomen as Campesino's arms, each littered with dozens of stab wounds, could do nothing but lie on the earth and bleed. With lightning speed Ritari riddled the gigantic warrior's chest and head with dagger strikes. Long after life had escaped, Ritari continued the barrage.

"He's dead, Captain," a Knight yelled as several others pulled him off. Chaos erupted as the temporary truce ended, skirmishes breaking out all around them. Ritari, and the Knights helping him, quickly found themselves fending off dozens of Agerian attackers. Luchar and a group of Knights quickly rallied forward, allowing Ritari to move behind the lines.

Scroll 10: Floating Lights are People Too

The rumor all over the Citadel is the Magicians and griffins took an absolute beating, Jumeaux thought nervously, traipsing to Veneficus' office.

Is he mad at me? Is it my fault? Have I not been training hard enough? Should I have gotten more information from Gimelli? For the first time, there were several Proliate guards outside Veneficus' door.

"This the one he's expecting?" one asked the others.

"Yeah, that's Jumeaux," another replied. After knocking, the guard opened the door.

"Oh, look—it's wonder-boy!" a Valo said, snickering.

"Oh, yes," another Valo added. "It's a *wonder* someone so annoying is still alive."

"He's not annoying," a third uttered, "when he's somewhere else, at least!"

"Hey, that gives me an idea," the first Valo said. "If we pledge to miss you, will please go somewhere super far away?"

"I assume you've heard of our defeat?" Veneficus asked somberly, ignoring the Valo.

"People are talking about it," Jumeaux replied.

"I see. 'People' are talking about it. Do you think we are chopped liver or something?" a Valo asked. "Just because we're floating, glowing heads without bodies we aren't 'people?' We have no rights or value? Is that what you think? Is that what you're saying?"

"Uh," Jumeaux started, but Veneficus cut him off.

"Did you also know Dark Warriors are attacking Temple Palvoa in the east?"

"I hadn't heard that."

"Jumeaux, the world is bleeding into chaos. I'm grateful for all you have done. However, now more than ever I need you to be my bridge to Bellae. Whatever the cost, *we* must end up with the Macht Crystals. We can't afford to run out of mindre crystals, especially with more battles looming."

"I'll do my best," Jumeaux said, smiling at the compliment while several Valo mockingly mouthed his words.

"I trust you will. Together, we must salvage the world. Make sure you do not fall behind in your classes, but I'll accelerate your lessons in the Magical Arts."

Jumeaux beamed.

Veneficus smiled back. "That's how important you are to our mission, and the future of our Magician way of life."

"Wow, boss, you do realize that if you pump up his ego any more, his head will be weighted to the floor?" a Valo mocked, chuckling.

"Will there be a room big enough for his overblown and expanding self-esteem?" another asked.

Veneficus stood up, eyes blazing, and the Valo retreated. One muttered, "Were those insults or descriptions?"

"I know," the first Valo whispered. "It's not our fault if those totally true statements were inconvenient truths."

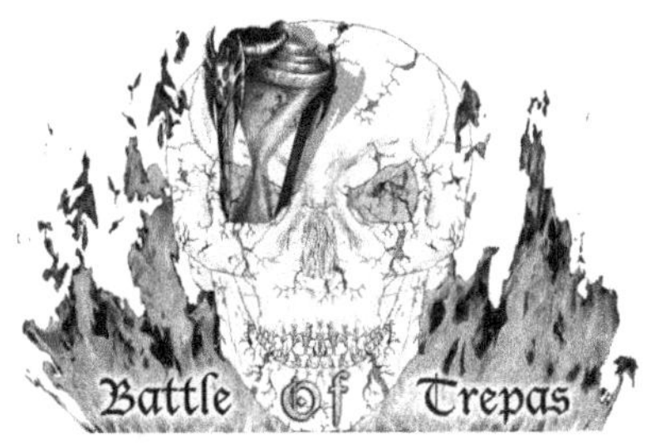

Scroll II: Hole of Death

The left flanks of both armies were in serious trouble of folding. The Knights' cavalry and the Elves of Creber were mauling the left end of the Confederates. The cavalry had surrounded the flank and was attacking from the rear. The Southern Dwarves and the Piscinians were wiped out, and Jaa was not far behind. The Elves used their staffs to smash the Jaa Warriors' Ko stones, which had been thought unbreakable.

On the Allies left flank the already battered Vioma Dwarves were being pushed back by the possessed fighting of the Proliate led by General Lidenskap. If they were turned back, the whole Allied line would be in jeopardy, despite the success on the opposite end.

"Where are the dragons?" Friar screamed, managing to pull back enough from the fighting to message his signalers.

Within minutes, the Vioma Dragons and Aer Ridire arrived. The flames of the dragons and bolts from their riders scoured the backs of the Proliate. In true military discipline, despite the odds of fighting so many dragons, the Proliate divided their lines, half turning to face the dragons.

Fierce squawking shattered the air as the entire force of Eaglians poured into the warriors of Jaa and Ager. The Confederate warriors were no match for an air assault from behind, and their numbers quickly fell. Princess Hamaza began creating a kuollut surrender flag. Her loyal soldiers died around her as she flipped the blue flag of Jaa upside down. The white Inukshuk and green waves looked odd inverted. Tearing part of her white undershirt, she tied it to the flag.

"Hurry, princess!" one of the warriors cried before being shredded across her face and chest by Eaglian talons. The sharp claws easily sliced through the tough Ko stones on her helmet and flayed open her chest.

In the south, the black flags of the Western Elves began cresting the hill. They had finished slaughtering the retreating warriors from the Rebelde Plains. As the flags continued to rise, the 12,500 Elves in their black and gold armor became visible. Their long bows were out with fearsome seven-foot halberds on their backs.

"That's a whole lot of Elves," Sorea said.

"Outnumbered a mere twenty to one? More for us to kill," Sarskil laughed.

Sorea felt exposed, having deferred the high ground in favor of the flat plain to allow the use of her sidus heulwch.

"Get ready with the sun stars. Make sure the grenades are behind the mantlets. I'm sure they—" Sorea was cut off by a barrage of arrows from the Western Elves.

The arrows riddled into the mantlets. Since there were not enough to cover everyone, the ranks of the already outnumbered Allies began to thin. Even though she had more tricks up her sleeve, Sorea knew they couldn't hold out for long against such a large force. As soon as the arrows stopped, a raucous clamor of shaking weapons came from the Western Elves as they brandished their long halberds—their tips ending in a weighted spear and axe blade.

"Get to the horses!" Sorea yelled. She had hooked three of her sidus heulwch onto teams of horses to be drawn across the battlefield. As the Western Elves plunged down the hill, she signaled them to pull the machines out. The rows of crossbows on the rotating cylinders began to move across the flat plain. Before they could get far, the Western Elves' arrows eliminated the Knights and horses of the first team. Several squads of Vasama Dwarves hurried over with crossbows to provide some cover for the second and third teams of Knights as the Western Elves continued to advance.

"Unleash lightning!" Sorea yelled. The Dwarves behind the mantlets readied the Lightning Line grenades she had developed, consisting of a twine net encasing a ceramic pot and wick. A rope handle attached to the netting to allow the pots to be thrown long distances.

Each pot contained ninety percent white phosphorous and ten percent naphtha. The Dwarves lit the wicks before hurling them. As the ceramic pots shattered, showers of red-hot shards extended like deadly flowers, spraying their venomous contents followed by white smoke. Screams of pain took flight as the Western Elves were splattered by the savage blend. Two-handed halberds meant no shields to fend off the deadly spray, which burned through armor and skin while providing a smoke screen for the Knights and Dwarves.

The two remaining teams of horses were moving again, still under fire from a few Western Elves remaining on the hill. They managed to hit the third team of Knights and one of the horses firing indiscriminately through the smoke screen of the grenades.

Sorea grabbed a few Knights to disconnect the dead horse and get the team moving again. Just as they started, a barrage of arrows rained down, instantly killing the remaining horses. All Knights, including Sorea, were hit. The arrow seared trough her leather chest plate, digging into her lung. Gasping, she fell.

"Get the...other...going," she said breathlessly. With each exertion blood gushed out of her chest wound. She crawled under the sidus heulwch and lost consciousness.

The only mobile sidus heulwch came to a stop as the Western Elves emerged through the smoke. The Dwarves fired the massive volley of bolts into the Elf lines. The crank turned to get the unfired crossbows into position, firing rapidly two more times, each round dropping large wedges of Western Elves.

The last of the Lightning Lines were thrown, and the Vasama Dwarves moved their last secret weapons, the Dragon Flame, into position. The flamethrowers used manual pumps to power the naphtha out of a narrow nozzle. A burning wick was placed in the path of the spray to start the stream on fire. When the Elves were thirty feet away, all four machines began belching huge flames with devastating effect on the front lines. Bellows of pain rose up from those coated in the burning, sticky residue.

However, the containers of naphtha were quickly depleted, and the overwhelming force of Elves neared the vastly outnumbered Allies. With no retreat possible, the remaining Dwarves and Knights formed up, bracing for impact from the Elves running downhill.

At the main battle, the few remaining Jaa Warriors quickly drug Princess Hamaza away from the battlefield. The Eaglians, seeing the kuollut, let them go to turn on the men of Ager. Their immense size and power, combined with the long reach of the pole flails, managed to keep the Eaglians at bay—several ended up with broken talons attempting to tear into the agrarian warriors.

The Knight cavalry began bearing down on the rear of the Ager lines. The Elves of Creber were attacking from the side while the Knights battled them from the front. The combination was too much, even for the imposing men of Ager. With the Southern Dwarves and Piscinians completely wiped out, and the few remaining warriors of Jaa fleeing north, the entire Confederate line was being rolled up and annihilated. The Saatana Dwarves were thinning their forces to avoid being cut off from the Vioma Dwarves, who were being thrown back by the rugged Proliate.

Figure 18: Battle of Trepas ICON V. The right flank of the Allied army is causing the Confederate's left side to fold.

A blue orb floated up to Lidenskap. “High Commander Storlax and I command you withdraw immediately, or your entire army will be destroyed. I have horrifying news! We just learned…” Lidenskap’s face contorted in horror as he listened to Veneficus’ message.

Lidenskap seethed. His well-trained Proliate were close to overrunning the Vioma Dwarves, despite the dragon attacks. He could see the stalemate in the center of the line between the Knights and Saatana Dwarves against the sarissa spears. He was not able to discern how the battle on the far flank was progressing. Looking over the battle lines, he could see the Western Elves about to overrun the measly force Friar had placed before them. *Victory is ours!*

“Destroy the Dwarves!” he yelled, lunging forward.

At that moment, a fresh group of dragons descended upon the Proliate from above and behind. Wave after wave of dragons plunged upon the Proliate lines. After several rounds of relentless attacks, the Red Guard were in serious trouble.

Being attacked on three sides by cavalry, griffins, Elves of Creber, and Knights of Toil Shaor, the men of Ager were compressed, unable to wield their pole flails, and completely annihilated. Friar turned to see the Western Elves slamming into the overwhelmed force of Knights and Vasama Dwarves.

As the last warrior from Ager fell, Friar dispatched the Elves of Creber, Knight Cavalry, and Eaglians to help Sorea.

“Ritari, go with the cavalry,” Friar instructed. “You take command.”

“Crebers against Western Elves? This should be interesting,” Ritari said.

“I wouldn’t bet against our allies,” Friar said.

Ritari joined the cavalry, charging south with the nimble Elves of Creber right behind and Eaglians soaring overhead.

“Knights and half of the Elves, to the western flank. Eaglians and the other half of the Elven army, to the east!” Ritari yelled.

The Elves of Creber split their forces with Kempe leading half and Ailante taking charge of the other. The overwhelming forces of the Western Elves were busy cutting down the Dwarves and Knights and caught off guard when the Knight Cavalry and Eaglians slammed into them. The shock was temporary but long enough to allow a significant number of the Western Elves to be cut down.

"Knight cavalry, disengage and slip behind the Western Elves," Ritari ordered.

The cavalry maneuvered around and began shredding the back Western Elf lines. Ritari began hacking his way forward when Herra Isanta, greatest of the Western Elf warriors, pointed her long halberd at him. "Ritari!"

Do I have a target on my chest plate? Ritari wondered, dismounting. Out of nowhere a Western Elf came charging at him from the side. Moving with lightning speed, Herra Isanta used her halberd to block the blow.

Nodding, Ritari smiled at the beautiful warrior. "Thanks."

She had long, sleek black hair that matched her dark eyes. Smiling back, she said, "I want to make you suffer before dying by *my* hands."

"I formally retract my thank you," Ritari said, as another impromptu ring of spectators formed.

She instantly began a blistering array of spinning attacks with her halberd—the weapon moving faster than Ritari could have imagined. Backpedaling, he did his best to deflect the windmill attacks. For seemingly no reason, she stopped, turning her back to him. Stunned, Ritari momentarily froze.

Suddenly, she exploded up into the air. With amazing finesse she did a back flip and spun around, slicing her halberd down with brutal force. Ritari managed to bring his sword up, but the force of her blow slammed it down while the spiked bottom of her halberd ripped into his chest, grating a scar in the panther head armor—sending pain shooting across his torso.

Another jumping and spinning move followed, but this time the axe blade split the panther head relief on his chest plate down the middle, gashing into his flesh deeply enough to draw blood but not break his sternum. Ritari was backpedaling faster, trying to catch his breath against the searing pain from the laceration. The two warriors moved away from the main battle, losing their spectators.

Meanwhile, the Knight cavalry continued gashing the back lines of the Western Elves. The diminished but still lethal Vasama Dwarves were putting up a brutal fight from the front. The Eaglians had landed behind the Western Elf line. With their swords slicing and talons shredding, they fought fiercely alongside the Knight Cavalry.

Ritari was just starting to get his breath as Herra Isanta caught him. Ritari tripped on a dead Dwarf, flailing backwards and losing his sword. Thinking quickly, he arched into a backwards roll, barely standing up before she was on him. Her halberd smashed down on his right forearm and hand, splintering his vambrace. His hand and arm screamed in pain as he stumbled backwards. One of her halberd blows flayed open the left side of his head and ear. Still struggling to breathe, pain screamed from all over his body as he crashed into a sidus heulwch.

"Can I tell you what a pleasure it is to kill you?" Herra Isanta smiled radiantly.

"Honestly, I'm not at my best. It's been kind of a rough day. Perhaps we could postpone?" Ritari quipped.

Herra Isanta smiled. "I don't think so. My only regret is that you will not live to see every Knight slaughtered."

Her face contorted in rage as she raised the halberd. Screaming, she lunged forward as a crossbow bolt sank into her throat. Herra Isanta's rage cascaded to shock as her weapon dropped. Ritari instinctively grabbed an object tossed towards him. He stared in wonder at Sorea's beak weapon. Quickly, he repeatedly jabbed the sharp edge into Herra Isanta's chest. The blade penetrated deeply, several thrusts searing into her heart. Blood shot out of her mouth, and pink froth squirted from the hole in her trachea. Ritari quickly found himself covered in blood as Herra Isanta fell forward, grasping desperately at Ritari before life passed from her and she collapsed.

Ritari bent down to see Sorea lying on the ground under the sidus heulwch, an arrow piercing her chest.

"Oh, man!" he said, seeing the arrow in her chest.

"Actually…woman," she managed.

"Ah!" he said in disgust, worry consuming him.

"I should've…taken the…high ground," she panted.

"Worry about that later! Right now you need a healer!" he roared.

"You…look…like shit." She motioned him closer. "You've had…

kind of…a rough day? Is that…the best you…could…come up with?" she whispered before passing out.

After checking her pulse, he sprinted towards the battle, yelling wildly for Aquila.

The Eaglian quickly descended next to him, covered in blood, his talons decorated with various body parts and gristle of those unfortunate enough to stand against him. "We'll soon have the day."

"No time. Sorea's hit and needs a healer!"

Without a word Aquila was in the air, gently grabbing her before heading to their southern camp where the majority of the healers were. Ritari watched until the two were safely away before sprinting back to the battle. Realizing he only had Sorea's beak weapon, he slowed. Removing his mangled vambrace, he sucked in air at the deep cut and bruise, but it did not appear broken. He found the sword of a dead Vasama Dwarf and rushed into the fight.

As he arrived, the last of the Dwarf Special Forces and original Knight Infantry fell. The Western Elves couldn't celebrate, finding themselves surrounded on bloodied ground, littered with dead Knights, Dwarves, and their own comrades. They quickly formed a defensive square as the Knights of Toil Shaor and a few of the Vioma Dragons diverted to help joined the fight.

Forced into a compact space and tripping on bodies or slipping on blood and guts, the Western Elves were quickly slaughtered until there was but one cowering Elf left, trembling in filthy golden silk. His ornate jewelry was so smothered in dirt and blood that they looked like warty sores instead of precious gems.

"What should we do with him?" one of the Knights asked.

"This would be good," Ailante said, driving the beak of his kama weapon into the back of the leader's neck. Bondi's head shot up, his eyes spread wide. Spurts of blood shot up around his head just before his body crumpled to the ground.

"Friar should have decided his fate," Ritari said.

"He needn't be bothered," Ailante replied calmly.

"Remind me never to make you Elves of Creber angry," Ritari commented.

With the Western Elves obliterated, the Knights, cavalry, Elves of Creber, Eaglians, and Vioma Dragons headed north towards the main battle site. As they neared, they paused at the horrific scene. Outlined by the burning siege engines was a scene of apocalyptic agony. The entire field was littered with dead and dying. There were occasional clusters where the bodies formed large mounds of slaughter.

"We found hell," Ailante said as they approached the last small pocket of fighting. A small group of Proliate had formed up around General Lidenskap, who was completely surrounded.

Lidenskap raised the kuollut flag for surrender—the once-proud flag of the Proliate—tied upside down with a white garment above it.

TABLE NINE Battle of Trepas

~~Dead/destroyed~~ *Reduced number* ***Out of the Battle***

Allies		**Confederacy**	
Knights of Liberum:	*3,500*	**Proliate Red Guard**	
Knight Cavalry:	*950*	(a corp + survivors):	*3,000*
(lightly armored from all three castles)		***Proliate Silver**	
~~Rebelde Plains:~~	~~0~~	**(other side of the pass):**	***10,000**
Eaglians:	*925*	Piscinians:	
Knights of Toil Shaor:	*3,000*	~~Retiarian Division:~~	~~0~~
(led by Veli Pingius)		~~Suoli Division:~~	~~0~~
Northern Dwarves:		~~Warriors of Jaa:~~	~~few~~
Vioma Division:	*3,500*	~~Southern Dwarves:~~	~~0~~
(Green)		~~Ager:~~	~~0~~
Saatana Division:	*3,750*	~~Proliate Red Guard from the north:~~	~~few~~
(Red)			
~~Vasama Division:~~	~~0~~	~~Magicians:~~	~~0~~
(Blue)		~~Griffins:~~	~~0~~
Rebelde Plains Dwarves:	400	~~Western Elves from south:~~	~~0~~
(skilled in prestidigitation)		~~Auxiliary archers:~~	~~0~~
Elves of Creber	*5,500*		
Vioma Dragons with Aer Ridire	*350*		
Total:	**21,875 (31,175 dead)**		**(78,025 dead) 13,000+**

"Allied troops, retract!" Friar yelled using the enchanted Huuto. The surrounded Proliate maintained their guard as the Allied army backed away. Friar walked, motioning for General Lidenskap to follow.

As they moved away, a small, but shrinking, seed in Friar hoped for negotiation.

"Aren't you the hero?" Lidenskap ranted.

Not good, Friar thought. "As you can see, no Dark Warriors fought with us," Friar said once the two were out of earshot.

"How is it you are allowed to live?" Lidenskap asked in a reviled tone, ignoring Friar's statement. "I don't understand how Tallcon can let you commit such blasphemy. Your honorless life of deception and evil will come crashing down around you...soon."

"General, no one wins if we continue fighting. Both of us will be decimated if we continue this path."

Lidenskap spat. "Your words are as poisonous as your dishonorable actions. I would sooner fall on my sword than trust you."

"You declared war on *us*!" Friar said.

"For the greater good of Verngaurd! You and your allies must be stopped. The only thing I learned this day is that you have no honor!"

"It's wonderfully convenient that you speak of a code of 'honor' with your overwhelming numbers. Such etiquette is a luxury affordable only to those standing on a position of strength. If we had not resorted to this planning, or deception as you call it, I find it hard to believe that you would have had any trouble slaughtering us to a Knight. Is that the honor code you speak of?

"I will not stab a man in the back, but I will use every means at my disposal to win victory," Friar continued. "Just because I don't worship your god does not mean that I have a lesser conviction, or right, to victory. I care about keeping my Knights out of the grave. You're thinking of war too righteously. The victory today allows me to provide my troops with optimism. Hope, easy to tear down, hard to build. Give someone a little gift of it, and all things become possible. I did what I needed to win victory and secure hope."

Lidenskap's face curled in disgust. "Tallcon states that you cannot be a deceiver in only one part of your life. You are either trustworthy or you are not. This deficit is part of your character, and not something you can put on and take off. As you recite your well-rehearsed speech of justification, I hope you realize how deluded it sounds."

"Those who make the rules for battlefields do so because of some advantage of strength in numbers or weapons that they want to keep," Friar said, his voice rising. "Your righteousness is not a luxury those greatly outnumbered can afford. I assure you everything I have said is true. You declared war based on lies, yet I still offer a chance to reconcile. Let's not fall for the tricks of those who would drive us apart. Together, we need to fight the real threat, the Dark Warriors."

Lidenskap laughed. "You burned my troops alive, forced them to fall into traps too cruel for an animal, and unleashed an avalanche on my friends. You wield the black art of prestidigitation to constantly mislead us. Worst of all, you took the image of Tallcon and used it in blasphemy to get us to lower our guard."

As General Lidenskap recounted the list, Friar looked down. *If everything went according to plan, why do I feel so heinous?* "We were forced into this. I only want the safety and security of Verngaurd."

The general scoffed. "The ears are not as sharp as the other senses. My eyes see evidence of your deception everywhere—one that cost me fifteen regiments. You also managed to destroy the newly reformed armies of the Southern Dwarves, Piscinians, Jaa, the Western Elves, and Ager." His eyes seemed to lose their focus, drifting to the lost soldiers.

"Allow me to return the favor you once granted me," Friar said. "I offer you safe passage to the Citadel as long as you travel north through Jaa."

Lidenskap's eyes blazed. "My heart feels your crookedness. Veneficus himself informed me the Dark Warriors, led by the White Wizard himself, attacked and destroyed Temple Palvoa today. You created the perfect diversion for them. Drawing our forces here to divide and thin our troops so that you both could achieve victory. Another example of your deviousness, and yet you stand here, casting black words, trying to fool me once again?"

The look of disbelief of Friar's face was obvious. His knees felt weak, and he almost reached out to Lidenskap for support. *How did the Dark*

Warriors know to coordinate their attack? It can't be a coincidence. Friar's mind murmured, unable to verbalize a response.

"Save your performance. I don't doubt your acting skills, but I will never trust anything you say. You and your Dark Warrior friends coordinated attacks—full stop. I accept your gesture of safe passage. If I could go back, I would have killed you when I had the chance."

A chill went up Friar's spine, and all he could do was nod.

"I swear on Tallcon's blood, I will see every Knight, Northern Dwarf, Elf of Creber, and inhabitant of the Rebelde Plains boiled, tortured, and killed. Every one of you is going to die." Lidenskap said in a low, ominous voice before storming away.

Friar stood, stunned, hollow. *How did we end up here?*

Suddenly, a naked and painful glimpse of the future pressed itself against him. Visions of full-scale war on two fronts danced in front of his eyes. Battles, pain, blood, despair, isolation, all flashed in his mind. Emotionally drained, he turned and looked up at the sky, letting his eyes follow the circling scavenger birds, so patient, waiting to feast on the flesh of the dead and dying.

Friar ruffled his hair. *I should shave my head to match those circling vultures. Those who feast on the blood of others have no time for such fancy decoration, as hair, or feathers, upon our heads. Scavenging is just too messy.*

Aquila came screeching towards Friar, signaling him to prepare for pick up. Friar put out his arms and felt the brisk, forceful pull as Aquila's leathery talons encased his shoulders.

"Let's tour the battlefield. Sorea is at the healers. Good news—the tip didn't lodge in bone and did not detach from the shaft."

Friar nodded gratefully, knowing that if the arrowhead detached, exploratory surgery to find it could be deadly.

"After making an incision, the healers removed it with arrowhead forceps," Aquila said.

"The Spoon of Diocles forceps work better than the old wire loops," Friar added.

"With the amount of bleeding, they did cauterize it. Luckily, she passed out from the pain before that."

Friar closed his eyes, sucking in a breath as the Eaglian briskly shot up into the sky. The immense pressure of rising finally subsided. He extended his jaw to pop his ears while opening his eyes—instantly wishing he had not. The scenes of horror punched up Friar's motion sickness, and he dry heaved, bile searing up to scorch his esophagus and throat. Even high above the battlefield, the smell of death and charred flesh seared his nostrils and stained his brain.

In silence they drifted around the islands of raging fire, still devouring victims, traced by vast stretches of the dead and dying, all coated thoroughly in the red sacrifice demanded by battle. Tears of regret plaited with those of despair, falling in windswept paths into the searing heat of the raging naphtha flames below.

"It looks like the whole earth is on fire, surrounded by oceans of blood," Friar said shakily as tears continued streaming down his face while his soul ached at the destruction. A deep-seated feeling of betrayal joined his already frayed emotions.

"We were *pushed* into this after repeatedly trying to avoid conflict. No one endeavored harder than you," Aquila added.

"After this, are we Knighted or benighted?"

Aquila simply shook his majestic head.

Looking down at his red-splattered body, Friar said, "The blood will be hard enough to wash off, but it will disappear infinitely easier than the guilt and self-reproach that seems to have seared their way into my soul."

"Friar!" Aquila squawked. "If you hadn't planned this, the Proliate would have easily overrun us and we'd all be dead."

"Perhaps. However, I fear we have reaped nothing but a colossal crop of sorrow and misery."

"I guess the one bit of good news is the Watchers have stopped casting their magical net. Their presence would have sincerely altered the balance of power in the air," Aquila said.

"It's more likely they want us killing each other," Friar replied, the thought weighing down his trampled soul.

After Aquila set him down, Friar walked to where Luchar was standing over an Elf lying on his right side with a large gash ripping through his face. Both legs were crushed and lying in unnatural angles. The Elf's right eye, wide with terror and pain, glared into Luchar as his left arm reached up to grab for the Knight. Friar noted that Luchar did not look much better off. His helmet was gone with blood streaming from his bruised and battered head. His unrecognizable armor was damaged and dyed maroon.

"Luchar!" his new squire called out. With one hand on his knee, he breathlessly held up a water skin.

Luchar grabbed the squire by the cloak so forcefully his feet went off the ground a few inches and the water skin fell.

"Despite what they tell you, nightmares don't come from killing men that are trying to kill you. They come from seeing this!" Luchar let go, and the boy fell right in front of the dying Elf. Coughing, the Elf sprayed blood towards the boy. The young squire stood up so quickly he was greeted by lightheadedness and nausea, feeling like he was bobbing up and down on a sea of dead with waves of frothy blood crashing all around him. Panicking, he scampered straight into Friar, who had just finished yelling for a healer.

Friar held him tightly, feeling his shaking sobs and allowing his body to shield the boy's tears. Leaning down, Friar whispered, "Don't fret about crying. Battle always requires a cascade of tears, traveling from the battlefield, washing its way across notifications to loved ones and friends."

Standing upright, Friar continued, "The real tragedy of war is the loss of potential. That Elf will never hold his family, never see his children again. For each life lost a hole will travel through time, an empty spot where he or she would have walked and lived, that will press itself against loved ones like a cold wind. Sometimes at a celebration they will feel like they have forgotten something, perhaps misplaced an object. That is the hole of death.

"Battle's other tragedy is on those cursed to survive. Every one of us, every day of our lives, will walk with a weight of guilt and remorse around our necks. No one ever asks for such a burden. These feelings and thoughts are an unavoidable obligation that all warriors must bear. We'll help you work through it."

Friar continued holding the young boy while gazing around at the carnage. The survivors had the faraway looks of exhaustion and horror that Friar recognized from his youth. *Different war, different people… same look.* He stared into their wide, vacant eyes. "If you want to see how important hope, love, friendship, and routine are, you need only gaze into the face of someone who has had those necessities forcefully stripped from their life. Like overused wells in the desert, their vitality does not easily come back. The stupor of despair is all too happy to fill the void of a damaged spirit.

"Why don't you go help the other squires?" Friar suggested when the boy's sobs stopped.

Reluctantly, the squire shuffled off, avoiding the countless dead and dying.

"I'm pulling you out, Luchar. Once back at Liberum you're confined to the infirmary until I say otherwise."

"Not a chance."

"I'm *not* asking. Think of what you just said to that squire. I'm telling as a friend, and ordering as Friar, stand down. If you don't, you'll have battle brain. You know those former Knights who can hardly talk, much less think?"

Standing as tall as he could muster, Luchar roared, "I'm a Knight and I will fight. What else do you expect? There's nowhere to run, no safe places in Verngaurd. Liberum is a splinter of what it once was, and there is no one to replace me, even if you wanted to get rid of me."

"Luchar, I've been seeing personality changes…" Friar started.

"As long as I have breath, I will follow every command you give except one, to back off. I will stand and fight as long as I have the strength and there are battles to be fought. If you force me, I'll go off and stand on my own—taking on the entire Dark Warrior army."

The weight of the future truly set in. *Today was no end—just a beginning,* Friar thought. "Luchar, there's truth to your words. Where can anyone go to avoid this war? The reality? Nowhere. However, there's also what happened in the Way of Trepas."

"I don't have any excuses."

Friar nodded, but his gaze was down. "There's no glory in killing lest the trapper and hunter be famous. Glory comes from acting honorably, from being on the right side at the right time. There is honor in defending virtue and freedom, even if that means taking lives in battle." Friar surveyed the fiery bloodbath surrounding them. *Have the Knights become what we despised?* "Justice is treating people with civility. Courage without justice and temperance is brutal savagery."

Luchar's eyes suddenly rolled up, seemingly in a sarcastic way.

"That's…" Friar began harshly. He did not finish as Luchar's eyes rolled completely back into his head as his body spasmed violently. He crumpled to the ground, every part of him shaking in savage, rhythmic jerks punctuated by occasional tonic contractions.

"Healer! Now!" Friar yelled.

Ritari saw Luchar fall and motioned frantically to one of the healers who had just been brought up from the south by an Eaglian.

"I'm here!" Leigh, the healer who helped Lontas at the squire games, said breathlessly. *I hate being a healer in wartime. It's just starting, and I already feel like I'm drowning in a sea of blood and pain.* Reaching Luchar, he immediately rolled him on his side. Using a padded metal spreader, he forced leather in between his teeth and supported his head with a discarded satchel.

"Is he going to be okay?" Friar questioned when the convulsing stopped.

"He had a seizure," Leigh answered of the now-limp Knight. "He needs to rest and avoid getting his bell rung."

"Come on!" Ritari chided. "This is Luchar! If no one hits him in the head, he goes nuts and does it himself."

"What you do with my advice is out of my hands."

Luchar's body suddenly stiffened in a tonic rigor, his entire body shivering in tight trembles as he hissed a gurgling yelp.

"Can you stop it?" Friar asked.

Without answering Leigh took out a vial with a tiny dropper. Seemingly in slow motion he gradually timed several drops under Luchar's shuddering tongue.

"What's that?" Ritari asked as Luchar slowly stopped seizing.

"My personal recipe: valerian, mugwort, groundsel, lily of the valley, passionflower, mistletoe, chamomile, and blue skullcap—to name a few. He's going to sleep for a long time, so you can see about helping elsewhere," Leigh said, not appreciating the audience.

Ritari and Friar looked at each other, the full weight of exhaustion pressing down on them. The adrenaline rush of battle had long since drained away, exposing the myriad physical and mental cuts and bruises from the battle. The deeper cerebral and spiritual wounds were harder to discern but destined to last longer than the physical traumas.

"Hey, Ritari," Leigh shouted. "Make sure you have a healer look at your chest, head, and arm. You look like hammered crap."

Ritari nodded as the two began to wade in the foam of dead and dying—shuddering as wave after wave of screams and howls ebbed and flowed against ear and heart with equal ferocity.

Friar stopped. "It's after the battle, surrounded by great warriors laid bare by pain and fear, when the thin veneer of armor and bravado are stripped away to reveal our frail truth."

Ritari closed his eyes, wondering if the sights, sounds, and smells would ever be cleansed. Friar took out his sword and stared. The incriminating blood lining the blade served as a glaring reminder of his role in the death and misery sounding off around them. A few bright red dribbles of blood began fleeing down the blade as if trying to escape blame.

"Quite the day, my old friend," Friar said. "After this, we need to get the Knights and squires back home and into their daily grind."

"Agreed."

The two began organizing the Allies to deal with the dead and help the healers' triage those in need. A tug of war began as scavenger birds and beasts began pulling at any abandoned corpse. Some of the dead were placed in pits and covered while others were burned in large mounds.

"The last of the injured have been ferried down to the southern port by the Eaglians," Ailante said, fatigue obviously pushing down on him. Like all the Elves of Creber, he was feeling uneasy being out of their forest. Many of his Varna warriors were starting to feel the pangs of separation sickness from their birth trees.

"Thanks, Ailante," Friar said. "We appreciate your help."

It was pitch dark as the head Archerian walked back to his troops. The Elves had volunteered to take the night watch—they didn't figure on getting much sleep in the exposed plain anyway. Although unlikely, the Allies were prepared for a counterattack by the Confederacy or Dark Warriors. The heaps of burning dead still lit up the battlefield as the last of the supplies were loaded on carts to be taken to boats waiting in the south.

"General Orel," Friar said, exhaustion hanging from his words. "Thank you for your invaluable service. Your Eaglians fought with honor and distinction."

He nodded but said nothing.

"I have one last request for you. I need to get word to Baiulus and let him know today's outcome."

"What was the outcome?" Orel questioned sagely.

"In some ways, this didn't feel much like a victory, did it?" Ritari added.

With tears in his eyes Friar sobbed quietly, "No. No, it does not." He wiped them away before continuing. "Did we just save the Knights and Allies, or lose everything: wisdom, courage, temperance, justice, that makes us Knights?" *Perhaps only courage from our creed survived this day.*

Orel rolled his neck. "I did not mean to offend. In reality, we were force fed war."

Friar nodded. "Perhaps."

"We can hope your former squires ultimately save the day," Orel said.

Friar bristled at the use of "former" for his beloved squires. *I guess they are.* "Tell Baiulus we defeated the Confederates but suffered great losses and failed to unite anyone. Inform him Temple Palvoa fell into the hands of the Dark Warriors as well. We need to get a force to Castle Taiheart and empty their granaries and weapon stores."

"Are you sure you want to give up one of your last three castles?" Orel asked.

"What did you have in mind?"

"Let the Eaglians hold it. If we get in trouble, we fly away."

Ritari shook his head. "General, no one doubts your fierceness, but you are invaluable. It would be devastating to lose you and your noble army."

"We would gladly concede the stones of a castle and the dirt beneath it before you and your Eaglians," Friar added.

Orel nodded, pleased with Friar and Ritari's words. "I shall deliver the message."

The symphony of battle was entering its adagio, and only the scattered call of the dying remained from the formerly raging tempest. Above the physically lost bodies hovered something even more desperate and forlorn. Severed dreams and dismembered relationships hung over the field like a vile, translucent fog. Deceased before they had a chance to be fulfilled, a mist of hopes, wishes, and dreams swirled over every dead soldier. They lingered, fruitlessly longing for a second chance that would never come before reuniting with oblivion.

Tacet-Vand lowered his crosier that had been rendering them invisible as he and IleZuri walked away.

"I know you have witness countless battles, but that? Brutal," IleZuri said.

The Wizard nodded.

"Friar surprised us and the Proliate standing against him." IleZuri paused. "Did you see the Watchers and Nishi?"

The Wizard's eyebrows rose as he made several hand signals. IleZuri had become adept at reading the mute expressions and gestures of Tacet-Vand.

"Exactly," IleZuri said. "They're letting the countries of Verngaurd kill each other, then they'll swoop in. Soon, the time when you can speak again, the conclusion of Na Cearcaill nears."

Tacet-Vand nodded, tears jumping up to stare, trembling, from the ridges of his eyelids. IleZuri was just one of countless companions who had accompanied him through the millennia. Each Defender of the Wizard passed the knowledge of Tacet-Vand's curse onto the next.

"You have been waiting a long time for this, my friend," IleZuri said, trying to comfort his companion. "You've suffered this curse for too long, all for trying to do what's right."

The old Wizard began to sob. One way or the other, this was going to end. It had to. The curse that had forced him to mutely walk the earth for all eternity could finally cease.

"Your hex, just for standing up to Na Cearcaill, seems excessively cruel," IleZuri said. "The unnatural long life isn't bad, but the muteness is."

The wizened Wizard continued to shed tears but nodded and thought, *Scourged to silently drift the world and endure each successive Na Cearcaill.*

Unsure of what to say, IleZuri gently held the Wizard's shoulder. After a moment, he spoke, "I'm sorry for the death and destruction you have endured. I promise I will do everything I can to release you from your bane and the world from this cycle of destruction."

Nodding, Tacet-Vand took a deep breath.

Scroll 12: Cut off...

Within the Citadel, General Lidenskap said, "I beg your forgiveness, Storlax. I accept any punishment, including death." Laying his blood-red sword on the ground before him, he knelt before the Supreme Commander with head bowed.

Storlax gazed at the general with mixed feelings. Part of him knew Lidenskap must have sinned against Tallcon to have lost so horribly.

However, Veneficus had warned him that the general was essential for the future of Verngaurd.

"I was informed of what happened," Storlax said.

"I cannot believe Tallcon allowed Friar's treachery!"

"Tallcon is all powerful," Storlax paused, "yet we are his soldiers and have to think and act on his behalf. The pillar of providence props up the conqueror, obscures the preparation, and cheapens the commitment of the victorious while serving as a crutch for the defeated, ignoring their responsibility. Fate is a buttress to hold up and bear the weight of responsibility when the blame is on *our* lack of preparation combined with the intense deceit of Friar, HK, or whatever he goes by. It is not because of Tallcon, or fate, that we lost—we were outworked and should have toiled harder.

"Friar's more dangerous than we imagined. We will *not* underestimate him again. Veneficus mentioned Friar's ridiculous planning to pull off his duplicitous victory. This clarifies that he has been plotting against us for years." Storlax's closed eyes fluttered wildly, sending waves of concern beneath his eyelids as he tried to imagine the future.

"At least we destroyed the Knights from Taiheart and the Rebelde Plains warriors. We could easily take over both territories," Lidenskap said, relieved. Despite his earlier words, he had been fearful of retribution.

"The simple fact is that all armies of the Confederacy, except ours, lie near ruin," Storlax replied. "We are greatly weakened by the loss of so many veteran troops. Even without adding more territory, we are stretched thin. Every nation in the Confederacy is clamoring for protection from the Knights and Dark Warriors. This puts us in a dangerous situation."

Lidenskap sat down, sighing heavily.

"What are your recommendations?" Storlax asked.

Lidenskap, surprised Storlax would want his opinion after the disasters of Ovest and Trepas, said, "Smash the Knights. Not just for revenge, but to end that threat. Only then can we focus on the Dark Warriors."

"We'll leave many Confederate nations exposed, but I agree. These defeats taught us we must change tactics: expand the ranks of archers, increase the use of the sarissa spears, and find a way to deal with their air power. The griffins are only able to provide a delay in the Eaglian and dragon onslaught."

"We also need a diversion. We should fake attacks on the Elves and Dwarves, then smash Liberum," Lidenskap said.

"Cut off the head, Friar, and the Alliance will fall," said Storlax.

"Exactly! Friar Pallium has been the force behind the Allies all along."

"I'm beginning to think Veneficus was right about you," Storlax said. "He quelled my anger after our great losses, stating you were put into unpredictable and unwinnable positions. For Tallcon, it shall be done."

"For our fallen comrades and for Tallcon, Liberum shall fall and Friar die like the dog he is," Lidenskap added.

Chapter Three

Desert Dessert

Scroll 1: Lots and lots of...

"The sand goes on forever," Lontas said. After making their way through the Báis te Pass, Kainen had been guiding the League to find the location mentioned in the prophecy.

"There's certainly lots and lots," Gimelli replied, sweat dripping from her forehead while staining her back and axillae.

"Shouldn't we have seen something by now?" Sankari asked, ignoring the former squires' cheerful tones. "I mean the first oasis you led us to was a total waste of time."

"The Siwa Oasis should be up ahead," Kainen answered, his eyes searing into the map.

Bellae looked over the seemingly endless ocean of sand, missing her friend. "I hate that we left Crann."

"He's near the Giant Redwood forest and a stream," Kainen said. "He has everything he needs and would have taken too much of our water."

Bellae nodded, smacking her thirsty lips together but instantly regretting it. The parched skin clung mercilessly together. Her dried-up tongue offered little help in breaking them apart. Wincing from the pain, she carefully pried her lips apart with her fingers. The drying mucous clung onto the back of her tongue and throat, which felt like they were on fire.

The irony of the windswept landscape resembling water made her smile. The wind rolled over the sand, curling it like frozen, moistureless waves bobbing across the scorched and barren landscape.

"I can't believe the stupid first oasis, which we were off track on, so it took longer to find, was dry!" Sankari huffed. "Now we have way less, thanks to..."

"It was an accident!" Scelto said defensively.

"Accidentally dropping two large water skins could have happened to anyone," Kainen said. "Plus, there are so few landmarks out here having to back track to the first oasis was not in anyone's plan. Now we just need to get to the next and ration water until we do."

Bellae let out a low groan at the inevitable. The tacky white mucous slid down further on the back of her tongue, demanding she swallow. Closing her eyes against the upcoming sting, she bent her head forward and willed herself to gulp. She felt the singe and burn as her bone-dry throat rattled a painful swallow full of slicing, and ubiquitous, sand.

"Sand is finding places to chaff I didn't know existed," Lontas said, walking with a wide-based gait.

While a few chuckled, Sankari went off on how, as a Fairy, with delicate wings, everything was much harder for her. Bellae looked up at the Luminos and Phoebus suns and stopped. They hung low on the horizon of the western sky. Scanning around her, she saw no trees or buildings to dress-up the suns, giving the landscape an almost naked, abandoned appearance. The stark blue above was just as barren as the never-ending sand surrounding them. "Even the clouds have sought shelter somewhere else, far from the blistering suns," Bellae mumbled.

The feverish sand sent sweltering waves dancing up from the desert, which made the suns wobble, as if embarrassed at being so precariously exposed in the stripped-bare sky. In celestial isolation the suns self-consciously dashed for cover behind the flat horizon, their bashfulness growing across the skyline in blushed reds.

Kainen looked expectantly at Arend. "Do you want to fly ahead and check for the oasis?" Arend simply shook his head. The heat was particularly painful for his wings, which drooped like parched foliage.

"I'll go," Sankari volunteered. Her little wings buzzed into action, and she shot over the dune, disappearing. Soon the League heard muffled screaming.

"She's found it!" Kainen cried out hopefully. The idea of water and the oasis gave everyone a boost of energy. Scelto, Gimelli, Lontas, Kainen, and Arend took off through the unsteady sand, each step flinging it outwards, yet large amounts always discovered a path to stow away in confidential places. The extroverted sand had no sense of modesty and with total disregard for their privacy wormed its way into every nook and crevice of their bodies until each step was an abrasive, prickly reminder of its omnipresence.

The League crested the dune, letting out a collective sigh of disappointment. Sankari was yelling and kicking at a shriveled palm tree.

"You've got to be kidding me," Kainen gasped.

As they moved closer, they could see evidence that Siwa Oasis was once lush and green with several watering holes. Now, however, they were nothing more than moist sand.

"Now what?" Sankari lashed out.

Kainen held his head and sighed. The strain of leading the League was getting to him. "Okay, Siwa is bigger than it looks. Let's search for clues."

"Oh wow! Searching this sterile bed of crappy sand was totally worth our time and effort!" Sankari said. "I loathe—loathe, I tell you—sand! The highlight was finding a puddle of salt water! Good job, valiant 'leader.'"

"It's not Kainen's fault," Lontas interjected. "Oases sometimes dry up and because they are usually well below sea level, sometimes are polluted with salt water. You see…"

Gimelli gently grabbed Sankari before she could reach Lontas. "It's frustrating for everyone, but we had to try."

"Let's rest for few hours, then head towards Oasis Vastaus."

"What?" Sankari screamed. "You expect us…"

Bellae was sick of yelling, fighting, thirst, and sand. Marching in the desert was a heavier burden than she anticipated. With nothing to distract her eyes or mind but emptiness and sand her thoughts painfully reached out for Finn, Stralande, and her unknown family. As the shouting match raged behind her, something caught her eye on the edge of the dried-up oasis. Drawing closer, she let out a gasp. She knelt down next to the fascinating growth of pink-colored rosettes. When she gently touched what she thought was a rose petal, the surface was hard, almost sharp.

"It's a proliferation of minerals common here—a desert rose," Lontas informed. Sitting down next to her, he emptied the sand out of his boots, knowing they would instantly refill.

"Bellae, Lontas, do you want to get in on this?" Kainen pleaded. The two reluctantly joined the rest of the League. "The prophecy states we need an oasis. The first two in Calor are dormant, with no rocks that look like a crown, so that leaves Vastaus."

"Why even go?" Sankari asked. "It's probably dried up too."

"The Vastaus never dries out," Kainen answered.

"Then *why* we didn't start there?"

"We talked about this, Kari. You know what lives there."

"We're close to death because of ferratus lanx?" she screamed.

"Kainen's right to fear them," Lontas said. "They're an armor-plated beast that knocks you out with a catapult-like tail before impaling you on its spiked head and slowly digesting you."

"Ewww!" Gimelli and Bellae whimpered.

Kainen held out his hand as Sankari was about to protest. "Fly home or go with us to the Vastaus Oasis. Those are your choices."

Bellae woke up to screams from Grym and Borb, her head throbbing and mouth painfully dry. Her eyelids, coated with sand, were still fluttering in arid pain when she noticed the ten-legged creature crawling out of the sand. It was tan colored except for its enormous pincers, which were dark brown. Bellae couldn't help screaming into the cool desert night. She shot up with her two mice friends holding on for dear life as the others awoke.

"It's a kameli spider," Kainen said groggily. "Not poisonous."

"They are not actually spiders or scorpions," Lontas said. "Although it *looks* like they have ten legs, it's actually eight with two sensory appendages. They are also distinct from scorpions, as—"

"Oh, wow, Lontas. Thanks so much. I can't express to you how much that really helps!"

"Enough, Sankari. I fell asleep on my watch so it's good Bellae woke us up," Kainen informed. "We head southeast towards Vastaus."

"We'll be dead in a day or two," Arend said weakly. He shivered his large wings, sending a cloud of sand out before rolling his neck. The sand had wormed its way into his all his feathers, making every movement painful and he was too exhausted to preen.

"It would take even longer to get back to the Báis te Pass. If we stay here, we die," Kainen stated. The League ate a light snack of mushrooms and drank their painfully small allotment of water. Scelto kept up his morose silence despite Gimelli's attempts at conversation. "Stop beating yourself up for spilling the water. It could have happened to anyone."

He simply shook his head as they set off.

After walking into the early afternoon heat, everyone was having trouble concentrating. In the desert, thoughts themselves seemed to evaporate under the baking warmth. The heat was stifling and growing bolder by the minute. The desert sand added to the misery by radiating heat from below to match the ferocity falling from the suns. The desert air stung with choking fieriness, burning as it burrowed into the passageways of their lungs. The dry heat sponged any moisture from their noses and mouths, jealously hoarding the smallest dampness.

"Isn't it cool?" Lontas asked.

"Not sure what you are going to say, but probably not to anyone but you," Sankari said. "Also, 'cool' is a spiteful choice of words for those traveling in the desert."

"I meant how the desert air shimmers. It's almost like it's being forced into a wavy dance under the lash of the unyielding desert heat." Lontas' head bobbed side to side with the pirouette of the sizzling air.

"His brain's broke," Sankari huffed. "He's more loony than normal."

"Look! Look there!" Kainen yelled, his voice sputtering in withered brittleness.

"Not another mirage," Sankari whined. All of them had taken turns seeing ghostly images of the oasis in the waving heat.

"No, kameli tracks," Kainen answered.

"Ah, why should we care?" Sankari asserted.

"These are the same ones I saw around the Siwa watering hole. They will lead us right to the Vastaus. Even kamelis need to drink once in a while. Look how their tracks head off in that direction. We should change course and follow."

"That makes sense," Lontas said. "I was thinking we were drifting too far south."

"Wait, wait. How do you know it's the same kameli?" Gimelli asked.

"Kameli all have unique grooves on their toes, so you can identify them by checking their footprints. See how one stepped in poop? I can see the ridges."

"Disgusting and waaay too much information," Sankari said before grumbling about "know-it-alls" sprinkled with obscenities as the others wordlessly trudged after the kameli tracks. As they continued to walk in the desert, despair began to weigh down as much as the sultriness. The unforgiving heat and thirst gnawed on their thoughts and feelings as much as their physical beings. The thin coating of caring and camaraderie had been grated away by the caustic sand and heat all around them until their exposed nerves were raw.

"Uh oh." Kainen sighed as the first scattered sand projectiles started pelting off his rough skin under the beckoning of a howling wind. "Here we go again, and no cover in sight."

"Oh fun, another one!" Sankari said, fatigue pulling on her sarcasm.

"Everyone knows what to do," Kainen instructed.

With well-practiced efficiency, they got out their blankets and began the process of hunkering down. Silently, they watched the approaching sandstorm. An intimidating wall of sand eclipsed the entire horizon, roaring towards them. The top part was a relatively flat wall while the middle bulged out like a nose sniffing for prey. It was majestic, and humbling. The wind's shriek angrily increased as the hits of sand surged.

"Wrap up. Take cover," Kainen said as the bulge of the wall of sand started to arch over them. "Don't forget to wrap cloth around your face to shield your eyes and filter sand from your mouth."

"How does sand still get everywhere?" Sankari huffed.

"It's small and angry," Lontas said. *Reminds me of someone.*

Everyone but Arend tucked completely under their blankets in a huddle. He sat with his abused wings facing the storm, covering them as best as he could with his blanket as the tinging hits briskly increased their sting.

Bellae quickly jumped up and went to Arend despite Kainen's protests.

"There," she said through her swathed mouth after adjusting his blanket.

"Thank you," Arend replied.

"You're amazing, and we need you, so thanks," Bellae said.

Arend grabbed her arm before she could leave. "My dad always says we Eaglians have the freedom of flight burdened by the heaviness within human knowledge of the vast and cold emptiness of eternity. No other bird has such a concern."

Bellae gave him a quick hug before hunkering down under her own makeshift tent.

Inexplicably, Arend started laughing.

"Are you crazy?" the muffled voice of Sankari cried out against the roaring wind.

The brunt of the storm hit, stifling his voice, "My father used to make me tread air for hours, hovering through the pain. He told me to keep fighting though the agony even when it felt like my back muscles and wings would fall off. He would ask, 'Opportunity or burden?' How you view something determines how you experience it. Perspective matters. Attitude matters."

"We can't really hear you!" Kainen said, cowering beneath his porous woven shield as the bitter shower of sand blasted into their backs while the wind thundered.

"All I mean," Arend screamed, "is that we *can* do this!"

They were too tired and too accustomed to sandstorms to cry out at the thousands of pinprick hits—there was nothing left to do but listen to the rattling waves of sand and take the abuse. After twenty minutes, the intensity of the storm began to soften.

"The dry air seems even more dehydrated," Lontas announced. "Plus, the temperature is actually rising."

"At least the massive sweating helps speed up the dehydration!" Sankari piqued.

"Stay covered. Stay down," Kainen yelled. "Even though the violent storm has moved on to terrorize a different section of the desert, the air is still choked with sand."

Hungry, thirsty, exhausted, and coated in perspiration and sand, the League fell asleep.

Bellae's lips were so dry when she woke they felt bulky and tender—deepening fissures encompassed the swollen curves. She carefully removed her sand-soaked cloth. Arend and Kainen were talking quietly. The Eaglian looked horrible. His feathers were tousled and beaten. For the first time since they entered the desert, Kainen looked dejected.

"Lontas, any suggestions on direction?" Kainen asked though a scratchy voice as Sankari scoffed.

"Not for sure," he replied, gazing into the haze around them.

"Does anyone else feel like we are literally being cooked over an open flame?" Sankari huffed, but her shoulders sagged, and her color was off.

"If I had to guess based on where I *think* the suns are, I would say that way." Lontas said, pointing.

"That's as good a direction as any," Kainen replied. "Good news: let's all take a really big drink. Bad news: this is the last of our water until the oasis."

Before they finished swallowing, a chilling bellow blasted the air. Kainen and Arend exchanged a telling glance just as another sound arose.

"It sounds like someone crying out in pain," Gimelli said.

Scroll 2: For the Birds

"What's that horrid noise?" Bellae asked.

"A ferratus lanx nabbed a kameli. The sound seemed to be coming from that direction. Looks like you were right, Lontas," Kainen said.

"We're going to die," Sankari said weakly.

"It's good news. The Lanx usually live near watering holes," Arend replied.

With little choice, the League set off, following the direction of howling screams. As the afternoon tumbled along, their hope began to dive as pangs of guilt wracked Bellae. *It's my fault we're stuck in the desert.*

"Let's lie down, just for a while," Lontas mumbled through cracked lips, his clothes hanging off his parched body. As if to emphasize his point, he fell where he was and pulled his blanket over his face. Although the hint of evening was visible above the Aard Mountains, it was still stiflingly hot.

Bellae settled down next to him in the omnipotent sand. "Maybe we should lay here for a bit," she added before promptly falling asleep.

Arend glanced at Kainen, the possibility of death growing larger. With sunken eyes and little energy, Gimelli and Scelto joined the other two squires. Silently, Arend moved toward the four of them and spread his battered wings out to block the sun. Closing his eyes, he imagined being back in his ancient nest of the Giant Redwoods. It had been in his family for centuries. *I call on the spirits of my ancestors for strength. I shall protect Bellae with my life. I am the League. Sacrifice for success.*

Several hours later, Kainen tried to wake the squires. "Let's move."

The cold desert night, rushing in behind the darkness, spread itself over the warm dunes. Just like its alter ego heat, the chill seemed to be constantly inviting them to lie down in the sand and give up. Arend had not moved all afternoon, relentlessly shading the rest of the League.

"I don't need to, but maybe I'll lie down for just for a second," Arend stated boldly, but he was asleep before his feathered ear hit the sand.

Bellae's eyes fluttered but wouldn't stay open. Gimelli smiled at her little sister encouragingly even though she felt exhausted and alone. Kainen started to protest but settled into the still warm sand as the cool night wind caressed their will from above.

Hours later, Bellae looked to the east and shivered. "Are you real?" she asked, meaning to shout, but it came out a withered mutter.

Two shimmering forms watched her from a distance. "Nishi?" Bellae wondered, not sure if she had spoken out loud. "You won't get me!"

The psychotic switch from blistering heat to arctic cold had her body stiff and fatigued. Bellae tried not to move to avoid feeling the scratchy sand. A hint of red was just reaching out across the flat skyline. This initial encroachment on the black sky was so slight it appeared morning was holding onto the bottom of the sky by its fingernails. Slowly, however, the red turned into orange and a buffer zone of white skirted in between the battling sunrise and darkness of night. The two figures shimmered and disappeared as the light awoke. *Was I dreaming?*

"Morning already?" Gimelli asked thickly.

Scelto managed a sluggish smile. Seeing Gimelli looking so fragile, he suddenly felt a burst of energy. They had to get moving and find the oasis before the brunt of the afternoon suns. Arend couldn't stand another afternoon of shading them with his body. Everyone but Kainen had blistered skin pocked with peeling red blotches. With a surge of spirit, Scelto lifted the League up one by one. With feeble groans of protest they stumbled east. The same unspoken question lingered in everyone's mind. *What if we don't find the oasis?*

The obvious answer: *Death.*

Lontas moaned, and Bellae looked up, realizing she was drifting south, away from the others. Looking down, she noted she had been dragging her feet, filling her boots with cruel sand, which dug and gritted into her skin unmercifully.

Finn! she screamed in her mind. It felt as if her body had been hardened from the desert cycle of baking and cooling. *Keep moving*, she encouraged her heavy and sluggish muscles.

What was I doing? she wondered listlessly as weariness and thirst clouded her mind.

Pretty, she thought, looking at the morning sky. She had the idea its beauty was distracting her but could not remember from what. The morning sun's paint had spread shades of yellow high above the horizon, complimenting the orange and hints of red still battling the dark near the mountains. Suddenly, her mind screamed, *Water!* She was standing in a pool of its refreshing embrace. Her yell to the others came out as a hoarse and splintered cry. She dropped to her knees awash with relief and hope. Her hands dug into the sand she saw as water, splashing, cooling, healing. The thought rejuvenated her. She trusted the others would hear and come as she splashed the sand against her face.

"Bellae!" Lontas croaked. He thought he was running but was actually stumbling. "We have to get back to the others."

"No, we made it. Water!" she replied.

"It's sand," he said. Seeing her look so fragile made him sad. *You're the one usually helping me.* The thought gave him courage, and he heaved her up.

"What are you doing, Lontas? I need to wash…" she murmured. "Oh, I see. You want me to see the birds?"

"Birds?" Lontas asked.

"Lontas, don't listen to her. Her brain is baked *waaaay* past well-done," Sankari said absently.

Ignoring her, Lontas followed Bellae's trembling finger.

"I don't believe it!" Kainen said. "It's phainopepla…desert birds! They are *always* near an oasis." The League looked up to see several crested birds, some black, some brown, flying north.

"We must have drifted south," Arend commented. "We can't be too far, guys! The phainopepla don't fly far from their oasis."

Stumbling on hope, they followed the birds. Within ten minutes, they could make out the outline of trees and rocks.

"Saved by a bird again!" Kainen said, looking at his old friend, Arend.

"Is that a giant mushroom?" Scelto asked as they moved closer.

"Kind of. It's a mushroom rock outside the oasis. Most sand blows only three feet off the ground and slowly blasts the base of the rock away. Even in sandstorms, which go up a mile, most of the sand is still concentrated near the ground," Kainen answered.

"How do you guys know so much?" Bellae asked.

"We learned to be able to help you," Kainen answered.

"Our whole lives have been preparing for this, to help you succeed," Arend added. Bellae felt overwhelmed at the thought that they had been training for years before she even knew anything about the prophecy. Kainen and Arend descended down into the oasis to fill up their water skins while the squires and Sankari rested under the shade of the mushroom rock.

"Drink in small sips. We can have as much as we want, but we need to take it slow. For a good two hours they rested, sipping water. On their third trip back, Arend and Kainen brought some apricots and dates. For the first time, Bellae noted the bundles of red dates clustering high above. They appeared to be snared by yellow strands arching down from the tops of the palm trees.

"Only the female trees produce dates. They are super sweet," Arend said happily.

When everyone was feeling bloated and happy, Arend left, returning with an interesting cactus on his sword. It was about three feet tall and looked like a green pickle lined with rows of red spikes and crowned with yellow flowers. "A barrel cactus," Arend said.

"Also known as the candy cactus," Lontas added.

Kainen smiled. "Correct."

Using his sword and talons, Arend cut the center pulp into cubes and handed them to the League. They slowly savored the sweet bites. Despite the afternoon heat, the League was finally feeling death's grip slacken.

After several days of recuperation, Kainen pulled out the Prophecy Scroll late in the afternoon. "All right, everyone. Now that we're back from the dead, let's make our plan for first thing tomorrow morning. I think Arend and I found what we're looking for.

Search then for the rock crown.

Go between the sprigs,
Of dates, olives, apricot, and figs.
There, discover a mystery you must solve,
Before the door will revolve."

"We saw several large rocks surrounded by olive, apricot, and fig trees," Arend explained. "They're covered in grape ivy that's kind of like a 'crown.'"

"Not that sitting here for days hasn't been just super fun, but can we please get moving so we can get out of this crap-fest desert?" Sankari huffed.

"You were just as worn out as the rest of us," Kainen reminded.

"Can we at least scout out that place you found so we can get an early start tomorrow?" Sankari asked. "I don't want to waste all day looking for the 'crown' tomorrow."

"That's reasonable," Kainen said as Arend nodded.

Moving between shade patches the League headed deeper into the oasis. After the barren and soulless desert, each tree, shrub, and plant was a beautiful and graceful reminder of life and revelation of hope.

"I never thought I would be so glad to see trees!" Gimelli laughed as the third sun, Phoebus, dove into the horizon of sand, highlighting the trees in an orange splash.

"Here are the large boulders…" Kainen paused, his Elfin eyes flashing danger. "Something's wrong."

A rumbling growl froze them in their tracks. A foul, acrid taste suddenly stung their noses as they caught sight of three beasts hunching low to the ground and armored head to toe. A massive tail was tethered by billowing flesh to two large spikes on its back.

"Oh, man," Lontas said. "They're insanely ugly."

"Ferratus lanx! Back," Kainen advised, motioning them to slowly move away.

"What's wrong with that one? It looks half kameli," Bellae said.

"The ferratus lanx's mouth is on top of its head. After it knocks the poor creature out with a catapult tail, it impales them on spikes around its mouth on the top of its head before slowly digesting the prey."

The other two animals stopped trying to move in and steal the suffering kameli. Their wobbly red eyes, on long stalks sprouting from the sides of their snouts, fixed hungrily upon the League. Massive spikes formed a ring around a repulsive mouth on top of its head complete with writhing tentacles to help scoop and trowel flesh.

Kainen and Gimelli took out their bows as two of the creatures rumbled towards them. Their awkward hips-out gait reminded them of the dreaded spraks. As the League began backing towards the rocks, the ferratus lanx sped up. Arrows bounced off the thick scale armor encircling the beast. The only soft targets, jiggling crimson eyes, were impossible to hit, surrounded by thick spikes and armored scales. On top of its cranium a sloshing mess of bones, muscles, and sickening digesting liquid sloshed within lens-shaped lips.

"Run!" Arend advised. He and Sankari flew, and everyone but Bellae ran towards large boulders.

Bellae felt frozen in the blistering sand, her heart tethered to the suffering kameli. Its pain radiated towards her, rendering her motionless as she stared in a daze at the fierce creature and suffering prey. Despite their awkward nose-down appearance, the ferratus lanx moved

Figure 19: Low to the ground, Ferratus lanx are surprisingly fast. Their main weapon is a hammer-like tail that can catapult forward at absurd speeds thanks to stretchable tissue that slingshots it forward. Once incapacitated its victims are slowly digested by a loathsome mouth and stomach on top of its head.

with surprising quickness, their thick legs paddling in the sea of sand. Arend landed on the closest rock and turned to inform them the top was all clear when his talon slid off. Falling, his right wing became lodged between two boulders.

"Ow!" he screamed, his wing buckling in the craggy vice.

The others quickly scrambled to the top, moving to helping Arend with his wing.

"How'd you manage this?" Kainen asked.

"You know, just bored," Arend protested sarcastically, wincing in pain.

It wasn't until they heard two bellowing roars that they realized Bellae hadn't moved.

Shaking her head, Bellae tried to overcome the searing pain radiating from the kameli impaled on the far ferratus lanx. *Why didn't I follow the others? So stupid.*

"What's she doing facing off against two ferratus lanx?" Sankari huffed.

The creatures maneuvered between Bellae and the boulders. The one digesting the kameli stayed put, seemingly content with its current meal. Stunned, the League could only gawk as Bellae slowly backed up, further away from them. With each step she desperately tried to communicate with the creatures.

"Please, stop. Talk to me!"

"Ainmhi Caint isn't working!" she yelled, occasionally swiping with her small sword.

Their mace-like tails were quivering, restrained by large stretchable bands.

Bellae screamed as the end of one tail catapulted forward, over the creature's head, like a hammer, slamming into the sand, sending up a shower of debris into Bellae's face.

Scroll 3: Time to Set Sail

Several mornings after the battle, Friar boarded his boat as a stiff wind, blowing in from the sea, battered his face. Regret and fear churned his insides. *Did the White Wizard send me those visions to smash the armies of Verngaurd, paving the way for his conquest?* The salty-tasting air and spritzing waves of the ocean peppered his face. The spunky tide jumping up on the sides of the ship reminded him of a puppy excitedly leaping to slobber his master after a long absence. There was a crisp freshness in the air, and it occurred to Friar that the sea affords a fresh perspective for all who leave by her shores. Looking back on the beach, the waves lapped against the sand, wiping away any traces of those who had just walked there. *Like a devoted servant constantly cleaning up after their liege, each tide washes the slate clean. If only it could clear my soul.*

A heavily bandaged Ritari gazed concernedly at his leader. Friar looked as if he were aging by the second. "What's on your mind?"

"Did we do the right thing?" Friar asked.

"Did we have a choice?" Ritari countered.

"That's what bothers me. Did *we* have a choice? If not, who's pulling the manipulating strings?"

"We make the best decisions we can with the information at hand. Our creed has been to not make enemies, but that does not mean we should tolerate disrespect from those who impose themselves as our adversaries."

Friar rubbed his head, his brain buzzing with frustration. "Wars. There are few and far between where right and wrong are clearly defined and you know exactly what you are fighting for. Lucky are those soldiers to fight, and leaders to command, in those battles. The rest of us are left to muddle through the grey mire of conflicts, leaving us wondering how we got here."

"You realize you don't have to bear the weight of the world," Ritari said. "We are part of a strong Alliance, and sometimes all we can do is all we can do."

Friar smiled dejectedly. "Tell that to all the dead back there on the battlefield. That alone, is enough to weigh a man down. Whoever said that the spirit is weightless has never ordered thousands to their deaths, forced for the rest of their life to bear the burden of those lost souls."

"Tomorrow will come, but today we can enjoy the victory. Shouldn't we?" Ritari said. "You should take pride knowing you led a vastly outnumbered army to victory."

General Lidenskap's words were ringing in his ears. *I'm not convinced about anything at the moment.* Friar stared intently at Ritari as if measuring him. "I know you are aware of my father's history."

Ritari shifted uneasily. *Of course. Everyone is.* "Under Friar Isa the Knights were repeatedly beaten and lost the majority of our castles and prestige." As he went through the details in his mind, Ritari seemed to understand Friar's obsession with victory and proving the Knights could win, especially under his leadership.

Clearing his throat nervously, Friar continued. "By chance and by choice I have distanced myself from my father and his reputation. I have purposefully redefined who I am, how I talk, what I read, how I train, the armor, or lack of it, that I usually wear, etc. I feel I have morphed hundreds of times since I was born, always trying to set myself apart from my father. And yet, when I stood exposed on that field of death, I felt all of the supposed changes were an illusion. I'm just a scared boy who desperately needs his father to comfort him and tell him everything's going to be okay."

Ritari turned to stare out at the waves, unsure of what to say.

"The truth of it is, Ritari, I don't know what's going to happen or if anything is going to be okay. Am I doomed to repeat my father's mistakes? Good intentions and faith are worthless if the outcome is lost. This battle didn't solve anything, and I feel the fool for thinking it would.

"It only served to pick open old sores and create new wounds. It's going to get dark now that war has awoken. It will demand ever more sacrifice without ever having its thirst for blood quenched. Our future is set, and we'd better be ready for the fight of our lives because it's coming."

Scroll 4: Eyes Close

BOOOOOOOOOOOM-BOOOOOOOOOOOM!

Both ferratus lanx repeatedly shot the clubs on the end of their tails at Bellae. Each strike moved with lightning quickness, exploding into the ground and sending up shrapnel of sand. Two extendible bands went from their largest spikes on their abdomens to large bony clubs, making a natural catapult capable of throwing forward their hammer tails with phenomenal power. Repeatedly, the creatures used their tails to stretch the bands, which when released, sent the bony weapons forward at incredible speed.

"Get me loose. Get me loose!" Arend screamed frantically as the League desperately tried to free his wing.

"Don't run, Bellae. They're faster than you think," Kainen warned. "Keep backing up slowly and avoiding those hammer blows."

"Oh, she should avoid the massive club on the tail that looks like it could kill her with one blow? Wow, thanks Kainen!" Sankari seethed. With her temper sizzling she transferred her frustration into yanking on Arend's wing.

"I'm going down after her," Gimelli cried.

"Me too," Lontas said.

"No!" Kainen screamed. "Let Arend fly to help. They'll kill you if you go down."

"I'll give you a few seconds!" Gimelli screeched, pacing on the edge of the boulder.

With a heave, Lontas finally freed Arend. He swooped upwards, shrieking angrily to startle the beasts. Distracted, their retractile cerise eyes scanned for the source of the noise.

"Bellae, skirt around them and head towards us once Arend draws them away. Keep an eye on the one digesting the kameli—it's still dangerous," Kainen advised, as Arend began to dive, then retreat from the beasts.

Bellae moved cautiously to her left, attempting get around the distracted pair of ferratus lanx. Feeling rejuvenated, Arend spun and tumbled through the air. Occasionally, when he got close enough, he scraped a talon against their massive armor. Infuriated, the beasts began to follow him away from Bellae, occasionally lashing out with their tails. Arend flew erratically, and the creatures became increasingly frustrated. Seeing Bellae move away, the beast digesting the kameli abruptly growled, warning the other two ferratus lanx. Spinning, they saw their easy prey clambering towards the rocks.

With a scream, Bellae took off in a sprint as the two beasts ignored Arend's near-constant assaults to take off after her. Even with his ferocious talons he could not penetrate the armor.

"Use your sword! Cut the giant tendons, and they won't be able to attack," Lontas yelled, panic filling every crevice of his body as he watched his friend scramble towards the rock.

Bellae could feel them right behind her as she jumped up to take Kainen's hand. While he pulled her up, Arend began hacking at one of their tails. The besieged ferratus lanx turned towards him while the other continued charging Bellae. Just as she made it to the top of the rock, the armored tail slammed repeatedly into the boulder. The section Bellae had just pulled herself up on shook violently, shattered, and broke into chunks. Her grip vanished in the cloud of dust. Screaming, she fell. With a violent thud she slammed into the sand, pain surging across her body as sections of rock showered down.

Just as Lontas started to scramble down to help, the ferratus lanx sent another barrage of blows crashing into the boulder, sending them scrambling back. Gasping for air, Bellae pushed the debris away and struggled up, hobbling away from rock and beast. Arrows from Gimelli's bow clinked uselessly off its armor as it headed for Bellae.

"Grab her and get up here, Arend!" Kainen yelled.

Arend flew towards Bellae just as the enraged ferratus lanx let loose his bleeding tail. Arend tried to dodge the hammer-like bone, but it caught his side, sending him tumbling through the air with shooting pain searing through his ribs. As he crashed to the ground, Bellae tripped, skidded, then clambered forward as the emboldened ferratus lanx picked up speed.

"No!" Gimelli yelled. Pushing Scelto into Lontas, she jumped off the boulder. The third ferratus lanx hurled the partially digested kameli off and bolted towards Gimelli. The incapacitated kameli moaned feebly, stiffly twitching on the ground. Barely clinging to life, its eyes stayed closed, flies lustily moving towards the open and raw back that had been partially digested. At the sight of it, Sankari vomited, coughing and gagging at the exposed muscle, bone, and blood.

"Gimelli, get back here right now or we'll lose you too," Kainen shouted, unsure of what to do. "Arend, get Bellae!" They had to save her, but going against one ferratus lanx was certain death. Trying to take on three nearly indestructible beasts was suicide.

Gimelli froze as the ferratus lanx who had been stalking Bellae turned to face her. Now she had two, closing in from either side. She started backing up. Suddenly, Lontas and Scelto jumped down on the other side of the boulder.

"Come get us!" Scelto shouted loudly while drawing his Proliate sword.

The two ferratus lanx froze, unsure of which victim to go after first, unused to so many choices of prey. The distraction served long enough to allow Gimelli to sweep around and clamber back on the boulder. Kainen helped Lontas and Scelto up as the two angry creatures charged the boulder, letting loose a barrage of tail strikes, rocking the large stone and vibrating the League on top.

A large growl from the third creature got the attention of those on the boulder but did not distract the two ferratus lanx who continued to slam into the large rock with massive strikes. They looked up to see Bellae sprinting towards the ferratus lanx attacking Arend. She began hacking with her small sword at the massive tendons that powered its hammer tail. Even though Arend had only been grazed by the beast's tail, it had broken several of his ribs, and he was struggling—every movement hurt, including breathing.

"Bellae's trying to rescue Arend!" Lontas howled.

"Arend, you're too hurt. Fly away, I'll figure something out," Bellae said.

"Not without you!" Arend said just as a blast from the creature struck his left talon. He screamed in pain as a loud *crack* spoke to more broken bones.

"Go!" Bellae screamed with authority. In agony, Arend hopped on one talon, taking to the air.

"You can't leave Bellae out there alone!" Lontas screamed over the crashing blows of the ferratus lanx, the resonating vibration making his words shudder. Lontas softened his tone once Arend landed and he saw the massive hematoma forming on his right side and the mangled left claw.

Bellae sheathed her sword, picked up a long stick, and began waving it at the massive beast while backing up. With one snap of its tail it obliterated the stick, her hands slammed into her chest, and her body flew backwards.

"Did it get her?" Gimelli asked.

"No, the force from hitting the stick sent her tumbling," Lontas said.

"What do we do?"

"I don't know," Kainen admitted, glancing longingly at Arend for help, but the Eaglian was gasping for breath while writhing in pain. "With his ribs and mangled claw, no way can he carry her."

"So profound!" Sankari said. "Can you tell us something else painfully obvious?"

Arend coughed, the retching hack sending up an offering of blood, splattering color over the insipid rock. Arend's eyelids lowered as the crimson shower slowed to a dribble over his beak.

The ferratus lanx began toying with Bellae—sending its powerful blasts all around her as she clambered backwards, weaving between desert trees. The other two were keeping the rest of the League cornered while intermittently battering the rock.

"What can we do?" Kainen begged.

"I don't know, but this whole boulder could disintegrate under their blows. We have to do something," Gimelli cried.

"I can try to distract one of them," Sankari offered.

"No, Kari. One hit, and you die. Look at Arend," Kainen said.

"If Bellae's going to die, I die next to her," Lontas said. Just as he was about to dive off the rock, a glowing white figure emerged into the increasing darkness.

"Is that a Nishi?" Lontas asked, somehow knowing it was not.

Before he could answer, the luminescent female figure pointed towards Bellae and the ferratus lanx while silently screaming. Her ghostly mouth exploded in fear and anger as the strands of her hair floated ethereally. Eventually, the spectral figure raised her arms in a silent howl before dropping down on both knees. Although no words could be heard, her mouth continued to shriek.

That's no Nishi, but I know her," Bellae thought. *Is that my mother?* Before she could move closer, two black skeletal hands clasped onto the ghostly figure's shoulders, and, in a flash, both disappeared.

A loud crack stung the League back as a whip-like tail slapped into the beast attacking Bellae. The ferratus lanx bellowed in pain as several more blows slammed into its head. The League froze in stunned silence, staring in disbelief as Crann suddenly broke onto the scene.

"He looks horrible and emaciated," Gimelli said of the dry, dusty figure of Crann.

"Go behind me and get up on the boulder," Crann neighed loudly to Bellae.

"I'm not leaving without you," she declared. *"No way!"*

Running to him, she jumped, desperately grabbing onto his neck. *"Get us out of here,"* she commanded. As the words left her mouth, she felt an explosion rack through Crann, vibrating to her body as the beast's hammer tail slammed into the horse. The force sent a shock wave of power cracking several of the horses' ribs and sending Bellae flying backwards. Crann neighed in pain as the agony of his shattered body lurched to the ground.

"Run, girl!" Crann managed, struggling to rise, fear swelling in his eyes from pain and comprehension.

"Get over here, Bellae!" Lontas called.

"We'll come down after you if you don't!" Gimelli screamed.

Despite his injuries, Crann clumsily rose. *"You made the right choice, child."*

"What does that mean? What choice?" Bellae howled as Crann made a move towards the ferratus lanx. Crann paused, looking back at Bellae, then he nodded before charging the beast.

Unaccustomed to being attacked, the ferratus lanx froze for a second—long enough for Crann to throw himself on top of the creature, entwining his whip-like tail around the ferratus lanx's bony tail. Enraged, the beast began to slam the hammer tail against Crann, trying to knock the horse off.

With fluttering eyes, Crann whispered, *"Run."*

As Bellae began to cry, he closed his eyes for the last time. The ferratus lanx was insane with fury. With Crann's cord-like tails completely entangled on the creature's, he could not bite into the horse or shake it loose. Finally, the beast went into a fit of convulsing spasms, stomping wildly up and down while slamming its tail against the beaten horse. Crann's insides were turned into a soup of broken bones, liquefied organs, and blood. His tail finally snapped, and the horse was thrown several feet away.

The beast quickly scooped Crann's splintered body up and began digesting it as Bellae bolted around and behind the boulders. She was sobbing as Scelto pulled her up. As her body hit the top, she shunned the horror of what was happening to Crann. Gimelli came and held her as tears exploded out, her body convulsing with misery.

"Don't look," Gimelli said, gently holding her sister's head against her chest.

"Don't have to—I could feel," Bellae wailed. "I shouldn't have left."

"He sacrificed himself to save you," Gimelli said in as soothing a voice as she could.

"We can't throw that gift away. Those creatures are too tough."

"It hurts," Bellae said, reliving the pain of both the kameli and Crann.

As Gimelli gently patted her sister's back, Bellae's body began to tremble instead of shake.

"You know, I'm going to miss good old Bucky the Beaver-toothed horse," Grym said after scampering out of Bellae's pocket.

"Seriously?" Borb admonished. *"That horse just sacrificed himself for Bellae, and in so doing, us!"*

"Why be angry? I said I'd miss him," Grym replied. *"I was trying to be kind."*

"You failed...miserably."

Scroll 5: This is...

"She's finally asleep," Gimelli said, still cradling her sister with a gentle sway. Arend was already sleeping after Lontas had made a makeshift splint for his broken toe.

"Bellae definitely *cannot* see Crann getting gnawed on," Scelto declared.

"This is totally surreal," Gimelli said numbly as two of the ferratus lanx feasted on Crann and the kameli.

"How did Crann survive the desert or even find us?" Scelto asked.

"What was that ghost, glowing thing?" Lontas asked. "I'm pretty sure it wasn't a Nishi."

"I don't know, but it pointed...almost as if it was leading Crann," Gimelli said.

A loud gurgling slurp was followed by a spraying sound as blood flashed upwards, the savage ferratus lanx continuing to engorge itself.

"That's seriously disgusting," Gimelli said. "That horse loves...loved her so much. Maybe he knew she needed him. Did you see how thin and dehydrated he looked? Crann barely made it here, but still put up a ferocious fight."

"At least the third one set off after some desert fox. How long until these leave?" Scelto asked.

"Soon they will likely head off into the desert just outside the oasis. There they will burrow down into the sand and hibernate while continuing to digest their prey."

"Nasty, nasty beasts," Sankari commented.

One by one, the exhausted League fell asleep on the hard rock. Still recuperating from their desert trek, they slept until morning.

Bellae woke up screaming, refusing to open her eyes. Even though the beasts had left, she kept recollecting the excruciating pain of

Crann and the kameli as they were slowly digested on top of the ferratus lanx.

"Hey, guys," Kainen said gently when Gimelli calmed her down. "I know yesterday was horrible, but Lontas and I think we've figured out the part about 'gem fit for any crown.' There's the group of rocks we were going to show you." He pointed to the northeast. "You can see flowers ringing the larger central rock. We believe that's the 'crown.' We should head there."

"How can that still be accurate if the prophecy is as old as they say?" Scelto wondered.

"Legend says each crystal set is protected by custodians," Kainen answered. "Their job is to keep the crystals safe and the path to find them recognizable."

Gimelli sighed, not happy about more surprises.

"We should at least try," Kainen said, his words shadowed by sadness. Bellae didn't even want to open her eyes, much less move.

Gimelli finally broke the stillness. "Maybe Arend and someone else should stay here and take it easy while the rest of us head over there?"

Kainen nodded, shushing Arend's protests. "We need you healthy. You need to rest your cracked ribs and organs."

"I haven't thrown up blood in a while."

"That's not exactly a high-water mark of health. Sankari, would you stay with Arend? You could fly to us if there's trouble." The fairy nodded, happy to stay on the boulder.

"Are you up for this?" Gimelli whispered to Bellae.

"You better not leave me, big sis. I said I'd go on without you, but I couldn't bear it," Bellae answered, her lower lip quivering. "I'm sick of everyone dying. Why does this keep happening?"

"I don't know," Gimelli answered. She looked to Kainen and Scelto.

"I know it's unfair, Bellae, but this is war," Kainen said. "However much we hate it, however much it hurts, we need to keep going. If the prophecy is right, you can help end the fighting."

Bellae nodded but was feeling nauseous. *If one more person tells me how important I am, I'm going to scream.*

After a breakfast of desert fruit and water, Gimelli, Bellae, Scelto, Lontas, and Kainen headed off while Sankari and Arend rested. Once they were closer to the other outcropping of rocks, they noticed an overgrown path between the various desert trees that led up to the center boulder. It had a wreath of green vines sprouting blue flowers ringing its top.

"Okay, now what?" Scelto asked.

"I don't know," Kainen confessed. "Let's look around for some sort of writing or symbol…"

"Up there," Lontas said, pointing to a notched area near the top of the rock formation.

"We could sure use Arend to fly up there," Scelto commented.

"He needs to rest. We can figure this out," Kainen declared.

Eventually, they decided to have Lontas stand on Scelto's shoulders.

"What do you see?" Gimelli asked.

"There's a bowl carved into the rock. I don't know how they did it, but it's set back *under* an overhang so that it is covered on all sides but the front. It's full of sand and debris. There's also writing carved up above it."

"Well, what does it say?" Kainen asked.

"I can only read the top part. The bottom bit is gibberish," Lontas replied.

"Hurry it up, Lontas. My shoulders are killing me," Scelto complained.

"Okay. There are only two paragraphs I can read:

To unlock the door,
You need read more.
Opening your eyes,
You may not see the surprise.
To crack the code,
Fill the load.

It is large enough to hold three suns and thirteen moons.
It weighs nothing, yet try to lift it? Buffoons.
It can be small as a drop or large as the ocean.
Despite the sizes, they hold exactly the same in devotion.

Right is left—left is right.
Top is still above, and bottom below—day or night.
Don't be confused,
Backwards will make it used."

"Is that it?" Gimelli asked.

"Great. At least it's nothing complicated," Kainen groaned.

"Yeah, the rest of it's complete gibberish, just random letters scrambled about," Lontas replied. "No, wait. Not only is it a whole bunch of letters thrown around—some are backwards."

"Backwards?" Kainen complained.

Lontas reread the riddle again before getting down.

"Obviously, we need to figure out some sort of cipher to be able to read the rest of the 'gibberish,' as Lontas called it," Kainen said.

"What in the world is big enough to hold three suns and thirteen moons?" Scelto asked.

"The sky is the obvious answer. Maybe the code has something to do with the position of the stars or something?" Lontas guessed.

"But you also told us it said that it weighs nothing and you could never lift it," Gimelli added.

"True, but it doesn't change anything. The sky is just black air that doesn't weigh anything, and you can't lift it," Lontas answered.

The League argued for over an hour about how to use the stars or sky to help read the bottom portion.

"Okay, Lontas, look again," Scelto said, hoisting him up.

"There's no hole or path for light to come down through the rock," Lontas said.

"So sun or moonlight can't be the answer," Kainen said.

"I can't see any connection or guide to the sky," Lontas added.

"I told you, the heavens can't be as small as a drop and are larger than the oceans," Scelto said defiantly.

"We're on the same team," Gimelli said. "I know everyone's nerves are worn thin after the desert march and Crann's death, but we need to work together."

Bellae remained silent. The pain at Crann's death weighed heavily and still had her stomach twisting into knots.

"Well, what can be both small and big? And what's up with the 'right is left—left is right' part?" Gimelli demanded.

"What was that?" Bellae whispered hoarsely.

"Hmm?" Kainen said, surprised at her finally speaking.

"What about right and left?" Bellae repeated.

"It said, 'Right is left—left is right,' but 'top is still above, and bottom below—day or night,'" Lontas said.

"Gimelli, do you remember when Jumeaux had trouble with left and right? You two would stand across from each other as you tried to teach him. He had so much trouble figuring out why your right hand was on the same side as his left hand when you faced each other," Bellae stated.

"That's right." Gimelli replied. "He finally got it when…" She paused as a moment of understanding flashed in her mind. "…I had him look at his reflection! The answer to the riddle is, 'Reflection!' That's large enough to hold everything you see in the sky and can be any size too. You can see a large reflection in a drop of water or looking down into the massive ocean."

"Just like when you stand across from someone, your left is their right, and vice versa, but the top and bottom are oriented in the correct direction," Kainen added.

Suddenly, Scelto began to laugh. "Oh, this is great!" he said.

"Hold it together," Kainen said, confused by his behavior.

Still laughing, Scelto removed the shiny shield given by Patuljak.

"He did help us!" Bellae said. Somehow, the fact he had done them a favor made her feel better.

"All right, Lontas. How about another go?" Scelto asked.

"This time, you need to face *away* from the inscription while holding the shield," Kainen advised.

"Oh, this is funny," Lontas said once he was staring into the shiny surface of the shield. "All the letters *are* backwards, but it's just more noticeable with letters like "e" than say "t." Okay, it says:

Clean the basin until it will glow.
Next, fill it, with what? Read below.
If you try and hold this in your hand,
Hold it tight, or it slips through where you stand.
It takes on many forms, liquid, solid, gas.
Guess right and you can pass."

"Is that it?" Kainen sighed.

"Yep," Lontas replied, getting down from Scelto's shoulders.

"Sounds like sand?" Scelto suggested. "Another, 'try and hold it in your hand and it slips through' things."

"I don't think so," Lontas added. "It's already filled with it, and sand can't be a liquid or gas. It's just a solid."

"I think it's something you eat, maybe," Kainen said. "You eat something and it's solid, but in your stomach, it gets turned into liquid and then comes out the other end as gas."

"Ew!" Gimelli squirmed. "Are you suggesting we fill the bowl up with gas or shit?" The idea was so funny they started laughing hysterically.

"I'm definitely *not* taking a dump on top of a boulder!" Scelto proclaimed.

"What if we can get you some torahammas milk?" Gimelli joked, sending them into another fit of laughter.

A fierce shriek tore through the skies, startling them. "Yee-weeent-weeent-weeent-yee-weeeent," Arend called as he and Sankari zoomed towards them.

"What's wrong?" Arend challenged, landing gingerly on one talon.

The others exchanged sheepish looks. "Nothing," Kainen said. "We were just laughing."

"You just gave your position away to any creature within a mile," Sankari chastised. "Do you want to see another ferratus lanx? Plus, you scared us half to death."

"It's nice to know you care, Sankari," Kainen said. Something in his tone of voice made them start laughing again. This only served to make Arend and Sankari more upset.

"Would you stop? My side's killing me, and my leg's throbbing. Why were you laughing?" Arend asked.

"Funny you should ask..." Lontas said, sending them doubling over in laughter yet again. "Do you feel like you could relieve yourself?"

It took several more minutes for the giggles to finally die down.

"I actually have known the answer for a while. It's water," Lontas explained. "Water can be solid—ice, liquid—water, and a gas—vapor."

"Brilliant!" Gimelli congratulated.

A short time later, they had the cleaned-out basin carved into the rock filled with water. Almost instantly, the water started to drain through tiny holes in the chiseled bowl. They waited, but nothing happened.

"Let's fill it up again," Lontas suggested.

After the third round, a loud *click* filled the air. Not long after, a stone door crunched and grated its way open on the far side of the boulder.

"That scraping makes my teeth hurt!" Sankari complained.

"Hey, I think there's a lit torch in there!" Sankari said, amazed.

"How could there be? No one is supposed to have been here for thousands of years," Gimelli said.

"Could be the custodian," Kainen said.

"Oh yeah. Let's find out," Scelto said, helping the hobbling Arend to the door.

Scelto drew his sword as Arend began leaning heavily on Kainen. They cautiously headed towards the opening.

"You'll have no need of that sword. In fact, if you don't put it away, I will be greatly offended," a voice called out from inside the doorway, but only Bellae understood.

"Bloody mess!" Lontas jumped in astonishment.

Everyone's jaw dropped when they saw the creature poking its head out the door.

Gimelli sighed. "Just what we need...things getting weirder."

Scroll 6: Seize the Day

"How's Luchar?" Friar asked, walking into the infirmary with the heavily bandaged Ritari and Lovag.

"About the same as when he arrived days ago," the healer Sanar replied. "Great to see you, Sorea!" he added as she rolled up in her rotasessius. "Your bed is right next to Luchar. I will change your thorax dressings next, and you need yours changed as well, Ritari."

"Ah, I'm fine! We should have been here sooner. Blasted travel by ship is too slow!" Ritari said, his eyes full of worry.

"The Vioma Dragons were exhausted and could only carry those with critical injuries, like Luchar, to Liberum," Friar replied.

The three Knights, Friar, and the healer hovered anxiously around Luchar's bed.

"Any more seizures?" Friar asked.

"Occasionally. Healer Leigh's anti-seizure drops seem to be working. Unfortunately, those seizures are the only movement we've seen out of him. If he doesn't wake up soon, he will die," Sanar answered, his voice sagging under the strain of exhaustion. "We're dripping small amounts of water under his tongue around the hourglass to keep him hydrated. The stablemates have been doing a great job. He has to be in lots of pain."

"Can't you do anything?" Sorea pleaded.

"Well…" Sanar said somewhat timidly, "at the Tournament a few Magician healers mentioned an experimental technique for blunt trauma to the head. Specifically, they focused on battle injuries causing bleeding inside the skull. If they could locate where the damage was sustained, then presumably the blood collection pushing on the brain would be under there. They then carefully drill a small hole in the skull, releasing an enormous amount of blood, relieving the pressure around the brain. This can result in the patient regaining consciousness." Sanar paused, his head wobbling.

"But..." Friar prompted.

"Over half of them died."

"What?" Sorea said. "Those don't seem like good odds."

"Compared to an almost 90 percent mortality in those not treated? Fifty percent's not bad," Sanar said. "Their technique has a good foundation of medical knowledge behind it. See how he has this massive bruise on the right side of his head? That's where we we'd go in. Given his symptoms, there has to be bleeding inside the skull right there."

"He'll die if you do nothing?" Friar asked anxiously.

"Luchar should have died after the dragon dented his head at the Tournament, so obviously, he had one tough head. However, it is my opinion..."

"Dwill a hole...I kill ewe," Luchar mumbled in a slurred and parched voice before drifting into unconsciousness again.

"Luchar!" Sorea cried as Sanar tried to rouse him without success.

"We wait and see what happens," Friar said. "I will not go against his wishes." Despite Luchar's toughness, he wanted to cry. Seeing this strong warrior reduced to incapacitation so close on the heels of Finn's death was hard to endure.

"He can hear us?" Sorea wondered.

"From what we know, some people in these unconscious states report hearing voices. That's why head healer Salus instituted a rotation of singing and reading times around the ward. It lifts the spirits of all who listen and may help healing," Sanar replied.

Several stablemates walked in, carrying a bucket of water and droppers.

"Good lads!" Friar said. "You should be proud of your work."

They nodded, but their halfhearted smiles belied the fact they were there because they had to be.

"I would like to read to him now," Sorea said.

"Of course. I want you staying in bed for *at least* a week, so you'll have plenty of time for reading," Sanar said.

Friar closed his eyes, knowing another battle would come soon enough. The idea of fighting without his stalwart Luchar made his uneasiness soar. The victories at Trepas and Ovest seemed hollow. *Such a high price for what reward?*

"What are you thinking, Friar?" Ritari asked.

"The sacrifice of the warrior when they defend the weak should be revered. When Knights live by our code of ancient virtues: search for wisdom, display courage, temperance, and defend justice, our actions are a privilege. For an honorable warrior there should be no fettering regret. Did we respect our Knights' Code? I'm thinking we won a true Cadmean victory. I surmise that we will lose, in the end, much more than we won."

Scroll 7: Unnecessary Riddles & Rudeness

"Are you coming in?" a voice coaxed as the League gawked in wonder.

"What did...a...it say?" Scelto sputtered.

"We should go in," Bellae answered. "But put away your sword."

There, standing in the newly opened doorway, was a creature with a lioness' head and a woman's body. Short, tan fur lined her face and ears save for some white around her eyes and mouth. She was wearing a form-fitting brown outfit and swinging her tail with a clawed hand. With stunned looks, the League reluctantly followed her in.

The entryway they were standing in had been chiseled from rock. A few small torches spit fragile light from the otherwise empty walls of the claustrophobic room. There was a set of narrow stairs leading down directly across from them.

"I'm Hamata. Which is the Chosen?" she purred, swiping her cinnamon-blushed paw.

"I guess...me," Bellae replied, stepping forward.

Figure 20: The League comes into contact with their first guardian, Hamata, after solving the riddle of reflection and water. The upright lioness has humanoid form with lion features.

"It's not something you guess at, genius. You are, or are not, the Chosen One," the creature growled. *"Let me help out your tiny intellect. Since you are talking to me, you are, in fact, the Chosen. Kay?"*

Exhausted mentally and physically from the journey, Bellae blew out a deep breath but remained silent.

"I don't want to put too much information in that miniature brain of yours. I would feel guilty, as it would surely be bored and lonely within the vast emptiness of your cavernously uninhabited skull, but follow me."

Bellae blushed slightly, embarrassed at the insults and grateful the others could not understand.

"What's she saying?" Gimelli asked defensively.

Bellae shook her head as the entryway door behind them thundered shut. The League jumped as the cramped room suddenly seemed even smaller in the shallow light.

The lioness woman touched her paw to a spot on the wall and began speaking in a language none of them knew, "Lifath alalihat." A hidden door scraped open. After ducking through, she motioned to Bellae. *"Just you."*

Before Gimelli could protest, Bellae dashed through, the door slamming shut behind her.

Gimelli began desperately pushing. "Help!" she called out. Despite Scelto joining in, the door remained closed.

Kainen sighed. "I guess we wait."

"Should we go down the stairs?" Sankari questioned.

"No, wait for Bellae," Gimelli replied.

"I'd better sit," Arend grunted, taking slow deep breaths, each one gifting a searing pain into his ribs.

After taking several steps down, Bellae found herself in a new room that was surprisingly spacious. Various scrolls and books lined two entire walls. Diverse statues and several maps littered the floor. Hamata sat in one of the two chairs within the room. The throne-esque seat had four lion paws ascending to a comfortable-looking cushion while two sets of wings served as arm rests and the back.

Using her clawed hand, she motioned to Bellae. "Sit."

"Wait, you know the common tongue?"

"Of course, but those dawdling bores you brought with you do not interest me. You do…a tiny bit."

Bellae cautiously sat down.

"So you figured out the water riddle? Hmmm? Proud of yourself? Are you? Water reflects what we want to see, but the image is ever so fragile—easily rippled into ugliness—and worse, its mirror-like reflection always hides the truth, concealing itself in the depths below the eyes peering out. Your true reflection is always in your actions.

"We like to convince ourselves there are answers to every problem," Hamata continued. "However, each answer simply breeds new questions. Cut the head off one problem, and many more grow—new lines of inquiry sprouting like a passionate rabbit's offspring."

The lioness laughed heartily.

Bellae simply stared. *What's happening right now?*

A light buzzing sound made Bellae pivot.

"Ah, Khepri! Come!"

Bellae's mouth dropped watching a nine-inch-long, colorful blue beetle alight on Hamata's shoulder. The beetle had two talons sprouting from his lower body, two ornate, blue-tinted wings, and two clawed legs from its sapphire upper body. Khepri whispered to the lioness, who immediately began laughing. "He thinks you look fragile and are going to die way before completing your tasks," Hamata explained, dissolving into laughter again.

The beetle flew up, hovering in front of Bellae. His eyes were large and not typical for insects but consisted of a rounded diamond shape bathing in irises that were various shades of blue.

"So you're the so-called Chosen?" the beetle asked.

Frustrated with being insulted, Bellae felt anger roiling within. *"So I've been told."*

"You have zero chance of success," Khepri hissed, his wings flittering loudly and claws gratingly scraping against one another.

"I don't remember asking your opinion," Bellae replied, frustrated she couldn't think of a better comeback.

"Sorry if you, like many humanoids, don't like the truth. Your belief does not change the fact you will fail, and die," Khepri said, buzzing around, studying her. Occasionally, he would make a judgmental clicking or hissing sound laden with disapproval.

"You are certainly entitled to your wrong opinion!" Bellae said, her face flushing with indignation.

Hamata giggled then snapped her finger, calling the beetle back to her shoulder. *"Well, the girl's spunky, isn't she, my beautiful Khepri?"*

"Thank you," Bellae said. Hamata looked up, confused. "I just wanted you to know how much I appreciate being talked about like

I'm not here. It has never happened before, and I am really, super enjoying it."

Hamata burst out laughing. "Okay. So, do you have the special bag from the dragon? *The one forged to hold the Macht Crystals?*"

"Yes. Did you know you are switching between the common tongue and Ainmhi Caint?"

"Don't care and glad you have the bag. I hope you truly can touch the Macht Crystals. If not, you will burn," Hamata said with a casual chuckle. "A lengthy, slow, and painful death that my dear Khepri would just love. Wouldn't you, boy?"

The beetle hummed with glee as Bellae angrily tilted her head, done with the rude lioness. Khepri hurtled towards her. *"Please slowly burn! I have not missed the vapid animal talkers."*

Bellae's eyes widened at his malicious words.

"I'm the first of five guardians you will meet. Of course, I'm the most important and oldest," she purred with no hint of modesty.

Bellae followed the beetle's path as it landed on an old, broken sign that read, "Rock of Aghurmi."

"Ah, you noticed the sign. This *desert* did not used to be so *deserted*," Hamata said, laughing at her wordplay. "The Rock of Aghurmi used to be in the Siwa desert, and a great oracle lived there. Kings and commoners alike would come, giving offerings to receive advice. Great tribes used to wander the desert." Hamata paused, seemingly lost in memories.

"Many would worship my mother, Sekhmet, and come for her powerful healing. Millennia ago, they stopped coming to the oracle or my mother. Several of the fresh-water lakes in Siwa became polluted with salt water, and the tribes eventually left."

Hamata's eyes flashed a mix of regret and hatred as her fangs gleamed. "However, being a descendent of a god is not too bad, hmm?"

"I guess not," Bellae said, feeling uncomfortably irritated and unbearably confused.

"Speaking of descendants, yours were quite annoying and dense." Seeing Bellae's interest, Hamata clarified, "Setting up this…farce, this shambles of an odyssey, is ridiculous. A quest full of riddles and games?

Ha! They paid us handsomely to be guardians of this prophecy, but it has grown exceedingly tiresome. I shall be quite grateful when you leave and could care less if you succeed or fail. Betting the world's future on you? Hopeless absurdity defined. There are many riddles you will have to solve, many perils you must survive. Should we try some riddles?"

Bellae performed two perplexed gestures that came across as confused as she was, nodding slightly and shrugging her shoulders. *Was that a question?*

"What says nothing of intelligence in the morning, at noon spouts nonsense but thinks it is brilliant, at late afternoon is slightly sage, but at the close of the day mumbles regrets?"

Hamata laughed at Bellae's confounded expression. "Not exactly a child prodigy, are we? You'll need more to succeed than conversing with animals."

Hamata spoke with Khepri, who flew to Bellae. *"Do you mind if I just call you 'girl who will die soon'? Great, and thanks. Do you realize that being born able to speak with animals is not actually a talent? You did nothing. No hard work or dedication required."*

Fighting tears, Bellae asked meekly, "I have to answer that riddle?"

"Oh, I change my opinion of you. That was a most insightful—genius-level, actually—question. *Yes*, the traditional response would be you answer, hopeless child."

All color drained from Bellae's face. *I'm going to fail the first challenge. I knew this was a mistake. The nasty beetle's right—what have I done? Nothing!*

Feeling her tensing up, Grym and Borb peeked out of Bellae's pocket. *"You know, just when I thought we wouldn't see anything stranger..."* Grym squeaked, gawking at the lioness with a sparkling beetle on her shoulder.

"Is lion-lady bothering you?" Borb questioned. *"Seriously, don't mess with us. We ate dead guy eyes to protect Bellae. Step off or feel the bite of our...bite!"*

"Bite of our bite? How eloquent," Grym said.

"I have to solve a hard riddle, and don't think I can," Bellae explained.

"Get Lontas. Klutz-boy is useful for stuff like this."

"Ah, get your backup, then you would totally succeed," Hamata said sarcastically before dismissively waving her hand and laughing. "Anyway, who's this Lontas?"

Bellae had forgotten Hamata could converse in Ainmhi Caint. "He's my friend and, like they said, very smart."

"Go get the blister of pus. Push the scarabaeus—the winged scarab button."

Bellae walked to the door, pushing the button. After a click, the door opened. "Lontas, I need you."

After a quick hug of reassurance for Gimelli, the two moved into the room with Hamata as the door closed behind them.

"This dopey boy is intelligent? Hmm, doubt it," Hamata purred.

"A winged scarab!" Lontas said excitedly. "They're supposedly masters of rebirth."

Sensing Lontas talking about him, Khepri fluttered over to study the boy.

"You are correct," Hamata said. "When my mother, Sekhmet, was killed, Khepri here was responsible for my birth. Like the Pegasus, there is only one of us at any point in time."

"You can speak the…"

"Obviously," Hamata drawled with irritation.

"Just ask this fool the question. He's going to die, just like the girl," Khepri said.

Bellae flashed the beetle a scolding look but did not translate for Lontas.

"What says nothing of intelligence in the morning, at noon spouts nonsense but thinks it is brilliant, at late afternoon is slightly sage, but at the close of the day mumbles regrets?"

Lontas looked down at the floor, shutting down his senses and thinking.

Grym scurried out to stand on Bellae's knee. *"I think his head's going to explode!"*

Hamata laughed, but Lontas took no notice.

"Based on the available data, I would say a human."

Hamata's expression fell into disappointment tempered with wonder.

"Many thinking beings, including Dwarves and Elves, begin without being able to converse intelligently at birth. That said, given their different phases of development, only human teenagers have the unique phase described as noon. In adulthood we are slightly sage, and once we get to our old age, at the end of the day, we often mumble regrets."

"Lontas! That's amazing," Bellae said. Even though he was becoming more confident, he was still her deferential friend.

Hamata stared at him, irate that he solved the riddle. "Think you're clever?"

"He's too humble to admit it," Bellae answered. "But I know how smart he is."

Hamata growled angrily before turning to Lontas. "At birth I am as tall as I will ever be. With age I grow shorter and shorter, puddling wider and flatter."

"Candle," Lontas answered immediately, unable to hide the smug smile fighting to erupt.

Khepri flew over, into Lontas' face.

"Don't let that insect intimidate you," Bellae said. *"Buzz off, menace!"*

Letting out a rumble of annoyance, Hamata said, "Oh, by all means, an eons-old magical creature who is sovereign of rebirth should be lightly ignored! What can never speak unless spoken to? It can articulate every language in the world, even if it has never heard the tongue before."

"I know this one," Bellae stated. "An echo, of course!"

Hamata's head bobbled side to side. "Oh, so shrewd! Who can dive into a massive lake headfirst and not get one hair on their scalp wet?"

"A bald person, or someone who has completely shaved their head," Lontas said, sighing and trying to act bored, knowing it would annoy the lioness. He squeezed Bellae's hand. *I've got you,* Lontas thought, trying to send good vibes through the touch. *I saw you were near tears when I came in.*

"What cannot move on its own, is full of infinite words, but never speaks?"

"A scroll!" Bellae said, laughing at the growing frustration of Hamata and her flying scarab beetle.

Khepri whispered something to the lioness, who nodded gleefully.

"When there were only one hundred Master Magicians in the old world, Magician Six lost his young apprentice to a tragic accident. Hundreds of interested candidates flocked to him, as there were few opportunities to train as a Magician and the job, of course, was coveted. Many were talented, and all eager to prove themselves. The sheer number of applicants posed a conundrum for Magician Six. So he held a contest to pick between such worthy contestants. He gave each an enchanted seed, a pot, and magic water. They were to plant their seed and water it. After six months, they were to return with the grown plant and any leftover water.

"When the time of judging arrived, Magician Six had them line up in two rows facing each other. As he walked between the columns, he found hundreds of beautiful plants, flowers, and even miniature trees presented. Seeming frustrated, he quickly passed on all of them, angrily dismissing them, until he came to the last two, each with barren pots filled only with dirt.

"An athletic, handsome male had a mostly full jar of the magic water, and a pot of dry soil. A young girl stood shyly at the end, holding a pot filled with moist dirt and a nearly empty pot of the given water. He chose the girl and chastised the others. Why was he interested in the two with no growth, and how did he know to choose the girl over the man?"

Bellae instantly looked to Lontas, who had his head down, eyes closed in concentration. Khepri began flittering around Lontas' head, trying to annoy him with his humming wings, clicking mouth sounds, and grating claw scratching.

Bellae joined her friend as a thin smirk blossomed into a full smile across his face.

"First, the Magician had given them small pebbles magically disguised as seeds, so everyone who showed up with plant growth had been fraudulent," Lontas said. "Then, left with the last two, the Magician could easily tell the man was lazy. His water container was mostly full—consequently, he had not spent any time watering the soil. Therefore, only the young girl, who had obviously tried to care for and water the 'seed,' was truly honest and hard working."

"Impressive. Good thing he's with you," Hamata said, plainly irked.

"Did we pass?" Bellae asked.

"Did you pass what?" Hamata asked, genuinely confused.

"Does Bellae get the first crystals?" Lontas said.

Hamata burst out laughing. "Oh, you foolish children. This had nothing to do with getting the crystals!"

Bellae and Lontas shot each other exasperated looks.

The lioness called over Khepri and whispered to him. He promptly flew to Bellae. *"You thought that was part of the quest? You really are imbecilic and going to die!"*

"Exactly how would we know that?" Bellae asked, squeezing Lontas' hand tightly. "I'm so grateful you're here."

When Hamata stopped laughing, she continued, "All I needed to do was make sure you could speak the ancient animal tongue."

"All of this was for nothing?" Bellae asked.

"Challenging one's mind is never 'for nothing,' little girl. I'm here to guide you through your first test, but please understand your ultimate success or failure does not affect me. I, in fact, love-love-love Na Cearcaill. Good riddance to the masses I say."

"So you survive it then? Na Cearcaill?" Bellae questioned.

"Obviously."

"I'm not sure you would feel that way if you weren't going to survive," Lontas replied, angry at what he saw as a ruse and the lionesses' arrogance.

Hamata laughed. "I guess we all feel a little more connected to the issue of our own mortality. Time, however, does not listen or care about the pleas of you mortals. Too often you wish things to remain stagnant, loathing the idea of moving back and fearing the endless march of time moving forward, which means, of course, the world moving past and beyond you.

"Eternity lets you measly creatures rise, but briefly, never stopping its movement forward, always changing. It is you transients that regret *yourselves* not being in the world, but the callous world does not mourn your absence."

Bellae and Lontas looked at each other, unsure of what to say.

Hamata shrugged. "Anyway, these riddles were just a taste of the challenges you will be facing. It wasn't actually part of your quest."

"Then why put us through that?" Bellae asked.

"Curiosity? Boredom? As you can imagine, ferratus lanx aren't exactly stimulating conversationalists, and kameli smell like scat. Plus, my ancestors were known for their riddles. Don't be mad at me. It's the wretched Ainmhi Caint that decided to put you through these tests."

"Why exactly did they do that? Why not—"

"Because they're simpleton dolts," Hamata interrupted, laughing. "Actually, like Magician Six they needed to make sure you are worthy to make the right choice at the end."

"So now we have to face the 'real' challenge?" Bellae asked, near tears.

"Yes. As first guardian, I have a whole list of things I'm supposed to tell you, courtesy of the half-witted Ainmhi Caint, but most of it's boring. This is a quest to save the world, blah, blah, blah, you can die, if you fail untold will die, blah, blah, blah, we are your ancestors, and you should try to succeed…etcetera, etcetera. The next part I do like.

"The sightless universe insentiently welcomes all lives, but not all who live have the courage to confront the reality of the infinite universe. Of those who dare to contemplate the vastness of infinity, some will turn their backs in horror, some will try, fruitlessly, to rage against the reality of the truth. The wisest amongst us see the supreme value, even if clothed in absurdity compared to timeless eternity, of our own brief life. They wake up to the reality of the supreme value of our life, our time here."

Bellae and Lontas shared a look of utter confusion.

"I should have known that would go over your embryonic brains. Well, you should get started. There's the world for you to fail to save and all," the lioness creature stated casually.

"Follow me," she whispered. All but Khepri entered the landing where the rest of the League waited. Wordlessly, the lioness headed down the stairs. When her form had disappeared, she yelled back, "Bird-boy stays. He won't fit down the stairs."

"I'll stay with him," Sankari volunteered.

Arend exchanged an odd look with Kainen. "She speaks common tongue, and Bird-boy?"

Kainen shrugged his shoulders. *Aren't the guardians supposed to help us?* Despite training for this their whole lives, they had been caught off guard by the demeanor of the creature.

"You guys, go ahead. Seems as if we don't have much choice," Arend groaned, looking tired and sore.

Kainen, Scelto, Gimelli, Lontas, and Bellae headed down the snug stairwell while Sankari fluttered next to Arend.

"How long have you been here waiting for us?" Kainen asked.

Hamata stopped on the winding stairway. "I'm a guardian of the prophecy, and my ancestors have been watching over the Seeing Crystals for thousands of years. There is a guardian at each of the sites you will visit. We are responsible for maintaining the structures and keeping things safe and prepared."

"Is your family here?" Gimelli asked since she had mentioned her descendants.

"I'm an Eviga-lejon—an eternal lion!" Hamata hissed angrily, as if this should be known. "My mother was the great and divine Sekhmet! However, like the Pegasus, there is only one of us alive in the world at any one time. Khepri will ensure the cycle will repeat when I die."

"Divine…but she died?" Gimelli asked tentatively.

Hamata laughed disdainfully. "What is born, dies."

Unsure of what to say, the League continued silently down the stairs.

Once at the bottom, Hamata stopped at a rectangular landing complete with a large door before spinning around. Her eyes suddenly blazed with hate, and a chill wormed through the League. Flashing her menacing teeth she spoke, "Since you asked about my family. How's your family, Bellae?"

"I'm her family," Gimelli said defensively.

"We didn't mean any offense in asking about yours. We've never heard of an Eviga-lejon," Kainen added quickly.

Hamata glared at them a little longer before pointing to worn-down inscriptions etched around the door. Time had rendered the series of symbols frail.

"Excuse me!" Lontas said, nudging past the lioness. "Okay, okay," he added excitedly. "So there are three etchings: one above the door and one on the wall to either side. While on the door, we have three sets of three emblems carved on what look like buttons—nine total. I surmise that each of the inscriptions are questions, and the answers are the on the door, like a riddle lock!"

"Oh, how I hate this kid," Hamata purred. "I despise arrogance!"

"Intelligence and excitement for knowledge are *not* the same as arrogance," Scelto said defensively, standing tall, face-to-face with Hamata.

"Careful, boy," the lioness said.

"If you knew Lontas at all you, would know how ridiculous 'arrogance' is," Bellae added.

"I'm guessing he's correct then?" Gimelli asked.

"Ask your friend. He seems to know everything," Hamata said. Glaring at Scelto, she moved up the stairs and sat down, detachedly picking at her paw.

"I think he's right," Kainen added. "I'm familiar with the symbols above the door but not the others."

"If you work on those above the door, I'll take the writing on the sides," Lontas said, smiling giddily.

Scroll 8: Graveyard of Splintered Dreams

"What's up, guys?" Jumeaux greeted, sitting down next to his friends. The dining hall was dim, lit by candles and torches instead of the usual bright magic. Cliques of students, mostly divided by the color of their robe, conversed around the large chamber.

"Hey, man. You been practicing with Veneficus...again?" Kaveri asked, a hint of jealousy coating the anger behind his words.

"Yes."

"What's he teaching you? You spend a ton of time with him, and little with us anymore."

"He told me not to talk about it," Jumeaux answered sheepishly.

"He probably didn't mean us," Chy said, forcing a smile.

"Really, he specifically told me not to discuss it," Jumeaux said.

Chy and Kaveri changed the subject and started discussing one of their classes, but their listless conversation seemed coerced and unwieldy.

"He genuinely warned me not to," Jumeaux interrupted.

"Hey, we get it."

"Yeah, don't worry about it," Chy added with mixed believability.

"Did you hear that they are rationing mindre crystals even more? Now, no practicing even for Master Magicians," Kaveri said, worry creeping into his expression.

"War uses up a ton of crystals," Chy said, nodding. "Apparently, there's a big attack coming up and they are moving intact siege engines."

Jumeaux looked down, embarrassed and ashamed at how many crystals he was going through with his extra training. *Aren't I going to help Veneficus reclaim the Macht Crystals from Bellae? Yes, of course, it's okay,* he justified internally.

"Yeah," Chy continued, crossing his arms angrily. "Now they are even limiting transporter use to emergencies. Do you know how far I have to sprint to get from advanced mathematics to defensive enchantments class?"

"They should add more time between classes. Without transporters most of us will consistently be late," Kaveri added.

Jumeaux nodded enthusiastically to let them know he was on their side.

"I guess the crystal shortage is finally catching up to us. I honestly didn't want to believe the rumors that things were this dire. What does Veneficus say?" Chy asked.

"He's going to get the Macht Crystals and save magic for us all."

Kaveri and Chy glanced at each other, a glimmer of hope fluttering deep below, still drowning under doubt and jealousy.

"I just worry about what this means for us," Kaveri said, looking around the dining hall longingly. "I don't have anywhere to go."

"Oh, and I do?" Chy said, his voice cracking with emotion. Jumeaux thought he saw the big man's eyes moisten before he turned away.

"You could do temple magic," Jumeaux added, trying to be helpful.

Anger briefly flashed across Chy's eyes before he softened. "Not really my thing. So what classes are you having trouble in?"

"It was alchemy, wasn't it?" Kaveri said, pulling out small pieces of parchment.

"Let's quiz you on the symbols. Also, make sure you study Jābir—he's super important. He single handedly organized alchemy from a chaotic shambles to a more scientific field. He came closest to the solving the riddle of an alkahest."

"How exactly would that work?" Chy wondered, smiling broadly. "If some alkahest substance could dissolve every material on the planet, like they say, wouldn't it dissolve its way through the container, and the entire earth for that matter?"

Kaveri laughed. "Remember Philalethes said the alkahest would only dissolve a compound into their purest elements. So a pure container would not dissolve and could hold it."

Chy scoffed. "Sounds like bunk. I believe in the alkahest as much as I do the Philosopher's Stone. I mean something that can transform base metals into gold? Nonsense."

"Jumeaux still needs to know it. You have to study chrysopoeia, the idea of transmuting baser metals into gold. Traditionally, this was done by finding the so-called, and likely fictional, Philosopher's Stone, but modern scholars think alchemy could do it. On the test they always ask about the historical trials. All failures, of course. Otherwise, we'd be bathing in gold."

Chy laughed before adding, "Make sure you know Zosimos of Panapolis and his distillation techniques."

"True," Kaveri confirmed. "They will give you the basic material, and you have to set up various distillation configurations."

"Boys," a grim looking Master Magician said after silently slinking behind them. "While I'm encouraged by your scholarly discussion, I need a word with my two Adjutants."

As Chy and Kaveri stepped away, Jumeaux spun around a codex that had been sitting next to Chy. A small piece of parchment peeked invitingly out of the middle. Jumeaux opened it to find a handwritten poem:

Dreams—
Ghostly, paradoxical aspirations:
To haunt with remorse, or animatingly inspire.
Their birth is free, born from ashes within our mind.
Too often they suffer to wither and die, untested.
Their realization,
If occurring at all,
Demands painstaking effort and colossal sacrifices.

I have *only* dreams.
Forsaken Dreams—
Dreams forsaken.
Despite my efforts, they starve,
Evaporating as to reality's heat they awaken,
Hope leaving as ambition flounders.

Dreams sit within my mind, scattered—
Fragile, cracked, bruised, mistreated, rejected, maligned, fading shards.
A few, though well worn by hope and aspiration, sit merely slightly bruised,
Seedlings struggling to rise towards the dreamers' sun.
Glowing internally, powered by rays of fading hope.

Time falls, unconsciously deaf to its repercussions.
My legacy condemned, eternally trapped in failure's amber.

Aspirations dying within my head—
A graveyard of splintered dreams.

Within my consciousness, their birthplace,
My dreams demand value, burdening with heft.
My soul shatters upon realizing outside me,
They hold no measure, import, or heaviness.
Who will grieve the death of my dreams?
Laying hidden, bathed in forsaken care,
Dormant in the cemetery of my mind.
The silent absence of replies,
To my noiseless screams?
Deafening.

Jumeaux jumped as Chy came roaring over to the table. "I'm so sorry. I was going to look at the book, and the poem fell out."

Chy sat down, some of his anger fizzling away as he held his head, eyelids bordering with uninvited tears.

"This is good. Outstanding, actually, and I'm not a poetry guy," Jumeaux said as Chy glanced up, eyes muggy.

"You think?"

"I know," Jumeaux said as kindly as he could.

After making sure Kaveri was still busy with their professor, Chy whispered, "Keep this between us. I don't want people to know I write poetry."

"Of course. No problem. But if you ever want someone to read your stuff, I would be happy to."

"Thanks. Anyway, this poem is about how I really can't handle it if this place closes down. Just like a lot of you squires…"

"Former squire," Jumeaux said defensively, lamenting his time at Liberum.

"Right—former. In any case, a lot of us are orphans, thrown away by our families and plucked off the streets to be given a choice between the Academy of Magic and the Proliate's brutal military school. When they found me, I was a begging on the streets of Maatila in Ager, half-starved and gloriously angry. Sometimes I act like I don't care, and flaunt attitude, but this place saved me. It can't shut down."

"They can't really close the Academy of Magic?" Jumeaux questioned.

Chy nodded. "Yeah, they really could and may have to. There's talk of going back to just one hundred Magicians. The mindre crystal shortage is desperate. I really don't know what I will do if I lose my place here."

Jumeaux nodded respectfully, unsure of what to say as tears streamed down Chy's face, all pretense of toughness long gone under orders from deep fears.

"What's going on here?" Kaveri said, sitting down as Chy quickly wiped his eyes.

"Too many onions," Chy said, folding the parchment with his poem and stuffing it in his pocket.

"There are a lot of onions around here these days," Kaveri said, sighing deeply.

Jumeaux felt guilty. He had been so caught up in his extra training and burgeoning relationship with Veneficus he didn't notice how worried and panicked his friends were. Knowing he was protected and "needed," Veneficus had shielded him from the worry inscribed on their faces.

Chy put his head down, his troubles manifesting as silent sobbing and sorrowful trembles through his muscular body.

"I hate bloody onions," Kaveri said, rubbing his temples.

Scroll 9: What Happens if We're Wrong?

"I've got the top question figured out," Kainen said. "Since there's no handle, I assume Lontas is correct and pushing some combination of the nine images on the door unlocks it." He looked at Hamata, who crossed her arms, absently drumming her clawed fingers against them.

"Aren't you supposed to help us?" Gimelli asked.

Groaning, the lioness rolled her eyes before staring at the ceiling.

"The door has three rows of three symbols. On the top row there's an ear, a mouth, and an eye. The second row has symbols representing the numbers five-V, six-VI, and seven-VII. The final contains a mouth with three slashes under it, a wavy pyramid on its side," at this, Hamata huffed angrily, "and a mouth with a half circle pointing down," Kainen said. "Let's assume the three inscriptions are questions. It seems logical we pick the answer by selecting three of the nine emblems to unlock the door."

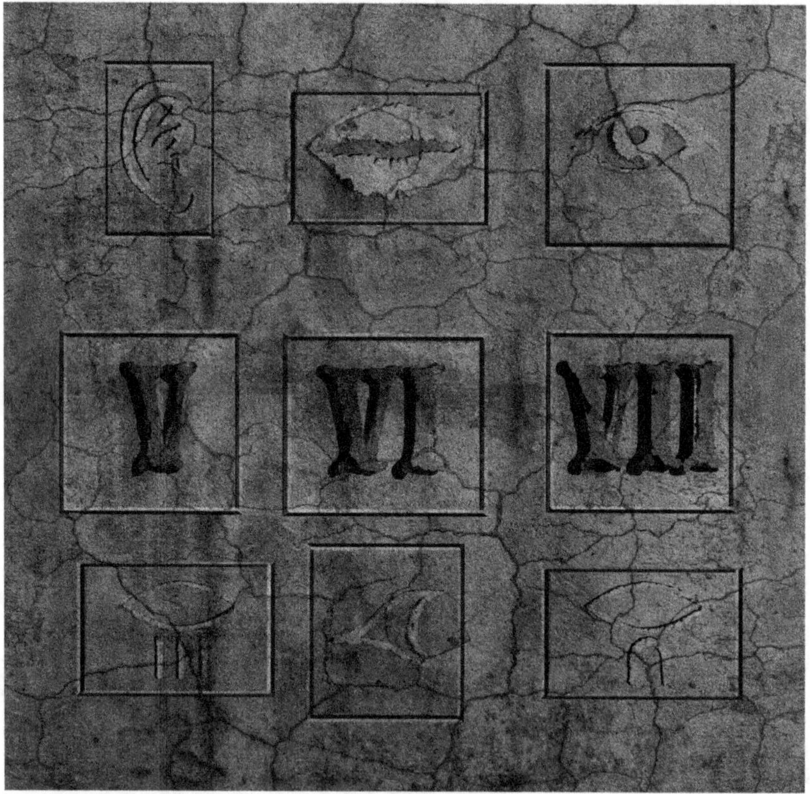

Figure 21: The League is forced to solve three riddles. The potential answers are represented by carvings within buttons which, if correct, will open the door.

"Do you know what your question is asking?" Lontas asked.

"Okay. The first part of the translation is hard, but I'm pretty sure it says, 'That existing in such fragility that speaking its name shatters it.'"

Lontas laughed.

Hamata moaned noisily. "How do you stand that twit?"

"Hey!" Scelto yelled. "Help, stay silent, or get out."

"Big tough guy, huh?"

"Yeah, I guess," Scelto answered as the others laughed.

"Just ignore her. Being cramped up here for eons has obviously made her unpleasant," Gimelli said.

"I recognize obnoxious when I smell it," Hamata replied.

"You have the answer, Lontas?" Kainen asked.

"Yes. Should I just say it?"

"No," Hamata roared. "You should just think and strain really, really hard until the answer comes out your arse!"

"So rude!" Bellae said.

"Silence–listening, that means we would press the ear of the top row," Lontas ventured quietly, his previous joy quenched by Hamata. "Silence–listening as opposed to talking or looking represented by the mouth and eye."

"Great job," Gimelli beamed, moving to block his view of the guardian.

"We have a one in three chance even without the answer," Scelto said.

"There are a trinity of sets each with three 'answer' buttons on the door arranged horizontally, which gives us twenty-seven possible outcomes for the triple answer required," Lontas informed. "It's true. With each row we have a 33.3 percent chance if we randomly guessed. However, I am one-hundred percent confident of the other two answers."

"Oh, bloody desert at noon, you just keep getting more endearing!" Hamata said, but the League ignored her.

"What are the other two questions?" Bellae asked.

"The one on the left is a series of adjectives: ideal, flawless, exemplary, peerless, utopian."

"Uh, what?" Scelto asked.

"That…isn't even a question," Kainen added.

"But look at the second row of numbers, the choices are five, six, and seven–represented by symbols on each of the buttons," Lontas said, smiling as if that would be an excessive explanation.

Bellae chuckled. "More?"

"Those words are synonyms for perfect," Lontas said grimacing in disappointment.

"Arend and I studied this," Kainen said. "It's six, isn't it?"

"Yes," Lontas replied, brightening. "Remember, we learned this in math," he said glaring optimistically at Gimelli and Scelto.

"I kind of remember that," Gimelli said.

Scelto shook his head. "Absolutely no clue. Just tell us."

"Number theory tells us a 'perfect' number is a whole number that is equal to the sum of its positive divisors," Lontas said, adding excitedly, "Excluding the number itself, of course!"

"Of course!" Bellae said, giggling.

"Since the adjectives listed are all synonymous for perfect, we need a 'perfect' number. Six's divisors are one, two, and three. One plus two plus three equals six, and six is, therefore, our first perfect number. What makes six super cool is, it is not only the sum but also the *product* of the first three numbers! I mean it's obviously not what makes it perfect, but one times two times three is also six. We have to wait until twenty-eight to get the next perfect number…"

Bellae put her hand on Kainen's shoulder, stopping him from interrupting while whispering, "Let him have this."

Kainen nodded as Lontas continued, "…positive factors are one, two, four, seven, fourteen, and twenty-eight. As we know, twenty-eight is excluded, so the rest add to twenty-eight. The next one is not until 496, then 8,128. Notice they are all even numbers. Uhm…should I stop so we can keep going? The next one is over thirty-three million…"

"Stopping your drivel would be a pleasant change of pace," Hamata said, narrowing her eyes, foot tapping displeasure upon the stair.

"What's that symbol on the right wall there?" Bellae asked, pointing to an etching of two men facing each other with one of the figures within a rectangle. "Is the one guy inside a box, or is he looking out a window? Also, what are they holding?"

"Notice the man outside the 'box' has a palm leaf in his left hand while the one 'inside' the frame has it in his right. The figure not in the square has a bunch of dates in his right hand. The one within holds them in his left. It's actually not a box but a mirror! There's one person represented outside, looking into a mirror, where the reflection makes left become right and vice versa," Lontas said.

"What's the round thing he's standing on?" Scelto asked.

"It's a circle with a one within it," Lontas answered.

"They are trying to say it's the mirror of unity, right?" Kainen said. "We studied that."

"Exactly. The inscription goes on to talk about several words with the prefix bi- and others with di-. Bipedal, bicentennial, bigamy, bilateral, among others. There bi- is meaning two or twice. Words with di- include diverge, dilemma, divide, and there are more meaning to split *or* two."

"So the answer is two? How does that help us with the last three symbols?" Gimelli asked.

"The reason angry guardian lady huffed when Kainen went through the last symbols is he had them wrong," Lontas said. "He was correct–the first one is a mouth with three slashes under it, and that represents three-fourths. The third is a mouth, but not a half circle below it, but a cattle hobble or yoke symbol. That represents ten in the ancient tribes of the desert, so it's one-tenth. The middle one is our answer–representing one-half. That is not a 'wavy pyramid' tipped over but a symbol for the inside corner of the eye–the sclera to the side of the center iris. Since two, when looking in the mathematical mirror of unity becomes one-half, we choose the symbol in the middle."

"How does an eye designate a fraction? That literally makes no sense," Scelto said.

"In the myth of the ancient desert kingdom, an archaic god's eye, Horus, was damaged, or broken up in battle. Even though it was restored by magic, the parts of the eye came to represent breaking into parts–fractions," Lontas said.

"So…ear-silence, six-perfect number, and part of the eye representing one half?" Kainen said as the others nodded, impressed with Lontas.

"Since I have absolutely nothing to do, and am so enjoying your company, I was hoping this could take longer," Hamata purred. "On the other hand, if you could finish in this century that would be super great."

"Go for it," Gimelli encouraged.

Kainen stepped forward and hesitated. "I never thought I'd use all those things my dad was trying to teach me. I was always more interested in learning to fight. Anyway, thanks for your help, Lontas. We couldn't have done this without you."

"Thank-thank-wel-welcome," Lontas said, blushing. I really just love to learn. It is—"

"I don't see how I could dislike you more," Hamata hissed. "Push the bloody symbols!"

"You seriously need a healer's help, Hamata," Kainen said, pressing the ear symbol. The emblem sunk in, and a loud click echoed within the door. "We're on our way, I—"

"And so quickly!" Hamata purred sarcastically.

After pushing the icon for six and the symbol for one-half, the inside of the eye, Hamata abruptly ran back up the stairs.

"Push the door or stand back!" she yelled. "I don't want to clean up squished brats."

Quickly Scelto moved forward, pushing the substantial door. It fell angrily forward, crashing onto the floor, sending a cloud of dust swirling into the air. They could see three locking mechanisms that had been holding the door up on both sides of the thick stone gate.

"The seeing seal is broken," Hamata said, scurrying back down and rudely pushing through the League, leading them into a large, dusty crypt. Descending into the large rectangular room, cooler air embraced their bodies, granular air greeted their eyes, and a thick mildew smell tunneled into their nares. The massive vault had three sides of tan stone. The fourth side was covered with unique carvings in white and black rock.

"Use ones in the stairwell to light the torches in here," Hamata instructed, pointing to Scelto and Lontas with her long, graceful claws.

As the light spread itself around the room, it became clear the fourth wall was covered in a series of shapes and lines carved into the distinctive dichromic rock.

"The Seeing Crystals, perception and deception, are within that wall," Hamata stated.

"Do you give them to us?" Kainen asked, excited to finally collect the first crystals.

Hamata cackled. "It doesn't work that way. Everything must be earned. Nothing shall be given. Did they mistakenly send the League of the Vacuous? This is the puzzle wall of Calor. It was meticulously carved from the du-a-gwyn rocks from around Mount Honoo. It is a white rock on the outside but black in the center. So carving into the rock creates shapes and lines that look as if they are written in black."

The League moved in closer to study the wall covered in a series of symbols. There was a thin ledge on the very top between the carvings and the ceiling.

"The majority of petroglyphs—carvings into the rock—are stars," Lontas said. "Each one has angled black lines cutting behind them and black squares surrounding their tips. There are triangles, pyramids, partial circles, lines, and some moons."

"So what do we do?" Scelto asked.

"Seriously?" Hamata seemed irritated. "I so want to kill them," she whispered.

"Why do you want to kill us?" Scelto asked angrily.

"I don't."

"You literally just said so," Gimelli said.

"Nope."

"Uh, yes, you did."

"Definitely no," Hamata purred.

"I mean, we unquestioningly heard you," Gimelli replied.

Hamata shook her head and rolled her eyes. "Doesn't sound like me."

"Remind me to avoid living alone in a desert oasis for eons. It turns you crazy," Gimelli said.

Figure 22: The first guardian Hamata proves discourteously unhelpful. After suffering through extraneous brainteasers, the League is confronted with a giant puzzle wall.

"I think we should read the inscription," Kainen said, pointing to writing above the ledge towards the ceiling. "I can't read it from here. Bellae, would you get on Scelto's shoulders?"

She nodded, climbing up as Hamata hissed. "Make sure you don't touch the rocks up there. It's *very* important."

"What rocks?" Scelto huffed as he edged Bellae to the overhang.

"There's a line of cylinder rocks actually sticking through the top of this ledge. They seem attached to something down below, but there's a lot of sand and dust. Each cylinder has a number carved on it. I can see: thirty, forty, fifty...but they keep going in both directions—getting smaller to the left and bigger to the right," Bellae advised.

"Can we look, Bellae?" Borb squeaked.

"Okay, but don't touch the rocks sticking up," she advised, setting them down on the ledge. The curious mice poked their noses into the cracks around the cylinder rocks sticking up.

"Each of these rocks is attached to something down below. It looks like if you press them, it will trigger something. Do you want us to check it out? Of course, for dangerous work like this compensation would be required," Grym said.

Bellae laughed. "The mice are telling me each of these rocks is attached to some sort of triggering device."

"Tell your rats to get away from them!" Hamata howled. "Once you find the answer to the riddle, you press the correct number on one of those answer stones, and the crystals will be revealed. If you press a wrong one, a trap is released."

Bellae collected the mice, carefully putting them into her pocket. *"Thanks, guys."*

"So wait, what happens if we're wrong?" Lontas asked.

"First, the room fills with whip scorpions that secrete acid from their glands and spitting cobras that can spit poison six and a half feet. Then, just for good measure, it fills up with sand to suffocate any who are still alive," Hamata answered tranquilly.

"That sounds lovely," Scelto commented.

"I guess we need to be right," Kainen said.

"Charming, and clever," Hamata said. "Just so endearing!"

Bellae began,

"To find the crystals of Sight,
You don't need muscles or might.
Wisely use your eyes.
Caution here applies.
Use all your Perception,
Don't fall for the Deception.
Count the ***STARS*** true.
Make sure to think it through.
Guess too many, or too few,
And you die.
There is no second try.
Get your answer Firm,
Then press the number to ConFirm."

"This will be easy. We just carefully count all the star symbols. Then Bellae can push the correct rock," Kainen said cheerfully.

"Ready to get down now?" Scelto asked, his shoulders starting to ache.

"No, wait!" Bellae answered. "There's something else. The word 'stars' is carved much deeper than the others. The letters are also all capitalized and sloping to the right. Also, the letter 'S' in Sight is carved a little deeper as well."

"They are just emphasizing it's the stars we need to count. Not the other symbols," Kainen explained as Bellae got down.

For the next half an hour, the League carefully counted and re-counted the number of stars on the wall. Everyone but Lontas had thrown themselves into the work. He kept asking Bellae to repeat what the riddle said.

"All right! For the fifth time, I count one hundred and fifty stars," Kainen said. "I know Gimelli and Scelto got the same number. I think we should go for it."

"Hold on. I think we're missing something," Lontas advised. "Bellae, can you get up and read it again?"

"Listen, Lontas, we just need to grab the crystals and get out of the desert," Scelto cajoled.

"Please," Lontas begged.

Bellae nodded.

Despite the frustrated sighs, Bellae climbed on Scelto's shoulders to reread the inscription. When she finished, Lontas had her move along the ledge and read all the number possibilities on the rock.

"They are arranged from zero to two hundred. They go up by tens under one hundred: zero, ten, twenty, thirty, and so on. Above one hundred they increase by fifty: one hundred, one hundred fifty, two hundred. So there are thirteen rocks all ending in zero, Lontas," Bellae said.

"We should press the one-hundred and fifty rock," Kainen declared.

"I agree," Scelto and Gimelli affirmed.

A loud grating noise startled the League. They turned to see Hamata slinking through a hidden door off the side of the cavern. "This is my cue to leave. Your success or failure is not my concern. Although personally I agree with the cleansing effect of Na Cearcaill, I do so hate to clean up messes."

"What do you mean?" Scelto asked.

"Nothing." Hamata purred as he backed out the door. "By the way, Bellae, the twins Gimelli and Jumeaux, are *not* your siblings. Just thought you might like to know." A loud caterwaul laugh spun through the room before she slammed the secret door shut.

Scroll 10: *Agree to Disagree*

"Not possible!" Gimelli screamed. "She's lying!"

Hamata opened a doorhole—only part of her face was visible. "It's true, vile child. I wouldn't waste a lie on you pathetic creatures!"

Gimelli paused, the secrecy around her parents' deaths, the small slip-ups where people had referred to mothers—plural—all coalesced to add credence to the lionesses' words.

"What was her mother's name then?" Gimelli asked as the others looked on, stunned.

"You think such insignificant details are important to me?" Hamata said, laughing.

"She's just trying to rattle us, you—Bellae. I was outside our house when you were born. It was right after that our parents died and…" Gimelli hesitated, a look of doubt unfurling upon her face. "We…Jumeaux and I, never got to see mother's body. The next thing we knew we were told our father killed himself. Then they ripped us out of the Redwoods, marching the three of us across Verngaurd to Liberum. But why…"

"I have known for a while," Bellae said.

"What?" Gimelli said, falling hard on her shaky knees under the harsh fatigue of shock. After sobbing for a moment, she said, "I need to speak with Bellae alone."

Bellae and Gimelli huddled away from the white and black wall as the others moved toward it.

"Stralande told me…along with many other things, when we met alone," Bellae replied calmly, despite the dread at many of his words of warning.

"What else did he say?" Gimelli asked, amazed at how tranquil Bellae seemed.

"He told me the truth about prophesies. They are just guides for future generations, and the so-called Chosen One is really just a title to be given to the first animal talker who appeared so that others would believe in me and help. If you had been born with the gift, you would be the 'Chosen.'

"He said the last descendants of the Ainmhi Caint have been hiding in the Giant Redwood forest for eons, waiting for the gift of the animal talkers to reemerge. When my mom was pregnant with me, she suddenly became fluent in Ainmhi Caint, among other talents. This meant I would be born with the gift. So they had to make me 'fit' with the prophecy while keeping the 'false' prophecy plausible. In order to do that, I needed a brother. That is how they paired me up with you and Jumeaux because your mom was also pregnant and due at the same time. I guess they switched me for your real sibling."

Gimelli's tears began flowing even harsher as she dove into Bellae, squeezing tightly. "You know," she sobbed, "now it makes sense why Kara-Rehe said she knew our *mothers*—plural."

Hamata's cackle conjured a deep anger within Bellae as she looked up to see the lioness peeking through a peephole in the larger door she had exited.

"Taking pleasure in others pain is the lowest and most heinous existence," Lontas said, moving over to stand near the small door she was peering through.

"Sounds like you have a lot of experience with people making fun of you," Hamata replied.

Lontas shrugged his shoulders. "It's made me who I am."

"I'm sorry I didn't tell you, Gimelli. Stralande told me not to. I think he knew Hamata would tell us out of spite and wanted it to be less of a shock, for me."

"He must have known she was evil," Gimelli said, glaring at the opening in the door.

"You know you're still my sister even if we didn't have the same mom and dad. Just because we aren't bound by blood doesn't mean we aren't family. You've always been there, always looked out for me, always been ready with a smile when I needed it, and always loved me." Bellae paused, trying to put into words the plaguing thoughts about her family since Stralande first splayed open the grisly truth. "I think loyalty, caring, love, giving hope, all those things, are stronger than blood."

Gimelli stopped crying. "Aren't you supposed to be the younger sister?"

"By the way the little brat of a Chosen One is reacting, I'm guessing the blue menace Stralande already told you," Hamata harrumphed. "He's always spoiling my fun. At least I got a rile out of the older one."

"What's wrong with you?" Lontas roiled, but Hamata shut the small door.

Lontas moved over, stiffly kneeling down next to them, forcing a three-way hug. "What Bellae says is true—sorry, I couldn't help overhearing. That makes us all family."

"Always," Bellae said but pulled away when she felt Gimelli stiffen and get that faraway look that comes from talking telepathically with Jumeaux.

"Are you eavesdropping?" she asked her brother.

"I didn't mean to, really. I just wanted to check on you. We hadn't spoken in a while," Jumeaux said.

"Did you hear what Bellae said?" Gimelli asked.

"No. What?"

"Never mind," she answered, a twinge of fear shivering through her. Gimelli was certain he heard and lied.

Jumeaux bit his tongue. Veneficus was watching closely. *I can't blow this.* He had, in fact, heard but did not care. His parents meant nothing, whether dead or alive. His family was here in the Citadel, not his twin or fake sister, Bellae. He was angry the Ainmhi Caint remnants deceived them, but it didn't change his opinion of them. Nothing could—they were traitors. The more time he spent with Veneficus the more he hated them. *Just keep playing nice.*

"So what are you up to?" Jumeaux asked. *"Any luck with the crystals?"*

Gimelli hesitated, knowing lying was useless. In fact, given the increasing number of flashing visions she experienced, she was convinced he could see a clear picture of where they were. *"We're in a cave in the Desert of Calor, figuring out how to get the first crystals."*

"Can I help? I just want you to be safe and get those crystals."

"Thanks, but we're okay. I better get back to Bellae."

There was an awkward silence as Jumeaux set the crosier aside and quickly updated Veneficus, leaving out the fact Bellae was not his sister.

"Cut it off," Veneficus recommended. "Don't push too hard."

"Okay, Sis. Good luck and let me know if I can help. Say hi to Bellae."

"The good luck was a nice touch," Veneficus commented after Jumeaux relayed the entire conversation. "Let's go practice some spells. You're improving fast."

"Thank you, sir!" Jumeaux said. "It's an honor to help."

Gimelli felt Jumeaux's presence leave. After taking a deep breath, she continued with Bellae. "Did Stralande tell you what happened to our mom and dad?" She hesitated. "I guess plural moms and dads."

"No. What *did* happen to them?" Bellae asked.

Gimelli turned pale, wishing she hadn't asked. *I ALWAYS knew something was off about their death. Our... my dad would never kill himself in grief even if Mom had died in childbirth.* "I don't know. Anyway, we should get back to the crystals," she added quickly.

"Wait. How did they die?" Bellae asked.

"My mom died in childbirth, and the story they fed us was that my dad killed himself in grief," Gimelli said plainly, no longer believing it. *There's no time to dwell on this now, but when this is over,* Gimelli thought, a smile hiding the coiling anger and resentment within, *I will come back to the Redwoods and find out.*

Despite Bellae's continued questioning, Gimelli insisted she had no other details. After a long hug, she said, "Sisters-in-spirit? Forever?"

Bellae nodded, and the three rejoined the others.

"Sorry about the news," Scelto said as Kainen nodded, both unsure of what to say.

Gimelli quickly hugged them both.

"Let's get back to the riddle," Kainen said.

"Listen, I feel strongly about this. You need to trust me," Lontas pleaded.

Kainen shook his head. "Everyone agrees, except you, the stars number one hundred and fifty, so let's push that and get going. We still have four sets of crystals to find."

Scelto and Kainen moved towards the wall when Bellae shouted, "No!"

The power in her voice triggered everyone to startle and stop.

"Tell me what you're thinking, Lontas," she requested.

"Hey..." Kainen started, upset at his leadership being usurped, again. Taking a deep breath, he nodded. "Lontas has helped us a ton. Go ahead."

"Well," Lontas said, "since we *die* with a wrong answer, I think we should be sure. There's something bothering me. I think I have it figured out but want to hear it one last time."

Despite the complaints, Lontas helped Bellae up on his shoulders.

"To find the crystals of **S**ight,
You don't need muscles or might.
Wisely use your eyes.
Caution here applies.

Use all your Perception,
Don't fall for the Deception.
Count the ***STARS*** true.
Make sure to think it through.
Guess too many, or too few,
And you die.
There is no second try.
Get your answer Firm,
Then press the number to ConFirm."

"Now, which words are capitalized that don't have to be," Lontas probed.

"Okay: Sight, Perception, Deception, Stars, Firm, and the "Firm" within the word confirm," Bellae answered.

"Anything else?" Lontas asked. "Anything else different?"

"Wait. Move closer," she requested. "I can't believe I didn't notice it before. There are three random letters that are carved deeper. I had noticed the S in Sight before but now I see there are two e's as well. The e in wisely and deception are darker."

After setting Bellae down, Lontas started laughing. *Wisely see deception! That's it!* he thought, awkwardly dancing around.

"Lontas, we all know you're more coordinated, but...what you're doing is giving me a headache," Scelto said, irritated at the riddle and stuffy chamber.

Ignoring him, Lontas grabbed Bellae, spinning her around in an impromptu dance. Bellae couldn't help laughing.

"There have been a few things bothering me," Lontas said after stopping. "It seems odd there's a number '0' as a choice. I mean, why have a zero? Then the line, 'Don't fall for the Deception.' What deception? There are stars, and you count them, right? No, no, and no. They are trying to trick us into rushing. Then the final clue was 'stars' and three letters being carved more deeply. The bolded letters spell, See. Sight: wisely, see, deception.

"The choice of words they put the bolded letters in is important. When you take it all together, the answer is obvious. Isn't it?" Lontas asked.

Blank expressions stared back at him, prompting him to move to the wall. "Come look. What do you notice about this so-called star?" he said, rubbing his hands across it.

"Help us, Lontas," Gimelli said.

"Okay, try this. Everyone run your fingers over it. Try and trace a complete 'star,'" he instructed patiently. "What do you notice?"

"Can't you just tell us, professor?" Kainen asked, impatiently.

Lontas blushed slightly. Well, Hamata said the outside of the rock is white, so the black is carved. Observe *what* they carved. They etched black lines and black squares missing triangular sections. They didn't actually carve *any* stars. Our minds *see* stars, but they are not there. It is only the absence of black carvings in the *full* shape of a star. The answer is zero."

"What?" Kainen and Scelto hollered.

"This is just a scheme to deceive us. They didn't carve *any* stars—not really. This riddle reminds me of the trick questions Friar used to ask us," Lontas replied.

The mention of Friar stopped the squires—his name a bell, calling increasingly distant memories to the forefront of their minds. Liberum, their stables, the Knights.... It seemed a million miles away. The cold distance of their former life added a somber tone to the chamber.

Bellae finally broke the silence. "Zero, it is," she declared boldly. "Let me up on your shoulders, Lontas."

"Whoa, whoa," Kainen said. "Lontas has helped us, but Arend and I have been studying our whole lives for this situation. I disagree."

Bellae smiled warmly at him from the vantage point of Lontas' shoulders. "Why don't you head up with Arend and Sankari, just in case we're wrong? However, I trust the person I've known *my* whole life. You know, the guy who used to break *into* the library...for fun."

Lontas looked down, grateful for her words, fighting tears. "Thanks," he whispered.

Bellae nodded, looking incredibly calm.

She really has that much faith in me, Lontas thought, quickly wiping away a leaking tear.

When Kainen and the others did not move, she motioned for Lontas to head towards the left side of the ledge above the symbols.

"Lontas isn't making sense! I can *see* stars," Scelto cried.

"It's your mind deceiving you," Lontas answered. "Not what truly is."

"Just go ahead," Gimelli encouraged. When Scelto turned to her, a little hurt, she continued, "I trust Lontas and my sister completely."

With a sigh, Bellae pushed the rock with "0" carved into it. A loud rumble moved through the room. To the left of the symbols a large rock dropped out, revealing a small vault. A dozen whip scorpions sprinted out.

"Scorpions!" Bellae screamed, flailing awkwardly before falling backwards. Scelto sprinted over to prevent her descent.

"I got ya," Scelto said, supporting her back before carefully setting her down.

As the rumbling abruptly stopped, a scroll and two dazzling crystals rolled onto the sand floor. The nine-inch-long crystals were glowing in rhythmic pulses.

"Crystals and the next scroll!" Bellae said cheerfully.

"Whew!" Gimelli smiled.

Scelto moved over, stabbing the few scampering scorpions. "Okay, we're good."

"Bellae, grab the crystals and scroll. Let's see what's next," Kainen said, smiling with relief.

Scroll II: Just Go Ahead

"Any word on the squires?" Friar asked Eaglian Aquila.

"The League of Truth is moving through the prophecy. They may even have the first set of crystals," Aquila declared, proud of his son.

"I guess they aren't our squires anymore, are they?" Ritari sighed.

"Being a squire is noble, but they have a greater purpose now," Aquila answered.

"What happens when they get all the crystals?"

"No one alive knows. That scroll was sealed eons ago when the Ainmhi Caint were dying. The Macht Power Crystals were concealed and protected by riddles, and eventually, the leadership of the League of Truth was taken over by dragons, Eaglians, Fairies, and Elves of Creber. The future of the Crystals will only be revealed to the Chosen One, once all five pairs of crystals are collected," Aquila answered.

"Why hide them? Why riddles?" Ritari ventured.

"For protection. The unique crystal pairs are powerful, but when all five combine, their unrestrained energy is indescribable. In the wrong hands? End-of-the-world power," Aquila said.

Baiulus entered without knocking. "We've got trouble. The large force of Proliate we have been tracking was nothing more than prestidigitation. The ban on black magic that the Proliate wanted is obviously over since we used it so effectively during the Battles of Ovest and Trepas."

Friar sighed. "Their force isn't heading towards the Northern Dwarves?"

"No." Baiulus said.

"Where are they?" Ritari thundered, his voice full of concern.

"It's not where they are going. It's where they've been. They wiped out most of the Rebelde Plains population and seized all of the stored grain to supplement their own. They captured almost all of the Dwarves skilled in prestidigitation. So, in addition to the Southern Dwarves, who are obviously skilled in false conjuring, they took our ability to effectively use it."

"Pumilus?" Friar asked.

"He's safe with the Northern Dwarves and about twenty others," Baiulus said. "In fact, that's how we found out the Proliate weren't camped around Mount Honoo. Pumilus was using prestidigitation to hide a squadron of Vioma Dragons heading out to torch the Proliate tents when they realized the whole Confederate camp was illusory. They did manage to capture a few Southern Dwarves, but that was it."

"Do we know where the Proliate army is?" Friar asked.

"Not yet."

"We'll have to risk probing attacks on any large force of Proliate from now on to confirm they're real," Friar stated.

"That doesn't help us with those that are hidden," Aquila said. "Perhaps, we unleashed more harm than good by poking the hornet's nest with prestidigitation."

Friar cringed, the act of second-guessing himself well-worn in his mind. "What of the Dark Warriors?"

"They are throwing frequent attacks against Jaa, with occasional sorties into Piscium. With Temple Palvoa destroyed, the Proliate are having trouble covering the population. There have been no major battles since that for Palvoa," Baiulus reported.

"I suggest we stay on alert and prepare for attack. With all this uncertainty I don't want to risk anymore campaigns," Friar said. "Any thoughts?"

"I agree," Ritari said.

After discussing a few more affairs, Friar focused on Ritari. "Shall we venture over to the infirmary to check up on Luchar's progress? Maybe they can look at your hand as well."

"My hand feels fine."

"I heard the healers were stunned Luchar awoke," Aquila said.

"Surprise quickly turned to fear and frustration at his outbursts and foul temper," Friar said. "The left side of his body is partially paralyzed and becoming littered with contractions."

"What do you mean he's with Hephaestus?" Friar asked the exhausted healer.

"Hey, if you want to go get him and bring him back here, go for it. However, you have to take care of him. No healer or orderly will go near him," Sanar stated defiantly.

"Is he still weak on one side?"

"Definitely. His entire left side is progressively tightening up while the right side of his face droops and does not move normally," Sanar replied.

"How's Sorea?"

"A model patient who listens and wants to get better. She's back to restricted duty and making great progress because she takes heed of what we say and doesn't attack us," Sanar replied.

As Friar and Ritari advanced on the armory, they could hear Luchar shouting. Hephaestus looked up pleadingly as they approached.

"What's going on here?" Friar asked.

"Hephaestus is going to make a custom manica armguard for my left side. It will be large enough to act like a shield, protecting my weak side, and then I can still wield an axe with my right hand," Luchar said happily. Despite his limp and contracted left arm, Friar and Ritari couldn't help smiling at his high spirits.

"May I talk with you alone, just for a second?" Friar asked.

The two went off, Luchar hobbling, to a safe distance.

"My fierce Knight, maybe it's time to release your anger and let others fight," Friar said. "You've fought enough battles."

Luchar's eyes had an odd mix of injected fury and sorrowful tears. "The problem with letting my rage wane is that allows memories to bubble to the surface. The faces of the dead, the horror, the flames—it's all I see when I lay in bed. As my hammer bludgeons or my axe slices, I relive them falling, but in the visions, they stare accusingly up at me. Always staring. If I let my wrath boil, I think only of the next fight, and what I need to do to prepare. That goal keeps the misery and haunting dead away."

"With changing circumstances, whether we choose them or not, we must adapt. Perhaps we could work with the healers on some relaxation tech—" Friar was cut off.

"War, battle...those are my calming home. With or without your permission, I shall fight."

Friar nodded, and the two returned.

"Should I make it, sir?" Hephaestus asked, looking at Friar.

"What are you asking him for? Do you ask Friar every time a Knight asks for armor or a weapon?" Luchar thundered.

"Go ahead, Hephaestus. Make Knight Luchar his armor," Friar answered. "However! You must agree to go back to the infirmary, promise to be a better patient, and follow the therapies they outline for you."

Luchar nodded, then unleashed a partial smile. Despite the fact that half of his face was paralyzed in non-participation, the joy fully radiated out. Friar grinned, but he was taken aback by his wild Knight's weakened appearance.

The body really is a fragile, rather unworthy vessel, flimsily holding the great spirits of the world, Friar thought.

Scroll 12: Here We Go Again...

Bellae stared at the two luminescent crystals pulsing with a bluish glow that lit up her face as she neared. Making sure there were no whip scorpions, she gingerly touched one—at first, quickly swiping her finger across it.

Nothing.

Taking a deep breath, she grabbed one. It flashed a brilliant red before going back to its rhythmic twinkle. Grabbing the other, her eyes rolled back as flashing visions blazed across her mind. She could see a pair of women in brown robes in front of galactic gas clouds and billions of stars. The brunette to her left had blood streaming out of blackened eyes while two tortuous horns sprouted from her head. Reaching for Bellae, she held out her right hand. Bellae gasped. Each of the woman's five fingers ended in sense organs—two eyes, two ears, and one mouth. *"Perception can be painful,"* the horned figure whispered to Bellae. *"Most prefer to stare benumbingly at the shadows dancing on the cave wall instead of facing truth."*

The second of the pair had red hair flowing over an ivory mask. Casually, she reached up and removed the mask to reveal a

Figure 23: As Bellae touches the crystals, she has visions of the physical manifestations of Perception-Deception.

half-skeletonized face. Her forehead had normal skin, but below her blindfolded eyes was a mix of stripped-bare bone and decaying flesh. The gaping hole of her nose had stringy flesh billowing down over rotting teeth and decomposing flesh. *"Deception is a sickly sweet, treacherous lie. Lies are duplicitous deceptions rotting the one flinging the deceit as much as those entangled within its treachery!"* the blindfolded woman hissed.

"We are here for you!" the crystals whispered. *"We've been waiting for you."* Bellae did not have to ask—she knew the visions and words were just for her. *"You can control all. Ultimate power can be yours."*

Slowly, her eyes began glowing red as her mind drifted past the twins, beyond the stars, and into a vast blackness so deep she could have never imagined it. In all directions, infinite, starless ebony surrounded her. Her ears began to ring with the indescribable silence that would forever change her definition of soundlessness. There was no peace within this quietude, but an intensely uncomfortable terror filled fear of death encased her brain, which apprehensively screamed in silent dread.

"Taste the acerbic reality of eternal shade," a voice from the crystals eventually said. *"Suffer the darkness awaiting if you do not embrace us and your ordained future. You were born out of the insensate shadow, and you are doomed to return to it…unless you open yourself up to the power of the crystals. Let us save you."* That voice abruptly drowned under an avalanche of mumbling voices.

Once the chorus of whispers stopped, the mind-numbing chime of complete silence enveloped her as true black swallowed her from every direction. Her breath quickened and heart raced as the crushing weight of eternal darkness swathed her with suffocating dread. A fathomless uneasiness washed over her, bathing her mind in cavernous disquiet. Time had no meaning as her lungs heaved ever more rapidly. Abruptly, Bellae found herself back in the cavern, her eyes no longer glowing red. Looking around, the others were smiling in the exact positions they had been. Slowly she inhaled several slow deep breaths.

"I really hate these crystals…and Hamata," Bellae muttered, shaking her head.

"You okay, Bellae?" Lontas asked.

She sighed. "Yeah, but I get the feeling this is going to be a long journey."

"We're with you, all the way," he said.

Bellae flashed a fraudulent smile, forcing it through the reality of what Stralande had told her and the bath of drenching darkness she endured. She took out the thick leather bag with ten pockets sewn inside that Stralande had given her and carefully put the two crystals in individual pouches. Pulling on a leather cord, she carefully enclosed the Seeing Crystals. Even through the sturdy bag she could feel the pulsating power.

"Make sure you don't touch these crystals," Bellae said emphatically.

"We serve you!" a voice from the crystals whispered.

That's not annoying.

"Is Hamata coming back?" Lontas wondered. "It's not like I want her to—just wondering," he added in defense of their scornful looks.

"I still hate you!" Hamata shrieked from behind the thick door that muffled her loathing. "Especially abhor the know-it-all! I do, in fact, hope you all die!"

Gimelli shook her head. "That lioness has serious issues."

"Can we leave?" Scelto asked.

Ignoring the occasional whispers, Bellae said, "Okay, next scroll." Once she retrieved it, they made their way up the stairs.

"Quiet. Arend's sleeping. So how'd it go?" Sankari whispered.

"Could have been worse," Gimelli said, chuckling.

"What does the next scroll say?" Sankari asked, fluttering nervously.

Bellae handed the scroll to Gimelli, who carefully unrolled it on the floor of the small landing, reading aloud as the others huddled around.

"The Seeing Crystals are in your hands!
Yet war devastates the lands.
The first tests are passed.
The trials remaining? Vast.
You were not fooled by Deception.
It's best to use your brain to filter Perception.

Far Forest Scrolls

Many creatures have vision,
Few truly see in their decision.

Strength crystals are Second.
Always a force to be reckoned.
Seek the crystals of **Power**.
Or **Weakness** shall rule the hour.

Every ending is a chance to begin.
There is a mountain no sane man has been.
A way divides this range.
Water on each end is strange.

Don't get stuck in the mire.
The opposite is what you desire.
Point your toes,
In the direction every map shows.

Get a bird's eye view.
Only **ONE** path will do.
Few have ever passed that way,
But from it do not stray.

The secret is what you have acquired.
They will help you be inspired.
Once you SEE, work quickly,
Or your situation will get prickly."

"This is even more cryptic than the first," Scelto commented as Kainen unfurled the map.

"Obviously, they want us to go to a mountain," Lontas said.

"Oh, brilliant. That clears it up. There are mountains all over Verngaurd, including the Proliate Islands," Sankari huffed.

"It's a start," Gimelli said calmly.

"You might be on to something with the Proliate Islands, Sankari," Kainen said. "It says 'Water on each end is strange.' That could be an island. The Ainmhi Caint were from there."

"What about a way divides the range?" Scelto asked.

"That doesn't really help. There are passes through all mountain ranges. Some are big, and some small," Kainen said, studying the Kissa Tuikea Mountains on the Islands.

"I don't think so," Lontas said.

Sankari huffed as Bellae asked, "What do you mean?"

"Well, it specifically says here that it 'divides' the range. That would suggest it is truly a larger pass in between the mountain range. That's not as common. I think it's the Tingij. The divided part is the Way of Trepas."

"What does, 'Don't get stuck in the mire. The opposite is what you desire' mean?" Scelto asked.

"I think Lontas is right," Gimelli said. "The Southern end of the Tingij rise above the Mohado Mire, and there aren't any mires on the Proliate Islands.

"Actually, the only other mountains near a mire are the lower mines of the Southern Dwarf Kingdom," Kainen added.

"Exactly," Lontas said, gesturing wildly. "It specifically says, 'Don't get stuck in the mire. The *opposite* is what you desire.' The mire is south of the Tingij, and we want the north end. The Tingij fit better because the Proliate Islands are surrounded by water. The Tingij range only touches water on either end, Lake Glasere in the north, and the mire in the south. The polar end of the Tingij also fits with the scrolls discussion of the direction on a map."

"What do you mean?" Gimelli asked.

"Look at any map," Lontas said. "They all have one direction, north. It may have the others, but north is always marked. So 'Point your toes in the direction every map shows' means north. So we need to go to the top of one of the Northern Tingij Mountains."

"That makes sense, it says, 'Get a bird's eye view,'" Bellae said.

"But which one? The Northern range is enormous. Are we supposed to climb each one?" Sankari huffed, her wing speed increasing as she drifted in agitated circles.

"No need. I know which one they're talking about," Arend said.

"You're up! We could have used you down there, but glad you slept," Kainen said.

"How are you feeling?" Gimelli asked.

"Like I was run over by a trompe from Ager," Arend replied. "My dad, Aquila, used to tell me about this mountain. Let me see the map." Groaning with discomfort, he pointed to the last peak before Lake Glasere. That's Kuolema Vuori, the death mountain. I think that's what the scroll means when it says, 'a mountain no sane man has been.' There are many legends about disasters visited upon any who tried to climb that last peak. People say it's cursed, leading to its name.

"There's but one path towards the top, and it's blocked by an unnaturally straight wall—likely created by the Ainmhi Caint. The top of that peak has more spikes compared to the others and zero place to perch."

"We were just near that peak not that long ago," Gimelli lamented.

"Well, we *obviously* need to go back," Sankari snapped.

Scroll 13: Black Dragon of Eternity

Bellae jumped as Lontas grabbed her arm. "Sorry! I didn't mean to scare you. The oasis views are beautiful, but you shouldn't be off the boulders at night, much less alone. We..."

Lontas paused after moving around to see tears streaming down her face. "You...okay?"

She nodded, but the drooping eyebrows angling down over her lowered gaze—wet with tears—and sulky expression disagreed. Lontas gently squeezed her shoulder as she leaned against him. The two stood near the edge of the closest freshwater spring. Plants and grasses of various shapes and sizes clung around the edge of the water for literal life. Several trampled paths, trodden by thirsty animals, gouged their way through the crowded fauna. Intermittently, bubbles would escape up, roiling through the water.

"You know, people used to report that the water would 'boil' at night in oases," Lontas said. "Now that's not impossible—there could be a volcanic vent or something."

Bellae chuckled, wiping away the tears while remembering how enthralled Lontas was to learn of the Dwarf irrigation system.

"It's actually gasses effervescing from fissures below," Lontas said, pausing under the knowledge Bellae was not interested. "Sorry about you and your sister."

"Thanks. Like I said, we're still sisters in the ways that matter, just like you're a brother."

"I know I'll never be as good as Jumeaux, but I'll try."

Bellae chuckled. "I do hope he's finding a home in the Citadel."

"All the times Scelto said he couldn't believe you were related…I guess he was correct. Although, plainly, Jumeaux's still Gimelli's twin." Lontas cleared his throat before continuing, "Hamata mentioned them, but there are lots of good stories about the great civilizations that used to live in the desert. Would you like to hear about those, or I could go into exquisite detail about the gaseous fissures?"

Bellae began laughing. "Is there a third choice?"

"You could tell me what's bothering you."

"Nice setup," Bellae said as they sat under a large palm tree, stretching over them in a thirstily yearning arch towards the water. Several olive trees, some immense with gnarled, disjointed trunks pocked with scars of age and hardship, clustered around as well, seemingly contorting themselves closer to listen. The sky was clear, and the stars glowed fiercely while the reflected light of several moons glistened off the silky rippling water.

Bellae recounted her experience after collecting the crystals. "I used to like looking up at the night sky. Now it draws me back to that immense, dizzyingly quiet darkness. I feel like the world's off balance and I'm whirling around—like I might fall any second."

After a long pause, Lontas sighed. "I've had similar experiences. For me, it usually happens during the quiet of night. I have these corrupted perceptions of darkness and an intense feeling I'm going to die."

"See...that's how smart you are. You didn't need infinitely powerful crystals to send you on that journey."

"That's why I read so much. It's something to do besides feeling helpless and small against the vastness of the world, while also searching for answers."

Bellae looked at her friend. "So it's an encounter with 'darkness' that made you a delinquent who repeatedly broke into the library's restricted section?"

"Yes...actually." He chuckled. "By the way, I named it."

"Breaking into the library? Bellae asked. "It's called being a criminal!"

"No, that pitch-black darkness and vertigo feeling, or realization of how minuscule I am. I call it the black dragon of eternity. Stupid?"

Bellae shook her head as he continued. "It's infinitely long and encompasses the entire universe. It spits us out for our brief life before swallowing us whole again. The black dragon of eternity. Sometimes I wonder...is that...like a preview of death?"

Bellae sighed, not really wanting to think about it. "I don't know, but it makes me depressed. Hey, thanks for cheering me up. Leave it to you to lift my spirits!"

Lontas laughed before faltering into seriousness. "I'm not sure exactly what I expected this journey to be, but nothing's turned out like I thought."

"All I know is first Finn, then Crann. You better not get any ideas about leaving."

"I'm not going anywhere."

"Hamata was so mean—especially to you. Sorry, Lontas."

"It didn't bother me. Plus, those riddles were fun."

"You saved us big time, especially with the don't-be-deceived, zero solution. The scary thing is," Bellae said, "we have no idea what the answers are going to be on this journey."

Lontas paused and looked out over the tranquil water. "Truth. That's what I hope we find."

"We may not *want* to find the answers," Bellae said, thinking of Stralande's words.

"To me, a wrong answer that makes us feel better holds no value. The life spent in pursuit of truth, even if some questions can never be answered, searching for honesty and accuracy, is better than bathing in the watery spa of ignorance. Whatever we find, when this is over, I will head back to my library. Even with Bestilla glaring at me, it's still my favorite place. I hope her legs are healed."

"Me too. However, going back to Liberum's not happening for me."

"You can't know that."

Bellae smiled outwardly. *I do know that.* She suddenly looked up at her friend, her face radiating terror and despair.

"What?" Lontas said, anxiously sitting up straight. "What?" he repeated. "Seriously, what?"

"Is it my fault my parents died? Did I kill them?" she sobbed.

Lontas' body recoiled slightly. "That's absurd. Why would you think that?"

"If my mom really died in childbirth, then it's because of me," she bawled. Her tears gushed as her body quivered in sorry.

Lontas held her trembling body. "You were a baby, of course it wasn't your fault. Please don't think that. That notion never crossed my mind. I know nothing about my parents or even if they are alive."

As the tears slowed Bellae wondered if knowing her mother died when she was born was better or worse than Lontas' situation.

"Have you thought this a long time?" he asked.

She nodded.

"Have you told anyone before?"

She shook her head.

"No one can blame you for being born," he said.

I can, she thought.

"You did nothing. You had no choice in being born."

Bellae took several deep breaths as Lontas went on to explain how she shouldn't hold herself responsible. He ended with, "…not a choice."

He doesn't understand. No one does. There are a lot of "no choice" situations going around, she thought before speaking out loud. "Everyone tells me there's a choice, we…I can just walk away, but that's not really true. Walk away and let the bloody Na Cearcaill disaster destroy everything? Yeah, right."

Lontas regarded his friend. "Why not? Let's walk away, leave this for someone else."

Bellae looked at him as if she were the older, wiser of the two, and he instantly felt remorse. "You could live with that?" she asked.

Lontas sat back, sighing. "Guess not. However, that's the point. We, and it is *we*, Bellae, are in this together, and *we* choose to keep going. It's what Friar said all the time: sometimes fighting for what's right *is* its own victory. So let's get this done, go back to Liberum, and the Na Cearcaill thing can seriously drown in an ocean of shite. We'll get through this dark journey together. It will be weird, but…"

"Also wonderful," Bellae finished. "Terrifying, but…"

"Exciting," Lontas laughed at completing her thought, then turned to stare at her, raising his eyebrows expectedly. "Who's doing this quest? Hint, the answer is *not* 'me' or 'I.'"

"We."

"Correct. *We* are doing this. All the way." After pausing to choose his words, Lontas continued, "I hate what happened to Crann. He was the coolest horse ever."

"Definitely the best. It feels like the last bits of Finn are falling away. I purposefully run through memories with both of them to keep them fresh in my mind."

"That's smart. How do you think Crann found us, and what was that apparition thing?"

"No idea. I know it wasn't a Nishi. It seemed to be talking to Crann," Bellae said, pushing aside a tear.

"Whatever it was, I'm grateful it showed up with him to save you," Lontas said. He continued speaking, but Bellae struggled to retrieve memories of Finn and Crann while fighting off the gut-wrenching punch of the reality they were gone from her life forever.

Bellae scrunched up her face when he finished. "Crann said something weird, like 'you made a good choice' or something. No idea what that's about."

"That's bizarre. Maybe he meant good choice to find the crystals?"

Bellae shrugged her shoulders, and they settled into silence. Some time later, Lontas became somber. "Are you going to tell me the big secrets that Stralande and all the others have told you when they pulled you aside?"

"Someday," Bellae answered, gauging his response. She could tell he was frustrated. "I'm sorry, but that's what I was told. Is that okay?"

"It will have to be."

"There are no ferratus lanx around," Sankari said, fluttering back to what had become their rocky home. "I'm so sick of dates, figs, and coconuts I could scream. Let's go!"

"We leave when Arend's ready," Gimelli said.

"Why would his opinion matter more than mine?" Sankari said, fluttering wildly.

"Uh...because he was battered by those insane creatures...twice!" Kainen said.

"But three weeks in this cesspool is twenty days too long!" Sankari complained.

"Arend? What do you think?"

"Eaglians heal fast, but I'm still sore."

Sankari huffed, but Arend waved her off. "However, I feel like I can go, especially with the splint you and Lontas devised.

"Every water skin is full, and all of us have drank to the point of engorgement. I think we're ready," Gimelli said.

After moving northeast through the oasis, the League reluctantly stepped across the invisible border between the oasis and the boundary land around it. A thin partition of scraggly growth, the last frontier of life, circled the lustier growth with better access to water.

"I'm nervous," Lontas said. "I feel like we're leaving land, sailing into an ocean of sand."

"We kind of are. I was thinking..." Kainen started, but he was interrupted by Sankari.

"That place is rubbish. Complete piffle!" the Fairy said angrily. "I can't wait to get out of here, and I never, ever, *ever* want to see, touch, or feel sand again!"

"Hold up, everyone," Lontas said. Realizing Bellae had stopped, he ran back.

"Look." She pointed to a cluster of cacti. Each short cactus had long tan spikes and stunning, three-inch pink flowers. "The middle of each flower has hundreds of yellow things and a large brown stalk with what looks like leaves—a mini palm tree."

"The yellow things are stamen, and the single large stem is the pistil. You see, the pistil is the 'female' organ of the cactus, or any flower. It's interesting..." Lontas stopped mid-sentence, seeing Bellae's disinterest.

"Isn't it stunning?"

"This hedgehog cactus tends to flower in the morning..." He stopped at Bellae's mock look of disapproval.

Grabbing his hand, she said, "Just enjoy it, my favorite bookworm. I think the Sight Crystals are saying slow down and *really* see the beauty around us. Asking questions is great, knowledge is awesome, but sometimes just enjoying all the splendor needs to, has to, be enough. The 'little' things may just be the most significant."

Lontas knelt down and truly looked at it before sheepishly saying, "It's super nice, but I still want to know how it works and as much information about it as I can."

"Are you two done?" Sankari asked, interrupting Bellae's chuckling.

Casually leaning down to smell the flower, Bellae whispered, "Beautiful. *Thank you.*"

Lontas shot her a questioning look, wondering, but not asking, if she could now speak to plants. The League briefly stopped at the edge of a large dune, looking back for a last glimpse of the oasis. The same disoriented and scared feeling the squires had when leaving Liberum came flooding back. They were about to set voyage into the monochromatic waves of sand, and the oasis seemed like the only anchor of reality, of hope.

"Well, here we go...again," Kainen said.

"Do you think we'll ever see the oasis again?" Lontas quietly asked Bellae.

"I won't," she said confidently.

"What do you mean?" he asked, still worried about everything she had not told him.

Bellae stopped, looking into her friend's eyes for a moment. "I mean I wouldn't come back to the desert for anything. Especially after what happened to Crann."

"Ya, sorry."

"Thanks." Realizing she was still holding his hand, Bellae gave it a squeeze as soggy tears drizzled down, only for them to be suffocated within the mercilessly arid desert.

Scroll 14: Time to Clean

They were grateful to see the Eaglians, Ekara and KovaKotka, gracefully fly down to meet them as they exited the Báis te Pass.

"I'm so happy to be out of the sand!" Gimelli said. "Priority one is a *long* bath to wash out the sand."

"The Maketa made you new clothes, which match your current ones but actually fit," Ekara said, looking critically of Lontas' high-water pants and unslinging a large sack of clothing.

"Are the Maketa coming?" Gimelli asked, suppressing her anger and wanting answers about her and Bellae's parents.

"No!" KovaKotka replied, seemingly aggravated.

Gimelli nodded, but the reply strengthened her desire to come back and confront them for the truth when this was over. Her outrage dissolved as KovaKotka informed them of the Battle of Ovest, Blodskogur, and Trepas.

"That enormous loss of life is...insane," Scelto added numbly.

"I'm sorry about Ragorsaf," Gimelli said sympathetically to Scelto, knowing he made friends there.

"The Elves are just defending their way of life!" Kainen said defensively. "The Proliate are trying to force Tallcon down everyone's throats."

Scelto gauged his new friend carefully. He had lived with the devout, but kind, Proliate at Ragorsaf. They encouraged him to learn of Tallcon but also let him leave. *The Proliate are just doing the same,* Scelto thought, *defending their way of life and beliefs.*

"It's a shame when anyone has to die on either side," Gimelli said calmly.

Scelto nodded. "You always know the right thing to say."

She smiled, blushing under his appreciative gaze.

"We'll take you to the edge of the Redwoods…or maybe the Fada River, but no further," one of the eight Eaglians said. "Ever since the Proliate rebuilt Ragorsaf, movement has been tough for us. They moved a lot of the griffins from Temple Aon Intinn over and they constantly patrol the skies. It was the new troops stationed there that leveled everything in the Rebelde Plains. They even brought out diezmars."

Scelto shuddered at the thought siege engines he helped with were used to kill civilians.

"Are you getting to kill griffins?" Arend asked, excitedly.

An older Eaglian shot him a stony glance. "There's no pleasure in killing such majestic creatures. We do it to protect our own."

Several of the younger Eaglians with obvious disdain for griffins disagreed, and pockets of argument broke out.

"I'm still finding bits of sand," Gimelli said to break the tension. "Even after several days of baths, rest, and new clothes."

The group feasted on black-tailed deer before being flown to the ruins of Cruinniú in the northern section of what was once the Rebelde Plains.

"What did they use this place for?" Bellae asked as they walked through the enormous rectangular rocks placed in a circle. It was obvious that the diezmar siege engines had destroyed most of them, as their boulders sat scattered amongst the chards of broken rocks.

"It was used in ceremonies to pass the seasons and elections of their triumvirate. The Proliate have sworn to kill everyone who fought against them at the Battles of Ovest and Trepas," one of the Eaglians stated somberly.

"What do you think? Can we fly them further north?" another Eaglian asked.

"No, we would draw too much attention. In fact, we need to get back to our forest now," General Orel answered, his feathered ears twitching. "I have a bad feeling we are about to have company. "You kids…" he paused, staring southwest for several moments before quickly scanning the area. "No place for them to hide. Lolar and Adelaar, get the crystals to the northern most edge of the Tingij, now."

While it did not seem to bother anyone else, Bellae was a little taken aback that the crystals seemed to take priority over the beings making up the League.

"What are they?" Arend asked.

"Hippogriffs. Lots of them," an Eaglian answered somberly.

"Eaglians, to the air!" Orel thundered. "We will try and hold them off as long as possible, but we can't guarantee you much time. There are too many."

With a solemn nod, Lolar, Adelaar, and Arend took flight. The three of them swung around as the League waited. Arend picked up Kainen while the much larger Adelaar gently grabbed both Bellae and Gimelli. Lolar took Lontas and Sankari.

"To fight and die!" Orel shouted. With loud shrieks the handful of Eaglians took off to meet the hippogriffs.

"Hippogriffs are fighting us?" Bellae yelled over the whir of rushing air.

"The winged beasts from the Isle of Hirmulisko seem to have been poisoned against us," the Eaglian answered. He kept craning his neck around to look back at his friends. "It has the head of a horse but with

Figure 24: Enchanted to fight by Magicians, the hippogriffs were rustled from their natural home on the Isle of Hirmulisko to replace the dwindling griffins.

feathers for a mane. The chest is that of an eagle—complete with talons and wings. The back half is that of a horse, except for the tail, which consists of feathers."

Bellae could see Lontas' mouth moving but could not hear anything. Lolar, the Eaglian carrying him, signaled to Adelaar. Without warning, the two Eaglians tossed Gimelli and Lontas. They crossed in mid-air, screaming their lungs out. Without disrupting their flight the Eaglians caught the squires so that Lontas was next to Bellae and Gimelli neighbored Sankari.

"Happy now?" Adelaar asked Lontas.

"Other than the fact that I just wet myself, yes, quite happy." Despite the dangerous toss, Bellae could not help laughing at her friend.

"I was trying to tell you that this is highly unusual. Hippogriffs are untrainable. They live on the Isle of Hirmulisko because they eat anything and everything, including intelligent creatures of the mainland," Lontas stated.

"They always have Magicians with them," Adelaar commented.

"As I suspected, they're under enchantment," Lontas stated.

"Adelaar!" Lolar yelled. "We're not going to make it."

Looking back, the League could make out the shapes of over thirty hippogriffs charging towards them.

"Looks like they killed twenty, but the prodigiosis volo enchantment speeds the rest towards us," Adelaar uttered.

"Where's General Orel?" Bellae asked, fearing the answer.

"Death's the only possibility—he would never retreat," Adelaar said somberly.

"What do we do?" Lolar screamed.

"No choice," Adelaar answered. "We set the League down and try to hold them off. Arend, don't look at me like that. You have your orders. Stay with the League. Once they get past us, and they will, you will have your chance to fight."

Bellae closed her eyes, fighting back another round of tears. *I can't stand the Eaglians dying.*

All three Eaglians quickly dove to the ground, only Arend stayed. Adelaar and Lolar streaked towards the thirty hippogriffs and two Magicians.

"Run!" Kainen yelled. The League took off across the vast grasslands north of the Rebelde Plains—completely devoid of places to hide.

To delay the inevitable outflanking, Adelaar and Lolar both banked hard to their left and began hurling their black throwing darts. Within a few moments, several of the hippogriffs were careening down. Bellae turned just in time to see a wave of hippogriffs surround the two Eaglians. The larger Adelaar began swinging his sword through ferocious arcs.

"Try to lead them away, Lolar," he barked.

Spinning wildly, Lolar managed to break from the swarm of attackers. Like a hive of angry bees, they shot after him. With an insurmountable distance in front of them and a horde of enchanted hippogriffs behind them, Gimelli had an idea.

Chapter Four

Have to Have a Little

Scroll 1: Last Hope

An aggressive, panicked pounding on his door startled Veneficus. He could hear shouting. Whispering an incantation, he magically threw open the door. Several Proliate guards were wrestling an apprentice.

"Cease!" he bellowed as they immediately stopped.

"Jumeaux?" Veneficus thundered. "What are you doing?"

"Sir, something happened…*is* happening. It's very important!" Jumeaux cried.

"Let the boy in and shut the door," Veneficus ordered, intrigued.

"Nice of you to join us, big guy!" a Valo light taunted. "You look like sh—"

"Enough! All Valo will remain silent!" Veneficus ordered. "Now, sit, Jumeaux."

"No time. Hippogriffs and Magicians are attacking Bellae north of the Plains! There are a few Eaglians but not enough to hold out."

"How do you know this?" Veneficus asked suspiciously.

"I have felt the connection with my sister growing, and I don't need the crosier anymore to communicate and see. The link must be getting stronger," Jumeaux said.

No, boy, it's you who are growing more powerful, Veneficus thought. He softly spoke an enchantment before grabbing two crosiers from a hidden closet. "This one will be for you after we land," he declared. Jumeaux couldn't stop beaming.

"Don't propose to it quite yet. It's just a loaner," Veneficus said as they ran out the door. "Let's see how well my tutelage has been sinking in.

"Hold on tight!" Veneficus instructed. "Übermensch!" he yelled as Jumeaux clung on to the Magician for dear life. Just like at the Tournament, flames exploded out of the bottom of the two crosiers. The Supreme Master Magician and former squire shot up into the sky, heading west towards the Tingij.

Despite the absurd speed, Veneficus and Jumeaux were in a bubble of serenity. "We must find and defend your sisters at all costs. I'll call off the hippogriffs and Magicians. Once they leave, we must not spook them. They need to firmly believe we only want to help."

Adelaar was completely surrounded. The Eaglian quickly threw his last several darts with one hand while slashing his sword with the other as the hippogriffs took turns attacking from different directions. Adelaar did not have a chest plate on, and the talons of the hippogriffs ripped and shredded chunks of flesh and feathers.

With hundreds of open and bleeding wounds splattered across his body, and close to exhaustion, Adelaar abruptly shot towards one of the hippogriffs. He managed to get on its back. Pulling on its feathered mane, he was able to exert some control on the beast. The other hippogriffs paused, unsure of what to make of the Eaglian riding one of them.

Adelaar took advantage of their pause and hacked several out of the sky. Their bodies whirled and spun as they hurtled towards the earth.

"Kill them both!" one of the Magicians riding a hippogriff commanded.

The hippogriffs instantly converged on Adelaar and his unwilling mount. Lunging in with talons and hooves flying, unrecognizable chunks of flesh, feathers, and blood showered outwards before roaring towards the ground. Bloody slabs of tissue that had formerly been parts of Adelaar and the hippogriff he was riding coagulated together, splattering to the ground in distorted heaps.

"Over here, you bloody demons!" Lolar screamed. He did several graceful somersaults in the air while taunting the hippogriffs.

The twenty hippogriffs remaining charged as one. As they neared, their tail feathers suddenly opened into a fan shape to help their maneuverability. They spread out into a wall of raging talons and hooves. Lolar hovered, smiling indifferently as they zoomed towards him. When they were about ten feet away, he unexpectedly charged, unleashing his last four throwing darts—all sinking deeply into the rushing hippogriffs.

Lolar shot through the gap made by the injured hippogriffs. Those closest chomped with their powerful horse jaws or struck out with their front talons. Once he was past, Lolar looped backwards, intending to come up from behind.

As he broke out of his move, he was instantly surrounded by a dozen hippogriffs. The feathered fan at the end of the hippogriffs tail allowed phenomenal maneuverability. Lolar managed to slam his sword into the chest of the first hippogriff. The mortally wounded hippogriff grabbed at the sword with its front talons, holding on tight to prevent Lolar from withdrawing it.

The other hippogriffs dashed in with teeth and claws bared. After sustaining several wounds Lolar took off, away from them—flying erratically to shake the hippogriffs. With each move he made, the more maneuverable hippogriffs drew closer.

Lolar banked hard right and dove to pick up speed before breaking up and to his left, hoping to circle around the swarm of hippogriffs. As he curled up, several hippogriffs slammed into him. One managed to severely damage his left wing.

Lolar spun violently towards the ground surrounded by hippogriffs, who continued to rip and slash. One tore off his feathered left ear. Another managed to sever his tattered left wing. The Eaglian's screams joined a burgeoning string of blood trailing out behind him. The hippogriffs broke away just before the lifeless body of Lolar smashed into the earth.

"There's one more Eaglian!" a Magician screamed.

"What do we do?" Scelto asked.

"We have no choice. I'll turn and fight to buy you time," Arend answered.

Kainen looked behind to see the charging hippogriffs. "Can you take Bellae and fly away?"

"You saw them run down Lolar. If he couldn't get away, I certainly won't, especially carrying her," the young Eaglian stated.

"You and I stand and fight. The rest of you, do your best to make it," Kainen instructed.

"No. Bellae needs you," Scelto said, drawing his sword and cracking his neck in anticipation. "I'll stay with Arend. You run. Run!"

Arend nodded gratefully as he crouched to take off. "I have an idea," Scelto added as the Eaglian picked him up.

As they neared the hippogriffs, Arend abruptly threw Scelto towards them while diving straight down. The surprised hippogriffs watched as the former squire pierced a hippogriff through the mouth with his sword. The beast could not even neigh as the two began to fall. Scelto pushed off the falling beast and slashed at an attacking hippogriff, managing to mortally wound it with a strike to its heart.

As gravity beckoned Scelto, Arend shot up from below, grabbing him before hurtling him towards another group of hippogriffs. This cycle repeated twice before a thunderous crack filled the air.

Veneficus burst over the eastern skyline with Jumeaux heading straight for Bellae, Kainen, Gimelli, Lontas, and Sankari, who were running for their lives.

"Bellae, Gimelli! Wait!"

"It's Jumeaux!" Gimelli said. As Veneficus slowed, Jumeaux jumped down with a crosier and ran to his sisters. Unsure if he was attacking or protecting them, Lontas stepped in front.

"Lontas! It's great to see you," Jumeaux said, awkwardly hugging the stunned Lontas before moving to clumsily embrace his sisters.

Bellae broke away and screamed, "Hippogriff!"

Jumeaux's eyes widened as he screamed, "Adtonitus!" A single lightning bolt flew out, blasting a blackened hole in the attacking hippogriff.

"Eat that!" Jumeaux shouted before twisting backwards to face two more. "Eldur hnottur!" Jumeaux calmly and expertly spread the five fire balls between the two hippogriffs.

Veneficus finished whispering his message, and a glowing blue sphere traveled towards the Magicians, directing the hippogriffs.

"It's moving too slowly," Bellae complained. Time seemed to crawl as they waited for the orb to reach the Magicians. After several painful moments, the hippogriffs broke off the attack and retreated.

Arend carried Scelto back to the League, both littered with bruises, bite marks, and lacerations.

"So much for our new clothes," Gimelli said, running to Scelto while Kainen darted to Arend to clean and dress their wounds. Jumeaux was left staring awkwardly at Sankari and Lontas while Bellae marched to Veneficus. "Sending hippogriffs after us?"

"Young lady, for someone recently rescued, you should be more grateful and respectful," Veneficus replied, trying to keep calm, his eyes magnetically drawn to her shoulder bag with the Seeing Crystals. He could feel the power pulsing, calling out to him—their rightful owner. *Patience,* he thought as his blood swirled with desire—the magic running through his veins throbbing towards the source of their power.

"Since when are Magicians using hippogriffs?" Sankari challenged.

"Since the Knights, Eaglians, and dragons saw fit to decimate squadron after squadron of griffins. We use them for defense only," Veneficus answered. "I'm sure they didn't know Bellae was with the Eaglians, or they wouldn't have attacked."

"We just came from the Rebelde Plains. The entire country was eradicated. What happened there, and here to us, sure looks a lot more like attacks and massacres than 'defensive' maneuvers," the bloodied and bruised Scelto murmured.

"Every single day, worse attacks come from the Elves of Creber, Knights, and Northern Dwarves. Plus, now we are dealing with the increasingly savage strikes of the Dark Warriors. You expect us…" Veneficus started.

"This conversation is not helpful," Jumeaux said, Veneficus nodded appreciatively at his maturity. "Listen, we just want you to be safe. I'm glad Gimelli reached out."

Gimelli left Scelto's side to hug her twin brother. "Thank you."

"Your brother fought his way through a pack of Proliate guards to get to me and demanded I help," Veneficus answered.

Jumeaux looked down sheepishly.

"I had a flash that you were in trouble and could see where you were thanks to your message," Jumeaux replied, amazed at how happy he was to see them.

"You've become stunning at magic," Lontas said.

Jumeaux nodded. "Veneficus is a great teacher."

"He's being modest. Jumeaux's a natural."

Veneficus and Jumeaux used their magic to create a fire. An uneasy silence ensued as they ate, each side eyeing the other suspiciously.

"Despite the war raging all around us, I only want to help," Veneficus said. "If there's anything I can do, please let me know through Jumeaux. Verngaurd desperately needs you to successfully fulfill the prophecy. Completing the quest is the only chance we have for peace.

"You have quite the brother. He's talented and has taken the Magical Academy by storm." Veneficus' face contorted into a smile, but his eyes drifted magnetically to Bellae's bag. She defensively clutched it close while the engorged Grym and Borb settled into her pocket.

"Thank you for rescuing us and the meal," Gimelli said. "Now, however, it's time for us to move on, and I'm sure you have important matters at the Citadel."

Patience, Veneficus said to himself. *Let the One do the hard work for you. I need all five sets.* "Of course, you're correct," Veneficus answered aloud.

After a taut goodbye, Veneficus and Jumeaux flew to the east.

"That was weird," Sankari said. "First Magicians attack us, then Veneficus rescues us?"

"I'll say," Gimelli commented. "We should rest here and let Scelto and Arend heal up a bit," Gimelli suggested.

"No time," Arend said, struggling to stand up. "You can't see it, but an Eaglian army is battling hippogriffs to the south. I'm sure they're trying to make sure we are safe. We should honor them by moving out now."

Scroll 2: Oh, Death? Nice Name.

"So why's this mountain called Kuolema Vuori?" Lontas asked.

"Legend says it's cursed by death herself. The tip is littered with incredibly sharp shards, making it impossible to land from above. A single path, supposedly cursed, winds its way towards the peak abruptly ending in a solid rock wall. There's no way to scale up or around it to get to the top," Kainen answered.

"Myth says a horribly painful death awaits those attempting it," Arend added.

"The wind here's as bad as I remember," Sankari said, struggling to stay aloft at the base of the last peak of the Northern Tingij with the wind off Lake Glasere roaring.

"Maybe Scelto and Arend should take it easy down here while the rest of us head up. The path gets super narrow," Kainen suggested.

"No way!" Scelto thundered.

"If there's only one path and no one can come from above, you two can guard the entrance," Gimelli added with a smile.

Kainen winked admiringly at her diplomacy.

"Scelto, can you please change the splint on Arend's toe?" Kainen added.

Scelto nodded as Arend took a deep breath. Every muscle in his Eaglian body ached after having to fight hippogriffs before his cracked ribs and talon were completely healed. The two hobbled members of the League of Truth moved inside the protected path while the others started up.

At first, Kainen, Gimelli, Bellae, Lontas, and Sankari appreciated being out of the wind, walking the walled-in path. Soon, however, each turn compelled the trail to tighten as they ascended. Before long, everyone but Sankari was feeling claustrophobically confined.

"I'm glad Arend's not trying to fit his wings through here," Gimelli commented.

"How long have we even been walking?" Lontas wondered. "I'm starting to feel disoriented."

"It's hard to tell how high up we are. Every part of this blasted passage looks exactly the same. Oh look, something different, rocks! There, a surprise, is rough rock!" Sankari huffed.

"The occasional changes in direction, or pitch to the incline, are the only breaks in the monotony. If it wasn't so tight in here, I would suggest we take a break. This is dizzying," Kainen added.

"I seriously can't stand much more of this!" Sankari said. "Plus, it's getting dark!"

"I almost miss the sand," Lontas said. "Almost!" he added as the others shot him dirty looks. *At least it was open.*

"We're here," Kainen added as the group finally arrived at a sheer rock barrier rising before them.

"Now, what?" Sankari huffed, as if she hadn't really believed the path ended abruptly in a solid wall.

"Get the scroll," Lontas suggested.

"Let's see...skip ahead," Kainen said. "Okay, here:

The secret is what you have acquired.
They will help you be inspired.
Once you SEE, work quickly,
Or your situation will get prickly."

"The secret is what you have acquired? Do they mean some sort of knowledge from the scroll?" Lontas wondered. "Maybe you should read the top part."

Kainen did so, but it did not help. Everyone searched the rock for hidden levers or symbols.

"Nothing. Now what?" Sankari asked, her frustration building.

"It isn't like thousands have tried to ascend this, so an easy answer would mean others would have beaten us up there," Lontas said.

"It's way too slippery and tall to climb," Kainen said. "Lots have attempted it."

"I think the 'what we have acquired' might be the Seeing Crystals," Bellae said. "Notice how 'SEE' is capitalized?" Slowly, she removed them from their pouches. "Stand back," she suggested, holding the two crystals glowing red.

The crystals began to pulse briskly before vibrating angrily.

"*Remember, our power is yours!*

You need only take it!

Accepting our energy is the only way to peace."

Oh, do shut up, Bellae thought to the whispers tormenting her mind. After several moments passed, she spoke. "My arms are getting tired from holding them up."

"Maybe touch the wall?" Lontas suggested.

Slowly Bellae walked towards the rock face. The rhythmic glow continued to gain speed as she neared. Just before they touched, an unusual symbol of squares and slashing lines appeared on the wall in front of them, glowing like the crystals.

Figure 25: An image appears in the stone, they will later learn it is a symbol of Strength.

"What the…is that supposed to be?" Sankari wondered.

"More importantly, what does it mean?" Lontas asked.

The symbol suddenly disappeared, and the Seeing Crystals went back to their baseline glow.

"It disappeared?" Sankari huffed. "We should have drawn it in the dirt."

Bellae meticulously put the crystals away. Just as she finished, a loud rumble shook the mountain as a section of rock began to shift. Gradually, part of the wall opened. Cautiously, Bellae peered in.

"It's a room," she advised, "but it's pitch dark."

"No Hamata?" Lontas said, half-joking, half-worried.

Bellae laughed. "I don't see anyone or anything, but it's super dark."

"Let me get a torch," Kainen said. As he was fumbling with his sack, a louder rumble rocked the mountain. The League had to brace itself as the violent quake continued to get more powerful. A thunderous noise rumbled a warning above.

"Avalanche!" Sankari yelled.

"Run!" Gimelli shouted, turning to bolt back down the mountain.

"No! No!" Kainen yelled, desperately grabbing her arm. "We can't outrun it!"

"We have to go through," Bellae warned. Without hesitation she sprinted into the dark room. Lontas quickly followed. Gimelli, Kainen, and Sankari joined them.

The entrance completely collapsed as the room filled with dust.

"There goes the entrance," Kainen said when they stopped coughing.

"Entrance? Our *exit's* blocked," Lontas said.

"Great! Now we're stuck!" Sankari hacked. "We should have run."

"No! That was quick thinking, Bellae. The crystals gave us a one-time entrance. No one can get in here again. If we bolted, the quest would be over," Kainen said, nodding at Bellae.

Just as their eyes were adjusting, a loud popping sound was quickly followed by a series of symbols glowing around the room. At first glance, they looked identical to the one at the entrance. On closer inspection, subtle differences became apparent.

"Now what?" Gimelli asked, her words echoing in the cold, dark silence.

"I guess we pick the symbol that matches the one on the wall we came through," Lontas suggested.

Everyone pick a symbol to study," Kainen said as they started to flicker.

"Oh, great, a time limit," Sankari "Which one?"

Bellae felt a chill go through her body and clutched Lontas' hand while trying to reassure the shivering Grym and Borb.

"It's that one," Lontas said, walking up to the symbol.

"No, I think it's that one," Sankari murmured. As the words left her lips, the flickering blue symbols faded completely.

"Uhm…anyone have any ideas?" Kainen queried.

Before anyone could answer, there was a loud click.

"What just happened? Did anyone do anything?" Kainen asked in a panic.

"I'm confident Lontas is right, and I pushed the symbol he suggested," Bellae said, trying to sound more composed than she felt.

"What?" Sankari protested. "If you're wrong, we all die!"

"It's as good a move as any," Kainen argued. "I doubt they're going to light up again, and the decision isn't going to get easier. Nothing personal, Sankari, but Lontas has been right most of the time."

"Most of the time? Most of the time! Oh, how reassuring," Sankari hissed just as a low rumble was followed by a large stone falling away, letting a foggy light creep into the room.

"Trust Lontas," Bellae said, heading through the new doorway. They followed her to find themselves instantly bracing against an enraged, rustling wind on a narrow overhang.

"Uh, this isn't what I expected," Lontas said, leaning heavily against the mountainside as the gale attempted to blow him away.

A cloudy mist hung close around them, obscuring their view, despite the bitter wind howling and whistling ominously.

"Between the fog and the darkness I can't see anything," Gimelli said.

"This wind seems like it's trying to push us off," Kainen said as the air hissed through the ruts of his skin.

"I got you," Gimelli said, gently cradling Sankari.

"The gale does seem to be taunting us," the Fairy said, shivering.

"Search for a walkway or secret door that'll get us off this ledge," Kainen said as Bellae let her mice skitter along the edges to search for cracks or air movement.

"Do you think there used to be a bridge or something? Maybe it was destroyed or covered by the avalanche or something?" Gimelli wondered.

"It's possible. As old as the prophecy is, anything could have happened. Each one is supposed to have a guardian to protect and maintain it, but since they function independently, it's impossible to know," Kainen replied.

"Should we go back to the other room?" Sankari asked, shivering close to Gimelli, afraid the harsh wind would blow her away.

Just then, Gimelli started laughing.

"What's wrong with you?" Sankari asked.

Gimelli wordlessly pointed to a carving that started above the doorway they had walked through before continuing around the side.

"At least we found this one a little easier," Bellae said, trying to sound cheerful.

"It's crazy long," Lontas said.

Kainen stepped forward to read,

"Nothing ended.
It's about to begin.
You must take the døde trinn.
Do NOT turn back the way you came.
Head the opposite, not the same.

The symbol of Strength got you here.
The next symbol will take you there.
Find it on rocky ledge.
Stand on it, the edge.

You need something vague,
A joy, a goal; light, heavy; an identity, a plague.
No one can give it to you,
But yours must be true.

Without medicine it can cure.
Some revile it, for others, it holds allure.
It can kill or save,
Whether king or slave.

Despite its power, it weighs nothing at all.
Yet it cannot be lifted by man or squall.

It can move people around,
Yet nothing solid can be found.

YOU can *have* it in people, places, things.
Do what comes next without wings.
Have confidence and belief,
Follow it for joy, not grief.

Now find the symbol behind you,
And forget what you knew.
Instead, use what you just heard,
And by it be stirred.

Only the Chosen can go.
It will give you wings of crow.
Take a leap of ______.
Answer found on the eighth."

"You've got to be kidding!" Sankari tantrumed. "I'm soooo sick of these brainless riddles!" In a huff, the petite Fairy flew out a little too far and was caught in a gust of wind. After a few tumbles, she began frantically beating her wings to get back.

Lontas stretched as far as he dared, but he was unable to reach her. Kainen appeared, clutching onto Lontas' waist, allowing him to grab the struggling Fairy. Once they pulled her in, she hid her face in embarrassment.

"Here should be good," Lontas said, positioning her next to the mountainside and a large rock. "I guess that was the 'Strength' symbol we saw before."

"I guess, but what's 'døde trinn'?" Gimelli questioned.

"That's what doesn't make any sense," Kainen said. "It's part of the legend of Death Mountain. It means 'death step.' Folklore says that there are hidden traps all over. If you take a wrong step and trigger one, you die."

"This prophecy is just full of lovely stories," Gimelli snickered.

"I found it!" The others whirled to see Lontas wiping off a section of rock near the edge of the overhang, his blonde hair lashing under the untamed gale. "It said 'the next symbol will take you there.' Well, it's here."

"What does it mean?" Sankari asked.

"No idea," Kainen admitted.

"It also says that the Chosen One should stand on it. Why don't you, Bellae?" Gimelli suggested.

Slowly, the young squire moved forward with Gimelli holding her hand. Closing her eyes, she reluctantly stepped onto it while everyone held their breath. Time slowly dropped away as they waited. After several moments, the anticipation evaporated, and they were left confounded in the impatient wind, which kept angrily flapping their clothes, encouraging them to do something. Bellae opened her eyes and stared into the clinging fog surrounding them. "I don't remember seeing clouds or fog up on the mountain from below," she commented.

"Yeah, I was thinking it's weird, and likely magical," Lontas stated. "Why don't you try holding the Seeing Crystals to the symbol?"

When that didn't work, they went back to studying the chiseled words.

"Obviously, we're missing something," Kainen said. "Look there. It says, 'You need something vague, A joy, a goal; light, heavy; an identity, a plague.'"

"Could that be any more confusing?" Sankari challenged.

"Wait, wait. The next sections describe what's required," Lontas said, rereading a large section.

"Could it be a dream?" Gimelli inquired. "It says it's 'a joy and a goal' there, and later it says can 'cure without medicine.' Sleeping and dreaming maybe?"

"So you're saying that Bellae should stand on the symbol, inches from certain death and fall asleep standing up…in this howling wind?" Sankari asked sarcastically, still desperately huddling against the rock. "Yeah, that makes sense. Get right on that, Bellae, dear."

"Come on, Sankari. It's not dreaming, but talking through this is how we're going to solve it," Kainen reasoned.

"Thoughts have power but don't weigh anything. Since actions start with thoughts, you could say they lead to killing or saving people," Lontas suggested.

"Also, 'kings' and 'slaves' think. You might be onto something," Kainen added.

"Everyone thinks? Apparently, not you guys," Sankari chastised. "Are you honestly telling me you think the reason nothing happened before was because Bellae wasn't thinking hard enough? Maybe she should squint and strain harder until something happens or shite oodles out her backside."

"Sankari, enough. If you can't be civil, be quiet. I can't think with you criticizing every suggestion!" Kainen bellowed.

"What do you think it means, Sankari?" Bellae asked softly. The quiet tone of Bellae's question took everyone off guard. While the rest of the League was annoyed, Bellae remembered the Fairy's defensive sadness.

Sankari stuck her nose up at Kainen. "She appreciates my talents, unlike others in this group." She flew up close to the words, gravely fighting the wind, finding crevices to grasp while rereading.

"The key's here at the end," she finally declared. Glaring at Lontas, she added, "The part that burned butt over there *didn't* re-read."

In spite of just having been insulted, Lontas couldn't help laughing with the rest of the League at the Fairy's catty remarks.

Sankari made a funny face before continuing. "Here, where it says 'use what you just heard…Only the chosen can go…give you wings of crow…Take a leap of…' Notice the blank line chiseled into the rock. Every other line has a word that rhymes with it except 'eighth.' What rhymes with eighth? Not much. In fact the one that fits perfectly, faith."

Her eyes twinkled with pride as she flew to face Kainen. "So, it's obvious…Bellae stands on the symbol and jumps off, taking a leap of 'faith.'"

Gimelli gasped as Lontas cried out, "That's not happening. No way!"

Figure 26: A symbol representing Faith is carved menacingly close to the ledge.

Sankari blushed, her pride at solving the riddle blinding her to the consequences.

"Wait, wait," Kainen said. "Let me think." He reread it repeatedly—each time becoming more convinced Sankari was correct. "Actually, great job, Sankari. That's it, but the notion of Bellae jumping off the cliff...seems crazy."

"Maybe we can go back and get Arend and have him fly down there?" Gimelli suggested.

"Great idea!" Kainen sighed, relieved, before remembering the landslide.

"Geniuses, there's the giant rockslide. Remember?" Sankari huffed. "Plus, it specifically says only Bellae should go. It's quite clear."

"Bugger that," Lontas huffed.

"Don't you remember what would have happened if we were wrong in the desert?" Sankari reminded them. "We would have died. If someone else goes down there, it could trigger an avalanche and kill us all."

"She has a point," Kainen agreed.

"I don't think they had an Eaglian in mind, though," Lontas reasoned. "If he flies down, there's no way it can know about it as long as he doesn't touch anything."

"It doesn't matter," Gimelli said, emerging from the darkened room. "There's no way down, and I doubt he could hear us even if we yell until our voices fail."

"I don't think the prophecy wants me to die," Bellae said, standing on the faith symbol and trying to control the tremble in her voice. The wind whipped her cloak around, highlighting her small and frail frame. Gently she took Grym and Borb out of her pocket. She smiled to push back the tears campaigning to be released at the cataclysmically lonely feeling encircling her mind. *Thanks to Stralande I know in the end I will be alone. Perhaps, when we think about it, we are always walking alone—trapped in our mortal body.*

"Go to Lontas. Unless you want to jump off the cliff with me?"

The two mice sprinted across the wind-swept ledge to Lontas, constantly readjusting for forceful gusts.

"Hold them for me, just in case," she said, smiling.

After a quick wink, she jumped.

"NOOOOOOOOOOOOOO!" Gimelli cried, sprinting to the edge.

Scroll 3: That Did Not Just Happen

The League watched in horror as Bellae disappeared into the dark mist.

"No, Gimelli!" Kainen implored, grabbing her before she jumped.

"Bellae's right. We have to believe the prophecy wouldn't do anything to kill her. If you jump, that would violate the riddle and could get us, and her, killed," Lontas reasoned.

"Six Verngaurd, seven Verngaurd, eight Verngaurd," Sankari said as everyone turned to stare at her.

"It said, 'Answer found on the eighth'? So I figured that meant something would happen after eight seconds," the Fairy explained.

"You're sharp today, Sankari," Kainen said.

"What's that? SHHHH!" Gimelli said. Lying on her stomach, she put her ear over the edge of the precipice. Grym and Borb began to squeak loudly.

"That was Bellae," Lontas said, relieved. "By the looks of how the mice are acting, I think they hear her as well. She has to be okay. If she had fallen all the way down, we wouldn't be able to still hear her."

Two Watchers hiding amongst the rocks behind them smiled.

"I'm sick of spying on these bratty fools," one said, his face twisting into a corrupt smile, releasing a dandruff shower of dust from his desiccated face.

"Soon, Brother," the other responded, "we shall rip the lawfulness of the world into chaos, sending these fools back to prehistory." He shook his head and closed his eyes as pleasant memories of past Na Cearcaills danced in his head. "Ah, the screams, the death—doesn't get any better."

"So what do we do now?" Gimelli asked, unaware of the two staring down at them.

"We wait," Kainen said. He trudged to the relative safety of the mountainside and sat, his eyes fluttering. *Despite training my whole life, it's more exhausting than I imagined. Even if Bellae somehow manages to "fly" back up here, we're only two-fifths of the way done.*

As Gimelli screamed above, Bellae reflexively began flapping her arms, knowing it would do nothing to slow her rapid descent. Her robes billowed with increasingly agitated anger at the gusts of air ineptly checking her fall. White fog whirring by in darkness was the only visual companion, while the stinging wind bit its tendrils into her skin from all directions.

Suddenly, her heels scraped something, prompting a little scream. Then her backside touched down. Soon her entire body was cradled in a half cylinder as her trajectory leveled out. She found herself sliding, more than falling, as Sankari's counting grew more faint. Abruptly, the track banked into a turn, and she began heading back towards the mountain, her speed continuing to slow so she could hike down her pushed up-robe.

"I'm okay!" Bellae yelled once gliding to a stop. "Stay up there!" She heard a few rumblings, mostly blanketed in the windswept gale.

Lovely, she thought, immersed in absolute blackness. As she rose, a series of torches magically lit, revealing an odd cave with many support arches germinating from floor to ceiling.

"Hello?" she ventured, watching the torch light dance angrily amongst the shadows of the cave.

A gloomy profile wisped between two of the pillars. Bellae froze—except her eyes, which scanned incessantly for more movement. A robed figure appeared then disappeared in confusing patterns. One moment, it seemed to be walking to Bellae's right, then, suddenly sprinting far to her left.

Dressed in an all black robe that hid his features, he eventually appeared in front of Bellae, carrying an odd staff that began to forcefully vibrate until it became a torrid blur. The oscillating staff floated away from the figure before shuddering even more violently. After several moments, the staff split into three separate ones: silver, black, and gold.

Bellae shook her head, afraid for what would come next. With a blinding flash of light, the black figure itself morphed into three. One looked identical to the previous form, wearing black, another was in flowing silver robes, and finally, one in gold. Each held out a mostly skeletal hand with tendons and exposed flesh, beckoning the staff of like color towards them.

All three seemed to be magically sucked backwards, their midsection a fulcrum as their heads and feet crumpled together. They abruptly stopped as a series of large multi-mirror structures, matching the color of their robes, appeared behind each of them. The succession of mirrors had ornate carvings framing them.

With a deafening sound the whole cave began to move, shuffling in small sections. All three, and their mirrors, were jumbled and rearranged as other full-length mirrors came into view. Sometimes the figures and mirrors would disappear before reappearing somewhere else. Bellae sincerely wished she had her mice friends. Without warning, the black mirror and black-robed figure appeared before her, and the cavern stopped moving.

"I'm Svik, and I present to you the black mirrors!" he said, theatrically waving a bony hand powered by tattered tendons and mangled muscles frosted with seeping blood.

Bellae leaned in but could barely see her reflection in the ebony surface. She was, however, stunned by the elaborate carvings and beauty of the piece.

"There are no selfish motives within my sable mirrors," Svik continued. "Enjoy the beautiful raven sheen and contemplate life without the egocentric, vanity-driven objects within 'normal' mirrors, which are, in reality, just conceited contrivances of one moment in time. The hubris-driven self-images of the gold mirrors are merely distractions, drawing you away from reality. So quickly give your first pair of crystals to me, and you are guaranteed to earn the next pair, the Strength Crystals! Go on. Touch the surface."

Bellae was taken aback, the robed figure coming across more like a charlatan street peddler than a guardian. Slowly she held out her hand, hesitating before touching the inky mirror. Svik nodded, and her arm moved forward again. As soon as her fingers touched the cold, dark surface, she found herself transported to a lavish hall. Luxurious pillows were surrounded by opulent statues, vases, and delicate paintings.

What am I supposed to do? Bellae wondered, sitting down on one of the ebony pillows. There was plenty of magnificent food and tempting liquids in elaborate goblets, but suddenly, she did not feel hungry, thirsty, tired, really anything.

Did I doze off? Bellae wondered, looking around the room. Everything was exactly the same, but she wasn't sure how long she had been there. *Shouldn't I be thirsty? Shouldn't I want to get up?* Some part of her grasped that time was flowing by outside of her, and she was missing it. Her body seemed to sink a little lower into the cushion, its comfort grasping, draining her will to move. Shifting, she touched Finn's Inion medallion and felt a surge of energy.

Springing up, she thought, *Where am I? What am I supposed to do?*

Even though she was not thirsty, she meandered over to a row of goblets and grasped an ornately carved black one. Raising it up, she looked into the metal, moving her face closer, turning her head side to side. *I can't see my reflection!*

Peering into the liquid surface within the cup, she could see the room's reflection but not her own. It reminded her of touching the black mirror. "I want out!" she screamed, instantly finding herself staring at the robed figure and wall of mirrors again.

"A little taste of the paradise awaiting you when you choose the black mirrors," Svik said. "Try it again."

When she did not move, even without being able to see his face within the shade of the hood, she imagined a scowl as the black mirrors and figure began to spin away from her. After several moments of the entire cavern rotating, the silver mirrors and figure appeared as the cavern's motions gratefully stopped.

"Your true reflection awaits you in my silver mirrors. My name is Fastus, and the classic mirror is your best bet to obtain the Strength

Crystals. It's not vanity to seek what is truly there. My images are simple—reality. Don't let the two deceivers swindle you. The dark mirrors never allow you to see yourself, or the truth, while the gold show you opulent fabrications. Please, touch the silver of my mirrors."

"I don't want to get trapped," Bellae answered, but Fastus remained still. When the silence became unbearable, she reached out, touching the silver mirror.

Instantly, she was ripped forward through a tunnel of blurring light. Portraits of the past smudged by at a blistering pace. She could see flashes of images and hear snippets of conversation from previous times as they flowed by with lightning speed. The rush of air made her eyes feel dry and painful as she surged ahead. Her body jerked to a stop, her head whipping forward. She felt dizzy and off-balance as the world wrenched into focus.

She saw Honey kicking the dagger from her hand. With the betrayal still puncturing her heart she zoomed forward again. Next, she came to a shocking stop to see herself cradling Finn as frothy blood spewed from his dying mouth. The pain of his death punched into her, and she felt like vomiting but found herself jolted into the tunnel once again. She made brief, lurching stops during which she experienced Lontas being bullied, herself being taunted. Over and over, horrible memories replayed.

The starting and stopping continued until she found herself deep within the massive Redwood Forest outside a small tent. Aquila, the beautiful Eaglian, came storming out before screeching a mournful howl that made her knees shudder. Rich tears came rolling out of his massive eyes as he fell back, his legs buckling, before his body landed forward.

"Even before your birth, you are doomed to die alone," Aquila screeched before continuing to pound the ground. Meanwhile, Bellae was whisked into the tent. As soon as she saw the woman who had just given birth, she knew it was her mother.

Dead.

Her mother's eyes were open, mouth frozen in horror, while newly minted tears journeyed down her cheeks, living out their brief existence, traveling on her perished body.

"You show me my mother DEAD?" Bellae screamed, her own eyes moist with heartache. Just as the words left her mouth, she found herself back in the cavern, staring at the silvery surface of Fastus' mirrors. Looking in the mirror, her haggard, sun- and wind-burnt face appeared gaunt and her eyes hollow after their horrific time in the desert—broken only by crisp tracks of tears streaking down her face.

"Did you have a nice journey?" the silver-robed figure asked quietly.

Bellae pivoted, her eyes ablaze. "You know I didn't. Is this fun for you? Do you like torturing me?"

"Everything you saw was truth," Fastus said, taken aback by her anger. "I don't alter, or filter, reality. I merely show it to you. Those so called 'negative' events created who, and what, you have become. Remove them—the past—and you remove a large part of yourself and who you are. You saw what you needed to see."

Bellae shook her head. "What exactly is the aim of…whatever this is?"

The silver hooded figure growled, "You should choose silver because it shows you undistorted truth. Quickly now—no need to see gold! You…"

He did not get to finish as the cavern began whirling again. The silver figure reached towards her, the sleeve of his robe retreating enough to reveal a raw skeletal hand complete with exposed beefy flesh clinging to yellowed bones. Once again, the images of mirrors—black, gold, and silver—moved in and out of sight. Sometimes she would glimpse a version of herself in a full-length mirror revolving around the cavern. Occasionally, the image was true. Other times, it was her as a toddler, or an adult. Once in a while, the likeness was flattering, while in others, her eyes were black and her body covered in blood.

Eventually, the gold-robed figure and auric array of mirrors appeared. "The best, easy choice, comes to you last. Beauty, allure, splendor, grandeur are all found here. The gold mirrors transform you into your finest self. Gaze at the powerful you, the one you were meant to be!"

A shiver of warning blasted through Bellae's mind. *Sounds like the whispers of the first crystals.* As she peered into the gilded mirrors, she was no longer haggard and drawn after the desert journey. In one mirror a bejeweled crown sat on her golden hair, which was clean and full-bodied. In another she was riding a beautiful horse across a field of flowers. In a third, ornate jewelry spread across her neck.

Panic tore through her mind, her head snapping down. *It's here!* She quickly began to rub her Inion medallion, instantly looking angrily at the gold figure. "I wouldn't trade my Inion for…all the riches in the entire world."

"Ah, that's fine, you don't have to! I am Nayttava, here to show you what the future *should* be. With the gold mirrors a better version of you, the best version, will emerge. A life of glamour, gorgeousness, a resplendent and powerful existence, a never-ending—"

"You don't know me at all, gold guy," Bellae interrupted.

The gold figure paused, taken aback by her response and lack of interest in wealth or beauty. "You still *must* touch the golden mirrors."

Increasingly lavish images of her future life, opulent images to the point of gluttony, flashed across the mirrors. Sighing, she reached forward, her fingertips brushing the golden surface.

Surrounded by complete luxury, massive quantities of riches, fine art, delicacies, and desserts, she was sitting next to chained slaves toilingly fanning her. Touching her head, she removed a lavish crown. She had to turn from the blaring brightness of the jewels and five sets of crystals around her. She could feel the hum of absolute power coursing through her from the Macht Crystals. Looking up, people were dancing and engorging themselves on the opulent food. Many were laughing while lounging in decadence. A shiver of dread at the hedonistic scene made her twist away.

"The world is yours, master," a servant bubbled, carrying a tray filled with luscious desserts.

Bellae gasped at the eyes of Veneficus staring out at her from the middle of the tray. His decapitated head sat like a gruesome decoration in the center of the plate. The servant laughed. "You are all powerful. That old fool is nothing compared to what *you* will become."

A second attendant approached. This one had the head of the White Wizard flowering from the center of a platter of food.

"Keep the crystals for yourself and rule the world!" a voice hissed. "Become *the* all-powerful ruler for all of eternity."

"I don't want that!" Bellae screamed, recoiling at the bloodied heads being pushed closer to her face.

"Only a fool would not jump at the chance of this much power! You will control the world! You'll rule eternally!" a voice asserted.

"Finn! Crann!" she screamed.

Without realizing how she got there, Bellae found herself sobbing on the floor. *What can I think of to replace those images of the decapitated heads garnishing trays?* She conjured an image of Stralande, and her tears slowed. A small smile crept out at his wizened blue scales. She imagined his voice. "Keep moving forward—one step, then another. Enjoy this time—enjoy the odyssey. Regrets have a way of haunting our minds and spoiling our thoughts in the form of sorrow and remorse."

Bellae stood up. "You really don't get me at all, gold," she cried, wiping away her tears. "Thanks, blue dragon friend."

The golden-hooded figure seemed taken aback. "Dragon?"

"A friend of mind, one who did *not* feed me false images like these."

"False images? You misunderstand," Nayttava seethed. "Keep the crystals for yourself, absorb their power, and this becomes reality!"

"I don't want any of that," she said.

"Then you're a fool!" Nayttava wailed before the ground started rotating again.

"I'm okay with that," Bellae said, smiling.

All three hooded figures appeared in a line across from her, their different colored mirrors serving as backdrop.

Without warning, Bellae found herself being yanked retrograde as the three figures began to shake violently and disappear. Unable to stop, her legs scurried her in reverse. Before she knew it, her body was sliding back up the incline that had brought her into the cave. Soon she was flying up through white mist as Sankari counted backwards.

She could hear Gimelli screaming, "OOOOOOOOOOOOOOON!" Eventually, she was back standing on the ledge, Lontas holding the two mice. Everyone was talking, but backwards and undecipherable.

Moving retrograde in time at increasingly blistering speed, she found herself back in the desert, staring at the lioness, but through the perspective of a mirror—in reverse, through a crystal-clear reflection.

Next, she was watching the likeness of herself back in the sandstorm, facing the Wasted Undead, staring at Stralande, crying at his secrets, fighting wolves in Creber, running from Dark Warriors, bawling while holding Finn, standing in front of the maimed and blinded dragon Hullus—weeping at his obscure words.

Bellae closed her eyes, immersed in damp darkness as her mind screamed, *Finn!*

"Esoohc dna rebmemer," a strange voice said.

"What does that mean?" Bellae asked, opening her eyes. "I don't want to see this again!" She relived it enough during the moonless landscape of her nightmares.

A shadowy, black-robed figure staring at her through a flowing mirror suddenly appeared. The finish of the reflective surface seemed to turn to water, rippling out in a wave, as his skeleton hand reached through, clasping Bellae's neck. His hand was incredibly strong, and she could not make a sound as the bony fingers squeezed air from her throat and slowed blood to her brain.

His head oozed through the now-liquid silver that was the mirror. His black hood leaked away to reveal an ebony skull with flaming red eyes. Bits of decaying flesh oscillated on his face, still clinging to the rough surface of his bones. Bellae croaked, struggling to breathe under the tightening grip. Her eyes flayed open in terror as her head started to spin in oxygen-deprived lightheadedness.

"Remember and choose!" the skull recited. A moment before she passed out, the skull's mouth opened, and flames shot towards her just as the hand viciously flung her backwards. Gasping for air, Bellae found herself flying faster and faster in complete darkness. She jerked to a stop, her brain and organs protesting at the abrupt deceleration. Glancing down, her whole body shone bright white. Looking up, she could see Crann standing nervously outside the Báis te Pass. The horse looked at her oddly but with a hint of recognition.

Figure 27: Alone, terrified, and forced to relive horrible moments from the past, Bellae faces the skeletal guardian of the mirrors.

A look of horror sculpted onto her face as she realized where she was and, worse, why.

"I will NOT do it! I will not!" Bellae screeched.

A sickly, corrupt laugh cackled behind her. The sable skull wafting within his black robe wavered, as if enjoying the pain frothing within her. "You have an incredibly uncomplicated choice. Sometimes the easiest choices are the hardest to commit to, having the longest consequences."

Crann carefully sauntered over to Bellae, bewildered by her glowing appearance and defensive of the black-robed carnal skeleton.

"Choose!"

Bellae shook her luminous head, tears flooding out terror.

"You understand the options before you?" Swaying in his dusky robe, his blazing eyes burned into Bellae with vicious glee at the alternatives bifurcating before her.

Crann neighed loudly but resisted touching the radiant form of Bellae before him.

As if powered by her tears, Bellae's head continued to swivel back and forth in denial of her decision. Looking up, anger replacing shock, she spoke, "That was me in the desert? I was the one guiding Crann? This whole time I led Crann to die?"

The skeletal figure laughed. "A puerile question. As of yet, you are still locked into a constricted view of time, seeing it, as frangible mortals do, only moving from point A to B. Where we stand now, you have not yet seen Oasis Vastaus or met the ferratus lanx.

"Each of the five tasks you must endure, and survive, along this journey are agonizing tests. These trials not only confirm you as the Chosen, but they evaluate your worth to possess the Macht Crystals. Most humanoid forms are greedy gluttons, who would rather immerse themselves in stupefying gratification and numbing pleasures than fight for enlightenment."

"You don't know us that well," Bellae said, thinking of her beloved Finn and the Knights.

He laughed and waved a boney hand as if swishing off her juvenile ignorance. "My role is to protect and guard the Strength Crystals.

What you seek can only be acquired after we test your resolve to complete this test, a *true* examination of your strength."

"My strength? How does leading Crann to his death do anything but torture me?" Bellae howled.

"Jumping off the cliff required vitality of faith, testing the sturdiness of your resolve. This choice determines your strength of will, determination. Going back to address your linear thinking, here and now, both futures are possible. Lead Crann to save yourself, and in so doing, you give yourself a *chance*, however small, to come to my mountain and ultimately save the world from destruction at the hands of Na Cearcaill. Or you can let Crann live, and you die in the desert—all hope of finishing this quest burns within the heat of the blistering suns as your flesh is agonizingly digested. Choose that path, and you will never live to meet me."

"How am I even here if I don't want to lead him to the oasis…that means I'm in the future before he rescued me…in the past?"

His two fiery eyes blazed in annoyance. "If you choose right now to let yourself die at the hands of the ferratus lanx, then nothing from that point until now will happen, or in your case, has happened."

"But I'm here!" Bellae said loudly, desperately stalling to find a way to save Crann.

Shaking his head in frustration, the skeleton's words leaked annoyance. "Linear time poisons your thinking. You have seen the outcome if you guide him to his death—you will make it to the Hall of Mirrors, and we meet. If you refuse in this moment, none of that will have happened, and you die, doomed to slow digestion."

Taking a deep breath, she tearfully explained everything to Crann, even though her head was spinning with the possibilities.

"That's an easy choice, girl," Crann said, nuzzling her sparkling form. *"Lead me to the oasis. I gladly give my life for yours."*

"No!" Bellae screamed. *"I won't lose you again!"*

Crann looked down. *"Sounds like we don't have a choice. You can lead me, or I will try and find that oasis by myself, because there's no way I'm going to wait around here while you die without fighting. I know you would save me if you could."*

When Bellae didn't move Crann headed towards the Báis te Pass. *"Lead me, or I go on my own."*

Bawling, Bellae turned to the skeletal figure. "Alright, let's do it."

"There is no us. It is only you," the robed being said. "This is all on you alone."

I'm so sorry, Crann. "I…I'm ready."

For Bellae, each moment seemed to be warping forward. However, she could see Crann growing weaker and thinner as if time for the horse was moving slowly and for her in giant leaps. One minute she would look up, and they were miles ahead.

I feel no thirst or hunger, but Crann suffers.

Suddenly, they were within the oasis. She could see herself being toyed with by the ferratus lanx. *"Go, Crann!"* she said with anguish, pointing to the beast. *"Fight as hard as you can. Try to survive,"* she said, knowing he was doomed to die.

"You fight! You survive, Crann! Find a way to win! Fight. You fight!" she screamed.

The robed skeleton appeared behind her, laughing. "You still don't get it girl! With this choice, he's already dead."

Bellae howled in anguish before dropping to her knees in despair. She could feel the bones of his skeletal hands clasp her shoulders before she was ripped backwards physically and temporally.

"How about a trip back to another death?" the skull said, an evil laugh hissing through his decaying teeth.

Instantly, she was back at the Tournament, holding Finn's bleeding body and sobbing. The world started to spin, and she felt lightheaded.

"Oh no," he said. "You don't get to take the easy way out." Instantly, he grabbed her throat again, and she was whipping forward through time, reliving everything again since Finn's death as an observing spectator.

The being controlling her cruelly showed all the experiences from the dragon battle to jumping off the cliff, to the pitches by the three robed figures. Coming to a stop, he released her. Grabbing at her throbbing throat, taking slow, wheezing, deep breaths, she stared around the cave. The different colored mirrors began to spin.

Without warning Bellae's body began to shake brutally. She clenched her teeth to stop their rattling. A flash of searing pain, and she was suddenly ripped into three separate perspectives. On the left she could see the gold-robed figure surrounded by gleaming flaxen mirrors. Wanton images and scenes flashed within the reflective surfaces. She saw herself collecting all the Macht Crystals, becoming dressed in ornate robes, kings and queens coming to pay homage, bowing down to her infinite power and beauty.

"You are the key to saving the world. Only when *you* control the power of the crystals will everyone be safe," a voice declared. "You are destined for ultimate power and to rule the world." The candied, aromatic voice continued to tell her of the riches and lavish life she could lead while rescuing the world from Na Cearcaill. "All strife can end now if you choose the gold mirrors."

At the same time, a different voice spoke from the center, surrounded by black mirrors. Shadows whirled and obscurely flashed across the ebony surfaces. Occasionally, reflections in the inky mirrors revealed glowing eyes complete with misty hands swirling out, its smokelike form gesturing her forward. In one mirror her eyes were cavernous and pitch-black. "Don't be hypnotized by the fleeting pleasure of wealth within the golden reflective surfaces. Riches rot the soul, defile virtue, and obscure truth. Avoid the conceited trap of the egotistical silver mirrors. The obvious choice is the modest sincerity, and veracity, of the black mirrors. Collect the crystals, give them to the One, and escape to a magnificently long life, ignoring Na Cearcaill."

Bellae's head was swimming as the three robed figures voiced competed for her ear. On the right, silver mirrors flashed images of battles, bloodshed, and death. "Candor and honesty await you in the silver mirrors. Turn away from shadow's ignorance. Avoiding reality is not productive. Dodge the self-indulgence, complete with sightless darkness, of gilt power and the fallacious prosperity of the gold. Choose wisely."

Looking into the silver mirrors, Bellae could see an Eaglian in the Giant Redwoods. His hands were covered in blood, and he was sobbing. "Your true beginning," the silver figure said cryptically. In another

Bellae wept, her chest blackened and her body covered in blood. Soon a tide of blood swallowed her image, frothing and bubbling up behind the mirror.

"Don't listen to the silver cretin. Do you want the bloody death that awaits you there? Some future! Forget about the darkness of the black dullard. The shadows contained there hold nothing but insentient incomprehension."

Their voices grew louder and louder until she couldn't make out anything but a roar of senseless noise. The images and shadows within the different mirrors began to hurtle by at a frantic pace. Seeing three massively different scenes and hearing the screaming voices made her head spin. Bellae closed her eyes and held her ears. Even with them shut, she could see visions, and with her ears plugged, she could hear the howling chatter.

"Enough!" Bellae screamed.

A solace of silence settled upon her, and she opened her eyes with a single perspective. The three robed figures crossed their arms, slipping their skeleton hands into the opposite arm's sleeve. The calm did not last. Everything began to move chaotically again. Mirrors, figures, and rock whirred by, all while the three figures resumed their incessant chirping, each one vigorously trying to convince her of their worth.

"You must choose beauty, wealth, and gold…"

"The selfless elegance of the black…"

"The true image of yourself within silver…"

Around and around the voices tumbled furiously as images raged across her eyes. It was maddening, especially as the volume increased.

Self, choose yourself…

Selfish is the poor's excuse for others' success. Don't…

Don't choose the false self…

The whispering intensified. *…false power…false self…true self…true selfishness…true selflessness…*

Bellae's heart was pounding, her breath racing, head spinning. Briefly, an image of Stralande appeared. His wizened smile creased into tarnished scales. The rustling voices calmed, replaced with the ancient dragon's. "Try not to get caught up in the trap of taxing stress or pestering pressure of this quest—they are lies and internal fabrications of our own minds. Do your best, and control your perspective. Change this from a horrible responsibility to a chance to help. Rework a daunting quest into an adventurous opportunity. Morph pressure and stress into excitement and enthusiasm. Keep moving forward—one step, then another."

Despite the maddening voices, she slowed her breathing and heart rate.

"How does this end?"

"Choose," a voice interjected. "Strength of mind is just as important as stature or burliness of muscle."

"You suck as a guardian!" she screamed. "Or guardians, whatever you are," she added, actually missing the discourteous lioness from the desert.

"The purity of your heart must be tested," a voice hissed.

"Jumping off a cliff was not impressive enough? Sending my beloved Crann to death isn't adequate to show my commitment? Do you really think it's okay to put all this on me?"

"It was not our, or your ancestors', intention that this task fall to a child. The world sometimes forces one's hand," the voice hissed.

The chorale of other voices exploded again. Dizziness and a wave of lightheadedness dropped her to her knees.

"Center yourself," a memory of Friar's voice cut through her mind. She searched for other memories of him. "Train your mind to be more powerful than any emotion: fear, excitement, jealously, anxiety, anger, indifference. If emotions overrun your mind, you lose. Unbridled passion rattling around in your mind corrupts sound decision making."

Bellae smiled, grateful for his wisdom. Focusing on his words quelled the guardians' voices. "Having the strength to face yourself as you are seems the only choice. Silver—I select truth over ignorance or false promises."

She paused, getting better at pushing their voices out of her mind. "Friar told me it is better to accept the truth, even if painful, than to ignore reality with a lie. The dark mirrors seem to ignore self-introspection, and the gold is full of insatiable gluttony."

When the rotating world sped up, Bellae shouted, "Stop! I chose!"

The three figures and their corresponding mirrors appeared in front of her—their voices still haranguing her mind.

"Silver!" she said, moving towards that mirror. Just before she handed the crystals from the desert, the figure changed to gold. She jumped back, sure it had been silver a second ago. Suddenly, all three began moving again.

She took a deep breath, *What a fun test.*

"Please stop."

The figures once again halted, but their incessant sermons continued. She moved quickly to the silver one, but it turned black. Before they could move again, she rapidly jumped to her right, to the "new" silver figure, and pushed the crystals forward.

All the voices stopped as the gold- and black-robed figures dissolved. The silver-robed form stepped forward. "Riches or death or ignorance? The options before you did not offer much of a choice. As you learned with the ancient dragon, you have to break the shackles of ignorance, stand up, and turn around to the truth if you want to grow. Even though we can never reach the peak of knowledge, there is always more to learn. We must strive for the truth. For all of us there is only one way forward, the future. Memories serve to teach, but we should not dwell on past victories, or be consumed by negative recollections."

His robe turned black as he pulled back its hood to reveal a skeletal head with decaying muscles and rotting flesh. "Long has been the wait for you. This decision is complete, but every day is a choice. Every time it gets tough, stand back up and go on. Do not ever give up. This is your journey. This test is now past, but you are not yet close to the end. Take what Stralande told you to heart—take one step, then another. Decide to keep going. You have everything in front of you, but you know almost nothing about what is truly coming. Only when you have nothing left in front of you will you know all that is required. Behind each choice is a consequence, often one we cannot see or fathom.

"Choosing self-reflection and truth was wise. Even though the image is inverted, only when we scrutinize ourselves, analyzing our actions and stripping the false pretenses we present to the world, do we truly see ourselves. Never critically examining who you are, or scrutinizing what you have become, hiding in the shade of the darkness—the black mirror would have been wrong. While garish and exuberant, the gold held no truth, only prideful debauchery. It is not easy to domesticate one's desires, but it is also not impossible."

Bellae shook from exhaustion and sadness. Knowing she led Crann to his death would forever haunt her. Seeing her mother's dead body and reliving Finn's death had torn off any scab of healing, releasing sadness, oozing out in the guise of tears.

"I know you're sad at the loss of those you loved," the skeletal figure said, as if understanding her thoughts. "But love is always a risk in all its forms and depths. Love is confronting uncertainty and the possibility of rejection and affection's demise. Love is laughing at the precariousness and taking the plunge anyway. Love can be painful. Love anyway. Death is certain. Live anyway. Swim in the immersive uncertainty and decide to be vibrant and happy with each moment gifted to us."

Bellae nodded, feeling guilty about loathing him after his kind words. "I'm just so tired."

"Once this journey is over, you might do just about anything to come back here and be with the living once again. To have so much of the journey left may seem like a burden, but may, soon enough, become your greatest wish," the robed figure said.

"Compelling me to send Crann to his death? Making me see Finn die again? That was mean," Bellae said.

His head tilted to the side as if in disbelief of her words. "Girl, you are still looking at the shadows dancing on the cave wall. Throw off the chains and turn around. There you will see that you *allowed* Crann to save you. If given the choice, which option do you think he would pick: let you slowly die while being digested on that desert creature or sacrificing himself to save you?

"Finn's death can serve you, if you let it. His ending is a chance for a new beginning. Such pivotal events, especially the ones that vault into our lives unexpectedly, uninvited, will always change us. How it changes you? That secret is, it's up to you. Grow from it. Let it motivate you. Live your life to honor his. If you let it, death will be all too happy to sour your vision so that all you can see is despair as it discolors hope and blurs joy. Don't let fear or sadness over death take your life metaphorically before it does physically. All of us, and everything, eventually submit to death. Mourn but move forward. Death's dark blossom is the world's greatest crop, blooming everywhere every day. Smile anyway. Just because death overcomes us in the end doesn't mean we should let it kill the time we have to live via worry and anxiety. It is okay to grieve on the inside but always beam on the outside."

His flaming eyes bore into her as he continued, "At the end of each day, we must pay a hefty toll, losing part of ourselves as we involuntarily contribute a portion of our lives into the past. Each of us is born with only so much currency to live with, to dream amidst, to love within. Each day, as more of our lives fade into memories, we are left a little poorer. Lighter is the coin purse embracing our days left to live. We pay this toll whether it was a good or bad day, an adventure or marked with laziness, filled with action or dulled with inaction. The cost must be paid, and it is not negotiable.

"Time, you see, is one of the few things that cannot be bribed, persuaded or pleaded with. Choose your course wisely while, and when, you can, for all of us are fading closer to our final payment when life manifested within us does cease. As the first sun crests the horizon each day, we have access to only one coin—the life toll for today." Twisting his skeletal head, several bones cracked. "The past, while we can learn from it, is not ours to hold, lost forever to the sands of time. The future? That is a fickle beast, ethereal and problematic, and never guaranteed."

He nodded, as if that was some sort of grand explanation for what happened to her and what was ravaging the world.

"Sooo...are you..." Bellae started, hesitantly, "...alive, or...?"

The figure laughed. "That is a question just as, if not more, relevant for those with additional flesh on their bones than I. Perhaps a question we should all ask ourselves. Am I truly alive? Do I truly live? What I have learned over a thousand of your lifetimes: Enjoy today. Live today. You never know how many more days you have."

With that he slid up his hood before one skeletal hand held out a bag containing the two new crystals.

"Will I have to face the darkness again?" Bellae asked, hesitating.

"You will hear the power of, and feel mortal frailty within, the eternal blackness. The best we can do is, while we have our time and strength, spread the light."

As she took them out, one of her eyes glowed orange and one yellow as the rustling promises of the crystals exploded in her head. Her eyes rolled back, and flickering images overtook her mind. At first, she saw a hand rise out dirt. A chain slithered its way towards the arm, slinking forward like a snake as the entire background morphed into a black night pitted with stars and smeared with orange and pink gas clouds. The chain wriggled forward, slowly writhing around the hand, which clenched into a fist before bursting into flames and sprouting wings, breaking the chain's grip. *"The Power to overcome,"* a voice whispered, *"the strength to conquer, gives flight to our soul and dreams."*

The broken link in the chain spewed forth splintered fragments of metal, which began transmuting into riches. *"The binding, snaring chains of weakness are inherently, internally decrepit. Riches, power, hedonistic delights, all whisper lies of freedom while coiling around free will, snuffing out all the light of who we are as they demand ever more. Ever more. Never enough. Love of wealth twists the psyche into covetous frailty, breaking spirits."*

The visions melted away, and she was instantly transported through the mountain and rapidly into the sky. Looking down, she could see Lontas, decades in the future, running, laughing, playing with his wife and children. Her smile evaporated as time whirred forward until he was on his deathbed, his children, now adults, weeping. She was forced to watch generations of his descendants grow old and die.

With tears flowing she was lifted upwards into space, watching the planet from above slowly stop and spin backwards. Tens of thousands of years passed with each minute. Mountains rose and fell. Lakes formed, dried-up, and reformed. The continents moved so Ifrean connected with Verngaurd. Eventually, the atmosphere sucked down into a mix of searing gases as the planet turned molten to be pelted by asteroids.

Live outside time, the voices encouraged as she was sucked backwards into the galaxy before moving forward and watching the process

Figure 28: Collecting the second pair of Macht Crystals sends Bellae a vision of strength and weakness.

speed ahead until she was back in front of hooded figure. After catching her breath, Bellae carefully put the new crystals in her bag from Stralande while trying to fend of the voices racing in her head.

Do I tell Lontas I watched him and his children's children live and die?

"The only meaning of life can be life itself. To live your life well and enjoy it, thumbing our nose at death, briefly, that is the best we can do. It is the only thing we can do. Some, the misguided and feeble, take that to be hedonism and greed. Others choose scholarship and a search for wisdom. What you decide to do will determine the fate of the crystals and the world," the robed figure said. He then handed her the next scroll while pointing to the back of the chamber and what looked like a solid wall of rock.

Unsure of how long he had slept, Kainen opened his eyes to see Gimelli pacing in animated conversation. Given her far-off look, he guessed she was talking to Jumeaux telepathically. His back and buttocks were protesting at having been propped up against the irksomely hard rock for so long.

"I *knooow* you saved us from the hippogriffs, but Veneficus sicced them on us in the first place!" Gimelli said before pausing to listen.

"You know what I mean. He ordered them to attack Eaglians."

More listening.

"Okay, Jumeaux. If we get into trouble, I'll contact you. I promise. I already told you, Bellae's safe, we're fine…Jumeaux, just get out of my head. I'll let you know."

"Trouble?" Kainen asked as she moved towards him.

"Sorry, was I talking out loud?"

"Yeah, but it's okay," Kainen said, standing up. "If I sat there any longer, I wouldn't be able to get up. Any sign of Bellae?"

Gimelli shook her head.

"What did your brother say?"

"He and Veneficus will do anything for us, but…the longer we talk, the less I trust his motives," she declared.

"They did save us on the plains," Kainen pointed out.

"You're right, and I've always said I'd never give up on him, but sometimes even giving all the love you have is not enough to break through self-imposed coldness. Jumeaux never makes it easy. I can sense, almost see, Veneficus sitting there. I'm not sure if Jumeaux cares for us, or…is being manipulated." Gimelli paused. "Is Veneficus supposed to get these Macht Crystals when we find them? Didn't the Ainmhi Caint steal them from him in the first place?"

Kainen wobbled his head. "They stole them out of his possession, but it was to protect them from a great evil that was supposedly coming to sweep across the land, Na Cearcaill—a cycle that's supposedly here again." Kainen quickly held up his hand. "I know you're going to ask about the great evil…no one knows. It may be we *are* supposed to give them to Veneficus when this is over. All I can tell you is that there's more to the story, and we won't know what to do until we find all the power crystals and the scroll that goes with them."

"It could get ugly if we *aren't* supposed to give them to Veneficus," Gimelli said, her eyes abruptly filling with fear. "That's one powerful Magician, and part of me thinks he's 'helping' just to steal them in the end."

Kainen shook his head, for the first time truly seeing all the obstacles at the end of this quest. "There's no doubt, when we finish, he could be a huge problem, maybe as big as the White Wizard himself. I guess, for now, we have no choice but to keep going." The young Elf shivered while scanning the rocks. "I keep getting the worst feeling we're being watched."

"By whom?" Gimelli asked, examining the cliffs around them.

"I don't know. I suspect the White Wizard is waiting to pounce on us just like we fear Veneficus will once we have the crystals," Kainen said. "I would definitely rather Veneficus get them than the White Wizard."

"Me too. I hope Bellae's up for this whole thing," Gimelli commented as a loud grating sound echoed on the ledge next to them. They turned to see a new, previously hidden, doorway opening, the diminutive Bellae poking her head through.

"Hey, guys," she said in a gravelly voice, exhausted but grateful.

Both Gimelli and Lontas instantly swarmed her as she came onto the bluff. She could barely breathe as they looked her over for injuries and asked a dizzying string of questions.

"Give me some air. Except for your smothering, I'm fine," she squeaked.

Don't tell them about Crann, Bellae thought. *I can't handle any more lectures, ridiculous expectations, and I am way beyond sick of sympathy.* The memory of leading Crann to his death forced her start to cry.

"I'm just so happy to be back with you," Bellae said before Gimelli could launch into an investigation of her tears.

Gimelli nodded, seemingly satisfied with the answer.

Just as the stone door Bellae walked through slammed shut, two Nishi slithered up to the Watchers behind the League. "The Evil One will be pleased the smelly urchin of a brat is making progress."

"You report to him. We'll keep watching the wretched children," a Watcher said.

"That's why they call you 'Watchers,'" a Nishi replied, her eyes going wild with rage.

"As soon as she acquires the last pair, we get to kill her!" the other Nishi hissed, her face contorting to reveal her teeth. "But oh soo slooooow. She dies nice and slooooow."

Scroll 4: Last of the Last

"We have confirmation!" Ritari bellowed.

It was predawn in Castle Liberum, but Friar Pallium had been up for hours, pacing and waiting for word from the Eaglians. Ever since the Magicians raided the Isle of Hirmulisko and enchanted the hippogriffs, travel for the Eaglians had become almost impossible. The hippogriffs and remaining griffins had totally abandoned fighting dragons. In fact, their new strategy was to rapidly flee. Now, they targeted Eaglians.

"Confirmed? By Aquila?" Friar questioned.

"Yes, sir. A massive force of Proliate is moving against us, not Creber, as we had thought. Apparently, those forces were a diversion."

"We are well fortified and stocked." Seeing the pained look on his captain's face, Friar asked, "What else?"

"We received confirmation that the Dark Warriors have overrun Ager—"

"What?" Friar interrupted. "All of it?"

"Yes," Ritari answered simply. "King Tarha was killed. His head is now on a stake over their capital of Maatila."

"How…?"

"Well…" Ritari hesitated. "We did wipe out most of their army, and with so few Knights, we can't protect them. The Proliate are obviously focusing on obliterating us before turning on the Dark Warriors. That leaves everyone vulnerable."

Friar sat. The forbidding thought that he had been played like a fool sat gloatingly on his mind.

"I can't imagine the White Wizard hasn't been planning this from the beginning. The Dark Warriors control a lot of the eastern seaboard with strongholds at Temple Palvoa, Castle Taiheart, and now Maatila. Only Toil Shaor, Pescare, and sections of Piscium remain unconquered."

"They control a lot of prime farmland and a great deal of the fishing lanes," Friar stated. "How large is the Proliate force?" he asked.

"We're still working out the numbers, but large. They are mostly Ultor or Silver divisions after the heavy losses by the Red Divisions."

"Are you blaming me for Ager and now this?" Friar asked bluntly.

"Just telling the facts," Ritari replied. "We had little choice at the time. You tried to avoid war and predicted the Dark Warriors were manipulating them…us. You were right."

"We should try and reason with Storlax or Lidenskap," Friar suggested.

Ritari shook his head. "Now that line of thinking I totally disagree with. Our last three messengers were killed, including an Eaglian.

Aquila mentioned they had been tortured and strung up on the walls of the Citadel."

"The Proliate are blinded by rage and ravenous for revenge," Friar commented.

"Sir, with permission I'll see to the preparations for the upcoming siege," Ritari stated. While we're well stocked, our walls won't hold up against their diezmar."

Friar nodded. *Bloody White Wizard! Now, hatred is boiling all around us and we have cultivated the perfect breeding ground for you to swoop in and take us over.*

"Ager has fallen?" General Lidenskap asked, riding at the head of the Proliate army heading to Liberum.

"Yes," High Commander Storlax replied. "Do you think we should continue? If we march against Liberum, we will have the Knights to the west and the Dark Warriors to the east. Could be a trap."

Lidenskap smiled. "I think this will work out nicely. After our diezmars reduce the Liberum's walls to rubble and the Knights are destroyed, we will turn and drive the Dark Warriors into the sea. With our Southern Dwarf friends using their prestidigitation to cover our troop movements, the Knights will not have time to prepare for our assault like they did at Ovest and Trepas. Now we choose the time and place of battle."

"With Veneficus magically moving the diezmars intact, we have a huge advantage. We can begin attacking their gates soon," Storlax said.

Lidenskap began to laugh.

"What?" Storlax questioned defensively.

"I can't wait to see Friar's face when we smash down his castle and force feed his brand of treachery down his throat."

Scroll 5: What Kind of Hat?

"It's nothing," Bellae hoarsely reassured.

"The bruises and scratches on your neck are not 'nothing,'" Gimelli said.

"Let's just say this guardian was not charming."

"Was there one or three?" Lontas asked.

"Not sure," Bellae replied. Seeing their confused expressions, she added, "The one split apart, I think. Or maybe there were three that merged into one? Anyway, I need to show you something."

The mountain wind was whipping furiously as Bellae took off the bag Stralande had given her. She carefully removed the two large crystals from the skeletal guardian. "These are the new ones, the Strength Crystals. Notice how they glow blue like the Seeing Crystals from the desert." After carefully setting them down, she warily took out the other crystals. "Watch what happens."

As the four crystals were moved together, each one changed color. The first two glowed a bright red, another radiated orange, and the fourth yellow.

"It's cool, but what does it mean?" Lontas asked.

"Not sure," Bellae admitted. "But I thought it was neat and may come in handy later."

"That's great. However, if you don't finish telling us what happened, I'll push you over the edge...again," Sankari said in a snit.

Bellae laughed, which made the Fairy angrier. "Okay, Sankari. I had to choose between three mirror sets of different colors. Each one showed me some part of the past, myself, or the future. Once I picked the right one, the skeleton guy pointed me to a back wall with lots of symbols. I tried pushing on them, I tried tapping them in different orders...nothing worked. I put the Strength Crystals up against the wall, and zilch. The door finally opened when I screamed in Ainmhi Caint."

"But how did you get back up here?" Gimelli wondered.

"There was a staircase behind the door. I walked up, using the crystals for light. You obviously couldn't hear me, but I was pounding on the rock, trying to get it to open. It wouldn't budge until I held up one Strength and one Seeing Crystal *and* said 'open' in Ainmhi Caint."

"So, without Ainmhi Caint you would have been stuck?" Kainen said.

Bellae nodded while carefully putting the four crystals into their individual pouches. "Do you want to see the next scroll?"

"We should get back to Arend and Scelto to check on them," Gimelli said before anyone could answer.

"Good idea," Kainen said, "but how do we get down?"

"Were there any other passages in the stairwell you came up?" Lontas questioned.

"No. Definitely not. I looked and felt around in there," Bellae answered. "Maybe the door to the passage we walked up on will be open?"

"I don't think even magic could remove that avalanche," Sankari said.

With no other options, the League walked into the room. The door to the ledge slammed shut, plunging them into total darkness. A short while later, the blue symbols they had seen before lit up again.

"Oh, no. Anyone remember which symbol we need?" Kainen asked.

Before anyone could answer, the emblems started to disappear.

"We're done for," Sankari wheezed. As her words trailed away, all but one of the symbols vanished.

Bellae shuffled forward. *"Open!"* With a loud screeching noise, a new doorway slowly ground open.

"That wasn't too bad," Gimelli said cheerfully.

The new path twisted around the mountain until a secret door let them join up with the trail that they had taken in the first place. Looking back up the mountain, they could see where a rockslide had completely blocked off the door they had originally entered.

After walking halfway down the mountain, they heard a loud rumble.

"What's that?" Gimelli asked, afraid of the answer.

"Another avalanche!" Lontas cried out. "Run!"

"Hurry!" Kainen shouted. The League took off, running until the grumbling rocks stopped. Looking back, they could see the entire upper part of the trail was covered in rubble.

"No one else will ever get to the top of Death Mountain again," Kainen said.

"Oh, what a shame," Sankari huffed. "It could have been such a popular vacation spot."

Once they neared the bottom, they could smell something wonderful.

"Arend got us dinner!" Kainen said, running the rest of the way to his old friend.

As soon as Gimelli turned the corner from the path, Scelto was right next to her.

"Hey!" he said, sheepishly.

"Hello!" she said, chuckling at his ubiquitous and succinct greeting.

"Are you okay?" Scelto asked.

"Yes, why?" she replied.

"You guys were gone two days!" Scelto said, concern radiating off his face.

"What? Are you nuts?" Sankari proclaimed. "We were gone about ten hours."

"I don't know, Sankari. I feel tired and hungry like it has been two days, and we had no way to track time up there, especially with the magic fog stuff," Kainen said.

"He's correct," Arend stated. "Scelto's been up and down the mountain at least sixty times looking for you."

"Aw, you missed us!" Gimelli said.

"You two lovebirds are going to make me puke," Sankari whined.

"There's obviously magic at work here," Kainen said.

"Come. Sit by the fire and tell us what happened," Scelto insisted.

After they had recounted everything that happened, they opened the scroll. Kainen read while the others ate fish Arend caught from Lake Glasere.

"Faith breeds courage—it takes courage to have faith.

Earth on Fire Ocean of Blood

You survived the leap of faith test,
Make every day, and act, your best.
True Strength is not war paint,
But Humility and Restraint.
Abuse of power is weakness,
Within life's briefness.
Courage is Strength *within Wisdom.*
Avoid blighting cynicism.

The **Time** crystals are Third.
In this world, it demands be heard,
Dominating each and every **Life**.
Death frees you from that strife.

Seek ones living in caves,
Riding mire waves.
Despite their flaws,
Find the ancient clan of jaws.

Go where admittance is exclusive,
And entrance conclusive.
Fashion for all—stone hats.
No sight, no chats.

It's ***the*** oldest of its kind,
Every one straight lined.
All eventually enter these.
Its master knows no appease.

They were different, now same.
No matter from where they came,
Once admitted, receive a cold embrace.
Still is the pace.

Time's no concern there.
In rooms—no windows or care.
No distractions, no paintings, no flowers, no food.
Yet no boredom, no loneliness, no hunger, or feud."

"Can we promise never to read these while eating?" Sankari asked. "They seriously make me want to vomit."

"I have to admit they're wearing thin," Gimelli stated.

"But we have to answer to win! See, thin and win rhyme," Lontas explained to their scowls.

"Is that your Jumeaux impression?" Scelto asked kiddingly.

Lontas blushed. Although more confident since beginning this trip, old wounds die hard.

"Okay, so the Time Crystal pair of Life and Death," Kainen said. "Otherwise, I have no idea what it's talking about. Seek ones in caves and clan of jaws?"

"Who lives in caves?" Arend suggested. "Dwarves, north and south, and Fairies."

"Didn't the Proliate live in caves before the Ainmhi Caint were exterminated?" Lontas reminded.

"It does say 'ancient,' so I guess we should include them," Kainen agreed.

"Wait, you're forgetting the part about 'riding mire waves.' Only one lives near a mire, the Southern Dwarves," Lontas said.

"You could be on to something," Kainen said, "but I don't understand this about flaws and jaws. The Dwarves don't have unusual jaws. Is there anyone else living there?"

"Let's back up and approach it from the mire then," Scelto suggested. "We have the Mohado and East Mohado Mire in the south, then there are the wetlands of the northwest."

"What lives near one of those mires with powerful jaws?" Gimelli questioned.

"There's the mire on the east end of the Isle of Hirmulisko, but Veneficus enchanted it eons ago so I think we can write that one off," Kainen said.

"Why did Veneficus do that?" Gimelli asked.

"Many dangerous beasts lived there when settlements of Dwarves and men tried to move in. Things did not go well. There was a lot of death on both sides," Kainen informed. "Veneficus declared it protected ground where no humanoid could settle, but also certain creatures had to stay there and not cross the Torpen sea onto the mainland."

"No one lives in the East Mohado Mire now, but…" Arend let his voice trail off.

"There was something that used to live there!" Lontas finished, his voice shrill with exhilaration.

"What are you talking about?" Sankari asked.

"The Daoine Crogall of course!" Lontas answered excitedly.

"Lontas, I don't think the rest of us know what you and Arend are thinking," Bellae informed gently.

"Okay, a long time ago the Daoine Crogall used to live where the Southern Dwarves do. Only back then the region was called Leuat, and the mires were much more extensive. Thousands of years ago, they stretched all the way up to Liberum. The mountains of the Southern Dwarves were like islands for the Daoine Crogall."

"Who, or what, were they?" Kainen prompted.

"They had heads of crocodiles but walked upright with humanoid bodies and hands. Obviously, they have powerful jaws, so that fits," Lontas answered.

"What happened to them?" Bellae questioned.

"They were tricked and killed off by the Southern Dwarves," Arend answered simply.

"That's right," Lontas said. "The Dwarves who would become 'Southern' either broke off or were exiled from the North. At that time, the mire was just starting to retreat, and they had discovered gold, the first of many treasures they would mine from the rich and diverse mountains of the south. Anyway, they promised to live in peace with the Daoine Crogall in exchange for exclusive mining rights.

"The Daoine Crogall were tricked. They thought they would get books and libraries and become as smart as the Kirvella dragons and agreed. That was a mistake."

"I'll say," Arend commented. "The Southern Dwarves betrayed them, destroying all the eggs in their nursery. Just like at the Battle of Petturi when they attacked the Knights—treacherous leeches from the beginning."

"The Dwarves blamed the destruction on the Saatana dragons with prestidigitation," Lontas added. "The poor Daoine Crogall thought the Southern Dwarves were protecting their babies. Finally, they convinced them to attack the Northern Dwarves and dragons. The Daoine Crogall did. Despite their strength, they were no match for dragons. Those that survived were killed by the Southern Dwarves when they returned."

"Thanks, you two! What a super cheery tale!" Sankari moaned.

"Anyway," Kainen continued, "we know we're heading south to the Southern Dwarf Kingdom, but that area is huge. We need to narrow it down. Let's reread the last bit:

Go where admittance is exclusive,
And entrance conclusive.
Fashion for all—stone hats.
No sight or chats.

It's ***the*** oldest of its kind,
Every one straight lined.
All eventually enter these.
Its master knows no appease.

They were different, now same.
No matter from where they came,
Once admitted, receive a cold embrace.
Still is the pace.

Time's no concern there.
In rooms—no windows or care.
No distractions, no paintings, no flowers, no food.
Yet no boredom, no loneliness, no hunger, or feud."

Scelto bent down, pointing. "No windows…cold embrace…straight lines," he read. "Sounds like we need to head into the mines."

"Couple things, bright eyes," Sankari said. "First, mines are not straight lines. Second, there are three mountain ranges and a large central mountain. Each has tons of mines, and only the biggest get a name. Every one of them has miles of paths that are dizzying, even for the Southern Dwarves who spend their whole lives down there. It would take decades to explore just a few of those mountains."

"Calm down, Sankari," Kainen advised. "Look, it says, 'Fashion for all—stone hats…It's ***the*** oldest of its kind.' That's the key. Once we figure out the 'oldest of its kind,' we have it."

"Are there any deep caverns with ice?" Lontas asked.

"What are you thinking?" Arend questioned.

"It says, 'receive a cold embrace. Still is the pace.' That sounds like they are frozen or something."

"There's nothing like that in the caves that I know of," Kainen answered. Seeing the Fairy sulking, he asked, "Sankari, you solved the last riddle. Any ideas?"

Sankari's face brightened, but she quickly recovered, hiding it with a grimace while moving closer. "Well, I suppose I can help. The thing that has me curious is this 'stone hats' business. That's bizarre. Also, why wouldn't you need food or drink?"

"You're brilliant, Sankari," Lontas exclaimed as she glared warily.

"You hit on the keys. At the Knight cemetery grave markers sit over the dead like stone 'hats.' When you're departed, you don't need food or drink and are still and silent!" Lontas said.

The League quickly reread the scroll.

"I think you're right. They usually line up the bodies in 'straight lines' and 'all eventually enter' when they die," Kainen said.

"Lontas, we'd be lost without you. And you too, Sankari," Bellae quickly added.

"Does this help us narrow it down though?" Arend asked. "A cemetery from the old kingdom of Leuat? A burial ground that was around when the Ainmhi Caint wrote this prophecy has got to be extraordinarily old. Is it still there?"

"Remember, the guardians maintain the sites," Gimelli added.

"Lontas, do you recall anything else about them?" Kainen asked.

"Let me see the map," Lontas requested. "My guess would be the Mines of Kavos. I know that it was called something else before the Southern Dwarves started mining it, but I can't remember."

"Why did you choose that one?" Bellae asked.

"Well, thousands of years ago, the southern string of mines were almost completely under, and surrounded by, a deep mire. That solitary mountain is by far the tallest, which the Daoine Crogall would have liked. It was also well protected. At that time, the mire and ocean were to the south and they had mountains on the other three sides. Nice and sheltered, a perfect place for a sacred burial site," Lontas declared.

Scroll 6: You Don't Understand

"They're here," Baiulus said, entirely too serenely. Exhaustion was pulling on his normally crisp and clean facial features. The Proliate and their Confederacy had been wreaking havoc on Knight intelligence gathering with prestidigitation. Since most of the Rebelde Plains Dwarves died, the ability of the Allies to respond with their own deception was severely limited.

"How far away?" Friar asked, sleepily, the first sun, Mardin, peeking through his window.

"You don't understand. They're at our gates," Baiulus answered.

"How's this possible?" Friar asked. Panic gripped his throat and squeezed as his heart thudded heavily. He exhaled quickly, the air whistling out as he struggled to calm his breathing. *Just like my visions.*

"They used prestidigitation," Baiulus answered, feeling calm and resolute about the impending battle. "The only reason we found them this early was the night patrols hadn't returned. When the morning ones went out, they were butchered by the hidden Proliate."

"My old friend, we're in for the fight of our life," Friar stated.

"Yes. Two paths: win or die," Baiulus said, as if either outcome was fairly equal.

Friar held his head, feeling as if he were back on the Torpen Sea, bobbing on turbulent water. Only this time, it would be the blood of his Knights they would be skimming over. "Is there any way out of this?"

"I'm the castle steward. You…are Friar," he said, his tone a reprimand.

"Don't play formal with me at a time like this. Is asking for terms out of the question?" Friar asked.

"I stand by what I said, win or die," Baiulus answered.

"Even with the Dark Warriors taking over the coast? Shouldn't that make Lidenskap and Veneficus consider a truce to deal with that threat?"

"They are convinced we're working with the Dark Warriors. I think they would kill any messengers and hurl their bodies over our walls," Baiulus said.

"We can't ask Toil Shaor for help. They have Dark Warriors all around them. If they send any troops out, they will likely be killed on the way, and their own castle overrun," Friar said anxiously. "The Northern Dwarves and Elves of Creber are embroiled in their own battles."

Just then, Ritari barged into the room. "Almost everyone's ready. Sound the Bells of Kadotus anyway?" he asked.

"I would. I'll join you on our false wall shortly," Friar answered, hoping his deception could save them. As Ritari turned to leave, Friar yelled after him, "How many diezmars are already assembled?"

Ritari craned his neck back to Friar without turning his body. "Over a hundred."

Scroll 7: The Bells Toll

Luchar stood in the dusty bell tower. Rhyfeler hadn't listened when he said he could smell a battle, and a big one, coming. *Who's laughing now?*

He had been in the belfry all night in full armor. *I can feel, and smell, a bloody battle!* A petit rim of frost clung to his new armor. Luchar knew he had one battle left in him, but only one.

This was it.

The healers had devised a special brace so his left foot would not scrape when he walked. "Sturdy," he said to himself, kicking it against the tower. He ran his good hand over the largest bell. *The cold metal feels good beneath my sweaty fingers.* The commotion below let him know they were about to ring the Bells of Kadotus. *About time,* he thought.

He moved out on the small balcony of the bell tower, reveling in the great view of the enemy. He felt a shiver of excitement. Looking at his contracted and weak arm, he willed it to move. It barely fluttered. *Worth a try. My broken body, headaches, and confusion won't matter for much longer.*

He didn't bother covering his ears as the Bells of Kadotus blasted behind him and the birds of the tower flew off in an angry startle. There was no need to worry about his hearing. He doubted he would live past the morning.

One last battle, he thought, sighing deeply. "I have served as death's handmaiden, as is the call of all warriors. We do its bidding until it is our turn to be harvested, so I stand in front of the overwhelming storm of doubt before an enemy ten times larger than ours. I say to you, even as the clouds of confusion rumble and turn black, I stand. I stand in front of uncertainty and scream, 'I will know you.' I will fight to know you. As long as I have breath, I will never let doubt or fear win. As long as I can move even one part of my body, I will fight, tear, and claw for Knight victory. When I heave my last breath, I leave no regrets."

The Bells of Kadotus finally stopped, and he looked at the large shoulder guard or manica protecting his paralyzed arm. "Let's go," he said. Turning, he started the long, painful journey down the stairs.

After going a few steps, he stopped and turned. "Hey, bells, don't go telling anyone the sissy things I just said. If you do, I'll come back here and melt you down into soup ladles for Cookie to yell at all day!" Luchar started laughing hysterically as he hobbled down the stairs.

Scroll 8: Battle of Liberum-Revenge!

"Archers, crossbows to the front walls, NOW!" Ritari screamed as Friar approached—a look of awe masking his face at the army in front of him. It seemed like every able-bodied Proliate was before Liberum.

"There has to be fifty thousand troops and hundreds of diezmars," Friar said of the war machines dotting the forest of soldiers before them. "If our scouts are right about the diezmars' destructive capability, harnessing resonance, our walls are in serious trouble. How did Luchar know they were going to attack? He's been saying the battle was going to start today for quite some time."

"He said he 'could smell it,'" Ritari answered. "The Proliate have griffins *and* hippogriffs. If they get a good look at our strategy involving the walls, they will discover our plan and it will be doomed."

"Sorea!" Friar bellowed with such ferocity many of the defenders startled.

"Here!" she yelled, coming over from directing the archers and crossbow-wielding Knights.

"Bring up the verndari!" Friar ordered. As she sprinted down, he turned to Ritari. "Captain, issue the death order."

"Omnes enim mori?" Ritari questioned, although with the force arranged against them, he knew it was true. "Everyone dies? So we're not getting out of this one?"

Despite the tears spying above his eyelids, Friar smiled. "Everyone fights until everyone dies. Get the squires up here with bows. Call up everyone, including anyone in the infirmary who can stand and is mentally fit. Grab *all* orderlies as well. I want any tutors, cooks, or professors who are able to move armed and up here or working on creating kill zones. Those tasked with it need to start constructing makeshift fortifications in series. Those barricades will funnel their troops into tight kill zones once they breech the walls. Make sure they follow the patterns outlined in omnes enim mori. Douse the designated buildings to be put on fire when they breach certain obstacles. Get Lovag to oversee the archers on the walls to free up Rhyfeler to control the defense of the gatehouse."

Ritari signaled a messenger. The courier cocked his head to the side, gesturing the sign to repeat. Ritari did so, then loudly slammed his spear against his shield.

"From a great distance battles are faceless strategies full of nameless casualties reduced to simple, guiltless numbers," Friar said. "Up close battles are sweaty with fear and reek of death—gauntlets of terror and horror warriors must enter. As war's naked essence washes over you, your true self is exposed, raw and stripped for all to see."

As the death order sounded, a burdensome silence gripped the castle. They were used to the Bells of Kadotus—they rang for practice routinely. However, the omnes enim mori was a different beast.

Cookie and others in the kitchen froze.

"That can't be real?" a cook wondered, his knife in mid cut.

"Clear out!" Cookie screeched. "Arm yourselves and report to your emergency post for the death order."

The other cooks paused, looking desperate and confused.

"Move!" Cookie screamed. Standing tall and nodding, her eyes flashed determination until the last assistant left the kitchen. Then, and only then, did she fall to her knees and let the tears come. Ri, the kitchen cat, began spinning in circles, feeling the anxiety.

"You might'en survive this, cat, but th'rest? Na," Cookie said.

Eventually, she slowly stood and readied the emergency cooking list. *Never thought I'd need this.* "W'ya come with me to the cemetery? That's where we make our last stand and hold out as long as possible," Cookie asked the cat. Ri cocked her head to the side in confusion while anxiously swishing her tail and flattening both ears.

"I know, it ain't been the same 'round here with no Bellae." Cookie stopped wiping the tears away. They were coming too fast now, and she had too much to do. "Our job, you silly cat, is to get cooking supplies across that rickety bridge. The Knights and squires will get the food from the storage caves."

In the infirmary, Salus froze on the stairs, about where the ancient Knight Necare and Jumeaux had landed so long ago. Patients and orderlies alike looked towards the head healer and surgeon. Gathering his strength, he declared loudly, "Empty out the infirmary. Anyone who can stand and hold a sword, in one group. Everyone else, across the bridge to the cemetery."

"The cemetery?" a young orderly said.

"Yes, child," Salus replied. "That's where we make our last stand, and if need be, cut the suspension bridge across it once all the other defenses have been breached."

"Omnes enim mori means we're all going to die," a large, thick orderly added. "The cemetery is as good a place as any to lose your life—not far to go in order to be buried."

"We still have a chance. It's likely just a precaution. Get to work now, both of you," Salus said. "Focus on your jobs." As activity exploded around him, Salus felt like he was stuck in a slow-motion nightmare. *How did it come to this?* Despite what he said, that bell only meant one thing—everyone was going to die. It was just a matter of how many of the enemy they could take with them.

"'Scuse me!" the patient who had terrorized Jumeaux, Crassus, yelled. He rubbed a mixture of belly-button goop and nasal sediment onto Salus' formerly pristine robe.

"Yes?"

"I fight hardestest. I big help Knights!" Crassus said, now rubbing his protuberant belly. "I'll slash, slash, and strike good!"

"I'm sure you would…" Salus started, cut off by Crassus.

"See! See?" he screamed at the orderly now trying to guide him away. "I do get to fights with the Knights!"

"You would best serve the Knights by guarding those heading to the cemetery. Can you handle that?" Salus stated diplomatically.

"When do I get my weapon?" Crassus asked before being led away.

In the forge Hephaestus stopped mid hammer strike, hoping the chronic ringing in his ears had deceived him. However, the omnes enim mori bells continued.

Calmly turning, he barked, "Alright, armor up. Shut down and close everything before getting to your assigned emergency posts."

Hephaestus fought tears while removing his honey leather apron in favor of cold armor. Once armed he slowly walked away from his home, knowing he would never work the forges again. The certainty of death spread out, blocking light from optimism.

Bestilla's left arm stopped mid-reshelf, her right leaning heavily on a cane supporting her healing legs as the book froze in crooked stillness, her head twisting to listen. "All right, everyone," she said shakily with copious tears streaming down her face, "out of the library." Whether it was the Dark Warriors or the Proliate attacking wouldn't matter. One group hated books. The other thought you only needed one to find truth. *Fools,* she thought before hobbling to barricade the castle library as best she could.

A smile cracked its way through the wetness weeping down her cheeks as she struggled to lower the metal gate at the back of the Athenaeum section. *I purposefully left this up night after night to let Lontas into the library,* Bestilla thought, chuckling at Lontas believing she was not aware. *I know everything that goes on in my house.* There were rumors circulating that those children were on a quest to save the world. *I'm not sure what you can do, but you loved learning more than anyone else I have ever known.*

Baiulus joined Friar, who was absorbing a mix of fearful and panicked looks on the top of the walls.

"They must have emptied out every castle on their island and most of the Temples here on the mainland," Friar commented.

"I agree, and inevitably the Dark Warriors will take advantage and conquer more territory. This will strengthen the Proliate delusion that we are allies with those maniacs," Baiulus remarked.

"Down, Friar!" Rhyfeler, the constable of the castle, yelled.

Friar and Baiulus ducked as one. They could feel the gush of air as a hippogriff and then a griffin streaked over their heads.

Rhyfeler's blue eyes blazed with intensity. Arrows and bolts slammed into the winged creatures, and the two spiraled into the castle bailey. Their lifeless bodies bounced and skidded, leaving a trail of blood and torn-up grass in their wake.

"Do we have any Eaglians?" Rhyfeler demanded. "We're getting pounded up here."

Just then, over a hundred hippogriffs streamed over the castle ramparts. They had flown incredibly close to the ground before rushing straight up and over the walls. While several were shot down, many grabbed Knight defenders before swooping up into the air, holding them in their ferocious front talons.

Without warning an equal number of griffins dropped out of the clouds, screeching down to catch the Knight defenders in a vertical pincer. The hippogriffs tossed the screaming Knights to the griffins, who impaled them with talons and beaks. Their hemorrhaging and perforated bodies were thrown at Knights still on the wall. The battlements became unwitting, gruesome canvases, splattered with body parts and blood.

After the winged creatures retreated past the line of Proliate trebuchets, the siege engines unleashed the mangled bodies of the dead scouts they had killed during the night and early morning hours. For greater revenge, they mixed the human remains with animal entrails and metal shards. Many of the mechanicians were stationed at the Citadel and hungry for vengeance.

"Friar!" Baiulus screamed, pushing Friar just as a putrid load slammed into the wall. As Friar tucked in behind a merlon rising protectively from the wall, Baiulus' body was battered with metal shards piercing deeply while bloodied body parts and soggy entrails hammered him off the wall.

"No!" Friar cried out as Baiulus' dead body hurtled off the walkway, plummeting to the earth. Friar scrambled to the edge, watching in horror as his steward violently received earth's embrace. Even if he had managed to survive the brutal fall, the rancid remains flooding his bloodstream with pathogens meant he would have been doomed to a feverish septic death.

"Cover! Shields up, and everyone behind merlons!" Ritari yelled. "Is this your first battle? You are Knights, and we will fight like it!"

Friar scurried back to the relative protection of the merlon as wave after wave of rotten projectiles hurled overhead and curled around, through the crenels. *Is there any way to save Liberum, the Knights?* Friar wondered, feeling sorry for himself. He focused on the ground below. Several healers took cover in between the two walls of Liberum. Sanar looked up at Friar and shook his head. It confirmed what Friar already knew—Baiulus was a dead man even if the healer could reach him.

We'll all join you shortly, my old friend, Friar thought as there was a break in the siege engines.

"Are you hurt?" Ritari asked, lifting Friar roughly. "We need you in this fight."

Shaking his head, Friar tried to clear the cobwebs. "Sorea absolutely has to get her verndari going. I'm sure they will send the hippogriffs and griffins in again whenever the trebuchets finish firing."

Ritari nodded and headed off.

"All right, time to send our last three Eaglian messengers to the Northern Dwarves," Friar said. Despite the projectiles and viscera once again raining down, Friar bolted across the bridge to the true wall of Liberum before heading down the stairs, dashing across the bailey.

"Be careful, Friar," Sanar said. "One hit from that slop, and you die."

Death will be the culmination for all of us. It's just a matter of the mechanism, he thought, huffing up to the top of the castle's keep.

"Örn, Ukhozi, Arrano," Friar said somberly as the three Eaglians prepared for battle. The closest one opened his beak wide, hissing a shriek of readiness.

"We're ready to fight," Örn said as the other fearsome warriors nodded.

"Your fighting spirit and prowess were never in doubt. However, outnumbered a thousand to one against griffins and hippogriffs are odds no one can win. You best serve us heading west. Once clear of the battle, break north and then east to the Northern Dwarves. We must have dragons here soon, or we all die. When your five brothers return from scouting, they can help us fight until you return."

"Should one of us head to the Elves?" Arrano asked.

"It would take too long for them to march here. With the huge number of diezmars, the Proliate brought, when they decide to unleash them, our walls will eventually be brutalized to rubble."

"We will be back with as many dragons as they can spare," Örn said.

Friar grasped each of their forearms warmly before sprinting back to the wall. The shower of body parts and shrapnel had stopped, for the moment.

"The verndari are rolling forward and will be in position soon," Ritari said.

"Great," Friar said. "Thank goodness for Sorea's mind. Those wooden structures resemble siege towers but will protect us against air assaults."

Ritari chuckled. "She was like a child when packing the tops of the towers and upper windows with all sorts of armaments in different combinations."

Friar nodded. "They'll hurl projectiles at the enemy outside the walls and help, but their true value will be protecting us from the winged creatures attacking from the sky. Without dragons or Eaglians, they control the air."

Sorea was busy on top of one of the verndari, barking orders. Some had smaller trebuchets, others ballista, and all were packed with archers and crossbows.

"Sir, they're preparing to charge!" Rhyfeler suddenly yelled.

"Without using the diezmar?" Friar questioned. "That's absurd! Unless they aren't working properly? Bring all available archers, including squires, to the walls."

A word was being chanted by the massive Proliate army slowly moving forward with their shield wall. At first, the noise was soft, barely audible...but it grew.

"*Trey*," fifty thousand Proliate hissed in a rumbling whisper.

"Trey."

"Trey!" they said, the volume rising.

"Trey!!"

"Trey-pass!!!" the entire Proliate army chanted ominously as one—the kind of sound that rumbles from the bowels of vengeance resonating with pure hatred.

"Trepas!!!!!" the Proliate howled, unbridled rage oozing off their words.

Finally, they switched words, "Revenge! Revenge! Revenge!"

The horns of attack cried out, and the massive steel beast that was the Proliate infantry surged forward as one.

"How close should they be before we fire?" Rhyfeler asked.

"Why, for the love of Verngaurd, would we wait? As soon as they are in range, release. If they want to keep chanting, let them try with an arrow through the throat," Friar said defiantly.

"Friar, the Eaglians on top of the keep are about to depart," Rhyfeler reported.

"Good." Friar swiveled to watch them take off from the central tower. The three creatures looked majestic—their beautiful brown wings gracefully propelling them westward, away from the battle. Friar smiled. *They'll make it,* he thought. *Soon dragon's fire shall obliterate those diezmars and give us control of the air. Perhaps we can get out of this alive.*

Just before he turned back towards the advancing Proliate, a hundred griffins descended from the sky, quickly overwhelming the three Eaglians. Friar could make out a few griffins falling, no doubt from the Eaglians' black throwing darts, just before the Eaglians were completely surrounded.

The swarm of griffins flew towards the Proliate lines. As they passed overhead, the Eaglians could be seen struggling in vain against the innumerable griffins clawing and pecking at their flesh. The Knights watched in profound silence as the pack of griffins stopped above the Proliate army, which was still chanting, "Revenge!"

The griffins hovered there a moment before quickly flying off. The three Eaglians started to fall like rocks from the sky. Their wingless forms sprayed a trail of blood behind the two wagging stumps on their backs as they plunged downward. A loud cheer went up from the Proliate as the Eaglian bodies smashed against the ground. They roared their approval again as the griffins paraded the wings they had ripped off the Eaglians. Friar quickly wiped away the tears welling in both eyes. They were born not just from the death of glorious creatures but at what their demise meant—the inevitable fall of Liberum.

"Sir," Ritari said dejectedly, "the Proliate are almost in range."

Are the Proliate really foolish enough to walk into our arrows? Friar wondered before yelling, "Archers, ready!"

The archers drew back their bows and waited. The Proliate advance slowed, then stopped.

"What are they doing?" Ritari asked.

Friar didn't have time to answer, as just then, wicker baskets packed with burning naphtha and metal shards slammed into the ramparts. Many within the rows of Knights with bows were obliterated in fire and fragments of hot metal.

"They used prestidigitation to hide this surprise," Friar said as he huddled against the ramparts with Ritari. Several of the verndari burst into flames despite being covered in animal hides pre-soaked in water. Friar could see Sorea fearlessly directing return fire. After multiple rounds of trebuchet fire, the bailey of Liberum was littered with waste, fire, and death.

The Proliate infantry again yelled, "Revenge!" This time their chanting teamed up with their spears pounding against their shields as they began to advance again.

"Archers, to the walls!" Ritari commanded. The remaining squires and Knights began to scramble. "Hustle!" he chided. "They'll be within range in seconds."

"Charge!" the Proliate yelled as one. The Mardin sun was coming up behind the mostly silver-clad Proliate. The mass of silver and red steel of the infantry took a few quick steps before stopping and backing up, careful to stay just outside the range of the Knight archers.

"Oh, no," Ritari mumbled. The shell-shocked Knights on the wall of Liberum were frantically scanning for the Proliate's next surprise. They didn't have long to wait.

With piercing shrieks, hippogriffs and griffins filled the skies. The hippogriffs came in a frontal assault while the griffins attacked from the rear.

Sorea had her verndari firing ballistas, arrows, and bolts to fill the skies. With the aerial pincer attack, the Knights were off balance and struggling to hit the constantly dive bombing and retreating war birds.

"Team up!" Friar shouted. "At least one shield and bladed weapon per archer! Watch each other's backs."

"Sir!" Lovag screamed, his bow constantly swiveling and firing. "I could use a shield."

Friar grabbed a soiled shield from a dead Knight and drew his sword. He and Lovag were constantly pivoting to allow him to shoot and Friar to shield his back. Initially, the method had a great deal of success. However, the enemy quickly adapted.

"Lovag, behind—five g's!" Friar screamed. The griffins had joined into flight sections of five to overwhelm the Knights.

As Lovag turned, the five griffins descended. Friar raised his shield and slashed at their talons—managing to sever one. It was quickly followed by a gush of blood and shriek of pain. Lovag quickly added an arrow in the heart to send the griffin spiraling down outside the castle walls. He hastily dropped another, leaving three.

The remaining ones flew over them before wheeling back. Lovag dropped a third while the other two launched an attack on Friar. One latched its talons on Friar's shield. The other grabbed his sword and right arm. Friar felt himself being ripped off the wall.

"Sorea! Sorea! Friar!" Lovag yelled.

Lovag put several arrows into the griffin holding Friar's arm. A Knight with a crossbow added a bolt to the eye to kill it. The one holding his shield briefly dipped lower when he had to carry Friar's weight alone. Sorea was manning a ballista on one of her verndari. She fired, and the massive bolt tore into the griffin. It entered just under its left wing and sliced through its body. The creature was spun upside down before tumbling to the earth. Friar's body hung briefly before speedily following it towards the ground.

"Cup shields! Ritari yelled to a group of squires. They quickly turned their shields upside down and moved to where Friar was falling. His body slammed into a shield, sending the squires sprawling like a wave around the battlements. Friar landed with a loud thud and groan.

"You okay?" Ritari asked.

"I'm…" he started breathlessly.

"You're not going to say, 'too old for this!'" Ritari said with a smile.

"No!" Friar said defiantly. "I don't think age really matters when you are dropped by griffins! I was going to say, I'm lucky to have you. My backside is bruised, and my arm scratched, but otherwise, fine."

In reality, Friar felt sparks of pain rattling up and down his spine. It was likely he had a few cracks in his back but nothing serious enough to stop movement.

Ritari began to chuckle. "Nice of you to join us, Luchar."

Friar looked up to see Luchar shuffling across the bridge that separated the two walls towards them. His weak left side was completely shielded in a large manica. His right hand held a small double-sided axe.

"Let's see if those turkeys can finally kill me instead of the tickling smooches they've dished out so far," he said. His unmistakable square helmet hid his smile, now deformed by the paralysis on the right side of his face.

"We can sure use you, buddy," Ritari said.

"Of course, you can," Luchar said, speeding up into a hobbling jog.

Release the flanking sappers!" Friar ordered. As Ritari went off to carry out the command, Friar and Luchar cringed as a loud *whhhhiiiiiiiiiiiiiiiiiiiihhhhhhrrrrrrrrr* from the diezmars pierced the air.

"Cover! Cover!" Friar screamed. The hippogriffs and griffins took off to the west as a series of "booms" rocked the castle walls.

"Everyone over now! Get off these fake wall-walks and back across the walkways to the real alures of Liberum!" Friar shouted as the wall crumbled. Over the preceding years, Friar had been stockpiling materials and building a false wall and moat. He had ordered its final construction as he was leaving for the Tournament of Flags. Now the Knights quickly scurried across the walkways to take cover behind the real ramparts of Liberum.

A large section of the fake wall was quickly destroyed by the diezmars, and since the true wall behind had been painted black, the Proliate assumed they had obliterated the real wall.

"Did you see that?" General Lidenskap commented to High Commander Storlax. "Behold the power of our technological advantage. Praise Tallcon! With your permission, sir?"

"Sometimes, it is the wretched soul that has lived with the bitter taste of defeat, and its vile reflux of pain, that is more determined than anyone to savor victory," Storlax seethed. "Unleash our revenge."

"Full assault on the breach in the wall! Remember, no prisoners! Kill everyone!" Lidenskap yelled.

"Sorea, get to the wall!" Friar commanded. As the Proliate troops streamed forward, she quickly headed toward the section of genuine wall with a good vantage point of the breach in the fake outer wall.

Friar limped his way to her. "Make it a blood bath. We need to kill at least twenty thousand with our ruses," he whispered.

Sorea nodded, her fierce eyes overshadowing the doubt swimming in her mind. *Five thousand Knights versus fifty thousand Proliate? Plus, the enemy controls the air and prestidigitation? Death embraces all within Liberum this day.*

As the Proliate were nearing the break in the fake wall, two crack groups of Knights emerged from different tunnels behind the enemy lines. The success of their gambit would decide if Liberum had any chance to persevere, or if they would all perish.

Leaders from opulent castles flick their wrists to send fighters to die as easily as they do to call for wine—each individual soldier but a numbered pawn. However, as long as they draw breath, a warrior's living afterlife is burdened with battles' hangover—nightmares.

There is a line between brutality and valor.
Where is that boundary? Who **defines** the divide?
The answer is often dictated by the perspective
Of which side of the battle, and which generals, you fight for, or live behind.
A brutal trap: military genius or heinous crime?
Guerilla warfare or terrorism?
Do the circumstances and conditions justify the means?
Does underlying motivation or the final conclusion warrant the tactics?
When the battle is over, only non-participants, often from a historical distance, see
Clearly defined victory and defeat.
Those embroiled within the tragedy bear the
Affliction of war
Whether their side won...or lost.

Critics of warriors sit in glass houses
Stuffed within a bubble of peace
Carved from the sacrifice
Of those whom they sanctimoniously condemn.
Under the righteous indignation of upturned noses
Their garish footwear stands on a
Foundation of blood and bones as
They condemn war, as if it were choice, while looking out at the world
Through a brief window of annexed tranquility, for...
...all who draw breath, shall see war.

Savage conflicts stormed through Verngaurd, under rune Teiwaz, leaving it bloodied and bruised. Insatiable war, still savagely ravenous, demands more as we take the last tenuous step on our journey.

Figure 29: Eihwaz comes from the warrior's (Heimdall's) second Aett. This complex rune represents the League's quest, and the perseverance required to see it to completion. It also symbolizes the battles ravaging inside each individual and realm within Verngaurd. Every country, even if it exists for ten thousand years, and every life, even if we breathe through ten thousand lives, eventually comes to an end. Eihwaz further represents rebirth: whatever happens to the League, and the wider scope of ruinous battles, the entire world shall be renewed.

It is just a matter of how.

Figure 30: The mystery of Na Cearcaill and the outcome of the prophecy await as we enter the embrace of Eihwaz, ending with Ingwaz, in Book Five: Tattered Shred of Eternity.

Is the world's background noise roaring too loud,
For you to hear anything of importance?
Between choice and circumstance lies the parchment that will hold the story of our lives.
We do not control the voice given to us,
Or the length of the paper to hold our tale,
But by the effort and determination of our dreams,
We designate the significance of the words writ.
Do we lament the end or smile with gratitude at the journey?
Each offering of consciousness
Is an inheritance of opportunity.
We must decide, and bequeath, life's value through our choices and goals.

www.ingramcontent.com/pod-product-compliance
Lightning Source LLC
Chambersburg PA
CBHW060540310726
48982CB00009B/1323/J

* 9 7 8 1 7 3 5 7 5 2 8 0 8 *